The Great Council

Path of the Ranger, Book 10

Pedro Urvi

COMMUNITY:
Mail: pedrourvi@hotmail.com
Facebook: https://www.facebook.com/PedroUrviAuthor/
My Website: http://pedrourvi.com
Twitter: https://twitter.com/PedroUrvi

Translation by:
Christy Cox

Edited by:
Peter Gauld

DEDICATION

To my good friend Guiller.

Thank you for all your support since day one.

Content

Map

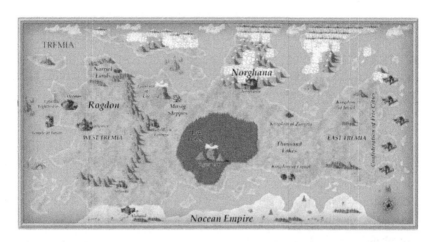

Chapter 1

"That looks like trouble," Viggo said with a grim smile. He was pointing to a spot of blood in front of them on the path.

"Don't even think about it," Ingrid warned him from where she was riding beside him.

"We need to get involved here, Blondie." His expression suggested that they had no other option, and he gestured toward the forest, following the trail with his index finger.

"Don't call me Blondie, or I'll give you what for. And we don't have to get involved. This situation's got nothing to do with our mission."

Viggo stroked his horse's neck. "Aren't you the one who's always saying the Rangers are the defenders of the people of Norghana, of the lands of the realm, of the defenseless, of the destitute, and I don't know how many more tear-jerkers like that?"

"Yes, we are, and they're not tear-jerkers. Didn't you learn anything at the Camp, and then the Shelter?"

"Of course I learnt something. That so much work and suffering, makes you old." He pointed to her face, and his look and smile said: 'I'm really sorry about that.'

"By all the Ice Gods! Why do I have to put up with him? Why?" she cried to the heavens. "You're insufferable!"

"Deep down, you're crazy about me. We both know these tantrums are just your way of hiding it." He gave her a nonchalant smile.

Ingrid took Punisher and aimed at him with the tiny bow. There was fire in her eyes. She seemed genuinely prepared to pierce his heart with an accurate arrow.

"Deep down, and on the surface, I hate you," she snapped back, without releasing her arrow.

"Wonderful. Now you've got your weapon ready, let's go and deal with this little matter. We've been riding for days since we left the Camp, and they've been incredibly boring. I fancy a little action. My muscles are getting cramped from disuse."

"The thing that's getting cramped is that tiny brain of yours.

We're not going to get involved! We're going to go on with the mission they've given us!"

"You'll thank me later," he said, and dismounted with an agile movement.

"Stop!" she ordered, but he was already making his way into the forest, following the trail of blood and cart-tracks. "If you insist on going, I'm not going to help you. You'll be on your own."

"See you in a while," Viggo replied. He raised a hand without turning his head, as if he were merely heading to the canteen for a good time.

"You're an unbearable pain in the neck! You're going to come to a bad end!"

Viggo ignored her comment and followed the trail into the bushes. There had been an attack here, he was certain. Judging by the marks on the ground, he guessed that a group taking three carts with a heavy load had been attacked at that spot on the road. They were so visible to the trained eye of a Ranger that there was no need for him to get off his horse to inspect them more closely.

He moved on a little, and this time he stopped to check the trail. It was one thing to be sure of himself and his skills as a Ranger, but a very different one to be so conceited as to go headlong into the wolf's den. He was what he was, but at the same time he always took good care to avoid mistakes, particularly when there were lives at stake, as was the case here. And apart from that, his own too would be in danger very soon.

He knelt down and studied the tracks. He counted five assailants, who were dragging the bodies of the men they had attacked and probably killed. They were big heavy men, he could tell by the depth and size of their footprints. These were bigger than his own, so he knew he was going to confront the kind of Norghanian who scared people. At least they scared most men, but not many things scared him, and a handful of huge Norghanians was not one of them. Still, he was aware that if he made a mistake it might cost him his life, so he was wary. He always was.

When he went deeper into the undergrowth, following the trail, he found the bodies of three men hidden amid foliage. He got down on one knee to examine them. They were armed guards, the kind you hired with gold. They must have been protecting the caravan. Unfortunately, that particular job had been the final one of their careers. Armed guards meant that the carts were carrying something valuable. He checked the trail, which here forked in two. On one side was that of the carts, heading north. On the other, that of the three men who were dragging another, heading east toward an ash-wood.

He decided to follow the carts and see what he would find there. In the city they always said you had to follow the gold, the valuable merchandise, which would inexorably lead you to the ultimate guilty party. He would soon find out. He checked the dead guards to see if he could find out more about them or their errand. Nothing. They were clean, having already been searched by their attackers. There was no more information to be had there, so he went on following the trail of the carts, taking care not to be seen or heard. The undergrowth was tall, but he was on open ground not in a forest and would not be able to hide so well. He looked up at the mid-afternoon sky, and the sun was shining between white clouds which did not threaten rain.

He saw a large projecting boulder and hid behind it.

"We're going to get a good sum for this little job," came a deep voice. It laughed abruptly.

"We'd better," said another man, with a higher-pitched voice. "We've had to come too far south. I don't like this area one little bit."

"That's because you've spent half your life attacking shepherds in the north. These jobs here in the south are much better."

"If you say so... All I can see is ugly clothes and cloth in these carts. Hardly any gold. What are we going to do with all this?"

"What d'you mean, what are we going to do? You idiot! Sell it in the black market! What else?"

"Don't you call me an idiot, or I'll smash your face in."

"You just try, and there'll be one less at dinner tonight."

Viggo, who was enjoying the argument between the two bandits, climbed up the boulder in a single agile, well-balanced leap. He took a good look at the two Norghanians as they searched the carts. He had not been mistaken: they were both big and ugly. They carried short axes and knives at their belts. The shorter of the two had a short bow across his back, which could be a problem. He waited for a moment in case another of the attackers appeared, but it seemed that the rest of the group was in the forest. He checked whether they could see him. They might be able to, but the forest was far enough away for him to notice if they attacked him. He decided that the best thing was not to wait any longer.

He stood up on the boulder with his hands on his hips. "Howdy, boys, sorry to interrupt this argument, but I have to order you to surrender."

The two bandits turned toward him with surprise and incredulity on their faces. "Who are you and what are you doing here?" snapped the taller and more unfriendly-looking of the two. He was already reaching for the axe at his belt.

"My name's Viggo, and I'd advise you not to resist, or I'll be obliged to use these," he replied. With an incredibly swift movement he unsheathed his knives.

The shorter one, seeing that Viggo was only a few paces away, reached for the bow on his back.

"If you don't get out of here this minute, we'll rip you apart!" the taller one snapped threateningly.

"I'm a Ranger. You, little man, don't nock that arrow, or you'll get a nasty shock."

"A Ranger? Here?" the taller one repeated. By now he had his axe in one hand and a knife in the other, and the look on his face showed that he could not believe his bad luck.

"Well, yes," Viggo replied with a shrug. "I was passing through when I saw the mess you left on the road. That was a stroke of bad luck for you, eh?"

"Whatever's going on here is none of your business," the shorter one said.

"I'd say it is. You're committing a crime of violence in the King's lands, and that's my business."

"Count Morsen's men are in charge of that, he's the lord of this county!" the tall one shouted furiously. "A Ranger has more important things to do!"

"Oops, that's true enough, and you're keeping me back, so drop your weapons and turn yourselves in right away."

"I told you we should have cleaned the blood off the road!" the short one said, and ignoring Viggo, he began to nock an arrow.

"What did I just say?" Viggo reproached him. He looked deeply disappointed by the bandit's attitude.

"I'm going to put this arrow in your heart!"

Viggo sighed in annoyance. "You wouldn't hit an ox at ten paces with that bow."

"Shoot the bloody Ranger!" his partner snapped at him.

Before the bandit could raise his bow to release, Viggo was already in motion. He got down from the boulder and took three steps at lightning speed. The bandit tried to aim, and Viggo rolled over his head. When he had finished the move, he was carrying his knives in his left hand and his throwing dagger in his right. He lashed out with his right arm, and the dagger flew dizzyingly at the head of the bandit, who tried to launch an arrow at him. Before he was able to release the arrow, the dagger caught him in the right eye. His head was thrown back from the impact, and before he knew what had hit him, his heavy body crashed backwards on to the ground. He had died without even seeing the dagger leave Viggo's hand.

The other bandit launched himself into the attack with a circular swing of his axe. Viggo, who was crouching down, rolled to one side to avoid the blow. The bandit went on to deliver several strokes with axe and knife, but Viggo kept moving from right to left as though sliding over ice on a frozen pond.

"Keep still and fight!" the bandit shouted angrily.

Viggo smiled. "Sure that's what you want? I was just warming up."

"I'm going to split you in two!" his attacker said, and came forward with axe and knife held high.

Viggo followed the bandit's example, raising his knives, then threw them at the giant with all his might as he was about to crash into him with all the momentum of his run. He tried to hit Viggo, who dodged swiftly.

"Uh-oh... nearly... but nope," Viggo said, a step away from his side, pretending to be sorry.

"You –!" the assailant began. He tried to turn, but at that moment he realized that Viggo's two knives were buried deep in his torso.

Viggo pointed to his opponent's chest. "That chainmail armor you're wearing is pretty sub-standard, not much use at all. In any case, my knives are quite capable of piercing it." He shrugged. "You really shouldn't run into pointed objects like a brainless brute. Well, in fact you'll never do it again."

The bandit stared wildly at the weapons buried in his torso, then at Viggo. He tried to say something, then collapsed forwards and was dead before he even touched the ground.

Viggo turned the body over with his foot and retrieved his knives.

"Let it be noted that I asked you politely to surrender..."

He shook his head as he stared down at them, feeling neither sorrow nor remorse. They were bandits and assassins who would never harm anybody again, and the world was a better place without them. And it was part of his job, protecting the innocent of the realm from human scum like them.

"Well, that was fun," he said to the two dead bodies. "I'll leave you now, I need to have a word with your comrades." Then he set off calmly toward the forest, wiping his weapons as he went.

He reached the first trees and at once felt better. In a forest, among shadows and vegetation, was where he felt most at ease. Clearings and open land were not to his liking. He was a friend of darkness and gloom. He crouched down, hid behind an oak and strained his hearing. Men's voices reached him from the east. Very carefully, with all his senses alert, he moved forward from tree to tree, hiding behind the thick trunks, slowly approaching the bandits, until he was behind them where they could not see him.

There were three: one of them was shouting at a poor wretch who was tied to a tree with a thick rope. Another one was beside him, while the third was checking the body of another of the hired guards, which was lying beside the man tied to the tree. They must have brought him here alive, then decided they did not need him.

"I swear... I have money... in Ostert..." the prisoner stammered. They had given him quite a beating, because his lip was split, he had two black eyes, and some of his ribs were probably broken. He was breathing with difficulty, and his right side was stained with blood.

"Yeah, yeah, you're just saying that to save your neck," said the one who looked like the leader of the band. He was the tallest and strongest of the three, with long, tangled blond hair full of clots of mud and dust from the road. There were two war-axes at his waist, and he looked like someone who knew how to use them. He was obviously as strong as a bull.

"I'm a trader in cloth... my business is going well... I've got gold on my estate... hidden..." the unfortunate man tried to explain, struggling to stay alive.

"I don't believe it. Kill him," said the one on the leader's left. He had the face – and almost the body – of a wild boar. He was dark and hairy, and like his boss looked filthy. None of these bandits could have washed in weeks. They smelt of rotten cheese.

"Let's hear what he has to say. There might be gold, from what he says," said the one on the leader's right. He looked a little sharper-witted, and a little cleaner. His head was clean-shaven, and he sported a short blond beard. In his hand was a composite bow, and on his back a full quiver. Viggo took good note of his eyes and his manner, and knew he was very dangerous. This was someone who could use his weapon.

The man with the face of a boar made a throat-cutting gesture with his long hunting knife. "Better kill him and leave with the load and his bag of gold before anyone appears."

"I'm the boss here," said the leader. "We do what I say."

"I want more gold than he was carrying," insisted the brighter-looking one.

"You shut up, or I'll tear your tongue out," boar-face snapped back.

The other nocked an arrow and raised his bow. "You try that and it'll be the last thing you do."

The leader spread his arms wide. "Stop that, both of you!" he roared.

"Don't kill me.... I'll give you all my gold..." the merchant muttered with difficulty, his tone a mixture of pleading and panic.

Viggo had already analyzed the situation and worked out what to do. He came out into the open and walked casually towards the three men. The leader's back was to him, and he did not see him. The other two realized, and spun round toward him.

"What the heck!" boar-face cried. He took a second long hunting knife from his waist.

"Who are you...?" the one with the bow began as he aimed at Viggo. He never finished the sentence. Viggo lashed out with his right arm and his dagger got the bandit in the neck. He dropped the bow and put his hands to his Adam's apple. Viggo knew that he was no longer a threat.

"I'll kill you!" boar-face yelled. He ran towards Viggo, while the leader reached for his axes.

Coolly, Viggo measured the distance between them and waited for the attack. The hunting knife flew toward his neck, and he threw his head back so that the steel passed two fingers away. Boar-face seemed to know how to use his weapons. He launched another circular sweep, and this time Viggo went down as if both his legs and

14

body were completely flexible. The stroke passed right above his head. He plunged his two black knives into the man's stomach, and withdrew them immediately. The assailant stared down at his stomach, fell to his knees and yelled with fury. He knew that he was dead. He fell to one side.

Viggo stood up and looked at the leader, who was waiting for him, holding his two war axes and apparently ready to slice him in two.

"Who are you?" he asked, more as an order than a question.

"Oh, how forgetful of me," Viggo replied from two paces away. "I'm a Ranger, and you're all under arrest. Well, your men are dead, but if you like, you can surrender yourself," he added casually.

"A Ranger?"

"One of the best. Before long I think I'll be the best in Norghana."

The leader arched one bushy eyebrow. "Well, that's our bad luck."

Viggo made an apologetic gesture. "Yup, rather bad luck, I can't deny that."

"I'm not altogether convinced you're the best. You don't look like much to me," the outlaw said. He was spreading his arms and showing off his muscles.

"I can assure you, I am. And in any case, hulks like you aren't much of a problem for me."

"We'll see about that!" he roared, and lunged forward. With both axes, he launched a terrible blow at his opponent's head. With absolute calm, Viggo stepped aside. The two axes missed completely, brushing past his left shoulder without touching him. The giant raised his two axes above his head, ready to strike again, but Viggo took a single step forward with tremendous speed and pierced his right side with both knives.

He yelled in pain and tried to turn toward his opponent, but Viggo, with another swift lateral movement, placed himself behind the giant's back and buried his two knives in the nape of his neck. A moment later the bandit fell to the ground dead.

"I ought to have told you I have a giant friend, bigger and stronger than you are, and I always beat him," Viggo apologized as he put his weapons away. "But you didn't give me time."

"Have you finished all that nonsense?" came a voice from behind which he knew perfectly well.

He turned and smiled from ear to ear. Ingrid was aiming her bow from beside a tree, partially hidden behind its trunk.

"You were spying on me, eh, you naughty girl?"

"I was protecting you, which is not the same thing at all."

Viggo gave her a deep bow. "Much appreciated."

"You didn't think I was going to let you get into trouble, when you were with me?"

"I didn't think so. I know that deep down you wouldn't be able to live without me." He gave her a captivating smile.

"Every day I'm more convinced that I'll be the one who kills you off before you drive me crazy with all your nonsense." She lowered her bow.

"Yeah, could be," Viggo said, fluttering his eyelashes. "Make it a sweet, loving death in your warm arms, by the side of your ardent heart."

"Stop playing the fool! They're waiting for us!"

"Yeah... yeah... the mission, I know."

"It's hard to believe they've chosen us for a very important job. We've got to do it. Gondabar himself chose us personally."

"Well, the two of us and a few others..."

"It's an honor."

"Bah, it seems pretty boring to me. It's just babysitting."

"It's providing protection for the leaders of the Shelter, bearing in mind the threat from the Dark Rangers, on their journey to the capital."

"That's what I meant: babysitting, really boring."

Ingrid looked up at the sky, raised her fists and muttered words not suitable for delicate ears.

"Free the merchant, then let's be off."

"Okay... maybe he'll reward me for saving his life, eh?" He was looking at the unfortunate wretch, who seemed frightened to death.

"We're Rangers, we don't accept rewards!"

"Speak for yourself... I need to think about my old age, once I retire as the legendary Ranger I'm going to be, and I need a castle, not to mention plenty of luxuries."

Once again Ingrid muttered a range of improprieties.

Once they were sure that the merchant was all right, they went on toward the Shelter. They were to accompany the Mother Specialist

and the Elder Specialists to the capital, for the Great Council.
And to prevent any possible trouble.

Chapter 2

Astrid and Lasgol rode into the main street of the little village of Skad. Behind them came Camu and Ona, camouflaged so that nobody could see them. Lasgol had asked Camu to use his skill as best he could to hide his partner beside him, so that with practice the power would grow stronger. Ona, who was not very happy, moaned with a sound which was half-protest and half-self-pity the moment she realized Camu had made her disappear.

"Thanks very much for letting me come with you," Astrid said with a smile of acknowledgment.

"You needn't thank me, I love the fact that you're with me," he said as he rode Trotter beside her. They were dressed as Ranger Specialists but their hoods were down so that their faces could be seen.

"It's your village... and, well, you know... these things..."

"Could the Assassin of Nature possibly be afraid to be seen with me in my village?" Lasgol said jokingly. He greeted a couple of villagers, who were staring at him with great curiosity. When they recognized him, they returned his greeting and set about commenting among themselves.

"Well, to be honest, I'm sort of concerned, yes," Astrid admitted, lowering her gaze. A couple of women were looking her up and down, trying to guess who she might be so that they could gossip about it later in the main square.

Lasgol smiled. "I don't know why you should be concerned, this little village is like any other in the north. You don't need to worry about anything." He greeted another couple of villagers who had recognized him and were welcoming him openly.

"It might be like any other village in the north, but it's your home. That's what's concerning me..."

He smiled. "Don't worry, I can assure you that you have nothing to worry about." He looked back to check that Ona and Camu were still invisible, and became aware that the villagers were stopping to watch and then following them.

"I know it's silly, but... what can I say... for you to bring me here

The Great Council

and show me the village is very touching."

"The fearless assassin has a heart after all," Lasgol joked. He was enjoying seeing Astrid blush. It was certainly not something that happened very often.

"I certainly have, and if you dare tell anybody I'll poison your food, and you know how good I am at that." She winked at him.

Lasgol pretended to be frightened. He swallowed hard as though he was afraid she might be going to carry out her threat, then he laughed.

Astrid not put poison Camu transmitted to him, along with a feeling that what the brunette had said was not true.

I know, pal, she's kidding.

Ona chuffed, sounding relieved.

Astrid good. Funny, but not much. Viggo more.

Yes, Astrid's very good, and she's funny too, but with a different kind of sense of humor. Different from Viggo's.

"Are you speaking to the little fiends?" Astrid asked him.

"Yes, how did you know?" he asked in surprise. He had not turned back to Ona and Camu to do so.

"Let's just say I'm pretty sharp. I could tell."

"Oh, I hadn't realized it was noticeable. Nobody's ever told me."

"It's not noticeable. I'm not really sure how I can tell, but sometimes I can feel it. It's something in you, in your gaze and expression, that tells me."

Astrid smart, came Camu's message.

Yes, she's smart, and what's more, she loves us.

Us, Trotter no.

What do you mean, Trotter no? Of course she does. Trotter too.

The strong Norghanian pony shook his head up and down and snorted.

Of course, Trotter, Lasgol said, and stroked his neck.

"Are they being good?"

Lasgol huffed. "As well as usual..." He shrugged and looked resigned.

Astrid smiled. "They're adorable. Charming."

"Yeah... exactly..."

They set off down the street which led to the main square, where the market was held and where the Chief's House was. Lasgol wanted to show Astrid the whole village, or at least its main areas. They were riding at an easy pace so that she could enjoy the place, even though it was nothing special, not very different from the other villages in the area.

"I see there are miners," she said, pointing to a group of workers who were coming back from one of the mines further north, covered in dirt from head to foot. You could only see their eyes. The rest of them was covered in black rock-dust.

"Yeah, Skad's a mining village. Count Malason has several mines in the area. Lots of the villages around make a living from mining. Also from the forests and farms, but the mines certainly offer more of a living for anyone who wants to work in them. A lot of Western Norghanians make a living from getting hold of valuable minerals."

"I see," Astrid said, and they exchanged a conspiratorial look. Egil had warned them before they had left to be careful with the Count.

"Do you think he betrayed our friend?" Astrid whispered discreetly, not mentioning any names.

"That's what the evidence our friend found in the Zangrian assassin's guild shows."

"The accountant might have lied to save his skin."

"Our friend doesn't think so. He's sure the accountant and the evidence he found are trustworthy."

"Well... this welcoming village of yours is exactly in the middle of the County of..." Astrid did not finish the sentence. She did not want to name Count Malason aloud. They had reached the main square, and quite a number of villagers were watching them curiously, not to mention the ones who were following them.

"We'll have to avoid problematic encounters and keep our eyes peeled," Lasgol whispered.

"You mean the way we always do," she said with a mischievous smile.

Lasgol laughed. "Exactly, as always."

He was very happy to be back in his village, and particularly to be able to spend some time with Astrid. Just looking at her green eyes, her beautiful wild face, to feel her presence close, filled him with happiness. The danger that always surrounded them seemed somehow less when they were together. They stopped in the middle of the main square but did not dismount, and Astrid looked at the buildings and the people who were approaching from the nearby lanes.

Lasgol greeted several women who addressed him by his title, Lord of the House of Eklund.

"Well, well, you're quite a celebrity," Astrid teased him.

"I'm the only Ranger, and lord of the biggest house in the village," he said defensively.

"You're forgetting 'hero of the realm'. I've already heard that a few times." She nodded in the direction of the butcher, who was speaking to the furrier, both in front of their respective establishments.

Lasgol smiled and looked toward the inn. Ulf would probably be inside, enjoying some *painkiller* and ranting about one thing or another. He thought about going in to see if he was there, but since more and more people were coming to see what was going on, he decided it would be better to see him later, more quietly. He did not see the Chief or his assistant among the inquisitive crowds, although he would definitely have liked to say hello to them. The rest of the village, not so much. The villagers were talking among themselves, and by now everybody knew that Lasgol was in the village, together with another Ranger. It would be news for days and probably weeks. In Skad it was not usual for anything interesting to happen, and this was quite an event.

Lasgol saw that the square was full of people by now. "We'd better go home. We're starting to attract too much curiosity among my dear neighbors."

Astrid nodded. "Let's see that estate of yours."

"Don't expect too much..."

"According to Viggo, it's a real mansion."

"Viggo always exaggerates. It's a traditional Norghanian estate, with a big house and a stable."

Like house. Attic very much, Camu transmitted.

Yeah, what you like doing is playing hide-and-seek up there.

Funny. Stable for Trotter.

The pony nickered and shook his head up and down. He had understood *Stable.* There was nothing he liked better.

Yup, Cabin for you and stable for Trotter.

Ona whimpered.

You're with me, don't worry, Lasgol assured her. He knew the panther did not want to be left alone.

21

"I can see it now, at the end of the street," Astrid said, nodding in that direction. "It's bigger than I'd imagined."

"You'll like it, you just wait and see. It's very quiet and cozy."

"Those two words don't usually go with us," she said with a smile.

He laughed. "Very true."

When they came to the gate in the high wall which surrounded the estate, they found it open, and Lasgol was surprised by this. Martha always kept it shut to protect the house from possible robbers, and particularly from snoops, of whom there were quite a few in the village. In fact a handful of them had followed them from the square. As for robbers, there were not so many of them in Skad, but snoops and gossips... as many as in any other small village.

"Let's get down. I'm surprised the gate's open."

"Trouble?" Astrid asked as she jumped off her horse and unsheathed her knives.

"I hope not."

"Just in case, let's be careful."

I investigate, Camu volunteered.

Lasgol looked inside, but saw nothing suspicious. Everything was quiet and in order, but he could not see Martha or anybody else. Had his efficient housekeeper left the gate open? Was it a mere slip, or was something up here? They were so used to meeting dangers at every turn of the road that almost instinctively, they imagined the worst in any situation they found suspicious.

Go on, then, but be careful.

I go.

Ona, stay.

The panther remained at his side obediently, then became visible as Camu moved away and she was left out of his area of magical influence.

"Shall we go in to check?" Astrid asked him.

"I've sent Camu. Let's wait and see what he finds."

"Fine," she said, and tethered the two horses to the gate.

They waited, watching the area inside the wall. Lasgol began to feel that something might be going wrong, though he did not really have any reason for this. The door of the house did not open, but he saw a window on the second floor opening inwards. It must be Camu, who had climbed up the wall with his adhesive paws and found a way in.

"I think Camu's gone in," he told Astrid.

She nodded. "I saw the window move."

Suddenly he received a mental message from Camu. *Come, quick!*

This gave him a shock. Something bad was happening inside the house. A terrible concern for the wellbeing of Martha and Camu clutched at his heart. Horrible possibilities assailed him, from murderers who had set a trap for him when he came back home, to sorcerers with evil powers who were waiting to kill him.

"Something's the matter! Camu needs us!" he told Astrid, with urgency and fear in his voice.

"Let's go!"

They ran into the building, at a crouch, zigzagging in case there might be a sniper in the upper floors of the house whom they could not see. With each step the fears in Lasgol's mind increased. The possibility of a trap destined to end their lives was becoming clearer all the time. They still had not found out who was behind the attempts on his life, and the perfect place for an ambush was exactly this one, his home, when he was coming back to enjoy a pleasant stay. The assailants would expect him to arrive feeling relaxed and happy, with his guard lowered. And so it was, except that because of everything they had been through they were now suspicious of everything, and the slightest thing out of place they interpreted as a possible sign that something bad was about to happen.

They went closer to the door. Ona was behind them, showing her fangs and ready to attack. She had picked up Camu's call and could sense Lasgol's worry.

Camu, are you okay? Lasgol asked very uneasily.

Quickly! Camu transmitted, along with a feeling of urgency which Lasgol felt as if it were his own.

"Inside!" he said to Astrid.

They positioned themselves on either side of the door, their backs against the stone wall. Lasgol tried to see inside through one of the nearest windows, but a thick dark curtain prevented him from seeing inside. He decided to use his *Owl Hearing* skill. There was a green flash around his head. He listened attentively, and something strange happened: he heard two people speaking in whispers which stopped at once. He had no time to understand what they were saying, but that was deeply suspicious. He listened for a little while longer, but

23

could not hear anything more. Whoever was inside was not talking or moving.

He communicated what was happening through gestures, and Astrid understood and nodded. Not wanting to go in without knowing what might be waiting inside, he decided to use his *Animal Perception* skill. Another green flash ran through his body, then spread outwards as if a pebble had fallen into the middle of a lake, creating a wave which spread through it. He could make out Camu in the middle of the room. He knew his presence perfectly well and it was not hard to identify him. Four people were with him, and he did not like that at all.

He indicated *four* with his fingers, and Astrid nodded. With another gesture he told her to get ready. They were going in. He could not allow anything bad happen to Camu. He drew his Ranger's knife and axe and prepared himself by calling upon his *Cat Reflexes* and *Improved Agility* skills to help him in the fight. Two green flashes told him they had been activated.

He counted with his fingers, and on the count of three he pushed the door open and they both rolled over their heads into the room. When they reached the middle, they remained crouching there, with their weapons ready to face the fight.

Chapter 3

"Surprise!" came Martha's welcoming voice, together with those of the others in the hall.

Lasgol stared at his housekeeper, wide-eyed. Where was the danger he had anticipated?

"By all the Icebergs! Now that's what I call a dramatic entrance!" thundered a well-known voice, deep and hollow.

Lasgol looked for the voice's origin and recognized its owner.

"Ulf..."

The huge Norghanian bear of a man, one-eyed and crippled, was watching him from the fireplace. With him were Gondar the village Chief and his assistant Limus.

"Lasgol, how wonderful! You're here at last! I'm so glad to see you!" Martha greeted him. She was holding a lettuce in one hand. Camu was beside her, happily chewing a smaller one and enjoying it.

Astrid and Lasgol looked at one another in silence and shared a look of confusion. "Is everything all right?" he asked, although he was beginning to see that nothing was wrong there, quite the opposite.

"Of course everything's fine! Martha's prepared a feast in your honor!" Ulf told him at the top of his voice, as was his habit. He was leaning on his crutch, and in his free hand he held a glass of wine.

Lasgol saw the Chief and his assistant staring at Camu in disbelief. Both of them looked as though they had seen a ghost. Even the Chief – who was as big and strong as Ulf and a true Norghanian warrior from head to foot – looked impressed. Lasgol remembered that neither of them had ever seen the creature before, presumably neither him nor anything remotely like him. Martha and Ulf on the other hand already knew Camu from their last visit to the village.

To finish making sure of everything, Lasgol scanned the room, and seeing the peaceful atmosphere, he concluded that there was nothing wrong there. They had prepared a surprise party for him, and he had mistaken it for an ambush. He felt deeply embarrassed, and a burning heat rose to his cheeks and ears.

"Everything seems to be okay," he said to Astrid as they stood up. They put their weapons away and tried to hide their embarrassment at their forceful entry.

Martha gave Camu some more lettuce and went over to Lasgol to welcome him with a big hug and an even bigger smile, while Camu gulped down the green leaves.

"You're looking so handsome! And so grown-up!"

"Thanks, Martha. You look great too," he told her, looking his housekeeper up and down, then at her sweet eyes. He hugged her again. "I'm really happy to see you looking so well. Time doesn't affect you."

"Flatterer! Of course it does, but I'll accept the compliment." She put a hand to her hair and tossed it back. "And this is...?" She gave Astrid a very inquisitive look.

"Oh, sorry, I haven't introduced you. This is Astrid, she's a colleague..."

"So pleased to meet you," Martha said with a smile, and took Astrid's hand in her own.

Astrid bowed her head. "It's a pleasure."

"Hmm, she's a pretty one, the Ranger!" Ulf thundered. "Is she your girlfriend? I hope so, although... well, you're not much of a thing... skinny and not very tall... don't know whether she'll be interested in you," he said without any qualms.

Lasgol blushed deeply, and was unable to hide the fact.

"Ulf! Those manners of yours!" Martha scolded him.

"What? What did I do?" He looked at the Chief for moral support.

Gondar shook his head. "You were just being you."

"Ah well, no problem then," Ulf said nonchalantly and took a long swig from his glass.

"Don't pay any attention to this ugly, crippled old crosspatch. Half the things he says are wrong and the other half inappropriate," Martha told Astrid, stroking her arm to make her feel welcome.

Astrid smiled back and nodded. "I'll keep that in mind," she said mischievously.

"Let me introduce you to the other guests," Martha said. "This is Chief Gondar Vollan and Limus Wolf, his assistant. They're in charge of making everything go smoothly in the village, and they do a really good job."

"The compliment is appreciated," Limus said with a bow.

"We keep the peace and make sure everybody obeys the law," the Chief explained.

"They're old friends," Lasgol explained to Astrid, who smiled and greeted them both with a couple of nods.

"Delighted to meet the powers-that-be of Skad. I hope I won't get into trouble," she said ironically.

"Hah! I like this girl more and more!" Ulf declared.

"I'm sure a Ranger won't get into trouble in our little village," the Chief said.

"You never know." She smiled and looked at Lasgol, who smiled too.

"Let's hope not," he said. "Astrid is a Specialist, an Assassin of Nature."

"An assassin, did you say? Well, now she really has won me over completely!" Ulf raised his glass as if to propose a toast, spilling some of the wine in the process.

"Ulf! Behave yourself!" Martha chided him. "And don't start making the house dirty. I had it all impeccable!"

"Oops..." Ulf apologized, and took another swig.

"Wait a moment while I wipe off this stain," Martha said, and went out.

Lasgol turned to Camu and glared at him. *Camu! Why didn't you say something?*

I say come quick.

You should've told me there was no danger! That everything was okay!

I want you come quick to friends meeting.

Don't pretend! You did it on purpose!

I behave well.

No way! This was mischief! You gave us a real fright!

Not my fault.

Of course it's your fault! You did it on purpose!

A little yes, the creature admitted and tilted his head. His eternal smile broadened even more.

Ona growled at him from the door. She had not come into the house yet and was waiting patiently for permission to do so.

Astrid moved to Lasgol's side. "You're scolding him, right?" she whispered in his ear.

"He just admitted he did it on purpose," he whispered back.

She smiled. "He's a rascal."

Camu began to flex his legs and wag his tail in the dance he so liked to do.

I rascal. Funny.

No! It's not funny!

"And you, please don't encourage him," he said to Astrid.

She smiled back. "But he's so cute."

I funny, cute, Camu transmitted to Lasgol and danced happily, very proud of himself.

"Ufff," Lasgol snorted. "Gods give me patience..."

"Deep down you love him and you know it," Astrid whispered in his ear so that Camu would not hear her.

"How about coming to the table?" Martha suggested. She had finished cleaning the stain at Ulf's feet, and while she was at it, another on his boot.

"You brought the kitty as well!" cried Ulf. He was pointing at Ona with his glass as she waited patiently at the door. Seeing that he was shouting at her, she growled.

"Ulf... remember, don't raise your voice... she's a cat," Lasgol pleaded.

"You know I speak loudly. It's because I have very big lungs. The mountain kitty'll get used to it, you'll soon see."

"It's your belly that's the big thing about you," Martha told him. She patted his prominent middle.

Lasgol smiled. Martha kept Ulf in line, and that was a very hard thing to do. He looked at the panther. *Easy, Ona. Come in,* he transmitted.

Ona came into the house. Gondar and Limus, who had not yet recovered from Camu's presence, could not avoid feeling intimidated at the sight of a snow panther beside Lasgol, in the middle of the room.

"She's very good and obedient," Lasgol assured them when he noticed their uneasiness.

They both nodded. They trusted Lasgol, but their expressions were uneasy.

Gondar was watching the big cat with interest. "She's bigger than the last time we saw her."

"More adult, I'd say," said Limus. "More dangerous," he added, and a shadow of fear passed over his face.

"Yes, I guess so," Lasgol had to admit. "It's been a long time since we last came to the village. She's grown." He stroked her head as if she were the huge kitten Ulf had called her.

Ulf pointed at Camu. "The one who's gotten really massive is that weird lizard over there!" he thundered.

Camu looked at him uneasily, his tail stiff. *Not lizard. Not weird.*

"He's grown again, it's true..." Lasgol admitted.

"And his skin's changing," Ulf added as he stared at him with his good eye.

"Is it?" Lasgol had not noticed this, perhaps because he was with his little friend all the time.

"He looks more silvery," Ulf explained. "Now he looks like a lizard with silver scales. What a really weird thing!"

I pretty scales. Not lizard. Not weird, Camu insisted grumpily.

"He's not a lizard, Ulf..."

"Well then, what is he? Because he's certainly no sparrow."

"We don't exactly know what kind of animal he is..." Lasgol tried to explain.

"Well, he does look like a giant lizard," Gondar agreed. He was watching Camu as if he were a real discovery.

No lizard! Camu said angrily.

"Well, he certainly looks a little like... like some illustrations I have in one of my books..." Limus began.

"What animal?" Ulf asked. "You've got all sorts of books of every kind, with some pretty strange things in them."

"They're not books of strange things, they're books about subjects that interest me. Reading enriches the mind and the soul."

"Then that's why I'm so poor," Ulf said with a deep laugh. "What enriches my mind a lot more than that is a touch of strong liquor." He laughed again.

Limus smiled. "Like most Norghanians. As for the creature – well, it's not the same. The illustrations show an enormous reptile with wings, and he doesn't have wings" (he pointed at Camu) "but the rest of his body is a lot like that of a... dragon..."

Dragon like! Camu transmitted.

You're not a dragon.

Might be.

No. Dragons have wings and fly – according to mythology, that is.

Might come out.

Wings come out of you now? I doubt it.

You not know.

What I do know is that you're not a dragon, and don't start being pigheaded.

Not pigheaded.

And anyway, dragons blow fire or ice out of their mouths, according to our folklore. You just blow out bad breath.

Not funny.

I think it was very funny. Lasgol had to hold back a smile.

"So then you're left with a giant lizard, which is what a land dragon is," Ulf said teasingly to Camu, who was deeply offended. He raised his head and tail and ignored Ulf.

"Now you've offended him," Lasgol pointed out.

"Bah, he'll get over it, the sensitive little dragon!" Ulf laughed.

"Stop making such a racket," Martha scolded as she shut the main door. "You make more noise than seven dragons."

"Me? Racket? That means I need more *painkiller*," Ulf said with a smile.

Before Martha could stop him, and with surprising agility given his size and the fact that he had only one good leg, Ulf grabbed the bottle of wine from the table and poured himself another glass.

"How wonderful to have the master of the house and his friends here for a visit," Martha said to Lasgol, ignoring grumpy old Ulf.

"And to be back home," Lasgol told her. He was really happy to be back in his parents' house and in such pleasant company. "By the way, how did you know I was coming? I didn't warn you..."

"No, master didn't warn me, but a friend of his did." Martha gestured toward the kitchen. "Better if master comes in to see."

Puzzled, Lasgol beckoned to Astrid to come with him into the kitchen. Once there, he was left flabbergasted. On top of the cupboard, he found a comrade with a very special temperament.

"Milton! What are you doing here?" he said delightedly.

Astrid too recognized him. "Well, well, it really is your owl!"

"The one and only," Lasgol smiled, He showed his wrist to the bird.

Milton clicked his beak several times, as if he preferred not to notice.

Astrid smiled. "He seems to be in the same good mood as usual."

"Come on now, I just want to make a fuss of you."

Milton clicked his beak again. This time he hooted.

"Don't be like that."

At last, Milton decided to cooperate, and flew to Lasgol's arm.

"That's better," he said, and stroked his feathers gently. Astrid did the same.

"You're so beautiful!" Lasgol told him.

Milton hooted even more loudly.

"He brought a note," Martha said, "from your friend Egil, telling me you'd probably arrive today. So I decided to prepare a welcome meal and invited some friends. And Ulf," she added ironically.

"Thank you very much, Martha. You needn't have bothered. Just the joy of being back home is more than enough..."

"Nonsense, it's no trouble. The master of the house comes back, and the least he can expect is a welcome in his own home."

"Thanks, I mean it," Lasgol said, feeling very honored.

"It's a wonderful idea, and we're very grateful," Astrid agreed. She could see by his eyes that Lasgol was very moved.

"Well," Martha exclaimed, "let's all start eating, because it's time to celebrate!"

"It's all sure to be delicious!" Ulf thundered as he lurched toward the table.

Lasgol shook his head and could only laugh.

Chapter 4

Before sitting down, they took care of Trotter and Astrid's horse. A Ranger should always take care of his horse first. When they finished they sat down at the large dining room table. Lasgol presided and to the right of him sat Astrid. Ulf sat down opposite Lasgol at the other end, with Gondar and Limus on either side of him. Martha was going to sit opposite Astrid, on Lasgol's left, at least for what little time she would spend sitting down, since she was busy running back and forth as she finished preparing the dishes they were about to enjoy, serving them, and a thousand other things so that the guests would be comfortable. Astrid and Lasgol offered to help, but she would hear nothing of this.

"You're the guests of honor, for heaven's sake," she said, and brandished her wooden ladle at them so that they would stay put.

"Ulf, you pour out drinks for everybody," Martha told him. "And I mean everybody, not just yourself."

"Of course, right away!"

Ona and Camu lay down in front of the fireplace and enjoyed the food Martha brought for them. Vegetables for Camu and fresh red meat for Ona, which they both devoured happily.

"And now, tell us all the adventures you've had," Martha said as she brought the starters to the table.

"That's right, tell us everything we've missed," roared Ulf. He poured out more wine for everyone, though Astrid and Lasgol declined it.

"Oh, yeah! I always forget, you Rangers don't drink. What a waste! Wine is the joy of life!"

"Sure, and all the nonsense you say and do when you're joyful is the sorrow of everyone who has to put up with you," Martha chided him with heavy irony.

Gondar burst out laughing just as he was drinking and began to cough wine. It even came out of his nose.

Ulf slapped him heavily on the back to help him get over it, and raised his glass. "No way! They don't know what they're missing! Let's all drink a toast! To Lasgol! Welcome home! You were sorely missed!" He raised his glass and took a quick swig, then went on: "To Astrid! Welcome to Skad! You're going to love it!" Astrid nodded, smiling, and raised her glass of water. Ulf took the opportunity for another swig and went on with his toast: "To the guests! Enjoy the feast!" and took another swig.

They all raised their glasses with him each time, some of wine, others of water. All except Camu and Ona who were of course unable to, but seeing them all drink they too did the same from the two bowls of water Martha had set down for them.

"I think half the county must have heard you, Ulf," Martha pointed out. "You're noisier than a whole group of Masig warriors on the warpath."

"It's just so they understand me properly," he said innocently.

"Please begin, everyone. And tell me what you think of the starters," said Martha with a broad smile.

"Delicious, Martha," Lasgol said as soon as he had tasted the first mouthful of salmon soup with bay leaf and rhubarb.

"A real delicacy," Astrid agreed.

"Really good," Gondar said.

"You're an exceptional cook," Limus added.

"It's... to die for..." Ulf mumbled with his mouth full.

"Thanks, all of you," Martha said. She went back to the kitchen, very happy and blushing slightly.

"And now, after the toasts, the stories," Ulf demanded. His one eye was wide open.

Astrid and Lasgol exchanged glances. "I think they'll enjoy hearing about what we went through in the Lost Islands of the Turquoise Queen," she encouraged him.

Lasgol nodded. "All right... well, you see..." and he began to tell them the story. They all listened with great interest as they gulped down the starters in the Norghanian style, as if there was no tomorrow and they had to enjoy everything at that very moment.

Halfway through the story Martha brought in the main course: venison stew with Norghanian tubers and wild berries.

"What a delicious smell!" Ulf roared, interrupting Lasgol, who had to agree with him. It smelt amazingly good, and their mouths watered.

"It'll taste even better!" said Martha.

"That's for sure!" Ulf said, not taking his eye off the main dish. It looked as if he was going to hurl himself at the stew at any moment.

"Gondar, will you do the honors for us?" Martha said before Ulf could do anything.

"My pleasure," he replied, and set about serving. Just as Lasgol had expected, it tasted even better than it smelled.

"Delicious, Martha, you really are an exceptional cook."

They all joined Lasgol in complimenting Martha on her wonderful culinary arts. She brushed it aside, but was very happy with the praise from her guests. Everyone knew that she must have spent hours cooking and preparing a feast like that.

Ulf begged Lasgol to go on with his stories about the Turquoise Queen, and so he went on telling them about their adventures in the lost archipelago. Ulf's comments helped to make the dinner very entertaining, and they all had a wonderful time.

The food was so delicious that Lasgol could not help licking his lips unobtrusively. Nor was he the only one, as Camu – and especially Ona – were doing the same. The life of a Ranger was full of thrills and adventures, but it was not quite so rich in family gatherings and the chance to enjoy feasts as enjoyable as this one. Because of this Lasgol was enjoying every moment, well aware that he would not taste a meal as good as that again in a very long time. The fact was that he would very rarely get the chance to sit at a table and enjoy himself so much again: not only the food, but also the excellent company.

By the time the dessert arrived, he was telling them about the siege and the destruction of the Frozen Specter, while Ulf and Gondar asked endless questions. Limus kindly helped Martha with the dessert, which was no less than a pie made of tart apples with honey and berries, a specialty of the county.

Once again, the guests showered their hostess with praise, since the dessert was delicious.

"A hot tisane to go with the slice of pie?" she offered.

Ulf made a face. "Tisane?" he said cheerfully. "That doesn't do much for the digestion. The best thing to go with dessert's the spirit called 'bone-warmer'."

Astrid glanced at Lasgol, and they both smiled.

"'Bone-warmer'?" Martha protested. "But the temperature's very mild."

"It helps what's in here to go down," Ulf replied. He rubbed his stomach energetically.

"That won't go down even if you chopped it off with an axe!" she retorted.

"Don't be mean, for goodness' sake." His gaze sought the agreement of the other two men. "Gondar and Limus would appreciate a good liquor too."

"I... well..." Gondar muttered. From his expression it was obvious that he would like it himself, but also that he did not want to upset Martha.

"Whatever the master of the house says," she said, and turned to Lasgol, waiting for his reply.

Lasgol looked around at the others at the table without saying anything Astrid was smiling at him in amusement. She was having a wonderful time, especially now that he was in a quandary.

"As this is a special occasion..." he said, looking at Martha, "I think a little strong drink to celebrate is appropriate."

"That's the way, laddie!" Ulf roared.

"Whatever the master says," Martha said, and turned to Ulf. "You know where it is," she said sternly.

"Me? How would I know?" he said, doing his best to pretend, but he did it so clumsily that it earned him a look of reproach from Martha and laughter from Astrid and Lasgol. Gondar and Limus hid a smile.

"Don't make me say anything..." Martha said threateningly.

"All right then... sometimes when I've come to see you.... I've stumbled on it accidentally..."

"Accidentally... of course," she said, and went to the kitchen to avoid saying something she would later regret.

As soon as she was out of the room, Ulf rose with the aid of his crutch and went to Dakon's old cupboard to fetch the bottle. Everyone at the table glanced at one another and smiled. Lasgol remembered that his father had kept exotic drinks in it which he had brought back now and then from his expeditions. He had completely forgotten, but it did not surprise him in the least that Ulf knew where there was strong drink in the house. Probably he was able to detect its essence from a league away.

"If you have time," Gondar suggested, "you might want to come hunting with me in the high mountains tomorrow."

"Going hunting is always a good thing to do," Astrid commented.

"It keeps your instincts and reflexes sharp."

"I think the Chief is referring to hunting on a large scale... beasts," Lasgol said.

Gondar nodded. "A huge bear, in fact. He's causing trouble for the woodcutters, and they've complained. The mines need wood, and it seems it's a very large animal."

"I'm up for bear-hunting!" Ulf roared. He took a swig of liquor, then poured some for Gondar and Limus.

"You're in no shape to go hunting bears," Gondar said. "That's a job for the young ones."

"I can kill a bear with my teeth!"

Lasgol put his hand to his mouth to muffle a guffaw. Astrid's eyes widened, and she shut her mouth tightly so as not to laugh.

"It looks to me as if you've had enough to drink," Martha pointed out as she took the bottle, ignoring Ulf's protests.

"We'd be glad to help," Lasgol told Gondar, "but we have to go on. We have to go to Count Malason's castle."

"You're going to visit the Count?" Ulf said in surprise.

Lasgol did not want to explain any further. "Yes, we've got a message for him."

"One of my assistants can do that for you," Chief Gondar suggested. "You can save yourselves the journey."

Lasgol shook his head. "It's a private message, and I have to deliver it by hand."

"Oh... I see."

"But thanks for the offer."

"Not at all."

"The Count is very busy these days," Limus commented casually.

"A busy nobleman, now that really is unusual," Ulf said mockingly.

Gondar smiled, but said nothing. The Count was the lord and owner of the entire county, including the village of Skad. The Chief could not afford to make an enemy either of the Count or his followers. He was not going to say anything against him openly.

"How busy?" Lasgol asked curiously.

"He's trying to double the production of the county's three mines," Limus explained. "There's plenty to be done, and people are coming from other areas to work. We've had to extend the southern part of the village and build houses for them."

"Yes, the village is growing, but with outsiders," the Chief said. "Which causes one or two altercations." He looked at Ulf and raised an eyebrow.

"What? It's no fault of mine if they're ignorant and think themselves better than we are. All I do is put them in their place."

"Sure... with your fists," Gondar complained.

"And how am I supposed to do it any other way? You won't let me use my sword!"

"No weapons at the inn, Ulf, you know that. You all drink too much, then the arguments end up in bloodshed."

"Bah! In my days a Norghanian made his voice heard with his war-axe."

Limus looked shocked. "It's a good job, times have moved on since then."

"No axes, and least of all your sword," the Chief warned Ulf.

"Well then, I'll beat a bit of sense into their heads," he said, and seized his crutch as if it were a club.

"Ulf, careful with that crutch, you're going to hit something and you'll spill something on the table," Martha warned him.

"How many times have I had to get you out of jail?" Gondar asked him.

"More than I can remember. But in my defense I'd say the fault's theirs, messing with people they shouldn't."

"Is it always their fault?" Limus asked mischievously.

"Nine times out of ten, at least," Ulf retorted defensively.

Limus smiled. "I'm not so sure about that..."

"Are you calling me a liar?"

"You see? You're getting into a fight already," Gondar accused him.

"It wasn't me! It's Limus who doesn't believe me!"

"Sure, it's always the other person."

"That's what I always say!"

Lasgol could not hold back this time and burst out laughing. Astrid joined him, and a moment later Gondar and Limus did the same. Martha went to the kitchen with a broad smile on her face.

"As for the Count," Gondar went on, "his second cousin Osvald 'the Whip' is giving his weapon free rein, and we've had to tend to a couple of injuries here in the village."

Lasgol nodded. "I remember... we had to throw him out of here, my home."

"Be careful when you go to see Malason," Gondar warned him. "Osvald'll be with him, and he has a grudge against you."

"Still? It's been years since that incident..."

"There are some people who never forget. They nurse a grudge inside them forever," Limus said. "I'm afraid Osvald is that kind of person."

"I'll take that into account," Lasgol said, and Astrid looked at him in puzzlement. "I'll explain later," he told her. "It's an old story."

"He's a cretin," Ulf commented. "Luckily he doesn't come to Skad very often."

"He's very busy with the mines," Limus said.

"Is there any reason why the Count has increased production so much?" Lasgol asked.

"Well, we're in the process of rebuilding after a war," Limus commented. "The noblemen's coffers are empty, and they need to generate some income. The mines are a source of wealth that might get Count Malason out of his precarious economic situation."

"I see..."

"And the mines can also be exploited for purposes of war," Astrid added, raising an eyebrow.

"True," Limus agreed. "The fact is that we're currently in a period of peace. The West is quiet. Count Malason doesn't need weapons now... in theory."

"I don't have much of a head for numbers and letters like my smart assistant Limus here," Gondar said, "but it might be because of both."

Limus nodded. "It could be, that's right. All the same, producing weapons will attract the attention of the East... of the King. That doesn't suit the Count, and he knows it. So I'm inclined to think he's seeking to fill his depleted coffers."

"That's because as far as you're concerned, the thing you most like in this world is gold," Ulf said laughing.

Limus smiled. "What man doesn't like gold?" he asked.

"Or woman?" Astrid said with a mischievous smile.

Limus gave her a nod. "Very true."

Ona and Camu fell asleep where they were after the feast Martha had prepared for them. Lasgol thought he could hear something akin to a slight snore coming from Camu's mouth. He knew Ulf's snores well, having had to put up with them more than a few times. The last thing he needed now was Camu to start snoring as well. He turned his attention back to the conversation at the table, which was becoming very interesting. Particularly on the subject of Count Malason, who was now a figure of interest for them. Of great interest. Lasgol listened to everything Limus had to tell him about the mining operations and the Count's business, both in the West and in the capital.

"Does he do business with the capital?" he asked with interest.

"Yes, he does. At least three important traders have come from Norghania to buy iron, coal and silver."

"The first two are for forging weapons," Astrid commented.

"And the third for paying for them," Limus added.

"Shouldn't the Count be dealing with traders from the West?" Lasgol asked.

"He did before," Limus said, "but things have changed since the war. Now he seems to be dealing more with the East..." He said this in a tone which suggested that the Count was betraying his own people.

"I'd imagine the Western League won't be very happy," Lasgol commented neutrally.

"There have been certain frictions," said Limus. "It's said that the most powerful Dukes of the West have visited Malason and there've been shouting and threats. All this, of course, is completely unconfirmed."

"Of course," Lasgol agreed.

What he was hearing put Malason in touch with the East. Not necessarily with King Thoran, but certainly with important traders who might very well either be in the pay of the King himself or else be transporting minerals for the Crown. This would interest Egil, and Lasgol decided to send Milton back to the Camp with this piece of news at dawn.

With the dessert and the liquor which Martha passed around again, the conversation became livelier still. Now and then Lasgol glanced surreptitiously at Astrid to see whether she was enjoying herself with the group. The smiles she gave him assured him that she was, so he could not have been happier. The meal stretched on to fill the whole afternoon, and they talked without stopping until it was almost night.

"It was a magnificent meal. It's been a long time since I enjoyed myself so much," Chief Gondar said as he said goodbye at the door.

"Incomparable," Limus added, "and a pleasure to have been able to enjoy it, especially in such good company." He gave Martha a slight bow, then Astrid and Lasgol.

"I'm glad you liked it," Martha said, looking delighted that her surprise party had come out so well.

"I'll try to come back more often, so we can do this again," Lasgol said with a smile.

"You can count on me!" Ulf thundered. "This old soldier loves parties and celebrations!"

"Are you sure you don't want to stay the night?" Lasgol asked him.

"Of course not! That would mean that I can't get back on my own foot to my own home after a celebration! Let me tell you, I've attacked walls and taken fortresses, and I can assure you I can get as far as my own home!" he roared to the heavens as he went out, leaning on his crutch.

"All right, then," Lasgol said. He had no desire to force the matter, because he knew very well what Ulf could be like after drinking a little too much, and it was not exactly a pretty sight.

Gondar, Limus and Ulf, set off toward the village and Martha went back into the house. Lasgol and Astrid stayed on the porch, watching them leave.

"What did you think of them all?" he asked her, a little afraid that she might not have taken to them.

"Exactly the way I was expecting them to be after what you told me about them."

"Ulf too?"

She smiled. "Well, Ulf's sort of indescribable."

"Yeah, there are no words..."

"I loved the old one-eyed bear," she said.

"Did you?"

"I did," she said, and kissed him.

Chapter 5

In the morning Astrid and Lasgol went for another stroll around Skad. This time they went without the company of Camu and Ona, who had stayed blissfully playing in the attic. Trotter was resting in the stable of the estate, well-looked-after and happy. Considering that every time Lasgol went somewhere, they all ended up running away at top speed from pursuers. The current situation was especially comfortable, and the strong Norghanian pony was enjoying it to the fullest.

Lasgol showed Astrid the places where he had spent his childhood. They stopped at every street, every square, every shop, and he told her about his adventures and incidents there. The memories were coming back to him in an attractive form now that he was happily walking around with Astrid, but in reality, many of those memories were bitter, even painful. His childhood had been a hard one, and the people of Skad had not behaved at all well toward him. Luckily all that was past, and now he did not remember the bad times as quite so bad, even though his subconscious warned him that they really had been.

"And here, at this street corner, was where one night Ulf fought off three bullies who'd been robbing one of the farms south of the village."

"Here? What happened?" she asked, looking around with interest.

"The Chief and his men were looking for them in the south, and they turned up here in the village. Ulf realized they weren't good people – he has a gift for that sort of thing – and he told them to halt. I was with him. It was during my first few weeks as his house-boy."

"He stood up to all three of them?"

Lasgol nodded. "He stopped them and demanded explanations in his usual angry-bear voice. The three outlaws didn't like it at all, and drew their weapons."

"And what did you do?"

"Me? I ran off."

Astrid threw her head back in surprise. "You fled?"

"No, Ulf whispered to me to run to his house and bring him his infantry sword. His house is in that other street, not very far from here."

"Did you get back in time?"

"I've never run so fast in my life. I knew unless I brought him his sword in time, something very bad would happen. I ran as if the three outlaws were after me, round the corner, down the street, and opened the door at top speed. I took the sword down from its hook, and I was so frightened about what would happen to Ulf that I cut my hand when I grabbed it wrongly. That I do remember. I brought him the sword with my tongue hanging out, fearing I wouldn't be in time."

"But you got there, right?"

Lasgol nodded. "Ulf distracted them long enough by shouting insults at them and all their ancestors. He seems to be impulsive, but don't be fooled by the old geezer, he has a good head on him."

Astrid smiled. "He looks more like one of those people who tear off somebody's head, screaming, without thinking about the consequences. It must be because of the way he yells and that ferocious look of his, with that red beard and hair, all so scruffy-looking. Well, everything about him's untidy. Not to mention that empty eye-socket that he leaves uncovered so as to be more frightening."

"Yelling, and with his sword," Lasgol said with a nod. "But I can assure you, he has a good head and he knows a lot, particularly about weapons, fighting and summing people up."

"Go on, what happened?"

"Well, I went round that corner with the sword in my hands" – he pointed to the corner between the two streets nearby – "and I found Ulf had already brought down one of the assailants with his crutch, hopping backwards on his foot all the time and wielding his crutch like a club. I shouted 'Ulf'. He turned his head and nodded, and I threw him the sword."

"You threw it to him?" Astrid's eyes widened in disbelief.

"The two assailants were already on him. I wouldn't have got there in time."

"Now tell me he caught it in flight," she said, deeply engrossed in the story.

Lasgol nodded. "That's right. With one hand, by the hilt. It really was worth seeing. He stretched out his right hand, while he kept his crutch in his armpit and caught it in mid-air."

"I can see that old dogs don't forget their tricks."

"You can say that again! Chief Gondar says he's a legend in the infantry. A legend with plenty of blots on it, but a legend all the same."

"And then, once he had the sword?"

"Everything ended there. With four precise thrusts he killed two of the outlaws and wounded the third one, who ran away. He has an incredible mastery of swordsmanship. He blocked, then thrust and feinted, then launched a deadly cut to the neck. As for the last attack, I couldn't see it, it was so swift. Impressive."

"Three cheers for Ulf! And without his right leg..."

Lasgol smiled. "And no spring chicken."

"Tell me more about yourself and your village," she said with great interest and a sweet smile.

"Let's go to the main square. I'll tell you a few more stories there."

"That'll be great. It's a pity we can't stay more than one morning, there are so many things you won't have time to tell me..."

He smiled back at her. "Duty calls. Besides, I don't want you to know all my childhood secrets." He chuckled.

"I'll get them all out of you."

They spent the morning going around the most characteristic spots in the village, the most unusual ones, and the ones which had a sentimental value for Lasgol. Astrid very much enjoyed the guided tour, and although the village was small and not very different from any other in Norghana, the stories and anecdotes Lasgol told her delighted her.

At midday Martha prepared another of her special meals for her guests of honor. Lasgol had begged her not to make anything special for them that day, since they had to go on with their journey that same afternoon. But in Martha's mind the idea simply did not register, so she prepared another feast. Ona and Camu were delighted, of course. Camu gulped down all the greens from the orchard that Martha gave him. Ona on her part was delighted with the colossal raw steaks the good housekeeper had got for her from the butcher that very morning.

Lasgol shook his head. "You're spoiling them."

"Poor little things," Martha said. "They're just skin and bone."

"Skinny? Ona even has a potbelly, and Camu looks like a little barrel."

Astrid laughed. "Don't exaggerate!"

Ona growled, unhappy about the comment.

I no little barrel! Camu transmitted.

D'you even know what that is? Lasgol replied, watching him crunch his greens with his strong jaws.

No... what is little barrel?

It was Lasgol who laughed now. *It's a small round container, a tub.*

I no little tub!

Yeah... yeah...

Ona growled again, but her anger vanished at once when Martha brought her another juicy steak.

"Martha, I'm deeply grateful to you, but if you keep giving us these fabulous feasts I'm not going to fit into my pants."

"But you're pure sinew. There's not a speck of fat in your body. I have to look after you, feed you well. Or what would Mayra say if she saw I wasn't taking good care of her dear son. No, no, no!" She shook her head and pursed up her lips. "My job is to make sure that when you come back home you're taken good care of. I can't let my best friend down. It's my responsibility."

Astrid jabbed Lasgol with her elbow to stop him protesting and let Martha have her way.

"I'm really grateful for all this attention," she said, and gave the housekeeper a small bow.

"Thank you," Martha said, looking pleased.

"Yes," Lasgol added, "it's much appreciated. You treat us like royalty."

Martha smiled at him. She stayed staring at him for a long time, as though she were lost in her own memories.

"You look more and more like your father," she told him, with a look of longing and fondness.

"Really?" Lasgol asked, unsure about this.

"You certainly do. Physically, every day that goes by. Although in spirit I think there's a lot of Mayra in you. Your mother had a special spirit..." She sighed.

"I hope there's a lot of both of them in me," Lasgol replied.

Astrid was gazing at him with her usual savage gaze turned gentle, which was very unusual in her.

"Are you going to follow in your father's footsteps?" Martha asked him as she cut some white bread she had baked herself.

"As a Ranger, you mean?"

"Yes, will you become a Royal Ranger, then First Ranger, like he did?"

Lasgol waved his hands in denial. "Oh no, not at all."

"Why not? Both positions are a great honor, and the next steps in your career as a Ranger."

"I won't say they aren't, but I don't see myself as a Royal Ranger. Most of them are huge, and very good specialists. Hardly anybody gets into that elite group that protects the King and depends on the First Ranger. And certainly I don't see myself as First Ranger, not in a million years."

"If you say so... I'm just reminding you that your father Dakon managed both," Martha hinted, implying that he too could do the same.

"My father was an exceptional Ranger..."

"And an exceptional person as well," Martha said with a smile.

"That too. Very true."

"If he made it, so can you," Martha said encouragingly. She ladled him another bowl of bitter Northern soup.

He blushed. "I'm not like my father..."

"You'll be better than him, whatever you choose to do." She ladled out more soup for Astrid, who was listening with great interest.

"You knew him, you know how special he was. How could I be his equal?" Lasgol asked incredulously.

"Because you're even more special!

"No, I'm not..."

"I know you are, because you've got him in you. And because your mother's spirit is in you too, and that makes you a lot more special."

Lasgol's spoon stopped half-way to his mouth. He did not know what to say.

"I agree with Martha completely," Astrid told him. "You're very special."

Lost for words, Lasgol finished his soup.

"Either way, I don't see myself as First Ranger. I don't want to be either, and from what I understand, to get there you need a very strong desire for it. It's very difficult to reach that position."

"Doesn't Ingrid want to reach it?" Astrid asked.

"Yes, she wants to be the first woman to become First Ranger."

"Well, as she's Ingrid, I'm sure she will."

Lasgol nodded. "Very probably. And that brings us back to where we started. I'm not going to be First Ranger. I don't have any desire to be."

"Well, that'll just be because you don't want to, because talent and spirit you certainly have to spare, as the son of who you are," Martha said as she brought out a meatloaf which smelt delicious.

"I absolutely agree!" Astrid said.

"You should listen to your partner more," Martha commented to Lasgol. She winked at Astrid, who smiled.

"I do listen to her..."

"Not enough," Astrid said, laughing.

Martha helped them both to large portions of meatloaf. They had no choice but to sit down to eat, because the aroma was so irresistible.

By dessert, which was a milk pudding with blueberries, Ulf made his appearance: to say goodbye, so he claimed. Martha's version was that he had been guided by the smell of food, like a greedy bloodhound who could recognize the smell of his own kitchen a league away. His beard was already spattered with the crumbs of the delicious dessert he was gulping down. Probably this was because he was talking while he swallowed, which was quite an achievement.

He puffed out his chest. "Sure you don't need a strong, determined bodyguard for whatever it is you're going to do?"

"I see you've come armed with your sword," Lasgol pointed out.

"Of course I have! In case you want company, to take care of problems. You know what I mean." He winked his one good eye.

Lasgol laughed. "Thanks Ulf, but I have company already."

"This company is too beautiful. You'd do better with someone with more character and the gift of the gab." He jabbed his torso with his thumb.

This time it was Astrid who laughed aloud. "Gift of the gab, you certainly have that!" She winked at him.

Ulf puffed out his chest even more. "And character aplenty," he added proudly.

She agreed with a nod. "You certainly have!"

Lasgol smiled. "Thanks for the offer, but I'll feel more reassured if you can take it on you to keep an eye on Martha and the estate. You know that now and then things get a bit involved here, and the Chief's usually too busy to look after everything."

"Don't you worry about Martha or the estate. I'm in charge," Ulf promised. He raised his hand to his sword.

"Thanks. That way I'll be feeling a lot easier when I go," Lasgol admitted. "And one more thing, Ulf. Could you ask Chief Gondar and Limus not to say anything about Camu? I asked them at the dinner, but you remind them. You know how superstitious and gossipy they are here in this village. All I need is for the word to get around that there's a dragon in this house..."

I dragon, Camu transmitted at once.

No, you're no dragon.

I be.

You're not, and drop the subject.

I drop, but I be.

Lasgol snorted under his breath.

"Don't worry, laddie. I'll have a word with them. You know they can be trusted."

"I know, and I do trust them. It's just to remind them not to mention the creature. There's enough talk about me in the village as it is. I don't want any more gossip."

Ulf nodded ponderously.

Lasgol got to his feet, and Astrid, Ona and Camu followed his example. The farewell hugs began.

"Take good care of yourself, Lasgol," Martha said. She hugged him tightly.

"You too, Martha." Then he whispered in her ear: "Look after the old crosspatch for me, will you?"

Martha smiled. "Don't worry, I have his favorite painkiller in the attic. He'll come to see me often enough."

"In the attic? So that's why I couldn't find it! I can't get up there with this leg of mine."

"That's exactly why I hide it there, so you can't reach it."

Lasgol smiled and hugged the housekeeper again

"Look after him," Martha told Astrid with a knowing wink.

Astrid smiled. "I will. I always do," she assured her with a determined look. Both women embraced.

Lasgol went to do the same to Ulf, who hugged him back and gave him two massive slaps on the back. "Take good care of your girlfriend, you don't deserve her," he said.

Astrid turned to Ulf, who gave her a wink with his one good eye.

"Girlfriend?" Lasgol repeated, trying to pretend.

"Don't pretend, laddie, you can see it from a mile off, the way you gaze at each other. Even a one-eyed old crosspatch like me can see that."

Lasgol blushed and looked at Astrid.

"He'll take good care of his girlfriend, and she of him," Astrid promised. She went across to Ulf and planted a kiss on each cheek.

The old soldier was delighted. "I like this girl more and more every day that goes by." He turned to Lasgol. "I really don't know what she sees in you."

"Nor do I," he said with a smile, blushing to the tips of his ears.

"You make a fantastic couple," Martha told them. "And you can tell three leagues off."

Astrid shrugged. "Oh dear, and we were trying to hide it."

"There are some things you can't hide. Love is one of them," Martha replied with a broad smile.

When the farewells were over, they set off for Count Malason's castle. They had a mission from Egil to carry out. It was one his friend had planned thoroughly. It was going to be risky, but then so were all Egil's strategies.

Chapter 6

Egil had Ginger and Fred on his cabin table at the Camp. He was feeding and looking after them with extreme care. They were two delicate species and they required a lot of attention or else they would not survive and losing them would be a shame after how hard they had been to get in the first place. Rare species were expensive and problematic to obtain. It had taken him a long time and a good sum of gold. On the table he had prepared a dozen jars and phials with everything he needed to keep his two pets.

"Don't worry, I know that most people find you to be horrifying creatures, but that's because they don't know you and therefore fear you," he told them in a whisper. "I know how special you are and the rare beauty that characterizes you."

Ginger, the pink dwarf viper of the Nocean deserts, slithered up Egil's hand, open on the table, and curled around his index finger.

"I don't know why they find you so repulsive when you are a beauty with those metallic pink scales and those little yellow eyes. I find you such a beautiful creature, and there are so few around. Besides, you rarely bite, you're most sociable," he said in a gentle tone while the viper's tongue went in and out.

Suddenly, there were two dull strong knocks on the door of his cabin. Egil did not need to ask who it was, he recognized the strength and cadence of the knock. Anyway, he asked to be courteous.

"Who is it?"

"It's me, Gerd."

"Come in," Egil replied smiling. He had guessed right.

Gerd came into the cabin and shut the door behind him. He saw what Egil was doing and went as white as the snow on the mountains that surrounded the Camp.

"You're with them..."

"Yes, looking after them. Aren't they fascinating?"

"Well... fascinating... what I'd call fascinating... I don't know..." muttered Gerd who did not move from where he was from the fear the two desert animals caused him.

"They're fantastic creatures, I assure you."

"If you say so…" the giant murmured making a face.

"Ginger is an exotic beauty. Look at her," Egil said and turned round in his chair to show her to Gerd.

"Yes!" he cried frightened, and jumped backwards, hitting his back on the door.

Egil smiled. "Easy, big guy, she won't harm you."

"Oh yeah, I believe you, it's just that my body would rather be very far from those two venomous creatures."

"It'll be your mind, your body only reacts to what your mind tells it to," Egil corrected him grinning.

"Well, so then all of me wants to stay away," Gerd replied raising his hands.

Egil laughed. Take it easy, they're not going to do anything to you."

"Don't know why, and I really trust you, but I don't believe it."

"Okay. Stay there then. I'll be done in a moment," he said and turned back to the table. He picked up a stick and very carefully, holding Ginger's head between two fingers, he opened her mouth and placed the stick under the two tiny fangs.

"Bite little one," he whispered to her and squeezed his fingers. The snake bit on the stick hard and from the fangs there issued a green substance which Egil gathered in a phial.

"That's venom!" Gerd cried horrified.

"Of course it's venom, she's a viper," Egil said nonchalantly without turning round and went on with the extraction process.

"You said she wasn't venomous!"

"I didn't say exactly that. What I said was that the viper had no venom, that I had extracted it."

"So, why are you doing it again?" Gerd asked him very excited.

"My dear friend, calm down, and use that rational mind of yours. What have they taught you in the School of wildlife about reptiles, and in that of Nature about venoms and antidotes for snake bites?"

Gerd blushed and began to think trying to overcome the fear that had him paralyzed.

"Snakes… produce venom… to kill or incapacitate their prey… you can prepare antidotes with the venom…"

"That's right. Very well," Egil left Ginger on the table and she immediately slithered to a jar where Egil kept live worms.

Egil combined the venom with two other liquids he had in

another phial very carefully. Then he added half a tablespoon of some roots he had pulverized in a mortar. He stirred it with a metal rod and waited for the elaboration process to finish.

"You're making the antidote..." Gerd said.

"Exactly. A wary man lives into old age," Egil grinned.

"And the viper has no venom... you extracted it..."

"*Fundamental*, my dear friend."

"I see. Sorry, I got nervous... I panic and then I don't see reason or anything."

"There's nothing to be sorry for," Egil said with a soothing wave of his hand, making light of it. "Every once in a while I have to extract Ginger's venom. Either that or pull out her fangs which I find cruel and would rather not do."

"Anyway, be careful, one distraction and it could cost you your life."

"That's why I prepare the antidote," Egil smiled broadly.

"And what about the king scorpion?" Gerd said pointing at it at the end of the table.

"Fred? Oh, he's very nice."

"Nice? It's a king scorpion! One of the most dangerous creatures in Tremia!"

"I did not say he wasn't also dangerous."

"What's it doing to that poor cricket?"

"It's his food."

Gerd put his hands over his eyes so as not to see.

"I guess that you came to my cabin for something..." said Egil giving him the cue for explaining the reason for his presence there.

"Oh, yes... when I saw those two, I forgot even my own name."

"I guessed as much," Egil laughed.

"Dolbarar wants to see us. He's waiting at the Command House."

"Fine, I'll put these two away and come with you," said Egil, who put on some kind of chainmail gloves and picked Ginger and Fred and put them in two tall ceramic jars which he covered with cloth and tied with a cord.

"Won't they escape?"

"No, they can't, don't worry."

"I'm not coming near those jars if you paid me to."

"I imagine," Egil said with a grin.

Shortly after, they arrived at the Command House. Inside were four Veteran Rangers guarding the door, which meant that the security measures inside the Camp had been increased. The situation was of maximum alert after what had happened to Dolbarar and the possible existence of Dark Rangers within it.

They presented themselves to the guards and they were let through. Inside they found the master Rangers Esben and Haakon, who were commenting on the complicated situation of the corps and by extension of the Camp.

"Hello Egil, Gerd," Esben greeted them with a welcoming gaze.

"Master Ranger," Egil and Gerd said respectfully.

"Everything okay?" Esben asked.

"Everything's very well, sir," Egil assured him.

"Nothing to complain about," said Gerd.

"That's the way I like things. Those of my School must show their worth and resilience," he told Gerd with a wink.

"Absolutely, Master Ranger," Gerd replied and straightened to his full height.

"Have you grown more again?" Esben asked him.

"I don't think so, sir…"

"I think you're taller…"

"Larger, he certainly is," Haakon noted.

Gerd, who was not sure whether that was a compliment or an insult, did not know what to do and looked at Egil.

"Gerd has a prodigious body," Egil commented.

"That of a true Norghanian," Esben said proudly.

"Has Dolbarar summoned you?" Haakon asked.

"That's right, sir," Gerd replied.

"Very well," said Haakon, and he became thoughtful looking at them. He was probably wondering what Dolbarar wanted with these two. Egil and Gerd were wondering the same thing. They had no clue.

"You may go up, he's in his office with Angus," Esben said with a wave toward the stairs that went up to the second floor. "They've been conferring all morning. They must have reached an important resolution," he added.

"Let's hope so. Inactivity in times of crisis leads to failure and death," Haakon foretold in a funereal tone.

"You say that because you're a man of action. Prudence also turns out good results in situations like this one," Esben replied.

"We have different points of view," Haakon said wrinkling his nose.

"Very true. We need a little diversity of opinions among the leaders," Esben said smiling at him.

"A strong leadership is what we need, and more so in this time of threats to the corps." Haakon replied back.

"The leadership is strong," Esben said looking upwards.

"If it were as strong as it ought to, the Dark Rangers wouldn't exist."

"The fact that this stain has befallen us isn't a sign of a weak leadership," Esben said spreading his arms looking as if those insinuations upset him.

"I think it's exactly that," Haakon snapped crossing his arms over his chest.

They saw Ivana appear, coming down the stairs. She looked like a blonde hunter semi-goddess with her frozen gaze and her northern beauty.

"I have the same opinion as Haakon," she said, with her usual frozen tone and gaze.

Egil and Gerd exchanged a veiled look that meant 'that's weird'.

"This situation will be resolved at the Great Council," Esben assured.

"Let's hope so," said Ivana who glanced at Gerd and Egil inquisitively.

"If we don't establish drastic measures the situation won't improve," Haakon assured.

"You'll have your chance to be heard at the Council. Expose the ideas and measures you're considering there."

"Perhaps they'll be taken into account," said Ivana.

"I seriously doubt it," Haakon shook his head. "My ideas are progressive and harsh,"

"That sounds aggressive and a little ripened. The proposals must be balanced and follow the principles of the Path," Esben told him.

"It's because of that way of thinking that they won't go forward. Our leaders are too traditionalist, they're still set on following the Path, when what we must do is change it, modernize it."

"Modernizing the Path is a good idea. There are passages anchored in the past that need to be revised and improved," Ivana joined in. "You can see that too, Esben, and don't say no just to protect the way in which things have been being done so far."

"I'm not saying that it can't be updated, improved, or modernized as you say. But we'd have to do it very carefully and always be respecting the way things have been done up to now." Esben said.

"Well, that's not a no, and coming from you is an improvement," Haakon said with a twisted grin.

"It's also not so strange that the youngest among the leaders seek to change things and modernize them a little," Ivana said.

"I'm not saying either that this is something we shouldn't study, I'm only saying that we must do it with respect and care for traditions," Insisted Esben.

"So much care is what's brought us where we are, said Haakon. "Now what we need is to take action and change things,"

Gerd and Egil looked at one another. They found themselves in the middle of a conversation in which they did not wish to take part, not even as listeners.

"If the Master Rangers will excuse us..." Egil said respectfully and gestured to Gerd to follow him.

Esben waved them off, "Of course,"

Egil and Gerd went upstairs to Dolbarar's office and left behind the conversation between the three Master Rangers, which appeared as if it was going to go on for quite a while, and most likely without reaching any agreement.

They found two more Veteran Rangers on guard duty at the office door. Nobody would reach Dolbarar with so many guards, and this was something to be thankful for after the attempt on his life. The Guards asked inside and after getting permission they waved Egil and Gerd in.

"Welcome, both of you," Dolbarar greeted them from behind his working desk with a big smile. Beside him, standing to his right, was Angus, the up-to-recently intern leader of the Camp. He was still helping Dolbarar, although soon it would no longer be necessary since he was almost fully recovered.

"You called for us?" Egil nodded respectfully and bowed. Gerd did the same.

"That's right, I wanted to talk to you about an important subject." Dolbarar replied.

"We're both at our leader's pleasure," Egil said.

"First I would like to thank you again for saving my life"

Dolbarar said, and his tone was of deep gratitude.

"It was our duty," Gerd said at once.

"And in my case, I owed you. There's nothing to thank us for." Egil said.

"Yes, there is. Angus has told me everything you did for me and that was going way beyond duty."

"We'd do it again without hesitation." Gerd said at once.

"Absolutely," Egil joined him. "It's an honor and a pleasure to see you fully recovered and leading the Camp once again."

"The truth is that these weeks of rest have been very good for me and with Healer Edwina's help I have made an almost complete recovery. Not that I was especially needed really... Angus did an amazing job in my place, leading the Camp while I was ill," Dolbarar said glancing proudly at Angus who nodded slightly accepting the praise.

"I also wish to thank you for everything you've done for Dolbarar and for helping me clear up all this ugly business." Angus said. "I must admit that no matter how much I like to think I have everything under control, there are situations that are totally unforeseeable and hard to prevent. Because of that I am utterly grateful to you for helping me save Dolbarar's life and unmasking the treacherous Eyra."

"We are very grateful to the intern leader for allowing us to leave in search of the information and for listening to our allegations," Egil said glancing at Gerd, who nodded.

"I must admit that when you proposed the expedition I did not have much hope that you would find anything useful. You proved to me that we must never lose hope and that we must follow any thread of it, no matter how frail or unlikely it might seem. This is a lesson that will remain engraved in my mind and never forget. It will serve me well in the future," Angus said.

"It was a pretty unlikely proposition," Egil confirmed nodding. "Few leaders would have accepted it," he said gratefully.

"But Angus is a good leader and he accepted it," said Dolbarar. "Thanks to that and to your friend Lasgol who discovered the cause of the poisoning, you uncovered Eyra's plot and I'm alive today."

"Thank you, sir," Angus said respectfully and Egil and Gerd joined him.

"And speaking of Eyra..." Dolbarar continued. "She's one of the reasons why I had you come."

"Eyra, sir?" Gerd said blankly.

"Yes. An order from Gondabar has arrived that she must be taken to the capital, to Norghania, at once."

Egil raised an eyebrow. He did not like the sound of this.

"The Great Council is in four weeks...Why is the Master Ranger being summoned now?"

"The plan was to all go together to the capital for the Great Council and that Eyra should travel with us as a prisoner," Dolbarar explained.

"But, our leader Gondabar, wants her transferred immediately," Angus added, and he indicated a scroll on Dolbarar's table with the Rangers' seal.

"That upsets all the plans we had already made, somewhat," Dolbarar went on explaining. "The day for the Great Council has already been communicated to all the Ranger leaders so we can't change it now. We've sent escorts to the Shelter so they may protect Sigrid, the Mother Specialist, and her four Elite Elder Specialists on their journey to the capital."

"We know. Our friends Ingrid and Viggo are two of them," Egil said. "Are you expecting trouble? Attempts on the lives of the Mother Specialist and her people?"

"No, be at ease, there are no indications that anything bad might happen, it's only a precautionary measure. Gondabar fears, and not without reason, that if the Dark Rangers have attempted against my life, they might do so against other leaders, himself included. That's why he's strengthened the safety and vigilance of all the leaders."

"Besides, the Dark Rangers will know about the Great Council," Egil mused.

Angus nodded in agreement. "It's been no secret, especially because King Thoran insisted."

"The King?" Gerd asked puzzled.

"It seems that our monarch was not at all satisfied with what has happened and is asking for responsibilities. He wants to put an end to the Dark Rangers at once and he's let it be known that he'll be present at the Council, to make sure that the measures taken are the ones he expects," Angus said with a troubled look.

Egil frowned. He did not like this. The Great Council was a gathering of the Rangers and only they could attend. Of course, the

King, as the highest leader in the realm, was also that of the Rangers, so he could attend if he so chose to. The problem was how far might Thoran interfere in the final deliberations and conclusions that were going to be approved.

"The King has the right to attend," Dolbarar said, "And I fear that the request for Eyra to be immediately transferred is also of his doing, although it may have been transmitted by our leader Gondabar."

"I see…" Egil said, as he wondered what the King could want with Eyra, he saw no direct relation between them. He would have to study it and find out what was going on here.

"And this leads us to you," Dolbarar said with a kind smile. "I want you to be a part of the retinue that will take Eyra to the capital. I need trusted Rangers who make sure Eyra reaches Norghania without any incident. You two and your partners of the Snow Panthers have proved on many occasions that you are to be completely trusted. That's why I want you on this mission,"

"Absolutely. It'll be an honor," said Gerd puffing his chest, touched to have been selected by Dolbarar himself for such a mission.

Egil raised an eyebrow. "Who else will come in the retinue?"

"I have chosen four Veteran Rangers to go with you and two others who will drive the prison-cart in which Eyra will travel," said Angus.

"Might we suggest someone else to come too" Egil, asked.

"Yes, of course. As long as they're at the Camp, there's no problem. I'll study who you ask for and if I approve, there will be no problem," Angus said.

"Eyra has refused to speak to anybody since we arrested her so she won't be a problem," Dolbarar assured them. "What I do want you to do, is that you watch her so she doesn't take her own life. She might try now that we're taking her to the capital."

"In order to take her secrets to the grave?" Gerd asked.

"And to avoid being tortured…" said Dolbarar. "King Thoran and his people are not as courteous as we, the Rangers are when it's a matter of obtaining information…I fear the reason why they want her might be that…"

"An interrogation in the Royal Dungeons?" said Egil.

Dolbarar sighed heavily.

"Everything points in that direction, yes. I'd like to avoid that situation, but Eyra refuses to speak to me, so I can't help her. What it does is confirm her guilt, something that still gives me nightmares every night. It's as if an older sister had stabbed me in the back..."

"We're very sorry, sir," Egil said; he felt bad for Dolbarar and the great betrayal he had suffered at the hands of someone he loved so much.

"Very well then. Get ready. You leave at noon," Dolbarar told them.

They both nodded, "We won't fail you."

"Good luck and we'll meet again in Norghania in four weeks," Dolbarar said.

The two friends left the office.

"Who do you want to bring with us? Nilsa is already in Norghania at Gondabar's request, working for him and the rest of our people aren't at the Camp right now."

"Don't worry, it's a special request..."

"I don't know why, it doesn't sound good to me."

"That my dear friend is because you're very keen."

Gerd snorted and shook his head, Egil was planning something again and it did not sound like it was going to be good.

Chapter 7

They did not have much time to get their things ready, although Gerd did not need it, and Egil had already foreseen that complications might arise which required his personal involvement, so that he was ready on time. All the same, something happened to delay them. Before they started, and just in case, he went to check whether there was any last-minute messages for him at the pigeon-house. And in fact there was. An albino owl had arrived from the capital. Egil knew who the message was from even before he opened it. He untied the message from the bird's leg and went to meet Gerd.

"Everything ready?" Gerd asked when he saw him in full gear and with his travel bag.

"Yup, everything ready."

"Short bow?" Gerd asked, pointing to Egil's back where he had slung his weapon.

"Yes. I ought to bring the composite one, I know... but who are we trying to fool by now? I can't hit anything beyond twenty paces, so why bother with the composite bow?"

"I was going to suggest you brought the long one," Gerd teased him.

"That one I can't even handle," Egil had to admit in embarrassment.

"Don't worry, I'll take care of shooting at mid-distance with the composite bow. You deal with anybody who comes close."

"I'll try, but I can't promise anything. You know weapons aren't my strong point."

"Your strong point is this," Ger said, indicating Egil's head. "It's a lot more important and lethal than a bow."

Egil acknowledged his friend's compliment with a smile. "Thanks. Let's hope my head works the way it should."

"It will, I'm sure."

Egil smiled again. "We have news."

"Oh? Who from?"

"From our favorite redhead," Egil said. He took the message out of his belt.

"From Nilsa? Fantastic! So what does she say?"

"I'll read it to you," Egil said, and looked around to make sure there was nobody eavesdropping. He could see a couple of Rangers a few paces away, but they were working, carrying supplies to the canteen. A group of Third-years passed in front of the Library at a run, but there was nobody else in sight.

Gerd too was looking around. "We're alone."

Egil began to read:

"Dear Snow Panthers. I'm writing this message to let you know I'm fine. The capital is nicer-looking and busier than ever. Since the end of the war there's been a lot of trade and business' prospering in the markets and the upper parts of the city, as well as a lot more people than before, so the city is flourishing. You have no idea of the many lovely things you can see in the stalls and shops. I could buy them all. The sad thing is that I have no gold, you know how tight a Ranger's pay is, and I don't have the time to go shopping anyway.

"Gondabar, our illustrious Leader, is keeping me incredibly busy. He tells me he's very happy having me back in his service, and that he's going to make use of my skills as long as he can and keep me working as messenger and liaison. I've barely had time to do any more than take a couple of strolls around the city. The rest of the time I've been working without a break. The preparations for the Great Council are keeping me so busy I sometimes even forget to sleep. You'll think it can't be as bad as that, that I'm exaggerating, but I can assure you I'm not. At first I thought it would be just another council, but it turns out it isn't. It seems the Great Council is a real event and is rarely called. Gondabar has told us that it's only convoked in times of crisis for the Corps of Rangers, like the one we currently find ourselves in. So, they're preparing fully and everything has to be perfect, because all the Ranger leaders will be there.

"I've also found out via rumors that King Thoran is very annoyed about the business of the Dark Rangers, and he may even attend the Great Council himself. I wanted you to know, so that you keep it in mind because of the repercussions it might have.

"As for the rumors of war, everything's pretty quiet, which is a novelty I'm giving thanks to the Ice Gods for. The Zangrians are still active and vigilant, waiting for an opportunity to try something, but once again they seem to be involved in skirmishes with the Kingdom of Erenal, so that gives us a breathing-space.

"As for the Frozen Continent, there's no news whatsoever. It's as if the ice had swallowed up its inhabitants. I don't know, but it seems strange to me. Could they be plotting something? The Wild Ones of the Ice aren't exactly the quiet

kind. It mystifies me. Well, there it is for you to analyze. As for the nobles of the West, they're behaving for the moment and King Thoran isn't taking reprisals. Mainly because a close watch is being kept on them and they're so overwhelmed with taxes to the Crown that they can't raise their heads above the parapet. Everything seems quiet on that front, although I'm sure one of our own people will know a lot more about what's really going on with them."

"Is anything going on with the nobles of the West?" Gerd asked Egil with concern.

"No, relax, my dear friend. Nothing's going on. For the moment..."

"What do you mean, for the moment? I don't like the sound of that 'for the moment' at all."

Egil smiled and went on reading: "*And that's all I have to tell you for now. I'll keep my eyes and ears open as usual. You know I have contacts in the Court, so I'll try to find out everything that might be of interest to you.*

"Lots of hugs and kisses.

"Take good care of yourself! See you soon!

"Nilsa."

"I'm so looking forward to seeing her," said Gerd.

"We'll be doing that soon," Egil pointed out. He tore the letter into tiny pieces and put them inside his belt to dispose of later on.

"Come on. They're waiting for us," he told Gerd.

Angus was waiting at the stables beside the horses. With him were several Rangers, ready to set off.

"Everything in order? Ready for the mission?" he asked them.

"In order and ready," said Gerd.

Egil nodded "Everything ready, sir."

"Right, Egil, I've accepted the name you gave me, to accompany us."

Egil nodded. "Thank you very much, sir." His eyes gleamed.

"You're welcome. I don't see any problem with it."

Gerd looked around intrigued, trying to identify who Egil had requested for the journey. His friend had not told him either who it was or why he wanted this particular Ranger to come along. Egil tended to turn mysterious now and then, and that only meant one thing: trouble.

"I took the liberty of adding an additional member to this escort, of my own choice," Angus said. "I thought it would be beneficial to the mission."

Egil and Gerd looked at one another, intrigued.

"An additional member?" Egil raised an eyebrow. This might be counterproductive for his own plans. Nor did he did like this coincidence. Coincidences were rarely what they seemed, there was always some reason behind them. At least, most of them.

"I don't think you'll have any objection. She's someone you've already worked with, and who brings skills that always turn out to be very useful." Angus turned and waved toward the center of the Camp, where a figure was approaching carrying two quivers full of arrows, one in each hand. She walked with a determined step which highlighted a graceful body. Her long blonde hair and beauty were unmistakable.

"Val!" Gerd called. He greeted her with a wave and a smile of pleasure.

"We have no objection, quite the opposite," Egil said, also smiling. Having Valeria with them gave him a greater feeling of confidence in their ability to carry out the mission.

"It looks as though they've given us a job of prisoner-transport," Valeria said as she reached them.

"I can see you're prepared," Gerd told her, gesturing at all the arrows she was carrying.

"Angus suggested I join you, and knowing the tight spots you two tend to get into, I decided to come better prepared this time."

Egil nodded and smiled. "A wary woman lives long and well."

"You won't have any trouble on this mission," Angus assured them. "Nobody knows you're leaving today, or the route you'll be taking."

"Good thinking," Egil admitted.

"I waited till the last moment to let the ones chosen know that they'd be taking part in this mission, precisely to avoid letting word get around." He indicated the Rangers who were getting ready in the stables. "It's not a good idea for it to be known that Eyra's traveling to the capital. Matters like this are better dealt with in secret."

"In case they try to rescue her?" Gerd asked. He looked skeptical.

"That's one possibility, yes..."

"And the other?" Valeria asked.

"That they try to silence her," Egil guessed.

Angus nodded. "Exactly. Dolbarar is worried that the Dark Rangers will try to kill her to stop her talking in the capital. It's been impossible for them to reach her here at the Camp, but away from this protected place... they might try, and all Dolbarar's efforts to keep her alive will have failed."

"Oh..." Gerd's face showed that he understood the situation and the problem they were confronted with.

"A strict protocol of meals and visits has been kept up, to make it impossible for anyone to kill her. Dolbarar planned it, and it's worked very well. All the same, everything has changed now. That's why this request to transfer the prisoner isn't to our liking."

"I understand that perfectly, sir," Egil said.

"We'll make sure nothing happens to her," said Valeria.

"And also that she doesn't escape," Gerd added.

Angus smiled. "I knew I'd chosen the right Rangers for the mission. Which reminds me, I haven't introduced you to the Ranger in command of the mission." He turned to the stable. "Gurkog, come over here, please."

A Ranger as big and strong as Gerd strode over to them. He was blond, with his hair in a braid on one side and the rest loose on the other. His face was Nordic, and a short blond beard decorated his stern face. His intense blue eyes studied the three of them without qualms. He gave the impression that he was a tough nut, and not only in appearance.

"This is Gurkog Gormsson, Specialist Ranger, of the specialty of Man Hunter in the School of Wildlife."

"I've heard of you," Valeria said suddenly, staring at him from head to toe with her head to one side. "They say you're a prodigy."

Gurkog nodded. "They're quite correct."

"Well, you don't seem to be exactly humble," Gerd commented with a grimace.

Gurkog stared hard into his eyes, as though challenging him. "I don't have a very good temperament either, and nor do I have the patience to put up with little jokes."

"Well, well, a real Northern charmer," Gerd replied without flinching, smiling the way Viggo might have.

Gurkog was not amused by this attitude and was about to say something, but Angus interrupted him. "Gurkog is in command of this mission. This transport and the prisoner are his responsibility. You're to obey his orders at all times."

Gerd said nothing more, but kept his gaze fixed on Gurkog, who seemed to want to tear his head off.

"Of course," Egil said soothingly. "We'll follow his instructions without question."

Gurkog looked at Egil and seemed to recognize who he was, because his grim expression softened. "I know you, you're... from the West..." He did not want to say who Egil really was.

Egil nodded. "So I am."

"I thought I'd recognized you. I'm from the West too. Make sure the big guy follows my orders."

"I'll make sure, don't you worry." Egil said, he nodded to Gerd, who nodded back.

Valeria smiled. "Well, this is certainly starting really well. It looks like a fun trip. Thank goodness it's not a very long one," she added acidly, chuckled and went to look for her horse.

"I'll get on with the last of the preparations," Gurkog said. He went back inside the stables with a heavy stride.

"He's very good," Angus assured Egil and Gerd, "and he has experience."

"I don't doubt it," Egil said. He had guessed as much from that brief encounter.

"Although he's not the kind of Ranger with the best disposition. I suppose you can't have it all."

"There are some who think they do have it all," Gerd commented. He was thinking of their friend Viggo.

Angus smiled. "Yes, those are the worst."

"In that we agree," Gerd agreed with a chuckle.

They heard the wheels of a cart approaching and turned to see them bringing Eyra, inside a barred cell at the rear of the cart. He had not seen her since her arrest and incarceration. It had been forbidden for any person in the Camp to have any contact with her, since they did not know who they could trust. Master Instructor Oden had been the one who took her meals to her, and the only one to see her. The cell she had been kept in had been watched by six Rangers, day and night.

The cart, drawn by two Norghanian draft horses, reached their side, and the two veteran Rangers leading them greeted Angus, Eyra looked poorly. She appeared to have aged to a hundred all of a sudden, and now looked like a shriveled old hag. She neither looked at any of them nor made any effort to communicate, which Egil found puzzling. She had not asked to speak to her friend Dolbarar or to the other Master Rangers, which was unheard-of as she had known them perfectly well for years and they were friends. Something was happening here, and he wanted to find out what it was. He would have to keep his eyes peeled.

"Ready to go!" Gurkog called.

"Have a good journey, and we'll meet in the capital," Angus said.

"Off we go!" Gurkog roared.

He and two Ranger Specialists led the way, with the prison-cart, with the two veteran Rangers following. Bringing up the rear were Valeria, Egil, and Gerd. As they crossed the gate, Egil looked back to see that Dolbarar had come out to see them leave. His expression was serious, his eyes showed concern, and Egil seemed to perceive something else in them: a deep sorrow.

He thought he knew the reason. They were taking Eyra, Master Ranger of the School of Nature, who had been his friend for many years, to the capital. There she would be interrogated, tried and sentenced. The first of those three would cause her great suffering, the second, shame and pain, and the last would cost her life, because she would be sentenced to death. Nothing and nobody could prevent that, and Dolbarar knew it.

At least, if she reached the capital.

And if she did so alive.

Chapter 8

When Ingrid and Viggo arrived at the foot of the Frozen Peak, in the most southerly part of the realm, the towering mountain looked as though it had come forward from the range behind it to act as a guardian.

"There it is, the entrance to the Shelter," Ingrid said.

"Good job, our orders are to wait outside. I don't fancy climbing that mountain one little bit."

"What you don't fancy is going past that dragon that's frozen in the ice," Ingrid teased him.

"Well, obviously I don't fancy it. You'd have to be insane to fancy something like that. One day it's going to wake up, and then you'll see the havoc it's going to wreak."

"It's just a figure in the ice that looks like a dragon..."

"It's a frozen dragon! You'll find out when it wakes up!"

Ingrid laughed. She knew the subject made Viggo very nervous, and she was taking advantage of it.

"I didn't know the great assassin was scared of mythological creatures."

"I'm not scared of mythological creatures, but a dragon is something else. Don't forget, it breathes fire, and conventional weapons won't pierce those tough scales."

"We don't know that. Nobody's ever seen a dragon in Tremia."

He pointed to the peak. "Well, that's one, and you'll find out when it wakes up!"

Ingrid laughed again. There were not many subjects she could use to annoy Viggo with, and this was one of them.

"You're unbelievable."

"So I am," Viggo said. He stuck out his chest.

Ingrid shook her head. "Come on, they're waiting for us."

They rode to meet the two Rangers on horseback who were waiting at the foot of the mountain. "Rangers," Ingrid greeted them.

"Comrades," replied a veteran Ranger, returning the salute. He must have been in his early forties, with a strong physique. His chestnut hair was long, and his bushy beard reached half-way down his torso.

"Are you here on the escort mission?" Viggo asked.

"That's right," the other Ranger said. He too was a veteran, a few years older, with long salt-and-pepper hair tied in a queue and a well-trimmed beard of the same color.

"Then we're all on the same mission," Ingrid said. "My name's Ingrid Stenberg, and this is Viggo Kron beside me."

The strongly-built Ranger with the chestnut beard introduced himself first. "Aron Almensen."

"I'm Ulrich Ulmonsen," the other said.

"Pleased to meet you," said Ingrid.

"Specialties?" Viggo inquired, raising an eyebrow.

"Tireless Explorer," Aron said.

"Forest Survivor," said Ulrich.

"Well, well," Ingrid said, "a Survivor. That's a very tough specialty. You must have some good stories to tell."

"I certainly do," Ulrich said with a smile.

"Having an Explorer will come in very handy," Viggo pointed out. "All this business of following trails and exploring isn't something I'm that good at."

"And what are you good at?" Ulrich asked him.

"Killing," Viggo said as if it was the most normal thing in the world.

"Assassin?" Aron asked.

"Natural Assassin," Viggo specified proudly.

Ulrich gave a long whistle. "Phew! Now that really is a complicated specialty."

"Remind me not to make you angry," Aron said with a smile.

"I will, don't you worry," Viggo said.

"What about you?" Ulrich asked Ingrid. "Judging by the bows you're carrying, you must be from the Specialty of Archery."

"Archer of the Wind."

"Hey, they've sent us a couple of Elite Specialists," Aron said. "That's important."

"Thanks," Ingrid said.

"And now we've all introduced ourselves, what are we going to do?" Viggo asked.

"Orders are to wait here," Ulrich said.

"I hate waiting."

Ingrid pointed northeast, where a rider was galloping toward them. "We won't have to wait too long. We have company."

Ulrich pointed to a second rider. "And from the East too,"

"You know how many of us there are supposed to be on the mission?" Ingrid asked.

"No idea," said Aron

"The usual thing is half-a-dozen specialists for a complicated mission," Ulrich said confidently.

"Then those two complete our group," said Ingrid.

"If they're Specialists," Viggo said.

They waited for the new arrivals to come closer. The first to arrive was wearing his hood up, so that they could not see his face until he was beside them.

They exchanged salutes. "Who are you?" Ulrich asked.

"An old acquaintance," replied the newcomer, throwing his hood back.

"Luca! What a surprise!" Ingrid exclaimed.

"How long it's been!" said Viggo.

He smiled at them. "Hey, friends! I'm very happy to see you too."

"What have you been doing?" Ingrid asked.

"Hunting men, bandits, outlaws, deserters and the like."

"That's what they prepared you for in there," Viggo said, gesturing toward the mountain behind them. "You must have had some fun."

Luca smiled. "Quite a bit."

Ingrid introduced Aron and Ulrich, and they greeted one another. "You look the same," Ingrid said.

"So do you two," Luca said looking them up and down. "How are the others?"

"They're all well. Nilsa, Astrid, Gerd, Lasgol, Valeria, all in one piece and doing well."

"I'm glad to hear it. I'd imagine you'll have been in trouble here and there, right?"

Ingrid and Viggo exchanged a smile. "Umm..." Ingrid said, "we'll tell you all about it. So many things have happened."

"Unbelievable things," Viggo put in.

Luca laughed. "As it's you, I'm not in the least surprised."

"So you two have a tendency to get into trouble?" Ulrich asked.

Ingrid nodded. "Yeah, a lot."

"Well, I want a quiet mission, so don't stir things up."

"Oh we're always quiet, but trouble finds us even when we're trying hard to avoid it." Viggo said, as if nothing that had ever happened to them were his fault.

"Oh, isn't that just great," Ulrich complained.

"Bah," Aron said. "Nothing's going to happen, this is just a simple escort mission."

"Nothing at all," Viggo said, and from his voice it was left perfectly clear to all of them that they were going to have problems of one kind or another.

"Here comes another rider," Ulrich pointed out.

As soon as he was close enough, Ingrid, Viggo and Luca all recognized him. "It's Molak," said Luca.

"Captain Fantastic... you've got to be kidding me..." Viggo protested under his breath. His expression had turned sour.

"Molak..." Ingrid murmured in surprise.

"Hi there, comrades," Molak said.

"Welcome," Luca said, smiling. "I'm very glad to see you, old friend."

"Same here," Molak replied with a smile. Then he noticed the others. "Ingrid, Viggo, it's been a long time. I'm glad to find you well."

"Molak," Viggo said coldly, with a touch of distaste.

"And I'm glad to find you well too," Ingrid said, a little taken aback by the meeting. "I wasn't expecting to find you on this mission."

"I wasn't expecting to be called either. I was at Norwek Fort, and a message came for me."

"What were you doing there? It's on the border, isn't it?" Luca asked him.

Molak smiled." Yes, on the border with Zangrian territory. They've got me doing long-distance archery exercises."

"Long-distance?" Ulrich asked.

"Molak is a Forest Sniper. A very good one," Ingrid explained.

"Ahhh... I see."

"Thanks for the compliment," Molak said, "although I think I'm pretty normal."

"What exercises do they have you doing?" Aron asked in surprise.

"Well... they're dissuasive maneuvers."

"I don't follow."

"He shoots at the Zangrians from this side if they come too close to the border. Most likely the officers," Viggo explained.

"Seriously?" Ulrich asked in disbelief.

"You know how these things go... confidential missions... I can't tell you anything," Molak explained apologetically.

"Probably ordered by Duke Orten," Viggo added. "He likes this sort of game."

"Some game," Aron muttered.

"I see you three are keeping well," Molak said to Ingrid, Viggo and Luca, although he was only looking at Ingrid. "I'm glad we're going to be on this mission together."

"Yeah, I'm delighted too," Viggo said with heavy irony.

Suddenly seven riders came into sight from the great mountain, led by a Masig Ranger. It was Loke Southern Wind. They recognized him at once by the reddish tint of his skin and the beautiful brown-and-white pinto horse he was riding. He was followed by five riders who were getting on in years. Getting on considerably. They were the Mother Specialist and the four Elder Elite Specialists. In fact they were riding very well for their age, although it was only at a trot. A little further back was a final rider who looked like a child. When they were closer, they realized that it was not a child but a dwarf. It was Enduald, Sigrid's brother.

The Masig greeted them with a nod, and the group returned the salute.

"It's a pleasure to see you again," Ingrid said to him.

"And for me, to see you all again."

"Well, well, an excellent group of my old pupils," said Sigrid, the Mother Specialist and Leader of the Shelter, as she came up to them. She looked the same as ever, as though she had not aged at all, even though she was over seventy and her once very beautiful face was lined with countless wrinkles. As was her custom, she wore her white hair long and loose over her shoulders. "I'm happy to see you again," she told them, and looked each of them up and down with her deep jade-green eyes as they bowed respectfully.

"I see two of mine among you," said Ivar, Elder Elite Specialist of the School of Archery, looking at Ingrid and Molak. Like Sigrid, Ivar was around seventy, although he was far more active and looked younger. He still wore his white hair very short. He was still thin, and was remarkably tall. He scratched his sharp nose and looked hard at them with his small grey eyes.

"Two very good students, who I imagine are great specialists by now."

"We try every day, sir," Ingrid said.

"It's an honor to be complimented like that by the Elder," said Molak.

"I see a Tireless Explorer of my School," Gisli said, indicating Aron.

Large and strong for his seventy and more years of age, with his white hair in a ponytail, he was watching his former pupil with sea-blue eyes in a broad, wrinkled, snub-nosed face. It was curious that for his age he still looked like a powerful man, capable of bringing down a strong young Norghanian.

"Master, it's an honor to see you again after all these years," Aron said, deeply honored that the Master Elder should still remember him.

He turned to Luca. "Also a Man Hunter with a good nose."

"Always trying to improve it," Luca said.

"I'm sure you've improved a lot."

"I try to, sir," Luca replied, equally happy to be recognized by the Elder.

Undoubtedly the oldest and frailest of the group of Elders was Annika, the Elder Elite Specialist of the School of Nature. She must have been eighty by now, although her barely-wrinkled face did its best to hide the fact, though the long white hair which came down to her waist did not. With her green eyes in her fair, delicate face, she was looking at them keenly.

"I know you," she said to Ulrich." You're one of mine, aren't you?"

"Yes, Ma'am, I'm a Forest Survivor."

"Ah, I thought I'd recognized you."

"You honor me, Ma'am, that was quite a while ago," Ulrich said gratefully, and Annika smiled at him.

"I recognize one of mine in the group as well," said Engla, Elder Elite Specialist of the School of Expertise. She was younger than the others, around sixty-five, and was in excellent shape. She was not a beauty, but was thin, sinewy and very nimble. She looked at Viggo with her intense blue eyes. The Elder wore her black hair straight as usual, held back from her face with a cord.

"Out of all those who've passed through my hands, they had to choose you for this mission?" she said to Viggo with a touch of reproach.

Viggo did not miss a heartbeat. "Who else? I'm the best Assassin."

"And you're still the humblest, as far as I can see."

"Humility is overrated," Viggo said with a sarcastic smile.

"The one who overrates his skills is you," Engla said. "I'd have thought the life of an Assassin and the missions you have to carry out would take the wind out of your sails. I can see that hasn't happened."

"Why would they take the wind out of my sails? I've carried out all my missions without shedding a single drop of sweat."

"Let's hope this one is equally easy."

"It will be," he said confidently. "I'm not in the least worried."

"Maybe we'll have time to practice a little. I'll make a point of putting you in your place."

"That would be wonderful," Ingrid muttered, unable to help herself.

Viggo narrowed his eyes as he looked at her, then at Engla.

"Of course, Ma'am, whenever you wish."

Engla gave him an acid smile.

"Good. Ready to escort us to the capital?" asked Sigrid, who had seen that her brother had caught up with them. Enduald was dressed as usual: entirely in black. His horse too was black, and huge. It was a contradictory sight, such a big horse and such a small rider, both completely black.

"Of course, Mother Specialist," Ingrid replied.

"It'll be an honor," Molak added.

"Don't you worry about anything, we're in charge," Ulrich reassured her.

"I'm sure we'll have no trouble," Sigrid said with an optimistic smile.

The group set off, with Loke leading them and the Rangers surrounding the Elders, with Ingrid and Viggo bringing up the rear.

Viggo nodded in the direction of the Elder Specialists "D'you think those old geezers will last the whole way?" he whispered to Ingrid.

"Viggo! Don't be disrespectful to them!" Ingrid reproached him, trying as hard as possible not to raise her voice and be overheard.

"Eh? Don't tell me you haven't wondered about it. They can't have come out of the Shelter in at least twenty years."

"They're our leaders," Ingrid snapped, "and we'll show them the respect they deserve. Always."

"I respect them."

"Well, it doesn't sound like it."

"I do it in my own way."

"Respect them properly!"

"I still say I don't think they're going to be able to keep up the whole way to the capital."

"You're wrong, and they'll show you how wrong you are. They might be old, but they're not like other people. They're Elder Rangers. They've spent their whole lives studying, teaching and training, and they've looked after their bodies. Even if those bodies are old, they'll keep up."

"Fine... if you say so. We'll see."

Suddenly Sigrid fell a little back and stopped in front of them. "The day we can't make the journey from the Shelter to the capital, that day we'll retire from our responsibilities," she told Viggo with a warning look.

Ingrid looked embarrassed. She had heard them.

"Let's hope that day's a long way off," Viggo replied, not much affected by the fact that he had been heard.

"Let's hope so indeed," Sigrid said pointedly. "We'll see how long *you* keep up." She smiled maliciously and went back to Loke's side.

"I'd forgotten what that old witch of a Mother Specialist was like."

"She's a great woman,"

"And very touchy."

"From having to put up with pumpkin-heads like you."

Viggo smiled. "Well, at least you didn't call me a numbskull." He fluttered his eyelashes at her.

"Don't look at me like that, and behave yourself. We're on a very important mission."

"It doesn't seem so important to me. We're babysitting a bunch of elders so they get to the capital without falling off their horses from exhaustion. It's going to be a slow, boring journey."

There was a spark in Ingrid's eyes. "I do hope Engla gives you a lesson or two. I'm going to have a whale of a time watching."

"We'll see."

"This mission is important. It's an honor to have been chosen."

"What's happened with you is that you're delighted with the mission because your little sweetheart Captain Fantastic has arrived."

"He's not my little sweetheart, or Captain Fantastic either, and don't start —"

"Okay, I won't start, but for me he'll always be Captain Fantastic."

Ingrid rolled her eyes, and they rode on in silence.

Chapter 9

As they moved away from the Frozen Peak, Viggo, who was at the rear of the group, was looking back. Ingrid, who was riding beside him, noticed this.

"Is there something wrong?" she asked.

"No..."

"All you're doing is looking back. What's up?" She knew something was preoccupying him.

"A few memories just came back to me..."

Ingrid turned to look at the mountain range in the distance, with the Shelter hidden behind it. "About the time we spent at the Shelter?"

"Yeah..."

"Don't tell me you've turned nostalgic," she said in surprise. Viggo was not the sort of person who showed a softer side over anything.

"I think I am, a little. We had some hard times in there..." He stared back again as the horses moved on. "Although we learned a lot too. I have to say I had a very bad time there, but at the same time I improved a lot and learnt things I'd never believed were possible. I'm rather fond of it, even if the scars I got there still hurt."

Ingrid too was gazing nostalgically up at the mountains. "It was a very intense experience, and a really valuable one. I'll always treasure it."

"Well, the mushy moment's over. On we go." He looked ahead at the group of Elder Specialists, who were making their way on at a trot.

Ingrid felt it was unusual that he should have had that moment of recognition. It was not a thing she had seen in him very often, if ever. She enjoyed finding out that not everything in Viggo was irony and detachment. There were things that reached his heart, which was probably the size of a green plum and as sour as a lemon.

The group set up camp at nightfall, with Loke organizing the watch. He wanted all the Specialists except Molak to make a circle around the camp at a distance of three hundred paces or so. Molak climbed to the top of the beech they had set up camp beside, and with his sniper's bow prepared himself to deal with any threat from a distance. Loke had chosen the site well. It was a wide area of open land with only four trees, which they had camped beside. If anybody came within five hundred paces from any direction, Molak would be able to bring the intruder down without trouble. Nor could they be taken by surprise at night, because even with little visibility, there was nowhere to hide.

Sigrid, Annika and Engla were sleeping in the center, by the fire. Ivar and Gisli were taking turns with Loke at watch-duty. They had insisted on this, even though there was really no need as the other Specialists were standing guard around the camp. Loke had had to give in because Ivar and Gisli were not going to budge and were his seniors, so that he had no choice but to do as they ordered. On the other hand it was never a good thing to argue with the Elders, because apart from always being right, they all had their tempers.

The first day of their journey had turned out quiet, and Loke, who was keeping a close eye on Sigrid and Annika to make sure they could keep up the gentle pace, had not needed to do more than stop for a couple of long rest-breaks. For the moment everything was going well, and it looked as if the Elders were going to stand up to the journey.

The weather was good, although gradually, with every passing day, it was obvious that they were entering autumn, and cold and snow were beginning to make their presence felt. When they arrived at the city of Denmink, they skirted it to avoid raising suspicion. Nobody knew that the group was on its way, which was necessary to guarantee the safety of the Elders, and things had to stay that way. On the other hand, certain secrets were very hard to keep. The departure of all the leaders of the Shelter and their journey to the capital to attend the Great Council was sure to be one of them.

"However much we dodge cities and travelers, I don't think the secret's going to stay secret much longer," Viggo told Ingrid, sounding worried. "If it still is a secret."

Ingrid was confident that the leaders had planned things well. "Don't be a bird of ill- omen. Nobody knows we're on our way."

"I'm not so sure..."

"You're always pessimistic."

"And you always think if you follow orders, everything'll be all right."

"Well, it usually is."

Viggo raised his eyebrows. "Not when we're around."

"Well..." Ingrid fell silent. She knew he was right.

Molak let himself fall back to their side. His horse was a beautiful white courser with little black and grey specks.

"Why the long face?" he asked Ingrid.

"We were talking about this mission."

"And what's worrying you?"

"That this mission might not be a secret."

"Hmmm... it should be... but it's hard to keep this type of secret."

"You too?"

"Wow, it seems I agree with Viggo. Wonders never cease."

"You can say that again," Viggo murmured ironically.

"Nothing's going to happen," said Ingrid, trying to convince both herself and her two friends.

"Sure, all we have to do is take the old geezers to the capital, it's easy as pie," Viggo said. He put on a horrified expression.

"Nothing's going to happen! Everything's been worked out in advance!" Ingrid insisted.

"I don't know..." Viggo said stubbornly.

"Better keep our eyes peeled," Molak said. "Ingrid's probably right."

"Funny you agree with her," Viggo said derisively.

"Our opinions don't always coincide," Molak replied with a glance at the blonde Valkyrie.

Ingrid said nothing, but went on staring at him.

Viggo did not like those glances at all. He began to feel a burning in his stomach that went up his trachea. It was jealousy.

"What's really going to kill us is this slow pace we're following, with boredom I mean," he protested, trying to quell his jealousy.

"We can't go any faster. Annika wouldn't stand it," Molak said. "She's doing well enough at this gentle pace. Her body's frail."

"Well then, she shouldn't have come," Viggo snapped.

"She's got to be at the Great Council, she's one of the leaders. In any case, we couldn't go much faster. Sigrid and Enduald wouldn't be able to put up with a faster pace either."

"Then it's going to take us forever," Viggo protested.

"Well, it's an important mission and I'm perfectly happy with it,"

Molak said. "The company's excellent." He looked at Ingrid, who smiled.

"That's your opinion," Viggo countered. He could now see what Molak was trying to do.

"We have very good specialists in the group, that's true," Ingrid said.

Her answer, which was partly in response to Molak's move, annoyed Viggo. "Lots of Specialists for nothing. We should be on some other more important mission, not baby-sitting old geezers."

"Shhhh," Ingrid reproached him. "Sigrid'll hear you."

Viggo frowned. "I don't know how she does it. I'm sure she's half-witch."

Molak smiled. "She's a wise-woman, not a witch."

"She's both," said Viggo, looking at her. Just at that moment the Mother Specialist turned in her saddle and stared at him for a single moment, as if she knew he had been talking about her. "She's definitely a witch," Viggo muttered, the moment she stopped looking at him.

Two days later Loke was in the lead, thirty paces or so ahead. Ulrich and Aron were fifteen paces behind him, followed by the group. Molak was in the center, together with Ivar and Gisli, followed by Sigrid, Annika and Engla. Enduald rode behind them, not speaking to anybody, and Ingrid and Viggo brought up the rear.

They were now approaching an important bridge which crossed the powerful river Rosteg. Loke went ahead to make sure everything was all right, and Ulrich and Aron went with him. The Masig reached the bridge and looked in all directions to make sure there was no danger. He began to cross, then stopped in the middle, looking down at the ground. It looked as if the bridge had been under repair, but the work had not been finished. Rocks and planks were piled on one side and the ground looked irregular for a good stretch of the center of the bridge, which was about thirty paces or so long.

Loke dismounted from his horse and began to inspect the ground. Aron and Ulrich saw the Masig crouch down to check the ground beside the pile of rubble, and reached for their bows. Something was up. Suddenly Loke stood up and looked toward the end of the bridge, picked up one of the rocks which had been piled up for the repair work and hurled it with both hands five paces ahead of him. There was a crack, followed by an explosion of fire. Loke leapt backwards, and a strip of the bridge began to burn intensely. He picked up another large rock and hurled it rather further away. There was another explosion, and another section of the bridge began to burn.

The Masig turned to Aron and Ulrich. "Fire traps!" he shouted.

"Go and tell the others," Ulrich told Aron, who galloped back toward the group. They had already suspected that something was wrong.

"Fire traps on the bridge!" he shouted as he ran.

Viggo looked at Ingrid in annoyance. "What was all that about nothing bad going to happen, eh, Blondie?"

"You're a jinx!"

"Oh yeah, sure, now it's my fault!"

"Well, yes. It's probably your fault for being a bird of ill omen," she said very seriously.

"To arms, everybody!" cried Engla.

"Where are they attacking us from?" Ivar asked. His composite bow was already loaded.

Molak rose in his stirrups and looked in every direction, trying to see where the attack was coming from. His sniper's bow was in his hand.

Suddenly, from a group of trees behind them, several riders appeared, charging at them. Ingrid and Viggo, who were the closest to them, were the first to spot them.

Ingrid was already aiming. "Here they come!" she said.

Viggo tensed his bow and aimed.

"What the heck..."

Behind the first riders there appeared another, then another, and yet another.

"There must be at least twenty of them!" he exclaimed.

"Who are they?" Ingrid asked incredulously.

Viggo took a good look at them as they charged. They wore brown hooded cloaks of a very everyday kind, and as they were also wearing brown scarves which covered their faces, all that could be seen was their eyes. They all carried composite bows, and some were beginning to aim as they galloped. Judging by the ease with which they rode and readied their bows, Viggo had no doubt about what they were.

"They're Dark Rangers!"

"So many? There can't be that many of them!" Ingrid exclaimed. She was concentrating on releasing against the first of them.

"Looks to me as though this mission has just turned rather complicated," Vigo said. He too was aiming.

"Now!" Ingrid snapped when she had calculated that the first riders were four hundred paces away.

Both of them released at the same moment. Ingrid hit the rider she had selected, and her arrow buried itself in his right shoulder. Even so, with his left hand he broke the shaft, leaving the tip in his shoulder, then with a grimace of pain charged on. Viggo's arrow flew straight to the head of the second rider, but with great agility he flattened himself against his horse's neck so that the arrow brushed past his hair without touching him.

"They're definitely Dark Rangers!" Ingrid said.

"Gallop!" came Ivar's call.

Ingrid and Viggo, who were already aiming again, turned to see the Elder Specialists galloping away.

Gisli's hand-language said: "To the East!"

Ingrid and Viggo looked at one another. "We release, then we follow them!" she said.

"Done!"

They released again at the two leaders. This time Ingrid hit the one she had already wounded in the chest, and the rider fell dead from his horse. Viggo's arrow grazed the shoulder of the second rider, who once again dodged it by nimbly shifting his position on the saddle.

"That cretin is good!" he shouted. "I'll get you with my knives, then you'll never get away!"

"Let's go"! Ingrid yelled. "They're on us!"

They raced after the group, which was already following the river to the east. Several arrows flew toward their backs, but they huddled down and changed direction abruptly to avoid being hit. One brushed past Viggo's head.

"You're getting me riled!" he yelled when he touched his head and saw that it was bleeding.

"Keep your head flat on your horse's neck and make it turn right and left," Ingrid said as two other arrows passed close to her body.

"This riding business isn't really my thing, and you know it!"

"Do as I say, you numbskull, they're Rangers, they know how to shoot and they're going to get you!"

Loke and Ulrich arrived from the bridge and joined the group of Elders, which was led by Engla. Surprisingly, they were riding like young Rangers, as fast as their horses could go. Molak was in the middle of them, and was constantly looking back.

"Wow, the old geezers are riding at full tilt!" Viggo said, seeing he could not reach them however hard he spurred his own horse.

"I told you they aren't like other people! Aren't you ever going to take any notice of anything I say?"

Viggo smiled at her. "Only when you tell me you love me, then I'll take some notice!" He looked back and saw that although they had gained a little, their pursuers were trying to bring them down with their arrows.

"Do you really think this is the moment for nonsense!" Ingrid shouted incredulously.

"It's always a good moment to fall in love," Viggo replied with a smile as he made his horse veer slightly to the left.

"You're a terrible pain!" Ingrid shouted as she veered to the right.

Three arrows flew between the two of them.

"A heartache?" Viggo said as they straightened and came together again.

"Shut up and ride!"

"Quickly, don't let them catch us!" they heard Ivar shout.

The pursuers were releasing, trying to reach the rear of the group, which delayed them a little, though not too much. They could not leave them behind, even though they were riding as fast as they possibly could, following the course of the river. They avoided a group of boulders and skirted a small oak-wood, with the pursuers at their heels. Engla tried to leave them behind by skirting two more woods, one of beech to the east and another of ash to the west, but there was no way they could shake them off. They turned toward the river, and the attackers followed them. The horses were beginning to tire, and nor were they alone in this: some of the Elders too, especially Annika, Sigrid and Enduald, were beginning to find things difficult.

Loke hung back to have a word with Ingrid and Viggo. The Masig was an impressive rider, certainly the best in the group by far.

"We're going to try to split them up!" he told them.

"Is that a good idea?" Ingrid asked unsurely.

"One or two of the group aren't going to hold up much longer at this pace! We're going to have to see if we can distract them with some maneuver!"

"How are we going to do that?" Ingrid asked. She was riding as fast as her horse could bear.

"You two, together with Luca and Molak, take Sigrid, Annika, and Enduald!"

"And the others?"

"I'll take the others, with Ulrich and Aron."

"Right! At your signal!"

"Good!" Loke said. He rode toward the group and reached it at dazzling speed.

"I'm not sure this is a good idea!" Viggo said dubiously.

"It's to try and save one of the two groups!" Ingrid pointed out.

"Yeah? Which one?"

"Ours, you numbskull!"

Chapter 10

Ingrid and Viggo rode toward the group as fast as their horses would go. The cool wind was blowing in their faces, and at the speed they were going it was not at all comfortable. They pulled up their hoods and covered their noses and mouths with their scarves. The sound of their horses galloping hard on the road, which was partly covered by the first snow, muffled other sounds around them, so that they were forced to shout to make themselves understood.

The Dark Rangers were coming closer. The group was not riding as fast as their pursuers.

Viggo turned to look and saw something he did not like at all. "There's a second group coming!" he warned Ingrid.

She took a quick glance back over her shoulder. "I can count over a dozen of them!"

"They must've been waiting for us somewhere else, but we spotted the ambush and got away!"

"We haven't got away yet, they're coming for us!" Ingrid said uneasily.

"I know, I can almost feel their breath at the back of my neck!"

"I can't believe there are so many of them!"

"I think we've underestimated the strength of the Dark Ones!"

"You've nailed it there!"

Loke had already passed on orders to everyone in the group, and gave the signal as they came to a large lake which opened out in front of them.

"We split up now!" the Masig yelled, and turned his mount to the west. Engla, Ivar and Gisli followed him, along with the Specialists Aron and Ulrich.

"The others, with me!" Ingrid shouted, and veered off to the east.

Viggo was beside her, and they were joined by the Elders Sigrid and Annika, together with the Specialists Molak and Luca, and finally Enduald bringing up the rear.

The group split into two like a river forking in different directions. The first sub-group set out to surround the lake by the east, the other by the west. Their pursuers were forced to hesitate, since when they reached the lake they had to stop to decide what to do. They made up their minds quickly. The first group of pursuers, the largest, followed Loke's group westward, and the second followed Ingrid's group eastward. Making this decision, and then communicating it among the group of pursuers gave their quarry a breathing-space, so that they were able to increase their advantage slightly.

"We can take advantage of their confusion!" Ingrid yelled.

Viggo meanwhile was constantly looking back. "We've got to lose them!"

Sigrid, Annika and Enduald, who to judge by their expressions were finding things hard, took up their positions in the center. They would not be able to hold up much longer, especially Annika and Sigrid. Molak and Luca took up their positions at the rear. They went around the lake, then on as far as another beech wood. At the edge of it, Ingrid veered to the east once again and skirted the forest.

"We're not losing them!" Molak warned them from the rear.

"I can count twenty!" Luca said.

"They'll soon have us in range!"

They went on trying to put a distance between them, but the

situation was getting worse by the moment. They could not go any faster, and were losing what small advantage they had. The pursuers were closing in.

"I'm going to take this narrow path between the two woods!" Ingrid told Viggo.

"Okay! They'll see us go in, but the trees'll give us shelter!"

"I'll try to lose them by making a sharp turn as soon as we're out of the wood!"

"Good idea! We'll have to cross it fast and take advantage of the fact that they won't see us when we're inside."

They took the path that separated the two woods. It was quite narrow, with room for only two riders, so that they had to advance in pairs. The forest around them was thick, with dense underbrush.

Ingrid was about to reach the end of the forest and turn abruptly toward the east when she heard a muffled moan.

"Annika!" she heard Sigrid cry.

When she and Viggo looked back, they saw Annika reining in her horse and slipping off it on to the ground. Sigrid dismounted and ran to help her friend, and the others stopped too.

"What's the matter with her?" Viggo asked.

"She's reached her limit," said Sigrid, who was holding Annika in her arms.

Luca glanced at the entrance to the forest. "What do we do?"

"Can't she go on?" Molak asked Sigrid.

"I'm afraid not. She's exhausted."

"If we can't go on, what are we going to do?" Ingrid asked her.

Sigrid looked at her from the ground. "We don't leave one of our own behind. Defend her."

"That's what we're going to do. We're going to fight!" Ingrid said.

"We need to prepare a defense," Molak said. He glanced at Ingrid.

"There are a lot more of them than there are of us," Luca said uneasily.

The blonde archer was thoughtful for a moment. She needed a plan, and quickly. A good one, because they were heavily outnumbered. Sigrid, Annika and Enduald did not count as fighters, because they did not even have bladed weapons. All three of them were carrying wooden staves, but those would not stop arrows and axes. Neither were they in any physical condition to do so, even though in their time they had been great Rangers. Age spares no-one. They had already done enough by getting as far as this. There were four Specialists against twenty or so Dark Rangers. The odds were not good.

At last Sigrid spoke. "I'll tell you what you need to do to get out of here alive."

Viggo did not look entirely convinced. "What?"

She gave him a stern look. "I'm the Mother Specialist, and I have more knowledge and wisdom in this little finger than you'll ever have," she said very seriously. Everybody knew she was being serious. Even Viggo.

"Fine. Let's hear the plan," he said without a trace of sarcasm, because he knew Sigrid, and deep down he knew that she was right.

"Dismount and come close, all of you. Quickly, there's no time."

"What are we going to do?" Ingrid asked.

"We're going to disappear," the old woman said very seriously.

They all exchanged puzzled looks, but Sigrid turned to her brother Enduald, who nodded.

Only a few moments later the first pursuers came on to the path. When they looked ahead, all they could see was the empty path.

"They've crossed the forest!" said the leader.

"Quickly," the next one said. "We don't want to lose their trail, we've got them now!"

The Dark Rangers rode into the forest in pairs as fast as they could in search of the end of the path. It was seven hundred paces or so long.

"It's clear! Forward!"

The path seemed to be deserted. Five hundred paces from the end of the forest, they heard a whistle. The two riders in the lead looked at one another, recognizing the sound. Before they could react, a huge arrow skewered the rider on the left.

"Archer!" shouted the one on the right.

"Where?" one of the others asked.

He raised his head from his horse's neck to try to locate the marksman. The only thing he saw was the arrow that hit him squarely in the torso and threw him off his horse.

The one behind, who was now in the lead, realized what was

happening. "It's a Sniper!"

"We've got to get to the end, that's where he'll be!"

Another arrow flew with a lethal whistle and ended the life of the one who had just spoken.

"Dismount! We've got to kill the Sniper!"

The riders stopped their horses abruptly and dismounted, but a new arrow finished off another of the Dark Ones who had had no time to get off his horse. The arrow struck him with such force that he was thrown backwards off his saddle.

"To the woods! Quick!"

"He won't be able to catch us among the trees!"

The Dark Rangers split up and went into the forest on both sides of the path. They moved through bushes and undergrowth at a crouch, seeking the cover of the trees, armed with both composite bows and short ones, ready to kill the first person they met.

Eight of them advanced on either side of the path. Once they had the Sniper, they would finish off the rest of them easily, since they too must be hidden in the forest not much further on. So they were thinking as they went on. As they neared the end of the forest, they split into two groups of four in order to cover more terrain and offer a less easy target.

Suddenly, on the left of the path, a shadow fell from a branch on to the two rearmost pursuers. It struck them with precise blows on neck and back. One of the Dark Ones died before he touched the ground, the other a moment later. Viggo had dropped from the top of a tree on to them and buried his knives in them as he hit them. The other two turned and released, but he lunged behind a clump of bushes like lightning and the arrows passed close to him without touching him. They ran to the bushes, but when they went around them, he was no longer there.

The four who were on the same side, a little ahead, turned at the sound of the fight. At that moment, from behind the tree where she had been waiting, Ingrid appeared with her short bow *Swift* in her hands. She released at the first of the pursuers, whose back was to her. Almost instinctively, the Dark One turned, and the arrow hit him in the side. He moaned in pain and fell. His partner had also turned and now aimed at Ingrid, who was moving with the speed and ease of the wind, as if she were floating above the difficult terrain of the forest. Two arrows crossed, aiming to put an end to their respective archers. The Dark One, who had not moved to avoid missing his shot, received Ingrid's arrow in the center of his chest. Ingrid, still in motion to one side, saw the Dark One's arrow graze her shoulder. Before the other two could release against her, she had disappeared behind a tree.

On the right of the path, the four at the front were almost out of the forest. There was nobody on that side. Suddenly an arrow pierced the air and hit one of them. The impact threw him backwards, so that he crashed into a tree and fell dead.

"Sniper!" yelled his partner.

The other three hid and moved forward toward the source of the arrow. Suddenly one of them stepped on a trap. There followed an explosion of earth, dust, and smoke which stunned and blinded two of them. Molak, perfectly camouflaged like the expert sniper he was, rose from the ground. He dropped his sniper's bow and reached for his second weapon, a short bow. He nocked at the same time as the Dark One, who had already stepped free from the trap and released at him. The arrow hit him in the waist, but though he gave a groan, he did not let go of his bow. He aimed just as the Dark One was nocking another arrow, but he gave him no chance to release again and hit him full in the face. The arrow killed him instantly. Then Molak went for the other two before they could recover, dropping his bow and taking out his Ranger's knife and axe. Like a wounded lion he killed them with precise, ferocious slashes.

The other four Dark Rangers on that side had found a trail in the middle of the forest and were following it. One of them stepped on something, and there was a click. From one of the trees fell an enormous net, which caught two of them.

"Man Hunter Trap!" one of them yelled.

The two who were still free were looking in every direction to locate the Hunter who had set it. As for the ones who were trying to get free, the more they struggled with the net, which was impregnated with a strange and very sticky substance, the more they found themselves tangled in it.

Suddenly Luca sprang up from behind a bush. He threw his short axe with tremendous force at the closest of the Dark Archers and got him in the forehead, so that he fell backwards and did not get up again. The other aimed at Luca, who was zigzagging through the trees in search of cover, and released. The arrow missed him by a whisker.

The Dark One nocked another arrow, but Luca had already vanished.

On the left-hand side, Ingrid waited till the last moment, when her two pursuers were nearly upon her, then came out from behind a tree with *Punisher* in her hands. The two Dark Ones looking for her were taken by surprise, but reacted fast and aimed. Ingrid released from her tiny bow almost point-blank against the first, and the arrow went through his heart. The other tried to release, but she was too close to shoot with his composite bow. He tried anyway, but she slid to one side as if carried by the wind and the Dark Ranger missed. She dropped Punisher and in the same movement brought out her Ranger's knife. He did the same, but Ingrid moved far faster and more nimbly. Her opponent had no time to use his knife, and she slit his throat with a clean slash.

The two Dark Rangers looking for Viggo moved on to the end of the forest without being able to spot him. It was as if the forest had swallowed him. Suddenly they heard the nickering of a number of horses, and looked at one another in surprise. There were no horses anywhere near. Those horses could not be behind them, since they had already checked, so that they could only be ahead – which did not make sense, because ahead of them were only trees. They stopped with their short bows in their hands, ready to release.

"There's something funny going on here," one said to the other.

Once again, they heard the sound of restless horses.

"The horses can smell us. But where are they?"

"The sound's coming from ahead of us."

"There's nothing there but trees."

They scanned the trees before them, without luck.

"Those trees over there..."

"What?

"They're oaks..."

"So what?"

"This is a beech wood."

They looked at one another and nodded. There was a trick somewhere there. They moved carefully until they reached the oaks, with their armed bows in front of them. Suddenly their bows met something that was not supposed to be there, and a large sheet of cloth fell to the ground in front of them. Hiding behind it were the horses they were looking for. And more than that: Sigrid, Annika and Enduald, who were hiding behind that strange camouflage sheet.

"Gotcha!" the first Dark Ranger said, and aimed his bow at Sigrid. The Mother Specialist unflinchingly prepared to defend herself with her staff.

"Good trick, but it won't be any use to you!" the other one said. He aimed at Enduald, who was also in a defensive posture by now, wielding his staff. Annika was stretched out on the ground, exhausted.

"Traitors!" Sigrid reproached them. "You're nothing but scum!"

"Shut up, you old hag! Your days are over!" the first one said, and aimed at her heart.

"We'll kill them and collect the gold!" said the other.

Chapter 11

Like a stealthy shadow that had come to life out of the night itself, Viggo appeared behind the second of the two Dark Rangers who were threatening Sigrid, Annika and Enduald. Without making the least sound, he buried his knife in the side of his neck, covering the man's mouth with his hand at the same time so that he would make no sound. The Dark One fell dead.

He saw that the other was about to release an arrow at Sigrid, and decided to call his attention.

"Hey, cockroach, over here!"

The Dark One turned and tried to release, but by now Viggo's throwing dagger was already on its way to his right eye. With a swift defensive move he put his bow in the path of the dagger, which hit the bow hard and deflected his arrow.

Viggo showed him both his knives. "Good defense. Time to dance. I'll give you a choice between the knives you'd like me to use," he added with an acid smile.

"I don't want to kill you," the Dark Ranger said as he reached for his knife and axe.

"Choose," Viggo replied and showed him his belt, from which hung three pairs of knives. "These are the Deadlies, the long thin ones I use for thrusts and slashes. These are the Lethals, the curved ones, for cuts and slits. And these, my favorites, I call the Fatals, the ones for throwing." He indicated them with his gloved finger.

"An assassin, eh?" the Dark Ranger said, and in his eyes Viggo saw the shadow of fear.

"That's right. So don't worry about killing me. That's not going to happen. It'll be the other way round." He winked.

"We'll see about that."

"Well, if you don't choose, I will. I'll use the Lethals." The moment he had drawn them, he attacked.

The Dark Ranger saw Viggo moving toward him and defended himself with two circular slashes with his knife, followed by his axe. With complete tranquility, Viggo threw his body back and let the slashes pass over him without touching him. He countered rapidly and slashed the Dark One in his right leg. Two new, rapid attacks tried to end Viggo's life, but he did not even flinch. He dodged them with great agility and wounded the Dark Ranger again, this time in the left leg.

"Looks like you're not going to be able to dance much longer," he said, gesturing at his opponent's wounded legs.

The Dark Ranger took off his hood and lowered the scarf which covered his mouth.

Viggo looked at him in surprise. This man looked familiar to him. He narrowed his eyes, looked closely at his face and recognized him as Jacob. He had been a fellow-Ranger, but had not managed to graduate at the end of the four years at the Camp.

"You?" he asked in amazement as he lowered his knives. "You're Jacob, of the Boars, from back when we were at the Camp."

"I see you remember me."

Viggo shook his head. "Why did you do it?" He remembered having spoken and trained with Jacob, and it seemed unnatural that he should be there in front of him.

"I didn't have much else to turn to when I was expelled from the Rangers."

"I remember your circumstances were rather like mine," Viggo said. He was remembering Jacob's past.

"Yeah. I was a convict. The Rangers were my salvation. I'd get the King's pardon when I graduated."

"And your plan failed."

"That's right. Without graduating, it'd mean back to a cell to serve my sentence."

"So the Dark Rangers recruited you."

"That's right. Me and others."

"How many others?"

"A lot more than you'd imagine."

"All those who were expelled during the last few years...·"

"And others who got tired of serving despot kings who don't deserve our loyalty."

"The King might be better or worse, but he's the King. It's not our job to judge him but to serve him." Ingrid said. She had come up to them with an arrow nocked, aiming at Jacob's torso.

Viggo nodded at her, and she nodded back.

"The Dark Rangers don't feel that way. You follow a leader who inspires you, not one who's been imposed on you."

"And your leader inspires you?" she wanted to know.

"That's right."

"And who is it?"

"You'd like to know, wouldn't you?"

"Are you going to tell me?"

"No."

"You're going to condemn yourself..."

"I don't think so. Today we're going to get rid of some of the Rangers' top brass. The end's getting closer for all of you."

"No way."

"We'll see."

"You shouldn't have joined the Dark Rangers," Viggo said, "whatever your situation might have been."

"It was this or the cell. This is much better."

"Can't see why. You're going to die in this forest without having accomplished anything."

"Your leader won't be able to defeat us," Ingrid told him.

"Our leader has gold, and very important contacts in the Court."

"How important?" Viggo asked.

"The most important."

"In other words, he's on nodding terms with the powerful."

"That's right, and he's very well-financed. He's offering a fortune in gold for the heads of the leaders of the Rangers. I could've lived like a noble after this mission."

"Pity you're going to die," Viggo said. He turned to Ingrid. "Let me finish him off."

Ingrid thought about it and nodded. "We don't have time for this. Finish him off."

Viggo prepared to attack.

"Wait, Viggo!" came Sigrid's order, and he stopped and turned to her.

"I want him alive. What he's been hinting at is very interesting. I'd like to know more."

"I don't suppose he knows much more than what he's already told us."

"Even so, don't kill him. We're going to interrogate him."

Viggo snorted. "Okay, then."

"Drop your weapons," Ingrid said to Jacob.

The Dark Ranger thought for a moment. He was losing blood from both leg-wounds. "All right, then," he said resignedly, and threw his knife and axe at Ingrid's feet.

"That's better," Viggo said.

They heard footsteps approaching from the east and turned, ready to attack. Molak and Luca appeared amid the undergrowth, both of them wounded and bleeding.

"Our side is clear," said Molak.

"And couldn't you have done it without getting wounded?" Ingrid asked them.

"Don't blame them, they're inclined to be clumsy," Viggo said with a glint of amusement.

"Very funny," Molak said.

"Yeah, I'd laugh if it didn't hurt," said Luca.

Sigrid was coming toward them. "Don't complain so much. They don't look like serious wounds to me, and you're grown-ups now."

Viggo laughed under his breath.

"And as for you," she told Viggo, "see if you can learn not to kill and to think a little."

"You're welcome," he replied. His expression suggested that he had expected gratitude for saving her life.

"Remind me to tell Engla not to be so benevolent with who she decides is going to graduate," Sigrid added.

This time it was Ingrid who laughed. Sigrid glared at her, so she avoided saying anything more, to avoid a poisoned comment from the Mother Specialist.

"Tie him up," she told Viggo.

Sigrid was looking through the trees toward the south. "Yes, and gag him in case there's anybody else left in the forest."

"I can have a quick look if you like," Luca offered.

"No, you have a cut in your arm that needs attention. Viggo, you go."

Viggo was about to protest, but Sigrid gave him one of her evil-witch glares and he swallowed his words.

"I'll be back shortly," he said, and disappeared into the forest.

"You two see to Annika," Sigrid told the others. "I'll tend to the three of you, you'll be fine in no time at all."

She set about preparing potions and ointments with the ingredients in her saddlebags. Ingrid kept a close eye on the surroundings. Enduald began to gather up the cloth he had used to trick the Dark Rangers. Ingrid noticed that as he folded it, the image it showed seemed to move.

"Is it enchanted?" she asked, remembering that Enduald was an Enchanted, a Wizard with the power to enchant objects, to give them abilities.

"That's right."

"How does it work?" she asked curiously.

"It's like a canvas with a landscape painted on it. Except that the landscape on it adapts to the environment it's in. In other words, it changes."

"Ohhh... wow."

"But I need to improve it. The enchantment tricked them at first, but I didn't manage to do it completely."

"I think it's pretty impressive."

"Not really. It's only an optical illusion created through magic."

"Even so, it seems amazing to me."

"The way you all fight so well seems more amazing to me. Unfortunately I can't fight."

"Not even with magic?"

"No... my magic's only for creating enchantments, I haven't any direct attack magic. I can enchant a sword so that it burns and creates more damage, but I can't wield it. I was never a good fighter."

"I see," Ingrid said.

Viggo came back presently after searching the whole forest.

"There's nobody left in the forest. We're alone."

"Good," Sigrid said. "Keep watch while I finish healing these two. Annika's better."

"Yes... quite a lot better," Annika said, speaking for the first time since the start of the pursuit. She had a better color now. She drank a potion Sigrid had prepared for her and sighed. "Give me a little more time, and I'll be able to go on."

"We're not moving until we know what's out there waiting for us," said Ingrid.

"We're staying here in hiding?" Molak asked. He was pressing his hand on his wound to stop the bleeding.

"Yes, I don't want to risk it." Sigrid turned to Ingrid. "I have a mission for you."

"Yes, Mother Specialist."

"I want you to go and find Loke and Engla and the others and bring them here. That is, if they've managed to get away. I hope so. I don't want to leave the forest and find the other group of Dark Rangers waiting for us."

"Right away."

"Be careful," Molak told her as she passed him on her way to fetch her horse.

"I will be. Don't worry," she replied as she mounted.

They waited for Ingrid's return while they recovered. Viggo was restless. He did not like being stuck there with nothing to do but watch, least of all knowing that Ingrid was in danger. He was aware that he could not leave the wounded and that he was the only one who was fit to fight. Molak and Luca did not have very serious wounds, but they were painful and would not let them fight as they knew how to, which put their lives at risk. As a result he had to resign himself to watch duty and be prepared in case he had to leap into action.

Night was beginning to fall when they heard horses approaching in the distance. Molak and Luca crouched down, their bows at the ready. Sigrid had disinfected, sutured and bandaged their wounds. Viggo hid in the shadows with his knives in his hands. Annika, Sigrid and Enduald hid themselves behind the enchanted canvas.

The horses stopped at the entrance to the forest, and they heard several riders dismounting. In silence, they prepared for whatever might happen.

"It's us," they heard Ingrid's warning whisper.

"Are you all right?" came Loke's voice.

"Yes, yes, we're fine," Sigrid called back from under the camouflage canvas.

A moment later Ingrid, Engla and Loke appeared beside them amid the tree-shadows, but Viggo did not come out at once. He stayed hidden a little longer in case it was a trap.

Molak and Luca came out to welcome them. "We're glad to see you," Molak said, looking at Ingrid, who nodded back at him. She was not wounded.

"Sigrid?" Engla called.

The Mother Specialist came out from under the canvas. "We're fine, a little bruised, but fine. These young Specialists have done very well."

"Thank you. Much appreciated," said Viggo as he came out from the shadows.

Loke turned to Viggo like lightning. As he did so, they saw that he had a cut in his cheek.

"Are you all right?" Sigrid asked him with concern.

"Yes, I'm fine..."

Her instinct told her that something bad had happened. "What was it?"

"We weren't as lucky as you were," Engla said.

Annika and Enduald meanwhile were getting up and looking at Engla, clearly worried.

"What happened?" Sigrid asked.

Engla sighed. "We fought them at the red wolves' gully."

Sigrid nodded. "I know the place."

"We managed to hold them back and make them run... but we've had losses. Aron and Ulrich are dead and Gisli's badly wounded. Two arrows: one in the leg and the other in the torso. That one nearly killed him."

"Oh no! We've got to get back to him at once!" Sigrid exclaimed. She glanced aside at Annika, who nodded repeatedly.

"He's with Ivar," Engla said, "not far from here. We'll go at once."

"Right, let's go."

Engla had seen Jacob gagged and tied to a tree. "And that one?"

"He's told us some very interesting things," Sigrid said. "He's coming with us."

"What for?"

"So that he can tell us some more," Sigrid said, and that evil-witch glare appeared on her face once again.

Chapter 12

Astrid and Lasgol rode very close together, almost touching, immensely enjoying their mutual company as well as the landscape on their way toward Count Malason's castle. They had to carry out the mission Egil had given them, and they hoped it would be one without too many complications. Although as it was them, and as one of Egil's plans was involved, they were both very much aware that things would probably get tangled. They said nothing openly, more than anything else to avoid attracting the bad luck that seemed to follow them wherever they went.

Behind them came Camu and Ona. Lasgol had tried to persuade them to wait for them at the estate with Martha, but there had been no way of doing it. They were not prepared to be separated from them for a single moment. Lasgol heaved a sigh. He was thinking of the day when because of a mission, or some other unavoidable event of life, they would be forced to be separated. It was going to be very painful for all of them. Ona and Camu would not understand, he was sure of that, just as he was equally sure that sooner or later it would happen, and he was afraid of that moment. Luckily, so far this had not happened, and he prayed to the Ice Gods that they would allow things to go on in the same way. The drama of separation from his two dear friends could reach tragic extremes.

Camu had permission to go without camouflaging himself as long as they did not come across anybody, and he was enjoying this. For some reason he liked to show off. Or rather, not for any particular reason, he liked to show off for the simple reason that he enjoyed being the center of attention whenever he could. Well, perhaps not as much as that, Lasgol thought, but it was true up to a point. He wanted Camu to use his ability to camouflage himself as much as possible. The reason was that the more often he used it, the easier it would become, the longer it would last, and the more beings he would be able to deceive with it. Lasgol suspected that although the skill worked perfectly well on mere humans like them, it would probably not work with all the creatures of Tremia. He was especially afraid that some Mage or magical creature like Camu himself might be able to see him even if he were using his skill.

On the other hand, the more he used his skill, the more powerful it would become. This principle which governed magic was one Egil had insisted he should internalize himself, not only for Camu's skills but for his own.

Lasgol looked at Astrid, then at the sky, and smiled. The weather was good, by the standards of what was usual in western Norghana at the beginning of autumn, and he was deeply enjoying Astrid's company in the beautiful landscapes of his native land.

"These ash forests and this smell of moist earth bring back a lot of memories," he told her, and breathed in deeply to fill his lungs.

"It's a very pretty area," she said, looking at both sides of the road.

"It doesn't look particularly beautiful to me, but it brings back some very good memories. I once made this same journey with my father, and passing this way again brings back vague fragments of memory of having been through here with him."

"Precious memories."

"Yes, they are. Very. The pity is that they're so slight and distant that they barely exist."

She smiled. "Enjoy them, even if they barely exist. I'll enjoy them later on when I remember this journey we made, you and I, all by ourselves."

"Alone with our children..." he joked.

She laughed. "Yes, in fact they do sometimes seem to be your children."

"But if I'm the father... you know who's supposed to be their mother." He glanced at her mischievously.

"No, no, no! I have enough to do looking after their father."

I no child, came Camu's complaint.

Oh no? In that case what are you?

I grown up. Ona too.

The panther chirped this time.

Oh yeah? Well, you often behave like little children.

Not true. We always like grown-ups.

Yeah, yeah...

No sooner had he transmitted this message than Camu saw a white fox and launched himself in pursuit of it. Ona, of course, followed him at once. Lasgol had told them over and over again not to go chasing after animals, but it was like speaking to... little children... He could not help smiling.

"I like to see you smile. It makes my heart sing," Astrid said, stroking his arm from her mount.

Lasgol looked aside at her. "Just looking at your beautiful green eyes makes me overflow with joy."

"Yeah, your compliments are.... just as clumsy as ever..." She laughed.

"Well, at least I try." He blushed slightly.

"It's a good thing I don't care much for that kind of thing, or you'd be in a pickle."

He beamed. "That's why I love you."

"Just because of that?"

"Well, of course not, for lots of other things..."

"Such as?"

"Huh... well... you're intelligent... determined... good..."

"Drop it," she interrupted him. "I'm just messing with you." She laughed aloud.

"Of course... that's you all over..." And he laughed too.

They were following the road toward the northwest. Count Malason's castle was not very far from Skad. If everything went smoothly, they would arrive the following morning. After visiting the Count, they were supposed to go on to the capital for the Great Council. Lasgol had asked permission from Dolbarar to go to Skad with Astrid first, and permission had been granted. With the proviso that he would be at the Royal castle for the day of the Council. Lasgol had not mentioned the visit to Count Malason, which was the Snow Panthers' private business, or rather Egil's, although it was true that it affected them all. What affected one of them always ended up affecting the others, as they were learning very quickly. As they were on a tight schedule they had not been able to stay in Skad any longer, nor could they afford to linger on their way.

Lasgol stroked the neck of his good old buddy, Trotter. "Good old pony," he whispered into his ear, leaning forward in the saddle.

"Just out of curiosity... doesn't it bother you that you look so much smaller than me when we're riding together?" Astrid said sarcastically as she looked down on him from her mount. It was a pure Norghanian horse, not a pony, and two hands taller than Trotter, which made her look as though she were much taller than

Lasgol when they were riding.

"Very funny. You may be taller and faster on that horse, but I'll go further on Trotter." He stroked the horse's neck, and the pony replied by moving his head up and down.

Astrid laughed. They went on teasing one another for quite a while about who was taller and who would get further. Now, though, they were not simply talking about their horses but about themselves. Afterwards they were silent, each lost in their own thoughts.

"Those comments about Camu yesterday have started me thinking," Lasgol said suddenly.

"About whether he's a dragon or not?"

"Yup..."

I dragon, came the message from Camu.

Don't you start... you're no dragon and you know it.

I dragon, you wait and see.

We'll see, yes.

Ona chirped twice, which meant 'no'.

See, Ona doesn't think so either.

Ona not know.

Trotter snorted twice.

Trotter doesn't think so either.

All you wrong. I know. You not.

"Camu's convinced he's a dragon now," Lasgol said sadly.

Astrid smiled. "In heart and spirit, he is."

"Don't encourage him, that's all I need."

Astrid know. She smart.

Lasgol rolled his eyes.

"Oh well..." Lasgol stroked Trotter's head, and the pony appreciated the gesture by nodding his head up and down.

"What have you and Egil managed to find out about him?"

Lasgol was thoughtful for a moment.

"We think he's a Drakonian species, related to dragons. That's to say a Drako, as they're commonly known by those scholars who study special creatures."

I of dragon family.

That's not clear...

I very clear.

Go and play with Ona so that Astrid and I can talk in peace for a while.

Okay, but I Dragon.

Lasgol snorted. *My, you're stubborn.*

"Is he still insisting?" Astrid asked as they took a fork in the road toward the east.

"Yes, very stubborn. When he gets something into his head, there's no way of dissuading him."

Astrid turned in her saddle and saw Camu and Ona playing in the grass chasing after each other. "I think he's sweet."

"Oh yeah... really sweet... and you've no idea how easily he changes his mind."

"No way, right?" she smiled.

"Absolutely none. Anyway... what we believe is that he's a Drako."

"Because he's like others of the same species?"

"That, and because my father had the book *Drakonian Creatures* with him, and we think this has something to do with Camu."

"Didn't your mother tell you anything else about him?"

"Yes..." Lasgol sighed at the thought of his mother. "She told me she'd got him for me, to protect me. She sent him to my father so he could give him to me."

"That makes sense."

"And then we know from Asrael, the Shaman of the Arcanes of the Glaciers and his creature Misha, that Camu comes from that region."

"Yes, I remember that. He said he'd seen a creature like him."

"The more I think about it, the more convinced I am that the only way to find out about Camu's origin is to look for it in the Frozen Continent."

She gave him a troubled look. "Are you thinking about going back to the land of the Peoples of the Ice?"

Lasgol sighed heavily. "Actually, yes, I am... it's the only way of knowing what's behind the mystery of his origin. I need to know what kind of creature he is, how my mother got hold of him, what I'm supposed to do with him... I mean how to look after him... I don't know anything about how I'm supposed to care for him so that he grows up strong and healthy."

"I know what you mean. But I'm a bit worried about this idea. It's a really dangerous adventure. Either the climate, or the Wild Ones of the Ice, or the Tundra Dwellers, or the Arcanes of the Glaciers would kill you the moment they laid eyes on you."

"Or the Creatures of the Ice themselves..."

"Yeah, those too," Astrid said. The look on her face suggested that it was insane to think of going back there.

"I know it's risky and there are all sorts of dangers..."

"When you talk like that you worry me... I know you, I know what you have in mind and that the danger won't stop you... If you go, promise you'll speak to me about it first."

"Of course I'll talk to you about it."

"Promise."

Lasgol sighed. "I promise."

"That's better."

"Don't worry, this isn't the moment..." Lasgol was thoughtful as they rode past an oak wood. "We've got more serious problems on our hands that we need to solve first. It's not the moment to set off on a new adventure, and a terribly dangerous and icy one."

"So we have serious problems as it is," Astrid said, as though she knew nothing about them. "You couldn't possibly mean the Dark Rangers' conspiracy? Or maybe you could be referring to the betrayal and murder attempt on Egil? Or maybe even the attempts on your own life?"

"Yeah... I mean that... all that..."

"Interesting... and on top of that, there's sure to be some bigger conspiracy we haven't found out about yet." She looked amused.

"I wouldn't say you're wrong, knowing our luck..."

"Or rather our bad luck..." She winked at him.

"I think I'm a bird of ill omen. I attract trouble. Viggo's always saying that."

At that moment a raven flew past their heads.

Astrid pointed to it. "Well, I never!" she said.

"You see?"

"In our mythology, the raven's also the bringer of news, the one who flies over the world and brings us news of whatever's going on."

"That's right. Whichever way, it's not the moment for setting off on new adventures. We need to clear up all our tangles first. After that there'll be time to look into Camu's origin."

"I'm glad you see it that way," Astrid said in a voice heavy with sarcasm.

Lasgol shrugged and smiled. "I'm glad to have you on my side."

"And I'm even more so. That way I can be sure you don't get

into any more trouble," she joked.

"I like that. You'll be my protector against new trouble."

"It looks as though I'm going to have my work cut out in this new role."

Lasgol burst out laughing. "Almost certainly."

Chapter 13

They spent the night beside a small river which flowed into a pond surrounded by beeches. Astrid and Lasgol slept in one another's arms under their travel blanket, wrapped in feelings of love and unfathomable happiness. Ona and Camu slept at their feet, as if they were two guardian creatures out of Norghanian mythology protecting the demigods who were their lord and lady.

With the first rays of dawn they woke and went to the river to wash before going on with their journey.

"What's the water like?" Lasgol asked Astrid, who was already splashing herself.

"Not very cold. I'd say it's even pleasant for this time of year."

Lasgol bent down and put his hand into the crystal-clear water to check the temperature.

"It certainly is. I almost feel like diving in."

"Why don't we go down to the pond and do that?" she asked, making it sound like a challenge.

"Are you sure?"

"Come on, it'll be fun."

Lasgol nodded, smiling. "Let's go, then."

They went to the pond and Ona and Camu began to run around the water, chasing each other like two overgrown puppies. Lasgol became aware that now Ona was much faster than Camu, who was still growing and had trouble moving with the same agility as his sister. The good panther was running more slowly to avoid embarrassing Camu and making him feel bad. Lasgol realized this, and was grateful for the gesture. Ona was a delight as partner and sister.

Astrid nodded at them. "They're having a ball."

"Yeah like a couple of siblings, playing the whole day long. I wonder what'll happen when they're older. Camu's growing out of hand, and Ona, even if we don't notice it, is growing up daily."

She laughed. "When they're older they'll get boring, like us."

"Since when are we older? And boring?" Lasgol shot back, pretending to be offended by the comment. He felt like a cheerful youth. At least on the inside.

"Well, we're growing too... even if you haven't realized... or don't want to realize." Astrid's smile was deeply ironic.

"No way. I'm still a laddie, as Ulf calls me."

"A laddie? I'm not so sure, you're twenty now... going on twenty-one."

"Well, I'm still playful and cheerful. A laddie inside, at heart!"

Astrid laughed aloud. "If that's what you want to believe... it won't be me who bursts your bubble."

Lasgol wrinkled his nose. "I'm cheerful, aren't I?" he asked her, and this time he was serious.

"Of course you're cheerful," she said. "Not the soul of the party, not that, but yes, you are cheerful. You make me smile all the time." She smiled from ear to ear.

"That's a pretend one!" Lasgol pointed an accusing finger at her mouth.

"Well, that one was, but most of them aren't."

"Most? What d'you mean, most?"

"Practically all of them," she said with a giggle and began to undress, ready to plunge into the pond.

"I'm still a lad and I'm very cheerful," he muttered under his breath while he sat down on the ground.

"Yeah, yeah..."

Lasgol began to take off his boots. For any dive you had to strip completely, because there was nothing more dangerous in the north of Tremia than putting on wet clothes. The icy wind killed more people who put on wet clothes than wild animals did. By the time he had his boots off, Astrid was already naked, looking at the water. She had her back to him.

"Don't peek," she said turning and covering her breasts with her arm.

"Of course." He put his hand over his eyes. "I'm a gentleman."

"Never doubted it."

"If I can't see anything, it's hard to take my clothes off."

"Good try, but like the gentleman you are I'm sure you'll find a way."

"Yeah, sure," he said while he took off his pants as best he could, without looking at Astrid, which was turning out to be quite a complicated business.

"Hurry up, it's for today," she urged him.

"Coming, I'm coming."

Before he had taken his shirt off, she was plunging headlong into the pond in an elegant dive. He followed a moment later, trying to imitate her style, but realized that she had done it more gracefully. In fact she did many things better than he did himself. He swam to her in the center of the pond. The water was not too cold – for a Norghanian, that is – and they could bear the chill that was biting their bodies. Probably in a week they would no longer be able to do this, as the temperature would begin to fall.

When he reached her, Astrid pushed his head under with both hands. Lasgol sank to the bottom, but luckily he was able to shut his mouth in time to avoid swallowing water.

"This is how you welcome me?" he protested when he resurfaced, shaking his head to get the water out of his hair while he breathed through his nose.

"Weren't you saying you were jolly and playful? Well, show it!" she teased him and lunged at him to push him under again.

They fought and laughed in the water like a couple of children, enjoying every moment, even though Lasgol ended up swallowing a lot of water in his struggle to stay afloat. Astrid was like a tigress in any environment, and water was no different. Her green eyes shone with that wild intensity she radiated.

Tired of fighting, they embraced in the water and kissed passionately.

"We should do this kind of thing more often," she said.

He smiled. "All the time."

They melted into another long kiss. And then Ona and Camu joined them in the water with huge splashes as they swam around them.

"For heaven's sake!" Lasgol reproached them. "Can't you see this is a private moment!"

Play in water, Camu transmitted as he splashed.

Lasgol tried to dissuade them by pointing to the shore. *Play over there!*

More fun here.

"By all the magical creatures of Tremia!" Lasgol grumbled, shaking his head.

"What's happening? They don't want to leave, right?" Astrid

guessed.

All together. More fun.

"No way."

"I can see that." Astrid was laughing at Ona as she put her paws on her to be close to her. She stroked Ona's head and brushed water off her eyes.

"Ona, beautiful," she said.

The panther appreciated the petting with a chirp. The four of them played in the water, splashing, leaping over one another, pushing each other under, and more, until they had no strength left and went back to the shore and their clothes, then lay down on the grass. Lasgol fetched a blanket to dry themselves with.

They rested a while and got dressed. Lasgol stayed staring at the surface of the pond and began to think about the mission Egil had entrusted them. Also about the plots that surrounded them and which they were still unable to resolve. Who was the leader of the Dark Rangers? What was his aim? Had Malason betrayed Egil? Who had paid the Zangrians gold to kill Egil? Who was trying to kill him? Lots of riddles to solve. Lots of worries.

He sighed. How he wished his parents were still there to advise him what to do. To help him choose the right way and not to make some mistake that might cost one of his friends their life. He did not fear for his own life, but for that of his friends. Especially that of Astrid, and also Egil, who he knew was very much in danger because he was who he was.

The surface of the pond now looked like a mirror. An idea came to his mind: his mother's pendant. He decided to use it and see whether he could call up some memory of his parents' lives which might help him at that moment. He was not clear whether this would work, but it always gladdened his heart to see his parents.

He took out the jewel he wore around his neck and looked at it for a moment.

Astrid had noticed this. "Are you going to use it?"

"I think so..."

She stroked his back in encouragement. "Go ahead."

"I don't know whether it'll activate itself. The last few times I've tried I couldn't get it to show me any memory. It's curious that I can't use it whenever I want to, when it's a gift my mother gave me to use."

"Maybe she was the only one who could use it when she wanted."

"Yeah... I think that's right. She and my father, because there are also memories of him in it."

"Maybe one day you'll be able to store yours in it too."

"You really think so?" he asked, without much confidence that this would ever happen.

"I don't see why not."

"You need some kind of spell to do that... My mother knew how to do it, but I have no idea. Egil doesn't know either. He hasn't found anything in the tomes he's consulted about how to store memories in objects of power."

"You have magic, just like your mother. She could do it, and one day you'll be able to as well. You'll find you can do it."

"We don't have the same kind of magic... I think... though I'm not sure. I've no idea how magic between mother and son works, how it's passed on... or inherited... or whatever it is that happens."

"She was a great sorceress, with a lot of power. I'm sure you could be one too. I'm sure you have it in your blood."

"I'm not so sure..."

"Didn't she tell you anything about magic, the basics, the way it would affect you?"

"No... she had to run away when I was very little. We never had the chance."

"Surely she must have known you'd inherit her power, at least part of it."

"Hmmmm, maybe." He was looking at the jewel. "But neither she nor my father ever told me anything about it. But it could be in these memories."

"If I were her and I couldn't teach you or transmit this knowledge," Astrid said thoughtfully, "I'd use the jewel to store it, and then one day you'd be able to acquire it. Yes, that's what I'd do."

"Perhaps they're in there... I'm going to try and reach them. I'd imagine that just like with my skills and most of the things to do with magic, the more you practice it, the more you learn and the better you get. Now I can't activate the jewel whenever I want to, and I can't search for the memories stored in them that I want to see. But something tells me that if I keep trying, the way I do with my skills, I might succeed."

She smiled. "You lose nothing by trying."

"That's true."

"If we don't count time and patience, obviously."

"Two things I have plenty of."

"Hah! Not time, for sure. Patience, yes. You're very patient." She kissed his cheek tenderly.

He looked at his mother's pendant on the palm of his hand. "The Marker of Experiences," he told her.

"Try activating it."

"Right." He moistened his index finger in his eye, then touched the jewel in the pendant. There was an intense blue flash.

"That's a good sign," he said.

He heard a protesting moan from Ona, who like Camu, though in a very different way, was also able to perceive magic. The panther through her feline instincts, and Camu because he could feel any magic which was conjured up near him.

Pendant magic, Camu messaged.

Go on playing, don't worry, Lasgol told them, and they looked at one another.

Okay, Camu as agreed, and ran off with Ona following him immediately.

A second flash bathed Lasgol's body. He began to feel nervous. It looked as though he was going to see a vision, an experience his parents had had. What would the Pendant show him? Would it be connected with his own life, with what was happening to him, in some way? The questions tumbled over one another in his mind. Whatever it was, very probably he would discover some new small episode in his parents' life. This filled him with expectation.

Suddenly there came the third flash he was waiting for, which was followed by the beginning of the vision. The image started out blurry, out of focus, which was what he had expected. It was as if the jewel were calibrating what it was going to project over the waters of the pond.

The image became clearer, and Lasgol had a sudden fright. The first thing he saw was the face of King Uthar. He was confused, because this was not quite what he wanted to see. Besides, Uthar appeared younger than he remembered him. The image went on becoming more definite, and he realized that the King was on horseback, holding a long spear. He was wearing a heavy bearskin cloak over his luxurious silver-scaled armor with its gold decorations.

From the melting snow around him it must have been the end of winter. After the King there appeared other riders of his personal guard, all armed with long spears. But the Norghanians did not use long spears, least of all on horseback. What was this scene he was watching?

He turned to look at Astrid, who was also watching the image on the surface of the pond, as if it were being projected upon it.

She pointed to four large hunting dogs passing in front of them. It's a hunt."

"Right. That makes sense. They used spears to hunt dangerous animals like big cats, bears, wild boar and so on."

He tried to think when this scene might be from. Was that image the real Uthar, the real King, or was it the Shifter who had taken his place? If it was the impostor, the scene would be closer in time. But if on the other hand the King was the real Uthar, the memory could be from further back. Nor did he know whether the memory was his father's or his mother's.

An officer was giving orders from horseback, and he looked familiar to Lasgol. After a moment's careful study of his features he recognized him as Sven, the Commander of the Royal Guard. Judging by his stripes, he guessed that at the original time of the scene he had been Captain of the Guard.

A rider came up to the King's group, who had stopped beside a river and was trying to work out how to cross it. Lasgol recognized him at once as his father. He was considerably younger. Seeing his father Dakon and Sven beside Uthar, he worked out that this scene must have taken place shortly after Sven had been appointed Captain of the Guard, so that Uthar must still have been the real Uthar and not the Shifter.

"The trail goes on eastward," Dakon said.

Uthar smiled. "You have an amazing eye."

"Ranger training, my liege."

"There's a lot more than training into what you see," Uthar said. "Very few men in Norghana – and I'd bet all the gold in my bag, in the entire north – can track like you. Not to mention that where you set your eye, you set your arrow: a quality which is not only sought after by others, including me – although I'm very bad with the bow – but also very difficult to master."

Dakon nodded respectfully. "You honor me, my liege."

"Does your majesty wish to kill the boar with his own hand?" Sven asked.

"Yes. Today I feel like getting a bit of exercise and giving my arm some work to do. It's a while since I used a spear, and lack of use is the worst enemy of muscles."

"You shouldn't take any risks, my liege," Dakon begged him.

"What kind of an example would I be giving the young ones if I weren't capable of killing a boar?"

"This is a very large animal," Dakon warned him, "and with dangerous tusks."

"I can do it, your Majesty," Sven said. "Boar-hunting is one of my specialties."

"The Captain has a reputation for being an excellent boar-hunter," Dakon insisted. "Let him be the one who kills this quarry."

"Your King is grateful for your concern. But a strong monarch must exercise and at the same time prove he's not a weak, useless King. Today I shall be the one who kills the quarry. Better still, I'll do it on foot, without the help of my faithful horse. That way we'll be more equal."

Dakon and Sven exchanged a look of concern. "Your Majesty, that's very dangerous..." Dakon began.

"Bah, nonsense. I've killed tigers with my bare hands. A boar, no matter how big, isn't going to make me quake."

"A boar's tusks can rip a man's stomach open, your Majesty," Sven warned him.

"Nothing I don't know already. It doesn't worry me. With this spear I'll pierce its heart."

"But if it charges, you won't have time to aim..." Dakon began.

"My marksmanship isn't half as good as yours is with the bow. Even so, it's enough to kill a wild animal, be it boar, tiger, or lion. I don't want to hear any more about it." Uthar was looking annoyed with all the objections Dakon and Sven were making.

"It's the real Uthar," Lasgol guessed.

"How do you know?" Astrid asked.

"Because the Shifter would never have dared confront a wild animal on his own. Too dangerous, and without any reward."

"Oh, I see."

They went on watching the hunting party. There must have been fifteen people or so in it, counting the King's guard, officers and dog-handlers.

"Send the dogs to search!" the King ordered the leader of the hunt. The dogs, very nervous because they could smell the quarry, were set loose to flush it.

Dakon shook his head. "Kings sometimes believe they're stronger and more skilled than they really are," he commented to Sven." Or perhaps they believe they still are after they've spent a while ruling."

"And very likely the truth is quite different... the constant days in the palace, with the court, weaken the body of the strongest nobleman... including that of his Majesty."

"Yes, and that's why we need to keep our eyes peeled and protect him."

"So we will," said Sven.

"Stay with me," Dakon said, "and when I find the boar, you kill it before the King arrives."

"All right... but the King'll be angry..."

"Yes, that's something we won't be able to avoid."

"Better for his Majesty to take it out on me, rather than give up his life with his guts all over the ground."

"That's exactly what we need to prevent," Dakon said. "I'll lead you to the quarry. Kill it quickly. I hope your reputation is well deserved."

"It is. I won't miss."

"Good. Let's be off."

Both riders set off after the dogs at a gallop.

Astrid was silent as she watched the scene. At last she said: "They're trying to stop the King from making a mistake and getting wounded."

"My father always protected the King, until he found out he was a Shifter and the perverse plans he had."

"Have you realized, we're not seeing the scene as your father would have seen it?"

"Well, no... what do you mean?"

"Do you see your father galloping?"

"Yeah."

"This can't be your father's memory, because it's not from his point of view. His memory would be of galloping with Sven, not of someone watching him galloping. What we're watching isn't just what your father saw and experienced. It's not only a memory... it's a whole situation, just as it happened, narrated from an external point of view."

"Wow... you're right. I hadn't noticed that until you mentioned it... but yes, it's the whole event, complete, not just what my father saw."

"It's as if it were amplified. The jewel stores your father's memory, but it's amplified by additional information."

"It must be because of the magic that's involved. It must store an amplified version of the memory. As if the scene was being observed from a higher point of view."

"Which is what we're watching now. Very interesting."

"Egil's going to love this new deduction."

Astrid chuckled. "He'll find it fantastic, you just wait and see."

They saw Uthar give the order to go on with the hunt.

"On we go, after the quarry!" he ordered, and the group set off.

The whole group followed the King, who waded the river showing off how skillfully he handled his powerful Norghanian steed, which was over seventeen hands high. It was a war horse, the kind bred for fighting. It could bring down other horses, men and animals with no trouble with its massive, powerful body.

The image went back to Dakon and Sven, who were a little ahead, following the dogs. The animals seemed to be confused now. They were going around a small pond half-filled with water plants, half with mud. They seemed to have lost the trail. Dakon leapt down nimbly from his mount. No sooner he had set his feet on the ground than he moved as if he were gliding over the grass and snow that still covered the area. Lasgol could now clearly see from the landscape around his father that spring was arriving and the snow was melting. Dakon knelt down at several points around the pond and examined the trails. Then he went back to his horse.

"Where to?" Sven asked.

"It's crossed the pond. It's heading north."

The two riders galloped away, while the dogs tried to recapture the animal's trail. When they had crossed the pond, they had lost it in the mud. They were barking and howling for help, but Dakon and Sven did not wait for them.

"They're leaving the dogs behind on purpose," Astrid realized.

"It looks like it. My father doesn't need them. He can follow any trail better than they can." As he said this Lasgol realized that he had used the present tense, as though his father were still alive. In fact as he watched the scene it was so vivid, so real, that it seemed to be true. He was made to feel that all this was happening there and then, when in reality it had happened a long time ago and neither his father nor Uthar were still alive. For a moment his heart wept for the loss of his dear father. It always happened when he saw those memories. On the one hand he felt deeply happy to see his father and mother, but on the other he knew that was all they were, memories, and never again would he be with them again.

Astrid pointed to the scene on the lake. "They're stopping."

Lasgol watched the two riders as they dismounted carefully. They were both carrying spears, like the others who were taking part in the hunt. Dakon was bending over now and then, following the animal's trail.

Dakon pointed to the east. "There it is," he whispered to Sven. Hiding among the bushes was a huge boar with long, twisted tusks.

"I can see it," said Sven. He got ready to attack.

"All yours. I'll help you if you have any trouble."

"I'd better do it alone. It'll charge me. It's safer."

"Right."

Sven hesitated. "The King'll be furious. I'll be punished for disobeying him," he told Dakon, as if asking for his advice.

"I know. But if you don't kill it, it might kill the King. Hunting accidents have left many kingdoms without a King. We're men of honor. We serve our King. We have to protect him at all costs. If we're punished for this act, so be it. We can't let him take this risk, particularly seeing that beast's size and its tusks."

Sven understood what he had to do and the consequences he would have to pay. "I'll take the punishment," he said, and stepped forward.

Dakon watched the scene, ready to step in, with his spear at the ready.

The huge boar saw Sven moving toward it, spear in hand, and just as he had predicted, it charged blindly at him. Sven waited for the right moment with spectacular sang-froid, since the animal was charging him at full tilt, and leapt to one side. He landed firmly on his feet, while the boar in its blind charge could not stop or change direction. Sven buried his spear in it from the side with a sharp, carefully-judged blow which reached the heart squarely. The boar continued its charge without realizing it had been killed, until its strength drained away and it fell dead.

"Impressive. You're a real expert," Dakon told him.

"Thanks. I am."

The pack arrived a moment later amid a deafening outburst of barking, followed by the King with his group. He saw the dead boar, and his face hardened.

"I said I wanted it myself!" he yelled at Dakon and Sven, who were beside the dead animal.

"It charged..." Sven tried to explain.

"Because you were where you shouldn't have been! And what a trophy on top of it! Which of you killed it?"

"It was me, your majesty," Sven admitted.

"Well you're going to pay for taking my quarry!" the King said threateningly.

"Your Majesty –" Dakon began.

"I don't want to hear another word!" The King turned and left at a gallop, followed by the group.

Suddenly the image began to fade, little by little. Lasgol knew the memory would vanish presently. He reached out his hand to the water, trying in vain to hold the scene back, to hold his beloved father back. He failed. A moment later the image had vanished completely and the water of the pond was once again nothing but water. He tried unsuccessfully to reactivate the jewel so that it would show him another memory, another scene from his father's life or his mother's, but as on all those other occasions when he had tried before, he could not make it happen.

Chapter 14

A slight cool breeze had sprung up as Astrid and Lasgol rode in silence toward Count Malason's castle and they had put up their hoods to shelter from it. They were very near their destination, which pleased them – though it also saddened them, as they would no longer be able to enjoy one another's company as they had been doing. They could make out four tall square towers of blackish stone in the distance. This was Malason's castle.

"Everything all right?" Astrid asked. "You've been very quiet ever since you used your mother's pendant."

"Sorry. I was lost in my own thoughts."

"You certainly were. You forgot I was beside you."

He smiled, slightly embarrassed. "No, never that. It's just that every time I have one of those visions, I wonder what it means."

"Mean? Why should it mean anything? They might just be random scenes, without any meaning or any connection with you. It's your parents' life, their experiences, not yours."

Lasgol shook his head. "I know. But I always have this strange sensation here" – he touched his stomach – "that somehow they mean something, that I see them for some particular reason, even if I can't say why."

Astrid shrugged. "That could be true, but don't torture yourself. If there is a reason, it'll come to you. One day you'll understand it. Don't beat yourself up about it, or else Trotter is going to take you straight into that mine and you won't even notice because you're lost in your own thoughts."

Lasgol looked up and saw that it was true, they were heading straight to the entrance of one of Count Malason's mines. Trotter nickered. He had understood his name.

He smiled at Astrid. "Well, you're right about that."

"Remember, I always am," she retorted gaily, and Lasgol laughed.

Camu, hide, and you too, Ona. There are strangers around here.

Humans?

Yes, humans.

All right. Camu used his skill and vanished. Ona, who was a few paces from him, did the same under his influence.

"A lot of movement around the mine," Astrid pointed out.

Lasgol surveyed the mine and the fifty or so people working at the entrance and around it. Mule-carts were waiting to be loaded with the ore the miners were bringing up from the depths to the mine entrance. Several foremen were barking orders to the workers, who were moving containers of ore from the mine entrance to the carts.

"Limus was right," Lasgol commented." There's a lot of activity, more so than usual."

"They're keeping up a good pace," Astrid said as with narrowed eyes she watched the miners outside loading the carts, cleaning the containers and sending them back to the depths.

"It's a hard job," said Lasgol. He knew about the life of a miner from what he had heard in the village.

"I suppose the ones who extract the ore from the depths of the mountain would say that this surface work is an easy option."

"Actually, it is. The ones you see working up here, it's because they have a better job. They know the foremen, or else some influential family, and they get them this work, which may be exhausting, but it's a thousand times better than swallowing dirt and mineral dust in the entrails of the mine. Plenty of them get lung diseases down there from swallowing so much harmful dust. Others end up with serious problems in their eyes from working for so many years like moles in the darkness of the tunnels, hundreds of feet underground. It's very hard."

"Sounds horrible."

"According to Ulf, only a fool or a daredevil can be a miner. He never has anything to do with them. Because if they're crazy they make trouble, and if they're daredevils, it's because they have no brains."

She laughed. "Ulf and his simplistic philosophy of life."

Lasgol smiled. "That's him. My father once told me that the work of a miner was probably one of the hardest and most dangerous of all. There are often cave-ins down there, and plenty of men lose their lives."

"In that case, why are there so many miners?"

"It pays much better than any other job."

"Oh... I see..."

"Then there are people who've lost their farms or don't have a trade, or families with problems getting enough to survive, and they have no choice but to accept this work."

"Well, there comes a bunch of miners, and I can count more than thirty of them," said Astrid. She indicated a group who were covered from head to foot in black mineral dust.

"They come up to breathe and rest a little," Lasgol said. seeing them being given water. "There are a lot of miners, that's true. More than usual." He had seen another group, even larger, come out after the first one.

"Plenty of miners, plenty of produce..." Astrid said knowingly.

"That means gold in the Count's coffers."

"Well, that's interesting..."

"I can also see a dozen armed men."

"The Count's guards, protecting the mines?" Astrid suggested.

"It looks like it. They're keeping watch, and one of them has seen us. He's pointing at us."

"Are we going to have trouble?" Astrid asked. She was readying her bow, just in case.

"We shouldn't. We're Rangers."

"We'll soon find out," she said, not altogether convinced.

One of the foremen went to fetch a man much better dressed than the others. He was presumably the man in charge, and his clothes revealed the fact that he came from a good family. He called half of the guards and beckoned them, then started walking toward Lasgol and Astrid. In his hand he carried a coiled whip. As he approached, Lasgol recognized him. He glanced at Astrid with a warning look, and her answering glance said *understood*.

"What are you looking at?" he asked as he came up to them. His voice suggested that he was looking for a quarrel.

"We're looking at the mine," Lasgol replied calmly.

"I know you're looking at the mine, clever guy. Why are you looking at my mine?" he asked again, this time more sharply.

"We were interested to see the miners at work," Lasgol explained calmly.

"Well, keep going, 'cos there's nothing here for you."

"We are on our way," Lasgol said. "We can stop to have a look. We're not doing anything against the law."

"Now look, smartass. I'm the law here, and either you go on your way or you'll regret it." He glanced at his armed men.

"The law in the kingdom is the King's, and we as Rangers" – Lasgol indicated Astrid and himself – "are the ones who see that it's obeyed."

The man threw his head back. "You're Rangers?"

"That's right," Lasgol said. He gestured at their clothes and their bows.

"Even so, here the law is Count Malason's and I, as his cousin, make sure it's obeyed."

"Oh, I thought your face looked familiar," Lasgol said. "What's your name?"

He showed them his whip and gave a cruel smile. "I'm Osvald, 'the whip'."

Slowly, Lasgol pushed back his hood and revealed his face. "My name's Lasgol Eklund. I don't know if you'll remember me..."

Osvald's face changed color. He began to go red, and his eyes gleamed as though they had caught fire. "Of course I remember you!" he said venomously.

"I thought you would."

"You and I have an account to settle!" said Osvald. He clenched his hand tightly on his whip.

"There's no account to settle. The law was on my side, and my family's estate was returned to me."

"You shed my blood! That I'll never forgive!"

"A grudge makes a very bad companion. You ought to be careful. And now, if you'll excuse us, we have to see the Count."

"Malason? What for?" he asked in surprise.

Lasgol was not prepared to give him any explanation. "Private business."

"I'm his cousin! I demand that you tell me the reason!"

Lasgol snorted. "You're his second cousin, or is it his third? You barely have any relatives in common. You can demand all you want, but I'm a Ranger and I don't owe you any explanation."

Oswald was beside himself with rage. "I swear you'll pay for this!"

"I wouldn't recommend you, or your friends" – Lasgol nodded at the guards – "to try any tricks. You'd end up in a very bad place."

"You arrogant Ranger!" Osvald's rage was so great that that he was foaming at the mouth.

"A pleasure," Lasgol said by way of farewell, and with a nod to Astrid they went on their way.

Osvald was left standing there, launching curses and threats at their backs.

"I see you have friends all over the place," Astrid joked.

Lasgol smiled. "Yeah, one or two."

From the last uphill slope they saw Count Malason's castle on the plateau. The fortress was not particularly large or impressive: a rectangular fortification with four square towers, one at each corner, and a large tower as its main entrance in the center. It gave the impression of being a solid fortress, built to bear the harsh Norghanian winters, and capable of resisting a siege for a long time.

"There's a lot of activity," Astrid said, indicating several groups of men with carts coming and going through the main gate.

"Yeah, I didn't remember it as being so busy. All the same, I do seem to remember the fortress from past memories."

"It's simple but solid. It'll hold up against the weather, and against a horde."

"That's true. Pure Norghanian rock and black granite from the northern quarries."

"I can see soldiers of the Count's on the four towers and patrolling the battlements."

"That doesn't seem suspicious to me. The count's always been a wary man, and he'll have soldiers protecting the fortress. It's to be expected."

"Okay. Are we going in, then?"

"Let's go."

They both rode up to the open area they would have to ascent to the castle on its plateau.

Camu, Ona, wait for us in that wood to the east, Lasgol told them.

We want go to castle.

That isn't a good idea. We might run into trouble.

Enemies?

No, not enemies. As far as we know, Count Malason is a friend.

Not understand.

Sometimes friends are not what they seem.

No? My friends, yes friends.

That's good.

Your friends not friends?

I hope not...

Count Malason friend?

That's what we want to find out.

All right.

You wait, and if in two days you have no news from us, it means something's happened to us.

Ona moaned.

Something bad, Camu clarified.

Yes, bad. I don't think it'll happen. Everything'll be fine, and by dawn we'll be back with you.

Okay.

The soldiers on duty at the castle gate stopped Astrid and Lasgol when they saw that they were not workers at the fortress or in its surroundings, nor were they traders. They identified themselves as Rangers and asked to see Count Malason, then waited until an officer came to speak to them.

"I know you," said the officer, who had blond hair and a goatee. He must have been in his forties, with very pale eyes and a direct gaze. "You're a friend of Egil Olafstone, King of the West."

To Lasgol it sounded strange that the officer would refer to Egil openly as the King of the West. On the other hand, they were in one of the main fiefs of the Western League, and although since the end of the war things had grown calmer, this area was still loyal to the West and as a result supported Egil's cause completely.

"That's right. My name's Lasgol Eklund."

"I thought I'd recognized you. I've accompanied Count Malason on a few missions..."

"I see," Lasgol replied, understanding that the officer had been with the Count to clandestine meetings of the Western League.

"My name's Alvis. I'm Captain of Count Malason's guard."

Lasgol introduced Astrid, and she and the Captain exchanged greetings.

"You'd like to see the Count?"

"That's right," Lasgol said. "We have an important matter to discuss with him."

"You're not the only ones. Some other important visitors have arrived too. I'll see whether he can see you. Follow me to the stables." He led the way.

Astrid and Lasgol followed him, still mounted. The inside of the castle was full of people coming and going busily.

"Plenty of activity," Lasgol commented to the officer to see whether he could extract some information from him.

"Yes, the Count has brought extra hands to help us with the mines. There's a lot of work."

"That's always good," said Astrid.

"So it is. More wealth for everybody in the county. We need to get back on our feet after the civil war."

"Very true. Are those traders from around here, or have they come from far away?" Lasgol asked. He was trying to avoid sounding suspicious as far as possible.

Alvis glanced at the traders by the barracks, who were preparing a caravan of several carts. "From all over the realm," he said succinctly.

Astrid and Lasgol exchanged glances. Those traders might be from the capital, but they were certainly not from the West.

They left Trotter and Astrid's horse in the stables to be tended, and Lasgol noticed that there were several horses of very high quality there. They were animals worth plenty of gold, the kind only the powerful nobles had. There was someone important here. Astrid noticed this too, and went unobtrusively over to one of the horses.

"Beautiful animal," she said, stroking its rump.

"It certainly is. We don't usually see many like this one." The officer did not mention who it belonged to, which was what they were wondering.

"The Count's?" Lasgol asked.

"No, it belongs to a visitor. Follow me, I'll take you to the Count. I can't guarantee he'll see you, he's very busy. But as you're who you are, I'm guessing he'll want to."

They followed Alvis, who guided them through the stone fortress to the second floor of the southern wing and Count Malason's office. There were soldiers posted along the lower corridors, which gave the impression that the Count was prepared to face some possible eventuality. Lasgol wondered what it could be.

The officer knocked on the Count's door and went in.

"The Count will see you," he said when he came out, and after saluting he went away down the corridor.

Astrid and Lasgol went in to find the Count behind his desk. He stood up with a welcoming smile.

"Lasgol, what a surprise."

"Sir." Lasgol gave a slight bow.

The Count came over to him and offered his hand. "How long

has it been?"

"Quite a lot, sir," Lasgol replied as he shook the offered hand.

"I'm glad to see you in one piece. You've come from Skad?"

"Yes, sir, I've been back to my estate, enjoying a few visits from friends."

"That's always comforting for the spirit. Particularly in your case, as Rangers don't often get the chance to go back home." The Count's gaze was on Astrid.

"Oh, excuse me," Lasgol hastened to say. "This is Astrid, Ranger Specialist."

"A Specialist, eh? Which Specialty?" the Count asked with interest.

"Assassin of Nature," Astrid told him.

The Count smiled. "Well, well. I was going to offer you my hand, but now I'm wondering whether I dare," he said teasingly.

She smiled slightly. "I'm not on an assassination mission."

"Well then, in that case, here's my hand," the Count said.

"A pleasure, sir." Astrid shook his hand energetically, and Malason looked at them for a moment thoughtfully.

"Receiving a visit from a Ranger is unusual enough, but a visit from two is really surprising, now I come to think about it. This isn't just a courtesy call, is it?"

Lasgol and Astrid exchanged glances.

"No, it isn't."

"Well, at least you're not here to kill me."

"Certainly not," Lasgol hastened to assure him.

The Count went back to his desk and sat down behind it, as if he had already begun to guess that the visit concerned something serious.

"So tell me, to what do I owe this visit?"

"We bring a message from Egil Olafstone."

"From Egil? Is everything all right? How is he?" The Count's voice was concerned. "I've heard that things at the Camp and among the Rangers are very chaotic. I've been worrying about it."

"They are, sir, but Egil's well."

"He'd better be," the Count said whole-heartedly. "He's the future of the West, the future of Norghana. Nothing must happen to him. He must be protected at all times. There's no-one more important for the West, for the future of Norghana."

"He is protected," Lasgol reassured him.

The Count seemed to be on Egil's side completely. At least he was showing himself to be, which ought not to surprise them. But now that it had been established that he was the one most likely to have hired the Zangrian guild of assassins to kill Egil, this could be a masquerade. He might be pretending, hiding his true intentions.

"It's not that I'm not glad to see you, Lasgol, but why has Egil sent you?"

"To give you this message." Lasgol took it out from under his cloak and handed it to the Count.

"In person?" the Count said in surprise. "He could have sent it to me by pigeon or messenger."

"It's an important and private matter," Lasgol assured him.

The Count looked at the sealed scroll. "I see."

He broke the seal, unrolled the message and read it carefully. When he had finished, he leaned back in his chair and was thoughtful for a moment. Astrid and Lasgol exchanged an unobtrusive glance.

"Do you know what the message says?" Malason asked.

"No, sir, Egil hasn't told us," said Lasgol. It was true. Egil had not explained either what it said or what he intended with it, although both Lasgol and Astrid knew that he had planned one of his plots.

The Count nodded. "Very well. Tell Egil I'll do what he's asked me to. You'll be staying for a few days?"

"We're very sorry, sir, but we have to go on to the capital. We're expected there."

"Ah yes, the Great Council... I've heard..."

"That's right, sir."

Suddenly there was a knock on the door.

"Come in," said the Count.

The door opened, and another officer came into the room. "I'm sorry to trouble you, sir. The Count insists on an audience immediately."

Malason's expression turned to one of distaste. "All right. Show him in."

"By your leave, we'll be going on our way," Lasgol said.

Malason raised his hand. "Wait. I'll introduce you to my cousin. I don't think you've had the pleasure."

The door opened and a tall, strong man in his mid-forties, with long blond hair and eyes blue as the ocean, came in decisively. He was a true Norghanian and for some reason Lasgol found him familiar, though he could not recall ever having seen him before. He was finely clad in silver-scaled armor, with a magnificent Norghanian sword at his waist.

He looked at Lasgol and Astrid from head to foot, then at Count Malason.

"Cousin," he said with a nod, and even though he was a good-looking man, his gaze was very unfriendly.

"Welcome to my castle. I trust the journey has been a pleasant one."

"You know I hate traveling," was the reply.

"Allow me to introduce you," he said with a glance at Astrid and Lasgol. "My cousin, Count Olmossen."

Lasgol swallowed. This was Valeria's father.

Chapter 15

Count Olmossen gave a slight nod. "These are the Rangers, Lasgol and Astrid..."

"Well, well, well, two Rangers," Olmossen said, looking at them with interest.

"Specialists, in fact," Malason added.

"You wouldn't know my daughter by any chance? She's a Ranger Specialist too."

Astrid and Lasgol looked at one another, and Astrid's gesture encouraged him to answer.

"Yes, sir. We know Valeria. We're... comrades."

"So you do know her. Interesting. Would you say she's a good Ranger?

Lasgol did not know what to say. Why would Olmossen ask whether his daughter was a good Ranger? It was hardly appropriate, and in any case he knew she had become a Specialist, which was something only the best Rangers managed.

"Yes, sir. She's a very good Ranger," Lasgol replied. He looked at Astrid, expecting some positive comment in support, but she simply pursed her lips and said nothing.

"What do you think, Astrid? Is she?" Olmossen insisted.

Astrid smiled slightly. "I wouldn't know what to say. I haven't had much to do with her."

Lasgol looked at her in surprise. It was true that they had not had much to do with each other, but after what Egil had told them about all the things Valeria had done to help him on his mission to Erenal, there was no doubt that she was an exceptional Specialist. He wondered why Astrid had not praised her in front of her father.

"I see my daughter is still making friends among men and enemies among women," Olmossen said candidly.

"I'm sure she's an excellent Ranger," Malason said.

"I doubt that. I've always said it wasn't her place. Anyway, she's never listened to me, and that's how she's gone on in life." Olmossen's tone was bitter. "On the other hand, her brother Erik is a worthy heir to my name."

"So is she, even though you're always like cat and dog with each other," Malason pointed out.

"The fact is that my daughter doesn't know – or rather doesn't want to accept – her place and her role. She wants me to appoint her as the heir to my title and possessions instead of her brother, which I'll never do. The males of the family are the ones who bear the title and maintain it in the name of the family. It's a Norghanian tradition that must be upheld."

"Some traditions are wrong, no matter how Norghanian they might be," Astrid said suddenly.

"Well, well, I see you're one of those who think like my daughter. Those women have a right to inherit the title." He stared fixedly into her eyes.

Astrid stood her ground. "I believe that. There shouldn't be any difference in inheritance because of the person's sex. Neither in inheritance, or in responsibilities, or the goals a person wants to reach."

"I see you're one of those..." Olmossen replied disdainfully.

"The ones who are right."

"We men are right, and that's the way things will always be."

"Isn't Valeria the eldest child?" Lasgol asked.

"That's irrelevant."

"If both siblings were male, the title would go to the firstborn. The fact that she's a woman ought to make no difference. It seems discriminatory to me."

"I think you've spent too much time with my daughter and this Ranger," Olmossen told him. "They've softened your brain."

"My brain works perfectly well," Lasgol snapped.

"Isn't Valeria a much better fighter than her brother?" Malason asked.

"Only slightly," Olmossen said with a dismissive wave.

"I've heard she's quite a lot better, and that was before she became a Specialist. Now she'll be even more so. I think that as she's elder and better-prepared, you ought to consider her for your title. It's happened in other families. It wouldn't be either the first or the last case."

"It would be a disgrace and a shame which I am not going to bring on my family."

"Well, it's your house, your name, your legacy for posterity. You must know better than anybody what's best."

"I do know, and I stand by it. My son will inherit because so he should. If Valeria wants to play at being a Ranger, let her."

Astrid and Lasgol exchanged a glance. She had not liked that "playing at being a Ranger" at all. What was at stake when you entered the Rangers was your own life.

"Perhaps a quiet, honest conversation could help," Malason suggested.

Olmossen shook his head. "I've already spoken more than enough with her. She's brought my patience to an end. She refuses to see the right way of doing things, and I'm tired of arguing with her. Let her do whatever she wants, and I'll do the same."

There followed a long, uncomfortable silence, which Lasgol broke at last.

"Well, we must be on our way," he said to Count Malason.

"Yes, of course," the Count hastened to say. "A pleasure to see you again, and to meet you," he said to Astrid.

They both nodded in return, then turned to Count Olmossen.

"A pleasure meeting you, sir," said Lasgol. Astrid limited herself to a brief nod.

"A pleasure. Say hello to my daughter from me if you see her. Tell her about this charming conversation we've had."

Astrid looked at Lasgol who returned the look in surprise. Count Olmossen appeared to want to annoy his daughter, taking advantage of any opportunity. They left the room and went away down the corridor.

"Curious encounter," Astrid commented.

"It certainly was. It doesn't look as though Count Olmossen and Val get along very well."

"I suppose you already knew that," Astrid said accusingly.

"Well, yeah... she told me about it," Lasgol admitted.

"She confided in you. I wonder why."

"Because we're friends."

She glared at him fiercely. "Yeah, sure, what she wants is to be more than friends."

"I don't think so... we've always been just friends," Lasgol said, trying to calm the situation.

"Just friends. Well, that little blonde had better stay away from you."

Lasgol raised his hands, pleading for peace. "You know you don't need to worry about me."

"It's not you I'm worried about, it's her."

"Really, there's nothing to be worried about," Lasgol insisted.

Astrid glared at him, looking decidedly unconvinced. Lasgol felt her glare piercing him. He swallowed, said nothing more about it and changed the subject.

"Was your father like that? Like Count Olmossen?"

"I don't know, quite honestly. I don't remember much about my parents."

"You haven't told me much about them," Lasgol said, trying to get some more information out of her.

"That's because I don't have much to tell. My father was a Ranger, and he died in action when I was eight. I never spent much time with him. He was away on missions almost all the time."

"He couldn't have been like Olmossen."

"In his way of thinking? I hope not. I wouldn't know what to say to you."

"And your mother? What do you remember of her?"

"Also, very little. She died a year before my father, when he was away on a mission. She was bitten by a venomous snake. That's what I was told, at least."

"I'm sorry..."

"Don't be too sorry. I barely remember them."

Lasgol nodded and stroked her back to show her his sympathy.

At the end of the corridors they found Officer Alvis.

"Have you finished?"

"Yes, we're on our way again."

"I can't let you leave without offering you a little western hospitality. Come with me to the dining hall. A nice hot meal will do you good."

Astrid glanced at Lasgol and nodded with the trace of a smile.

"We can't refuse the Count's hospitality," Lasgol said to her. "A hot meal sounds great."

"Good. Come with me."

They followed him down long corridors, then down a flight of stone stairs, to a large dining hall with long oak tables, each of which could sit a dozen guests.

Alvis gestured. "Sit right here. I'll go to the kitchen to order them to give you the best they can put together today." He winked at them and left through the north door.

They sat down opposite each other and turned their attention to the other tables, which were half-empty. A few soldiers were eating at a table to their right, another few at two tables at the far end. It was late for lunch by now, so that these must be the ones who had been on watch duty until the midday change of guard.

Alvis came back after a moment. "Everything's fixed. They'll serve you a couple of specialties that'll have you licking your fingers."

"Thank you very much, Alvis," Lasgol said.

"You're welcome. Your horses will be ready at the stables with their saddlebags full of supplies by the time you finish eating,"

"Thanks again."

"A pleasure. The least we can do for the friends of the True King." With those words he left them.

"It looks as though Egil has a lot of followers round here," Astrid said. She was a little surprised at all the support.

"Yeah, they don't forget who the legitimate heir is and what happened to his family. I don't think they ever will."

Astrid nodded. "They're loyal to the West."

"And the True King."

They ate peacefully, and just as Alvis had promised, the dishes were delicious. Not as good as Martha's, not remotely, but for soldiers' food they were very good. Probably they had been prepared as though for Count Malason and his guest.

They were enjoying dessert when someone approached from the side of the table.

"Well, well, well, look who we have here," came an unpleasant voice. Lasgol turned to see Osvald with his much-feared whip in his hand. Behind him were half a dozen soldiers as big as wardrobes.

Astrid gave Lasgol a look of warning.

"Osvald. I didn't think we'd see each other again so soon," Lasgol said calmly.

Osvald raised his voice so that everyone in the dining hall could hear. "You really thought you'd get away so easily after you'd insulted me?"

"I didn't insult you," Lasgol said quietly.

"Yes you did, and you're going to pay for it! This is my domain, and I'm the one who's in charge here!"

"Count Malason's the one in charge here, and you serve him. If you're looking for a fight without any real reason, I wouldn't advise it."

"You don't advise me about anything!"

"I'd appreciate it if you stopped yelling," Lasgol said. "You're upsetting everybody else." Lasgol could already see that this was going to end up in a fight. He sought his Gift and activated his skills, *Improved Agility* and *Cat-like Reflexes*. Two green flashes that only he could see ran through his body.

"I'm going to teach you a lesson you'll never forget!"

"You don't have enough friends with you to teach me a lesson." Lasgol nodded at the six huge Norghanians. "So I suggest you don't get yourself into trouble. The warning goes for them too. If they attack us, they'll be in serious trouble."

"You're the one who's in serious trouble! Go for him!" Osvald yelled.

The six enormous soldiers took no notice of Lasgol's warning, but split up into two groups. Three went to Lasgol's side, the other three to Astrid's. Osvald uncoiled his whip.

Lasgol stood up and leapt on to the bench as the first soldier stretched out his arms to grab him. Lasgol leapt forward with his knee up. The movement caught the soldier by surprise as he took the knee on his chin. His head shot backwards and he fell back unconscious. The second soldier delivered a right hook to Lasgol's face, but he dodged the punch with a movement of his waist. The soldier delivered a cross-left hook with all his might, but Lasgol let it pass in front of his nose by bending backwards. As he recovered he launched a kick at the soldier's right ear, leaving him totally stunned and clutching his ear.

Astrid, seeing two of the soldiers approaching her, gave an agile leap. Like a panther, she climbed onto the long table and launched a tremendous kick which caught the first soldier squarely in the nose as he was reaching out to grab her. There was a crack, and the soldier drew back his hands to reach for his face. She had broken his nose, which was bleeding profusely. His eyes were watering, preventing him from seeing anything. The second soldier tried to grab her leg, but she slid to one side. Then, keeping her balance, she launched a tremendous kick at his temple. The soldier fell like a hollow log. The third hesitated a moment. Astrid took advantage of this moment of doubt and jumped off the table with her right leg stretched out so that the heel of her boot hit his neck. The impact set him coughing. Unable to breathe, he bent over and fell to his knees in an attempt to get the air into his lungs.

Lasgol dodged first a crossed right hook, then a left, which the third soldier delivered straight to his face. With his skills active, he could dodge the big man's blows without too much trouble. To begin with, the soldier's size meant that he was not quick in his movements, and with Lasgol's skills active it seemed to him that his opponent was hitting as though he were half-asleep. Lasgol heard a *fssst* and knew it was Osvald's whip. When he saw it out of the corner of his eye coming toward his face, he pulled his head back. The tip of the whip scratched his ear and stung sharply.

"I'll deal with the soldier. You get rid of the cretin," Astrid said as she went to his aid.

Lasgol nodded. Dodging the soldier, he went for Osvald. The soldier spun round to follow him, but Astrid jumped on him like a great cat and brought him down. Before he could fight back, she had punched him hard and accurately in the neck, nose and temple, leaving him out of action.

"You always had a bad temper," Lasgol said as he moved towards Osvald. "And that's not a good quality."

"You're going to get what's coming to you!" Osvald yelled. He lashed his whip toward his opponent's face, but Lasgol saw it coming and crouched with almost inhuman speed and agility. The whip went over his head. He rolled toward Osvald, who was yelling and launching another whiplash at his back. Lasgol hurled himself forward with his arms folded in front of his head and his legs stretched out behind him. He hit both Osvald's shins with his forearms at the same moment as the whip hit the floor by his legs, without touching him. From the impact, Osvald's feet left the floor and his legs buckled. He fell forward toward Lasgol, who rolled to one side, and his chin hit the floor with a massive impact.

Lasgol leapt back to his feet and stepped on Osvald's right wrist to make him drop the whip he was clutching tightly.

"You're going to pay for this!" he muttered, and Lasgol saw that he had cracked his chin open and was bleeding heavily.

"Hey, you're bleeding."

"Where?" Osvald asked with fear in his eyes.

"Here," Lasgol replied, and kicked him hard in the face.

Astrid arrived at his side. "Well fought."

"He deserved it, for being a bully."

Astrid nodded in warning. The soldiers who were eating in the dining hall had stood up and were watching them.

"This has nothing to do with you. It was an old debt," Lasgol told them.

The soldiers stared at them without a word.

"I don't recommend you try anything," Astrid said as she drew her knives.

One of the soldiers, a little older than the rest, sat down and nodded to the others. They followed his example.

"Let's get out of here," Lasgol sad to Astrid, and they left. A little while later they had left Count Malason's castle behind.

"Nice visit," Astrid said teasingly.

"You can say that again. Let's fetch Ona and Camu and go on to the capital."

"That sounds a really good idea."

Lasgol smiled. "Let's see what we find there."

Chapter 16

Egil watched his back warily as he rode along the road. He had the feeling that at any moment somebody was going to attack them. It was a feeling he had been unable to shake off ever since they had left behind the safety of the Camp. Several days had gone by since then, and he could not help feeling uneasy.

"Nothing's going to happen. This is going to be a very boring journey," Valeria said from where she was riding beside him. She winked.

"I don't know... I've got an ominous feeling."

"Nonsense, nobody knows we're here escorting Eyra to the capital. Angus and Dolbarar have kept it secret and didn't tell anybody about it till the very last moment. There's nothing to worry about."

"Still..."

Valeria turned to Gerd, who was riding behind them. "Have you got the same bad feeling too?"

"I... well... if Egil's restless, then so am I," the giant said with a shrug.

"You're both worrying too much. Norghana's too big for them to find us by chance."

"It won't be by chance," said Egil.

He was watching the cart which held Eyra rattling on ahead of them. He was not very happy with the one they had chosen to transport her. It was one thing to be a prisoner, quite another to be transported in a cart behind bars like some dangerous animal. It was not that she might be dangerous – though she was – but the danger was not the physical kind. Instead it involved her intelligence, her knowledge and her wide experience. She could have been transported in a normal cart, completely enclosed. That would have been more intelligent. Nobody would be able to see her, and the journey would be safer. Besides, if anybody tried to kill her they would have a better target now than in a cart whose roof and doors were of solid wood. Arrows have a tendency not to penetrate wood.

He sighed. No, it was not an ideal form of transport. He had not realized this at the Camp, but now, on the road, it was obvious. The Camp leaders had not shared the plan with him, otherwise he would have realized the problem. But he could not blame Dolbarar and Angus for not telling him. They were being very cautious and had been right not to talk about it with anybody. Whether this was the best plan was another matter.

"Well then, how?" Valeria asked him, bringing him back from his thoughts.

"There are certain kinds of news it's very difficult to conceal, however hard you try to keep the secret."

Valeria frowned, looking thoughtful. "I don't see how anybody could have found out."

"There's always some way of getting hold of information. The difficult thing is keeping it secret." Egil recited this as if it were a mantra.

"I think you spend too much time among books and planning things, and you're a little paranoid."

Egil smiled at this. "I wish that were true."

"Just in case, I'm keeping on the alert," Gerd said. He was turning to check behind them now and then.

Valeria moved to one side to look at the Rangers at the head of the group. "Gurkog's leading the way, and there are two Specialists with him. Do you know anything about them?"

"Funny question for someone who isn't distrustful," Egil said ironically.

"It's not that I suspect them, I'm sure they're two seasoned and completely trustworthy Rangers, otherwise Angus wouldn't have chosen them." She went on watching them carefully.

"The taller one with short chestnut hair is Enok Underson, and he's an Infallible Marksman," Egil said.

"Wow! That's a Specialty you don't see very often. When we stop for a rest I'll have a word with him."

Gerd raised an eyebrow. "How come you know him?"

Egil turned in his saddle with a smile. "I'm a good observer, my dear friend."

Gerd was not entirely convinced by this reply. "And what have you observed?"

"He's a veteran, and he passes by the Camp now and then. Most of his missions are given to him by Gondabar in the capital."

"Have you ever spoken to him?" Valeria asked. "Did he tell you?"

Egil shook his head. "No, I don't think I've ever spoken to him. On the other hand, as Dolbarar's assistant I have access to information about certain missions that are handed out..."

"Oh... I see," Valeria said with a smile. "What a rascal you are."

"More than a rascal, well-informed," Egil replied with a mischievous smile.

"And what do you know about the other one?" she said as she watched him riding on Gurkog's right. The road was deserted, and they were passing a beech wood. The cart was going slowly, with its large wheels turning far more slowly than the Rangers would have liked, so that they had plenty of time to chat. They wished they could have been going at a gallop, or else taking a short cut through some dense forest. Unfortunately they were hampered by a heavy cart and a prisoner, which made it impossible.

"The other one, the one with long fair hair and brown eyes, is Fulker Inservand. He's a veteran Specialist and doesn't usually come to the Camp, so I guess they'll have made him come especially for this mission."

"What's his Specialty?" Gerd asked with interest.

"Natural Marksman."

"Wow! Wonderful. Another Archery Specialist. What a coincidence that including me, there are three Specialists of the same School in the same group..." As Valeria said this, she realized that it did not fit.

Egil smiled at her. "Coincidence, you say?"

"It's not a coincidence, is it? We've been specifically selected for this job."

"That's right. One of the hardest Man Hunters there are – if not the hardest – to lead the journey, and in case the quarry escapes and we need to hunt it down... and three Archers with ideal Specialties to protect the quarry in case they try to kill her before we get to the capital."

"Wow... I hadn't even thought about that," Valeria admitted.

"Nor me," said Gerd.

"And the other two leading the cart, are they Specialists as well?"

"No, they're veterans. Experienced. They're in charge of the cart and the draft horses."

"And tending to Eyra?" Gerd asked.

Egil shook his head. "I'm afraid not. We're forbidden even to go near her."

"Even now, during the journey?"

"Now more than ever. One of us might kill her or help her escape."

"Oh… gee…" Gerd's expression showed that he had never even considered the possibility.

"Irrefutable, my dear friend," Egil said with a broad smile.

"Irrefutable, rubbish," Valeria shot back. "What happens is that your mind is always thinking about the possible disasters that could happen to us. One day it's going to burst with so much thinking about twisted things."

"I also think that some good things are going to happen to us," Egil retorted with a serene smile.

Valeria looked doubtful. "Are you sure?"

"Of course I am," he beamed at her.

Valeria turned to Gerd for corroboration.

"Although it's hard to accept it, he does think that good things are going to happen to us," he assured her. "What happens is that we're always caught up in awkward situations…"

"You don't need to tell me that. I don't think there's a group with more trouble dancing around them in the whole of Norghana."

"We're a group of characters who tend to attract interest." Gerd said with a comical grimace.

"Our Egil here is number one, and don't start me talking about Lasgol – and by the way, where is he?"

Gerd smiled. "I'm not saying anything."

"Won't the brunette let you tell me?"

"Let's say it's better for my physical and emotional health if I don't tell you anything about Lasgol."

Valeria looked peeved.

"What about you, Egil? Has that cat eaten your tongue too?"

"She's more a tigress than a cat," said Egil, with an apologetic shrug.

"It doesn't matter! Don't tell me anything! That harpy won't be able to hide him from me for very long! I know he'll be at the Great Council. Just about all the experienced Rangers who are currently active have been summoned. Lasgol'll be there, and that'll be my opportunity."

The anger vanished from Valeria's face, which once again glowed with an enticing beauty. She rearranged her golden hair, looked at Gerd and Egil and said: "Lasgol won't be able to resist me forever."

Gerd and Egil exchanged a look that said *trouble's on the way,* but did not utter a word.

At the beginning of nightfall Gurkog gave the order to halt. The cart stopped, and with it the whole escort. The leader of the group pointed to the right of the road, at the end of the forest they had just left behind

"We'll set up camp in this clearing. Pull the cart up beside those trees so that it's not visible from a distance," he told both drivers, "but don't go into the forest with it."

The younger of the two nodded and led the horses away. Gurkog signaled to the rest to follow the cart, then dismounted.

"We'll set up camp here," he told them, and sent the two specialists to search the area.

Valeria, Egil and Gerd dismounted in turn and tethered their horses to the nearest trees.

"I'll take charge of them," Gerd said. He loved animals and always enjoyed looking after them and "giving them a bit of affection", as he put it.

"Gerd is a softie," Valeria commented to Egil.

"Particularly with animals. And especially with dogs."

"But it's funny, he's so big and strong it's surprising that he's so gentle and sweet."

"Especially in our beloved kingdom, where the bigger a Norghanian is, the more brute and brainless he tends to be."

Valeria gave a small chuckle.

As if he had guessed that they were talking about him, Gurkog came over to them. "Elemental Archer, you track the northern area, then take up your position, well hidden, and keep watch from there."

"Yes, sir," Valeria said. She picked up a quiver of elemental arrows and went to her post.

"You two, look after the draft horses," he told the two veterans who were guiding the cart. "Then get a campfire ready. I'm going to take another look at that forest. I don't want any surprises," he added.

"What about me?" Egil asked helpfully.

Gurkog looked at him for a moment.

"You keep an eye on the prisoner. Don't let anybody or anything near her. On this mission, you'll be in charge of looking after her. You and you alone. Nobody else. You're to prepare the food and drink and serve it to her. You're to look after her needs. That's your job."

"Oh. Wouldn't it be better if Valeria did? You know, she being a woman...

"I do not believe in such things. A prisoner is a prisoner. Whether the prisoner is a woman or a man does not matter to me at all."

"Understood. I see that you trust me."

"I know 'who' you are, and I trust you."

"Oh. Interesting."

"Anyway, the fewer people who deal with her, the less risk of an accident or an escape."

"That's a wise and prudent attitude."

"I can also tell you, I haven't lost anybody, nor has anybody ever escaped from me, and this mission isn't going to dishonor me."

"Understood. I'll do everything in my power to keep things that way."

"Taste the food and water before you give it to her. Even if you've prepared it yourself, try it before you give it to her. All the Rangers on this mission are trustworthy, but you never know... I don't even trust my own shadow. One of them might be a Dark Ranger."

"You might be one too," Egil said, to see his reaction.

"Quite right. That's why you're not going to let me come anywhere near the prisoner. Neither me nor anyone else."

"This is going to be interesting..."

"I know you're a friend of the big guy. If you need him to establish order, use him. That guy's a mountain of muscle, he can take care of anybody."

"Even you?"

"Me, I doubt it, but you'd be two against one."

"And numbers are always an advantage in a fight or in war."

"So they say."

Egil bowed slightly. "All right. I'll do as you say."

"I'm glad we understand each other. Here's the key to the cage."

Gurkog nodded in the direction of the cart and handed over the key. "It's yours now. You're the only one who can open it, so the responsibility's yours."

"Right." Egil took the key, which was a large and heavy one, and put it in his Ranger's belt.

Gurkog saluted him with a nod, then took his short bow and went into the forest to search for tracks.

Egil waited until the fire was ready, then began to prepare Eyra's dinner. It would not be anything otherworldly, since he was not a very good cook and the supplies they carried were only campaign rations, but at least it would be hot and he would make sure there was no poison in it.

The Specialists covered the whole area, then took up their positions so as to cover the whole camp from all four directions. Gerd finished attending to the horses and went to eat with the two cart drivers.

"My name's Gerd," he said as he sat down by the fire.

The taller of the two offered him his hand. "My name's Ibsen." He was a veteran Ranger with a weathered face, his brown hair short and straight. Silver glints were beginning to appear in it, and his short beard showed plenty of white at the chin. He was not so much strongly-built as athletic.

"Pleased to meet you," Gerd replied. He shook his hand hard in the Norghanian style.

The other Ranger was putting wood on the fire. He turned to Gerd and offered him his hand.

"Musker Isterton," he said.

"Gerd Vang," Gerd said. The name sounded familiar to him, but at that moment he was unable to place it. He was strongly-built, though not very tall. His hair was dark, which was not common around there, and his beard was short and dark. He must have been in his mid-thirties and his snub nose looked as if it had been broken. He gave Gerd the impression of being a tough guy, not only because he looked like a bulldog but because of something in his gaze. His brown eyes had an intense, hard look about them.

"Need any help?" Ibsen asked Egil.

"No thanks, I'm fine on my own."

"You can't help him," Musker said sharply. "Nobody's to go near that food."

Ibsen looked at him blankly.

"It's for the prisoner's safety," Egil explained. He showed him the soup in the pot which he was adding a few final touches to.

"Oh... I see," Ibsen said. He was looking at his own Ranger's belt. They all carried various things in them, several of which were poisons of different types, from paralyzing ones to the kind which left the victim unconscious, and some of them were deadly.

Egil finished preparing Eyra's dinner a little distance from the fire so that nobody could pour any strange substance either into the food or the drink, then got up to take it to her.

Musker crouched down to go on feeding the fire. "My rear end is flat from all that riding in the cart," he complained.

"Mine too, that's no way to travel," said Ibsen, joining in the complaint as he rummaged in his supply sack, trying to decide what to have for dinner.

"We're Rangers, not cart drivers," Musker grumbled as he too rummaged in his bags.

Gerd looked at Musker and opened his eyes in amazement. Now he knew why his name rang a bell! He was the one who had been spying on Egil at the Camp! And he was there with them! He looked at Egil and gestured insistently at Musker's back to warn him. His face showed the unease he was feeling.

Egil returned Gerd's look, and to the big guy's enormous surprise, smiled at him. Gerd was flabbergasted. Why was his friend smiling? Egil nodded, then turned and went nonchalantly over to see to Eyra.

Gerd was shaking his head. What was going on here? None of this made sense. And at that moment he noticed another detail, and an important one. He had just realized who Egil had requested Angus to include in the group: Musker! And if Egil had asked for him, it must be for a reason. Some reason which Gerd realized at that moment was part of one of Egil's elaborate plans. This meant one thing: there was trouble ahead.

He looked up at the sky and breathed out heavily. Better get ready. Now he had no doubt whatever that this journey was going to be a pretty eventful one.

PEDRO URVI

142

Chapter 17

Egil took the food to the cart, a campaign bowl in each hand. Eyra was sitting on the floor with her back against the box where the two drivers were sitting. The back of the cart was really a barred cage. There was no other way to describe it. The floor and ceiling were of metal, half a palm thick. The sides and door were of thick steel bars. There was no way of taking the prisoner out of there unless you had the key, and now he himself was the only one who had it.

He had the odd feeling that this image should not exist, that this woman should not be inside there as a prisoner. Because of the person she was, or rather had been. Remembering the past, she had been the Master Ranger of the School of Nature for half her life, one of the most intelligent and knowledgeable people in Norghana. Egil respected Eyra for her wisdom, for her great intelligence, for all her experience. It had been a fiendish job to unmask her, and she had nearly killed Dolbarar. She was a formidable enemy, even though now she appeared defeated.

He wondered how many young Rangers who had passed through the Camp she had seduced to the Dark Rangers' side. How long had she been doing this? Dozens of years? Or was it more recent than that? Why had she done it? What was the aim of the Dark Rangers? Who else was involved among the leaders of the Rangers, or the Norghanian Court? All these questions and more came to his mind every time he thought of Eyra and what they had found out about her and the secret organization she belonged to. She was not the leader, he could sense that, but she was certainly a second-in-command. But if so, who was her boss? Who was in the shadows, leading the Dark Ones?

Even knowing the danger she represented and what she had done, it saddened him to see her locked in that square steel cage. The old woman did not look good. The ashen color of her face and the purple circles under her eyes and around her lips did not bode well. He shook his head to clear it of these feelings of empathy. Eyra must go to the capital as a prisoner in that transport, however out of place it might be and however much it might give the impression of ill-treatment.

He could not let himself be tricked by the Master Ranger's frail appearance, or by his past feelings of affection for her. He must not allow his empathy to overwhelm him, or else he would make a mistake which he could not allow himself. It might very well be a trick – although at that moment it seemed rather farfetched, seeing her in front of him as an old sick owl, trapped in a cage she could not escape from, on her way to her end.

He walked a little further along the side of the cart, letting Eyra see him, although she showed no interest. She barely glanced at him, then went back to looking at the floor and huddling inside her cloak. One thing Egil was learning with time and experience was that some people's tricks – as well as their evil – often went beyond what was imaginable. He would stay alert to any possible trick, even if he had to shut down the good feelings of his heart until the situation was over. It was something he would have to do more and more often. He could not go on being "good old Egil" all the time. Situations like this, and others which were even worse which he would have to face in the not-too-distant future, would force him to turn into "tough Egil", at least until the situation was on its way to a satisfactory resolution. He did not enjoy revealing this other personality, colder and more calculating, but the risk he was taking was forcing him to.

"I'm bringing your food," he announced to the Master Ranger.

Eyra said nothing, but raised her eyes and watched him for a moment. Then she looked down again. Egil was expecting this reaction, so he went to the door of the cage. He left the food on the ground carefully so that it would not spill, as he was not exactly the most coordinated of Rangers. He unlocked the steel-barred door slowly, as if there were some danger to his life, as if Eyra were suddenly going to jump on him and slit his throat, which was practically impossible as her hands and feet were tied with tough ropes and expert Ranger knots, and she had no weapon to attack him with. Apart from the fact that she was a weak old woman who was no match for him.

He picked up the food and put it inside the cart through the open door. Then he went in, took both bowls of food and set them down in front of Eyra on the floor. She ignored him completely.

"You need to eat," he told her, crouching in front of her so that his head would be level with her own and he would not seem to be looming over her arrogantly.

She glanced at the food, then at him, and said nothing.

"It would be better if we communicated. There's no reason not to. I'm not going to try and get any information from you, and I'm sure the Master Ranger of Nature isn't going to tell me anything she doesn't want to."

Eyra stared at him, and Egil could see that she was considering his words. Would she speak to him? He was not trying to trick her into confessing anything, and he knew perfectly well that if Dolbarar, Angus and the other Master Rangers had not made her talk, he was not going to succeed himself. So far Eyra had not wanted to confess, even though the evidence was so incriminating. Dolbarar himself had tried to make his old friend talk more than twenty times, always unsuccessfully. Ivana and Haakon had tried half a dozen times, appealing to honor, to the Rangers' traditions, to the principles and rules that guided them, to the Path, but she had refused to speak at all. Even Esben, to whom she had been united by great friendship and companionship for years, had had to give up. Nothing had succeeded in drawing any words from the veteran Master Ranger.

"Hmmm..." she mumbled all of a sudden.

Egil watched her hopefully. It was not much, but it was a first start at communication, and it encouraged him. He tried to make her go on talking to see if he could draw her out of her silence.

"Talking is always helpful, even between opposites or enemies. Especially in this thorny business. I don't think I'll be a problem now we've got this far."

Eyra suddenly smiled, a malicious-looking smile. "You've done enough already," she told him in a voice heavy with sarcasm.

Egil gave the trace of a shrug. "Circumstances drove me."

"Circumstances... now they're different ones..."

Egil saw no hatred for him in Eyra's eyes, which surprised him. He had expected her to be eaten away inside by hate and resentment, and that she would burst out against him. Nothing could have been further from reality. She remained calm, thoughtful, without showing any feelings, which made him think. At least he had managed to make her speak, and that was a major first step. Nobody in the Camp had managed to do that. The fact that he had done so did not fill him with pride, it made him suspect her. He was not the one who had made her talk. If she had spoken, it had been because she herself had wanted to, and there must be some reason for it. What she had said about the change in the situation must have been significant.

She indicated the food with her tied hands. "You taste it first."

"I prepared it myself," he explained, to reassure her.

"Even so."

"And I've already tasted it."

"Do it in front of me."

Egil nodded, picked up the wooden spoon and used it to sample the soup.

"A little spicy. I think you'll like it."

"The meat," she said with a glance at the other bowl.

"Okay." Egil tried the stewed meat. "It didn't come out too well. I did what I could. I'm not a great cook."

"You can leave the food and go."

Egil shook his head. "I have to stay and make sure you eat what I've brought you."

Surprisingly, Eyra smiled: a twisted smile, which made her look like an evil witch. "I don't trust the food not to be poisoned, and you don't trust me not to poison it, myself."

"That's right," Egil agreed with a nod. "I can't let you die. Neither by poison from my people" – he waved in the direction of the Rangers by the fire – "nor by your own." He pointed to her clothes.

Eyra nodded. "If I'm making sure you're not poisoning me, why would I poison myself afterwards? That doesn't make sense."

"It does if this test you just made me carry out is just a trick to make me trust you, then when I turn my back you poison the food yourself somehow."

The Master Ranger gave a brief, sour cackle. "I've always liked you. Did you know that?"

He smiled. "I didn't know, but I suspected it. Although after what I've seen, I'm not sure it wasn't a sham."

"In your case it wasn't," Eyra said. "You're very intelligent. More than that, you're extremely shrewd, which isn't quite the same thing."

"No, it isn't. Thank you for the compliment."

"Right now you're asking yourself whether this compliment, this approach, this conversation, are all a sham, or whether there's actually some truth in them."

"That's right."

"You're doing the right thing. Don't trust. Never. Advice from an old wise woman."

"Not even now?"

"Now less than ever."

"I won't," he assured her.

"You've been given the job of getting me to Norghania alive, right?"

"That's right."

"That's a difficult job. They want me dead. Important people. They don't want me to talk and give away their names."

"I can imagine."

"Dolbarar has chosen well. You're a very skillful lad, and he trusts you. You're a guarantee. You'll do your duty."

"That's what I'm going to try to do."

"And yet we both know you're not entirely to be trusted, eh?"

"I don't know what you mean."

"Oh yes, you do. You're the future King of Norghana, or that's your ultimate purpose. Your secret that you don't want to be revealed."

"Thoran's the King, and I'm not after the crown. I'm a Ranger, nothing more than that."

Eyra smiled very sourly. "If you say so. Time will tell."

"You could speak now. You could name the conspirators," Egil went on, to try and wring more information out of her.

"If I speak, my life is worthless. It would be like committing suicide."

"Which is another possible way out of this situation, bearing in mind what's waiting in the capital."

"Right, my young Ranger, but you don't know whether it's the one I'm going to take or not."

"I hope not."

"We both know what's in store for me in the royal dungeons. That brute Orten carries them out personally. He loves torturing helpless people. That's not something I have any desire to experience at this point in my long life."

"Torture is mean and cowardly. Gondabar won't allow it."

"I'm afraid our leader has neither the power nor the capacity to stop the King's brother. Still less the King himself. He won't be able to protect me. Nor do I expect him to."

"All the more reason to speak now. The King and his brother won't need to use dishonorable means to get the information if you've already confessed..."

"Good try, but I'm not going to confess anything. Nor can I assure you that I'll arrive in Norghania alive."

Egil was thoughtful. He knew Eyra was planning something, but what? She was not going to talk, but neither was it clear that she would not end her life to avoid going through what was in store for her in the capital. Doubts assailed him. Would the Dark Rangers kill her to stop her talking? Would she take her own life? Would she try to escape? He was not at all sure what was going to happen, and this made him uneasy. Eyra was very clever and dangerous, and he could not afford to be distracted even for a moment. This conversation proved it.

"I'll be here. Watching you. I won't let you die."

"I know. I expected that."

"Don't try anything. It won't work."

Eyra gave a little laugh. "If you say so."

"I can assure you of that."

"We'll see. Now if you don't mind, I'd like to eat my food before it gets cold."

"Go ahead. I'll watch you."

She nodded. Egil pushed the bowls closer so that she could reach them and gave her the spoon, but did not loosen the ties on her hands and feet. The ropes held her wrists and ankles, but that would not prevent her from eating if she held the spoon with both hands.

He sat down in front of her with his legs crossed and watched patiently while she ate, very slowly. In fact extremely slowly, which he found strange. He said nothing, but waited until she had finished, noticing that she had eaten it all.

"Delicious. Who says you're not a good cook?" she teased him.

"The spoon," Egil said. He had realized that it had vanished. There were only the two bowls, with no trace of the spoon.

"Oh, the spoon... yes, of course, how absent-minded of me," Eyra said untruthfully. She handed him the spoon, eyeing it as though it were a weapon she could try something with.

He put it away in his belt. A wooden spoon could not be used as a weapon. Or could it? Probably, in some way. He was not going to risk it, in either case. Unthinkable things had happened because of less than a spoon.

"You haven't asked me," she said distrustfully.

"Asked what?" Egil said as he picked up the two dishes and inspected the floor to make sure he had not missed anything, that Eyra had not tricked him in some unexpected way.

"Come on, ask me."

"Ummm... whether you hate me for having found you out and exposed you in front of everybody?"

"Well.... that too... but no, not that."

"Do you hold a grudge against me?" he asked, honestly intrigued to hear her answer. He guessed that it would certainly be "yes", but he preferred to wait and see as she watched him with a strange look in her eyes.

"Grudge, no. It's something else," she said, tilting her head as she went on staring at him strangely.

"Then it's hate."

Eyra shook her head. "No, I don't hate you. In fact what's happened to me has been my own mistake. I should never have helped you to stay among the Rangers, and particularly not to work with me, in my School. A mistake which I'm now paying for dearly."

"In that case, why did you help me?"

She laughed with a perverse witch's cackle. "Curiosity. I always knew you'd make trouble, considering who you are... what you represented... the West of the kingdom, the true king. I thought it would be something worth seeing, and that you'd make trouble for the King and his people. I wasn't wrong, you did make trouble and you're still doing that. Your career is a very interesting one, and it's provided me with the chance to make more out of some very awkward situations. That head of yours, that exceptional intelligence, is the thing I didn't foresee. In fact I thought you wouldn't survive the civil war. But what with your own ability and Dolbarar's help when he interceded on your behalf, in the end you didn't hang by the neck, which is how you should have ended."

"Something for which I'm deeply grateful to our leader."

"And because of which, you took pains to save his life."

"Exactly. I'd never let him die."

"And which has led us to this moment. One I'd hoped to avoid. But curiosity killed the cat." She cackled again. "What's to be done about it? I yielded to my curiosity, and now treacherous fate is making me pay for it."

"You can still save yourself," Egil insisted. He was trying to get her to tell him what she knew and was keeping hidden, even though he seriously doubted whether she would confess anything.

"You still haven't asked me."

Egil stared into her eyes, which were looking at him in amusement. He thought about it. What was it that he had not asked her? He was silent, puzzling over it. Then, all of a sudden, the answer came to him with intense clarity. He knew what it was.

He narrowed his eyes, and with an interrogator's questioning stare asked: "Why? Why the betrayal?"

Eyra smiled from ear to ear.

"That, my very intelligent young man, is precisely the question."

Egil waited for her to go on, but he knew she would not. She would leave him with that doubt in his mind. So he would go on probing. He picked up the bowls and the spoon, left the cart and locked the door. As he went to rejoin his comrades by the fire, he was thoughtful. The conversation with Eyra had not left him at ease. And now the question echoed inside his head:

Why?

Chapter 18

Egil slept all night by the door of Eyra's cage, to make sure nobody tried to help her or kill her – including herself. It was a particularly complicated situation, but he knew that what he had to do was to stay alert and not let her out of his sight for a single moment. If he could manage that, everything would be fine. Or so he hoped. Certainties in the lands of northern Tremia were becoming increasingly scarce.

He barely managed to rest, and had nightmares in which Eyra poisoned him and pushed him into the river so that the water would carry him away to a horrible death by drowning. He woke up at first light drenched in sweat. Eyra was looking at him with a twisted smile from inside her cage. Her expression seemed to be asking" Did you sleep well?" and Egil was aware that his own was replying" not at all".

Gerd came up to him. "What are you scheming?" he asked him in an inquisitive whisper so that Eyra would not hear him.

"I'm not scheming anything," Egil said with a shrug.

"Don't play innocent with me, pal." His voice was one of muffled outrage. "That one over there by the fire is Musker Isterton!"

"That's quite right. It is."

"He's the Ranger you caught spying on you at the Camp."

"Quite right as well."

"You're not going to tell me he's here by chance. You asked Angus to put him with us."

"Right again."

"Then you're planning something!"

"Irrefutable, my dear friend."

"This is no moment for your plans and stratagems!" He jabbed his thumb at Eyra. "We have enough on our plates as it is!"

"It's always a good moment for an excellent plan."

"No it isn't!"

"You take it easy, big guy. Everything'll turn out well."

Gerd looked horrified. "But things never turn out well for us! I'm just pointing out that he's a veteran Ranger and he's highly valued!"

"Every kind of 'well' is a relative concept. Don't you worry. Leave it to me."

"You're going to get us into a mess!"

Egil put a finger to his lips. "Shhh, they'll hear us."

Gerd was red by now and about to burst into a fit of fury which in all probability would culminate in a flood of words not fit for sensitive ears, but he could see that both Eyra from inside her cage and Ibsen and Musker from the campfire were watching him, and he was forced to contain himself.

"I'm keeping an eye on you, so be good," he warned Egil.

"Of course, my dear friend. This journey is going to be fantastic."

Gerd put his hand to his forehead and muffled an impropriety.

They broke their fast with something hot around the fire, and Egil took a bowl of hot porridge to Eyra before they set off again. Gurkog, Enok, Fulker and Valeria had come back from their watch-positions around the camp and were having breakfast too.

"Ibsen, Musker," Gurkog ordered, "get the cart ready. We're leaving shortly. Let's see if we can make faster progress than we did yesterday," he added to the others. "We're going far too slowly."

"It's not us, it's the cart keeping us back," Enok said.

"I know, but the delay's the same."

"We're not behind time, Gurkog," Fulker said. "It's just that you want us to get to the capital earlier."

"It's the same thing," Gurkog replied bad-temperedly.

"Perhaps they can drive the cart a bit faster," Valeria suggested, to try and stop Gurkog getting even more annoyed.

"Yes, that's a good idea. I'll talk to those two and see if they can speed up the horses. It makes me sick, having to go so slowly." Gurkog raced off to where Ibsen and Musker were tethering the horses to the cart.

"It doesn't look as though he's in a very good mood," Valeria said to her two Specialist comrades.

"He never is, but particularly today," Enok said.

"Have you known him long?"

"Yeah, well, just in passing. We've crossed here and there on missions, but we've never shared one."

"And you, Fulker?"

The Specialist shook his head. "No, me neither."

Valeria was looking around at the other comrades in the group. "And with any of the others in the group? Have you ever shared a mission?"

"Not me," said Enok.

"Me neither," Fulker agreed. "I've seen them at the camp and in the capital, but I've never shared a mission."

"You?" Enok asked Valeria.

"I have. I know Gerd well, and I've shared a mission with him." She nodded in the direction of the giant where he was bringing their horses. "And with Egil too," she added with another nod toward the cart where he was watching the cage door and the prisoner.

Fulker was curious. "And what are they like?"

"They're great. Gerd is a force of nature, and for his size he's very quick up here." She pointed at her own head. "As for Egil, you've all heard all kinds of rumors about him. All I'll tell you that he's awesome with plans and strategies, apart from being a walking encyclopedia."

Enok nodded. "Yeah... the giant seems capable of dealing with anything."

"And about Egil," Fulker commented, "it's true, there are all sorts of outrageous rumors making the rounds... I'm glad to know he's good at strategy and knowledge, that's always a welcome bonus for a group."

Valeria smiled. "Yeah, charm and personality aren't in short supply among the Rangers, but wisdom isn't exactly something we're over endowed with."

The two other Specialists smiled. "You can say that again," Enok agreed.

It was not long before Gurkog gave the order to set off again. They took up the same places, with Gurkog, Enok, and Fulker in the lead, Ibsen, Musker driving the cart and Valeria, Gerd and Egil bringing up the rear. They noticed at once that the cart was going faster than usual.

"We seem to be in a hurry," Gerd commented. "That's not good for those poor draft horses."

"Gurkog wants to get there as soon as possible," Valeria commented. "He's restless."

"That's understandable," Egil pointed out, "considering his mission and the dangers hovering over the load we're transporting."

"Nothing's going to happen," said Gerd, as if he were trying to convince himself more than the others.

Valeria smiled at him. "Let's hope so."

"Have you found anything out?" Egil asked her.

Gerd gave Egil a worried glance. "Find out what?"

"Egil asked me to get some information for him," she explained nonchalantly.

"And what for, Egil?" Gerd asked suspiciously.

"In order to be prepared, my dear friend."

"Are you planning anything?"

"I'm always planning something," Egil said with a smile. "On this occasion I'm trying to limit the risk we're taking with our current comrades."

"Oh..." Gerd looked slightly surprised.

"One of them might be working for the Dark Rangers. "I'm trying to gather information that'll help us find out whether that's so."

Gerd refused to believe this. "It won't be..."

Valeria smiled. "It's better to be cautious and clever like Egil and keep your eyes peeled. I've asked everybody – casually, don't worry – whether they know each other, and in fact they don't. Except for the three of us, the other five only know each other by hearsay, and they've never worked together."

"Interesting..." Egil was looking thoughtful.

"Why is it interesting?" Gerd asked. "It's good news, surely?"

Valeria nodded in agreement.

"It's true, the fact that they don't know each other isn't exactly bad news," Egil agreed. "But we can't discount any of them as a possible traitor, because we don't have enough information. On the other hand, if they don't know each other, there's less chance that there's a plot between several in the group. Although it's not completely impossible."

Gerd wrinkled his nose. "Surely not. How could there be several traitors here?"

"We've seen more unlikely things," Valeria said.

"We can't discount that possibility for now. There might be one or several traitors in the group."

"Even though they've been personally selected by Angus?" Gerd said skeptically. "I don't think so. It sounds impossible."

"That's because you're honorable and good-hearted. Too good." Egil smiled at him fondly.

"So are you."

"Oh not even half as much as you," Egil assured him.

Gerd waved his hand in disbelief. "Bah..."

"On the other hand, that makes me a better investigator of possible betrayals," Egil went on. "I can be rather more malicious and twisted than you, and that helps me in situations like this."

Valeria smiled sarcastically. "I can be very straightforward, so when you need to corroborate a suspicion, tell me and I'll deal with it."

Egil smiled in his turn. "I'll try not to be over-hasty in my judgment, so that I don't find myself in trouble."

"I can't believe we could have a traitor from the Dark Rangers among us," Gerd went on, refusing to believe in the possibility. "They're all veterans and Specialists. Besides, if you think about it, the odds that one of those five could be one of them is all-but-nonexistent."

"Not nonexistent, but very low, it's true," Egil corrected him. "I'm not saying you're wrong, but after finding out about Eyra's betrayal, we can't trust anybody. It's as simple as that."

"And sad..." Gerd added, sounding downhearted.

"You can't trust everybody, big guy," Valeria pointed out.

"Not everybody, but you can trust experienced Rangers... or at least I ought to be able to..."

"You could before, but not now," Valeria replied.

"How many has Eyra recruited for her secret group in the years she's been at the Camp?" Egil wondered, more to himself than to his comrades.

Valeria nodded firmly. "Quite a few, for sure."

"Yeah... that could be," Gerd was forced to admit. He did not like the idea, but the truth seemed to indicate it.

"It could be and it has been, no doubt about that," Valeria said.

Gerd sighed in disappointment. "Which means we don't trust any of the five..."

"Irrefutable, my dear friend," was Egil's reply.

"Who do you think the traitor could be?" Valeria asked, looking very interested.

"It's difficult to say at this moment," Egil said. He was unwilling to point a finger at any of the group.

Gerd gave him a reproachful glance. "Don't pretend, Egil, it has to be Musker."

"Why does it have to be him?" Valeria asked.

"Because Musker was spying on Egil at the Camp. He found him doing it. Just like Uliskson."

"Hey! Now that really is interesting." Valeria gave a start on her saddle and frightened her horse. She realized what she had done and calmed him by whispering affectionately in his ear.

"The interesting thing is that Egil asked Angus to include Musker on this mission," Gerd said. He was still eying Egil intensely.

Valeria smiled. "Our dear Egil, is he plotting one of his masterly plans?"

"Irrefutable, dear Val."

"See, he doesn't deny it."

"I see. In that case our number one suspect is Musker, because if Uliskson was watching you and turned out to belong to the Dark Rangers, we can guess that Musker, who was also watching you, very probably belongs to the secret faction too."

"Good guess, although we can't establish that link as yet. We need evidence." Egil was shifting his seat in his saddle. He still found it hard to adapt to long journeys on horseback.

"We'd better watch him closely and not let him out of our sight," said Gerd. "If he's going to try and free her, it'll be at some moment when we're distracted."

"I'm afraid freeing her might not be the only action he could take," Egil said. "He might have been given a more conclusive order..."

"More conclusive?" Gerd looked at him in surprise. He had not caught the nuance.

"Egil means he might have been ordered to kill her so that she doesn't talk," Valeria said flatly.

"Oh...!"

"Yes, that's a possibility we can't discount, and which we need to watch out for even more carefully than the possibility of flight."

Valeria leaned toward Egil from her saddle. "Which do you think is the more likely?"

"Rescuing her, right?" Gerd said, and it sounded more like wishful thinking than certainty.

Egil smiled at him, shaking his head. "That big heart of yours. The most likely option, because it's the easiest to carry out, is to put an end to her."

"No..." Gerd cried, and tugged at his horse's reins. That was exactly what he did not want to happen.

Valeria nodded. "Makes sense." She nodded at the cart. "It's easier to kill her than to get her out of there."

As though she knew they were talking about her, even though she could not hear them because they were too far behind for their voices to reach her, Eyra looked at them. She smiled that twisted smile of hers and once again looked like an evil witch.

"Anyway," Egil said, "we need to be ready to face any possibility, whether it's a rescue or an attempt to kill her."

"I'm going to keep very alert," Gerd said determinedly. "Nobody's going to escape or die while I'm here."

"Well, I'll go on digging to see what else I can find out," Valeria said. "It's one of the many advantages of being me. Boys tend to talk more with me. Generally too much." She smiled coquettishly and shook her long blonde hair.

"Yeah, with me I don't think their tongues would wag so much," said Gerd.

Egil gave a chuckle. "Let's keep our eyes and ears open and try to find out whether we have a Dark One in the group. I'll go on planning possible future actions."

Valeria and Gerd nodded and went on their way. All three of them had the feeling that soon events would come to a head, which would mean having to confront unexpected dangers.

Chapter 19

Gerd never took his eyes off Musker. When he was traveling at the rear of the group he would crane his neck to see the veteran's head on the box of the cart. Egil had already noticed this and had asked him to be more unobtrusive, but unobtrusiveness was not exactly Gerd's strong point.

They had been travelling for several days now, and although nothing of notice had happened, he was very restless. That was why he was not letting Musker out of his sight. During the day he kept an eye on him, while at night he helped him with the draft horses and sat down beside him by the campfire. As Egil would say: "Keep your friends close and your enemies even closer". That was what Gerd was doing, and for the moment Eyra was still intact inside her cage.

"Did you find out anything interesting last night?" Valeria asked Gerd as they were riding at the rear.

"About Ibsen and Musker?"

"Yes, obviously, you spend the evenings talking to them." She brought her horse closer to his.

"Nothing particularly interesting. They're not the kind who talk a lot."

"Don't ask too many questions, or they'll turn suspicious," Egil said.

Gerd bowed his head. "I try not to. I hope they don't notice."

Valeria winked at him. "Well, you're very friendly. They probably think you're trying to be friends with them."

"I hope so. I'm not much good at this spying business."

"Don't try too hard, or they'll realize you're after something," Egil warned him.

"Understood. I'll be a little less friendly... The thing is that just thinking Musker's a Dark Ranger turns my stomach." The giant was craning his neck to get a better look at the veteran.

"Suspected of being a Dark Ranger," Valeria corrected him. "Isn't that so, Egil?"

"Correct. It's not proven yet. He might not be."

"To me it smells bad," Gerd said. "When I asked him what he did at the Camp he gave me pretty evasive answers... missions of supply and logistics for the daily needs of the contenders... it didn't sound convincing to me at all."

"It's a good excuse," Egil said. "There are a number of Rangers, usually veterans, who are in charge of those jobs. That's unglamorous work and not highly valued, so it's not strange if Musker doesn't want to talk about it. As a rule, both in the army and among the Rangers, work in the quartermaster's department is considered a punishment rather than anything else. Nobody's proud that they've been given it."

"It could be that" Gerd agreed, but he did not sound convinced. He patted his horse.

"What did you find out about Ibsen?" Egil asked with interest.

"He's been on the southern border doing surveillance missions. He's glad of the company, because he spent the last year by himself."

"For reasons of practicality and efficiency," Egil pointed out, "most of those types of mission are entrusted to a single Ranger."

Gerd nodded in acknowledgment. "And also because there aren't many of us..."

"That's true," Egil agreed.

"He's not happy about having to drive the cart," Gerd went on. "He protests a lot about that. He says it ought to be you and me driving it, Egil."

"Oh, really? And why's that?"

"Because we're the lowest in rank. First come the Specialists, then the Veterans, and then you and me."

"Oh... I see."

"He doesn't understand why they, as veterans, should be doing the least gratifying work, while you and I keep watch on horseback."

"He has a point," said Valeria.

"You think that too?" Gerd asked her in surprise.

She smiled. "Well, the hierarchy's there to be respected."

"Gurkog's in command," Egil said, "and he assigned jobs to each of us. Well, Gurkog and Angus, who were the ones who chose us."

"They both respect Gurkog," Gerd went on. "Or rather, they respect and fear him. He has a very good reputation among the Rangers of being almost infallible and also very tough."

"Could he be the one who's been infiltrated?" Valeria asked Egil suddenly, as if the thought had just occurred to her,

Egil scratched his head and considered this.

"I doubt it. His reputation goes before him. All the same, we can't rule him out. Sometimes the most outrageous option is the best one. He's the person we least suspect..."

Gerd shook his head. "I don't think it's him."

"What do we know about the other two Specialists?" Egil asked.

"Well, I've managed to get them to tell me quite a lot," Valeria said with a seductive giggle, very proud of her achievement. She tossed her hair to one side, smiling roguishly.

Gerd laughed. "I haven't the slightest doubt about that."

"Listen. Enok is an Infallible Marksman, and he's been carrying out missions for the Court. To be exact, for King Thoran and his brother Orten."

"Well now, that really is interesting," said Egil.

"At first he didn't want to tell me who he was carrying out those missions for, and would only say they were for leading members of the Court. But he couldn't resist my charm, and in the end he told me."

"What kind of missions were they?" Gerd asked. He brought his horse close to Valeria's.

"The kind you can't talk about... without losing your head..."

"Oh, wow."

"He didn't go into detail, but he did say they were missions of intimidation and extortion to other Court nobles."

"Of the East or the West?" Egil asked. He sounded serious now.

"From what I could work out, mainly the West. So that they pay taxes to the King, which must be pretty heavy, from what he told me."

"So they are. It's a way of keeping the Western noblemen under control. Robbing them of all their gold in the form of taxes, then threatening them with death if they don't manage to pay."

"He's also been on missions in the East..."

"That doesn't surprise me either," Egil said. "Thoran has rivals among his own Eastern allies. He'll have sent them messages so that they stay quiet as mice."

"That's right. From what Enok said, his job was to give those noblemen a good scare."

"Yeah," Egil agreed, "and there's nothing better than an Infallible Marksman for doing that."

"I don't know much about them. Why is it a good choice?"

"Because where he puts his eye, he puts his arrow," Valeria explained. "If he puts it in your ear..."

Gerd nodded. "Oh... I see..."

"Infallible Marksmen are capable of hitting a fly on the wall," she said.

Egil nodded. "That would frighten the boldest of the noblemen."

"It looks as though he's done a good job, or at least so he told me. This mission gives him a change of air, and he's happy. In fact he's dying for someone to try something against the convoy so that he can put an arrow between the eyes of whoever dares. If there's more than one of them, even better. From the way he said it, I think he's very serious about it."

"Wow, that Enok..." Gerd said with a whistle.

Egil was listening attentively to what Valeria had to say. He seemed to be taking mental notes. "What can you tell me about Fulker?" he asked her.

She waggled her hand in emphasis. "I thought he was even more dangerous."

"Just wonderful," Gerd commented.

"He's a Natural Marksman, and from what I heard Gurkog say, he must be one of the best, if not the best. Imagine someone as good as Ingrid, or even better."

Gerd shook his head. "Better than Ingrid? I doubt it."

"He has a reputation for being very good. Enok told me that too. I haven't managed to get any more details about his missions, except that they were given to him by Gondabar and that they're usually very complicated ones. He usually goes with Man Hunters and even Assassins when it looks as though things are going to get messy. What he did tell me was that his specialty is rescuing hostages."

"Well, that sounds interesting," Gerd said.

"Yes, it seems that when they have to go into a well-guarded building and rescue someone important, he's one of the best. He can go in and start to take out a whole band of outlaws all by himself, though he usually has two other specialists with him so that there's less risk for the hostage. What I came away with was the fact that he's capable of going into the lair of a guild of thieves one quiet night and finish them all off until he gets as far as the chief."

"We should've brought him with us to Zangria," Gerd said mischievously, with a glance at Egil.

"On our special missions, only people we really trust can come with us," Egil replied. He winked at the giant.

"You could also have explained what you had in mind before we started the mission."

"Ouch, that hurt," Egil said, pretending to have been hit by an arrow. He clutched his horse to avoid falling off.

Valeria laughed out loud. "Both of you are really entertaining!"

They arrived at a tight bend on the road and lost sight of Gurkog, Enok and Fulker, who were leading the way. Suddenly the cart stopped in the middle of the bend. Gerd and Egil exchanged glances of alarm.

"What's the matter? Why are we stopping?" Valeria asked Ibsen and Musker.

Ibsen turned and pointed ahead. "There's a fallen tree in the middle of the road."

Gerd looked to right and left. On the right a beech wood spread as far as they could see, while on the left was an open area, with an oak wood further away. There was no-one in sight.

"Spread out!" came Gurkog's order.

"Better separate and be careful," Egil told them.

Valeria was looking in every direction. "I can't see any danger."

"Nor me," Gerd agreed.

Egil took a wary look. "Trees don't fall down in the middle of the road all by themselves..."

Gerd nodded and went to the left to see what was happening, while Valeria did the same to the right. Egil rode up to the cart and watched Eyra's reaction in search of a possible clue. The Master Ranger was lying on the floor, as if she were asleep. The door of the cage was locked. There was no way she could escape.

"The tree's been cut down!" came Gurkog's voice. "It's a trap!"

At the same moment an arrow struck one of the bars of the cage with enormous force. Egil had to hold on hard to his horse to avoid falling. He managed to regain his grip and looked around, but could see nobody.

"Look out! Ambush!" Gurkog shouted.

"Who's attacking us?" Gerd asked.

A second arrow flew into Eyra's cage and out of the other side. Egil realized what was going on, and why she was lying on the floor.

"Archer!" he yelled at the top of his voice. "An Archer!"

"Everybody on the ground! On the ground!" Gurkog yelled.

Valeria leapt off her horse and raced into the forest. Gerd slipped from his horse and stayed lying on the ground. Ibsen and Musker leapt off the cart on the side of the forest and hid among the vegetation. Egil dismounted quickly and crouched beside the door of the cage. He could not see Gurkog, Enok or Fulker, who were at the end of the bend, but he imagined that they were lying low.

A third arrow flew in search of Eyra's body, and this time it brushed her head.

"He's shooting from the oak wood to the west!" Gerd yelled. He had seen the arrow fly past him.

Immediately Egil took shelter on the right of the cart, huddled behind one of the wheels.

"They're coming for me," Eyra told him.

Egil raised his head slightly. "Do they want to kill you?"

A new arrow passed close to her body where she was staying as flat as she could, stretched out on the floor on her face to avoid offering the marksman an easy target.

"I know too much... Help me, Egil, or else I'll die here," she pleaded.

"Enok, Fulker and Gerd, we're moving to that oak wood to get the Archer," Gurkog ordered. "The rest of you, cover the cart."

Valeria appeared beside Egil. "What do we do? Is it a lone Archer?"

"Looks like it. We've got to get Eyra out of here, or he'll hit her sooner or later."

A new arrow hit another of the bars and ricocheted at high speed.

"He's using a powerful precision bow," Valeria pointed out. "Definitely a Forest Sniper."

"One of ours?" Ibsen asked. He was lying on the ground with his bow in his hand a few paces away.

"I fear so. One of ours, working for the Dark Ones."

"Well, that's all we need. Better not raise our heads, or he's going to blow them apart."

Egil turned to Valeria. "We have to get Eyra out of here or she'll die."

"Do you want to risk your life for her?" she asked, tilting her head.

"Well, I don't exactly want to, not really. But I can't let her be killed like this."

"Why not? She's a traitor. She deserves to die. In fact she'll be judged and then die in any case."

"I know, but... nobody deserves to be murdered."

"Don't forget, she's probably murdered innocent people, quite apart from trying to murder Dolbarar."

"True... but I can't let her die like this..."

A new arrow grazed Eyra's head, and she screamed in anguish.

"Will you be able to cover her?" he asked Ibsen and Musker.

Both veterans armed their composite bows and released in the direction of the oak forest. The arrows fell short.

"Too far, "Ibsen said with a grimace.

"It's certainly a Sniper," Musker reasoned. "You need a long-range bow for that distance.

Valeria snorted and looked Egil in the eye. "Fine. Although I don't know why we're risking our lives like this. If that sniper puts an arrow in my head, let's see how you explain that to my father. Don't forget, he's not entirely on your side..."

"Very true. You'd better try not to get hit."

Valeria rolled her eyes.

"You open the door and I'll get her out."

"All right."

Egil stretched out his hand to the lock, trying to keep as much under cover as possible, which was not much as the back of the cart was the barred cage and did not offer much to cover behind. He managed to turn the key by reaching as far as he could, while Valeria crawled to the door of the cart like a snake through grass.

The moment he heard a click, he gave her the warning. "It's open."

"Coming," she said, and stood up smoothly. She pulled the door open and jumped inside the cage. An arrow passed close to her back.

"Phew!" she gasped.

"I can see Gerd and Gurkog!" Ibsen warned them. "They're getting near the oak wood!"

"It might be too late," Valeria said. She seized Eyra's ankles and pulled her out sharply.

"Careful now," Egil warned her. He was watching the spot in the forest where the arrows were coming from.

"Is he going to shoot at them?" Musker wondered. He was

pointing at Enok and Fulker, who were also approaching the oak wood, running at a crouch and zigzagging to avoid being hit.

Egil already knew the answer, but said nothing. He turned to Valeria. "Get her out, now!"

Valeria dropped down out of the cage and tugged Eyra hard. An arrow buried itself next to where she had been a moment before. It missed her by a finger's-breadth.

"Come on, get her out! The next arrow'll kill her!"

Valeria tugged with all her might, and she and Eyra dropped to the ground behind the cart. Just as Egil had guessed, an arrow buried itself in the back of the cage where Eyra had been.

"They're getting there now!" cried Ibsen.

"Now they'll hunt him down!" said Musker.

Egil crouched to see how Valeria and Eyra were as they lay flat on the ground. "Are you all right?" he asked Valeria.

"Pretty shaken, but well."

"Eyra?"

"I've had a couple of massive bumps, which at my age aren't exactly advisable, but considering I was going to die, I won't complain."

"Your head is bleeding," Egil said.

"It's a scratch. One of the arrows came too close."

"Stay flat, Egil. Just in case," Valeria said.

"The Sniper won't shoot again," Egil told her.

"How d'you know?"

"He knows because your comrades have got as far as the forest," Eyra explained. "And the Sniper will have fled to avoid being caught."

"Oh, wow."

Egil nodded. "We'll wait a moment to make sure that's true. Don't get up, just in case."

They waited, unmoving, to see what was happening in the oak wood. Everything seemed too quiet. Their comrades had gone in among the oak-trees from different directions, and it was as if the trees had swallowed them up. Egil was staring at the edge of the forest, hoping to see Gerd or the others appear, but for some reason nobody was visible.

Valeria too was staring at the wood. "Will they be okay?" she asked from the ground.

"They should be," Egil reasoned." The Sniper won't confront them. He knows he'd die if he did."

"They're taking too long," Musker said from the other end of the cart.

"I don't like this," Ibsen said. "They should've come out by now."

Valeria, unable to stay stretched out on the ground any longer, crawled toward Egil.

"Be careful..."

"Don't worry, it's just that I can't stay lying down waiting to see what happens. I'll drag Eyra under the cart. She'll be under better cover."

"Good idea."

Valeria got under the cart. Taking Eyra by her tied wrists, she dragged her under with her and then stayed beside her. Eyra held up her tied wrists.

"Thank you... couldn't you untie me, given the situation?" she asked.

"Don't mention it. It's my duty and no, I can't untie you. Sorry." She glanced at Egil, who had gone back to shelter behind the wheel.

Suddenly they saw Gurkog coming out of the center of the oak wood. A moment later Gerd and Fulker came out too.

"There they are!" Musker cried.

"Thank goodness, I was beginning to get nervous," said Ibsen.

They waited until the two reached them before leaving the protection of the cart.

"Did the prisoner survive the attack?" Gurkog asked urgently as the moment he arrived.

Eyra said nothing, so Egil answered for her. "She's okay, a little bruised and with a head-wound. She came very close to dying."

"Hellfire! They've wounded my prisoner! My responsibility!" Gurkog shouted furiously.

"The ambush was very well prepared," Fulker pointed out. "That tree in the middle of the road, right at the end of the bend so that the cart would be in the open at this point – that was a good bit of thinking."

"The Sniper was good," Gurkog added. "Presumably one of our own."

"Did you catch him?" Musker asked.

"No, he ran away the moment we came near the wood."

"We chased him as far as the other end of the oak wood, but he ran like a hare," said Gerd.

"We'd have followed him," Fulker added, "but Gurkog made us stop and come back."

"There could have been more danger there, and I didn't want to risk it," Gurkog said. "Hunting that traitor wasn't the priority. Transporting the prisoner is. I've sent Enok after him. He'll hunt him down. He's an Infallible Marksman, and at short range he'll easily get the better of that Sniper. He won't bother us again."

"So there's no danger anymore?" Valeria asked from where she was still by Eyra's side under the cart.

"No, you can both come out."

Valeria leapt out, then helped Eyra, who had some trouble getting back on to her feet.

"Egil," Gurkog said, "tend to that wound, and those bruises and scratches. Valeria and Gerd, you stay with Egil. The others, clear the road. I want that tree on one side in the blink of an eye."

"Yes, sir!" said Fulker, and they both set to work.

Chapter 20

Egil loosened the ties on Eyra's wrists and ankles and attended to her carefully. All the Rangers had learnt first-aid skills and field healing, so he did not have too much trouble. In addition he loved potions, brews, ointments and things of the sort, curative or not, and was an expert. Lately he had spent more time studying poisons and antidotes than anything else, but everything connected with the School of Nature interested him deeply, even the traps, which he was not very good with. He would have to talk to Lasgol and get some practical lessons in placing and hiding them.

"I'm glad to see some of my teachings have taken root," Eyra told Egil as he was busy tending to her.

Valeria and Gerd, bows in hand, were on watch duty a few paces away, each with an arrow nocked ready for danger.

"Healing is an art I've always liked a lot. I've studied all the tomes on it in the library."

"It certainly is an art. It's a pity you like it so much. There's so much trouble we could have avoided if you hadn't taken an interest in my School."

Egil was intrigued. Why was she saying this? Suddenly he realized.

"You mean because of Dolbarar and his poisoning."

"Precisely."

"Will you tell me the reason why, some day? Why you did it?" he asked her while he gathered up the ointments he had been using.

"Maybe... or maybe not..." she replied enigmatically.

"If you don't tell me, at some point I'll find out," he said, as though he were challenging her.

Eyra smiled her twisted smile. "You might manage to find out, but it won't be easy for you. And in any case, even if you do find out, I doubt whether you'd understand."

"I've always tried to keep an open mind and have a broad view of things. You might be surprised by how much I understand."

"Maybe. We'll see... If you don't mind, I'll lie down in the cart. My head aches, and this bandage you've put on is tight."

"It's to stop the bleeding. I'll check it later and change it for a new one with more disinfectant ointment."

He helped her to get as comfortable as possible in her cage and tied her wrists and ankles again with Ranger knots.

"Is it really necessary?" she protested.

"I'm afraid it is."

"It won't help if they try to kill me again."

"I'm sorry. I can't let you loose." He jumped out of the cart and locked the barred door.

"Everything quiet?" he asked his comrades.

"Seems to be," Gerd said.

"Only one archer," Valeria added.

"One archer, yes, but there were several people carrying out this attack," Egil said. He was looking at Gurkog, who was on his way back.

"You're not wrong there," the Man Hunter said. "I found the trail of at least three people by the trees."

"Then the tree didn't fall..."

"No, it was cut down."

"A well-planned, well-executed ambush," Egil said. "Luckily the Archer didn't get as far as the prisoner."

Gurkog snorted in relief. "Thank goodness. I don't like the way she's so exposed," he added.

"I was thinking the same thing" Egil said. "We ought to cover the cage."

"What with? We don't have any canvas..."

Egil smiled and pointed to the undergrowth. "We have a forest," he said. "We can camouflage the cart."

"Great idea!" Gurkog said. He turned to Ibsen and Musker. "You two, come with me. We'll cut a few leafy branches."

Both Rangers stared at him blankly. "What for?" Musker asked.

"To cover the whole cart with them. You others, stay in position and keep watch."

Fulker took up a position in front of the cart, while Valeria and Gerd went on covering the rear, one on either side. Egil sat down on the ground in front of the door and set about checking the ingredients he was carrying in his Ranger's belt.

Gurkog, Ibsen and Musker covered the whole cart and Eyra's cage with a variety of branches and shrubs so that it was impossible to see the prisoner inside. They tied the branches tightly with ropes and cords, and even rocks to hold down part of the cage roof. It took them some time, but once they had finished it looked so good that even Egil congratulated them.

"Camouflage is one of the things I'm best at," Musker said.

"It's come out very well," Ibsen said. "Let's hope it holds up on the road."

"If we lose part of the camouflage, we'll stop and replace it," Gurkog said. "You're in charge of it. I don't want anybody to see what our cargo is. And now we'll be off again. We've wasted too much time."

Valeria went over to Egil. "Do you think that marksman will try again?"

Egil scratched his temple. "He might. He didn't manage what he was after. He could have picked out a second position further along the way and then try again."

"That makes me pretty uneasy," Gerd said. He had just arrived with their horses.

"He won't be able to hit Eyra if he can't see her," Valeria pointed out.

"Not her..." Egil began.

"But us, he could," Gerd finished for him.

"I fear so. He might try to eliminate us so that he can get as far as the prisoner, although I doubt whether he'd be successful. There are a lot of us, and once he got the first one we'd almost certainly spot where he was."

"Tell that to the first one he hits," Valeria said. From her expression it was clear that she did not like the idea at all.

"Yeah," Egil agreed, "that one won't live to tell the tale..."

"Best keep our eyes peeled," Gerd said.

The three mounted and rode on. For a long time nobody spoke. They were all worried in case either the Sniper tried again or they ran into another ambush. They found it difficult to relax enough to be able to chat a little. They were beginning to understand how dangerous this mission was, and they were afraid things might get worse.

Gurkog, who wanted to go faster, turned to Ibsen and Musker every now and then. They were going as fast as they could, but the camouflage hampered them. The road was in poor condition, and every bump threatened part of the camouflage on top of the cage.

They lost a fair amount of it when it finally fell off as night was approaching, forcing Gurkog to stop. He decided that the best thing would be to repair the camouflage and spend the night where they were. They would set out before dawn to make up the time they had lost.

Egil hurried to see how Eyra was and tend to her wound and her bruises. It was the first chance he had had to do this all day. The rest of the group set up camp. Gerd took care of all the horses, with the exception of the draft ones, which were Ibsen's responsibility. Musker built a small fire so that they could cook the food they were carrying.

"How are you?" Egil asked Eyra as he went into her cage, which was now covered with forest foliage.

She mumbled something unintelligible.

Egil was surprised to find what she was saying incomprehensible. "Is anything wrong?"

"I... wrong..." she stammered.

When he was at her side, he realized that she looked terrible. She was as white as snow, her lips were purple and her eyes feverish. He put his hand on her forehead three times at equal intervals of time, and it was clear that she was running a very high fever.

"Valeria! Gerd!" he called. He took off his cloak and rolled up his sleeves.

Valeria's head appeared at the door. "Is there anything wrong, Egil?"

"Eyra's pretty bad. She has a very high fever."

"Fever? She was all right this morning."

Egil took off his Ranger's belt and left it on the floor in front of him so that he could work better with the ingredients he was carrying. "Can you bring me some water?"

Valeria nodded and raced off.

Gerd's head appeared at the door. "What's up?"

"Eyra's running a very high fever. Get a fire going right here. I'm going to need it to prepare some tisanes and potions."

Gerd nodded and turned. "Wait," Egil added. "Tell Gurkog. I need to speak to him."

"Have you been hurt in any other part of your body?" he asked her as he checked her arms and legs very carefully in case he had missed some other wound which had become infected. He knew very well that any wound that went untreated, however small, if it were infected, could give a high fever which could even put a life in danger. It was often said that more soldiers were killed on the battlefield by infections than by enemy steel. The most common infections among the people of the north, when there was no war on, were dental ones. If a gum became infected or a tooth decayed, as often happened, it could spread throughout the body and even kill. That was why in Norghana and other civilized kingdoms of Tremia, healers and surgeons pulled out bad teeth. And if none were available, teeth were pulled out by friends or relatives, however much it might hurt.

"Wound... don't know..." the Master Ranger mumbled.

Since he could find no other wound – apart from the one on her head, which he had already treated – he had to undress her. Very carefully, respectfully and with great modesty, he examined her fully. At her age she was only bone and deeply-wrinkled skin. To his puzzlement, he found no other wound. She had bruises and scratches from Valeria's efforts to get her out of the cart and then pull her underneath it to safety, but they were not infected. He took out the disinfectant ointment and put it on all the scratches, even though they did not appear to be infected and could not be the cause of the fever.

Gurkog appeared at the door of the cage. "What's up? Problems?"

Egil told him what was happening succinctly. Gurkog grasped the bars and got into the cage, then knelt down beside the patient. He wrinkled his nose as if he could smell trouble.

"She looks very bad. I don't like this at all."

"They're killing me... murdering me..." Eyra muttered in her delirium.

"What's she saying? Who's killing her?" Gurkog asked, looking seriously worried.

"She's delirious because of the high fever," Egil explained. "It's hard to understand her. She's having nightmares where someone's trying to kill her."

"Delirious? Then she has a very high fever which could be deadly."

"Unfortunately that's right."

"She can't die, Egil. We've got to save her and deliver her to the capital alive."

"I'll try, but I can't guarantee she'll survive the night."

"By the lightning of the Ice Gods!" Gurkog swore, and left the cart. Outside, it took him a while to calm down, then he climbed in again. "We need her to be judged in the capital, in public. If she dies here all kinds of rumors'll be unleashed, and the first of them will be that we took justice into our own hands."

Egil looked at him with a frown. "Yes, it might look like it if the prisoner dies mysteriously of some fever."

"That's why you've got to save her! It's not only our reputation, it's that of the whole Rangers' Corps. Things are bad enough with this business of the Dark Rangers to have this come down on us on top of it all." He shook his head and snorted violently.

Egil nodded. "I'll try," he promised. He was mixing the ingredients he needed for a tisane, to bring her temperature down.

Gurkog jumped off the cart and set off determinedly to tell the rest of the group what was going on. Valeria brought the water Egil needed.

"Thanks, leave it by the fire Gerd's making." He indicated the front of the cart, where Gerd was making a pile of dry wood.

"If you need me to help with anything, let me know," she said. "Potions and ointments aren't my thing, but I'd be glad to help you any way I can."

"Get me a pot. Ibsen or Musker are carrying campaign utensils at the front of the cart. Under the box where they sit."

She nodded and flew off like an arrow.

Gerd had the fire going by the time she came back with a pot and a long iron spoon, together with an iron trestle to support the pot on the fire.

Without having found any other noticeable wound, Egil prepared to change the bandage on Eyra's head-wound, which he had already tended to after the assault. He took off the bandage, and the smell of putrefaction assailed his nostrils.

"What the –" he exclaimed. This was something he had not expected. He checked the wound, which was completely infected and looked horrible. But that was impossible. He had treated it himself, left it clean and protected with ointment. It should not have turned infected, particularly in such a short time.

It was getting dark, and he asked Valeria to bring an oil lamp so that he could see the wound better. Valeria helped him by holding it over Eyra's head.

"This looks very, very bad..." Egil commented, though he was really thinking aloud. It was obvious that it made no sense to him.

Valeria was staring at the wound in disbelief. "How could it have gotten so infected? Wasn't it a clean cut?"

"It was. The tip of the arrow grazed her from here to here." He showed her with his finger. "I cleaned the wound very carefully myself. I don't understand how it could have turned like this."

"Perhaps a dirty hair got inside? Or there might have been dirt on the bandage?" she suggested, without much conviction.

"Maybe, but it shouldn't have turned so bad in such a short time."

Gerd's head appeared at the door. "Need anything?"

"Water, soap, disinfectant and clean cloths. Look in my travelling satchel, the second one, the largest one, brown. I carry a bit of everything in there. Don't put your hand in the black satchel, the smaller one," he added seriously.

"Don't worry, I won't put my hand in," Gerd replied with a look of horror on his face. He could imagine what there was in that satchel.

Egil went on looking at the wound. An idea which had not occurred to him at first, because of the strangeness of the infection, came to his mind.

"There might be a different explanation..."

"What?" Valeria asked as she wiped the sweat off Eyra's forehead with her scarf.

"That the arrows were smeared with some noxious substance."

"Poison?" Valeria asked excitedly.

"It might be some type of poison, true."

"That would explain why the wound's turned so ugly so quickly, for a simple graze."

"That would explain it, but it complicates the situation."

"If it's poison, we'll need an antidote."

"The problem is, we don't know what it is."

They were both quiet and thoughtful as they watched Eyra, who was delirious, shivering in nightmares.

Gerd appeared at the cage door with Egil's satchel slung over his shoulder and a basin of clean water in his hands. He left it all on the floor before he climbed up, to avoid upsetting the water. His huge body could barely squeeze through the door. Egil turned round to give him a hand.

"I've brought the whole satchel, just in case you needed more things."

"Good thinking. I think I will. Do me a favor and call Gurkog. I have worrying news for him. It might be poison."

The giant snorted. "Wow... this is a foul business."

"It certainly is. In the meantime I'll clean the wound again and prepare some antidotes."

Gerd jumped down from the cart and ran to fetch Gurkog. Egil got down to work immediately. Very carefully he washed the wound thoroughly, leaving aside a sample of green pus to analyze in more detail at dawn in the daylight to see if he could identify the poison that had been used.

The leader of the group came at once. He had already guessed that it was not good news.

"What is it?" he asked Egil unhappily, without climbing up into the cart.

"The tip of the arrow might have been poisoned."

"By the Norghanian mountains! Are you going to be able to save her?"

"I don't know... the wound isn't deep, which means not much poison can have got in, but it might be a very potent one, to judge from her adverse physical reaction."

Gurkog shook his head. "This woman looks terrible. It must've been a very potent poison, to make her as ill as this."

Egil nodded. "I'm going to prepare several antidotes, some with a wide spectrum and some others I happen to have the ingredients for. By dawn they should have taken effect."

"Right. Anything new, you let me know."

Egil set to work, and with Gerd's and Valeria's help he prepared the antidotes while the Specialists kept watch around the cart. Musker took over the post Valeria had vacated, while Ibsen took Enok's.

Gurkog appeared several times during the night to see how the prisoner was doing, and Egil briefed him on what little improvement there was. With dawn, and after giving her the antidotes he had prepared, her fever was still high. They had not managed to bring about any improvement.

"I fear she's going to die," Egil announced to Gurkog when he appeared at the cart with the first rays of dawn.

Chapter 21

"Is she going to die?" Gurkog asked. He was staring in disbelief.

"We can't seem to lower her temperature. What I'm afraid of is that it'll consume her completely in a couple of days, and she'll die."

Gurkog shook his head, refusing to accept this. "That simply can't be allowed to happen. It's my responsibility. She can't die under my watch."

"I'm sorry I can't give you better news, but without knowing the type of poison used – and it must be a very strong one – there's no way to stop her body from burning with fever. The infection's a severe one."

"There must be something that can be done."

Egil gestured at the surroundings. "With what we have available here, I fear that's not very much."

"Suppose we took her to Icelbag? It's a major city. There are surgeons and healers there. We'd be delayed a couple of days, but if it saves her it'd be worthwhile."

"It's a good idea... but on the other hand I don't think she'd survive the journey. She's in a very fragile state, and with that high fever..."

Gurkog scratched his chin thoughtfully. "The other option is to do it the other way round. To bring an expert surgeon here as quickly as possible."

"We could try that. Certainly a surgeon or a healer would have a lot more knowledge than me, and might be able to save her."

"In that case that's what we'll do." He turned, in readiness to take action.

"There's a problem, though," Egil added.

Gurkog threw his head back. "Another one?"

Valeria and Gerd were listening beside the fire they had brought back to life. They had barely been able to get any rest during the night, but this was something Rangers were used to. They would rest when they had the chance to, and this was not the moment. Egil had not slept at all, but nobody could have guessed it.

"If we don't bring that fever down, the surgeons or the healers won't get here in time to help her."

"Well then, we'll just have to bring her temperature down!" Gurkog burst out, more loudly than he had intended. The rest of the group stared at him from their watch-positions, which they had not left all night.

"We'll have to if we want to keep her alive, it's true."

"So how do we do that?"

"I've given her two different potions which should have brought the fever down. They haven't worked. The poison must be enormously toxic."

"So what alternatives do we have?" Gurkog asked. He was afraid that Egil's reply would confirm his suspicion that there was nothing more they could do.

Egil was silent for a moment, looking around him. To the north was a high mountain with a snow-capped peak, and beside it two other peaks, lower but also snow-capped.

"I have an idea..."

"What? Whatever it is, tell me," Gurkog urged him.

Egil pointed to the nearest of the mountains. "How long would it take you to reach the lowest peak?"

Gurkog turned to look at it. "I don't know exactly, but we can ask Fulker. He's from this area, and he knows it well."

"Then let's ask him."

"Fulker! Come quickly!" Gurkog called.

The Natural Marksman came quickly to their side, and Gurkog pointed to the mountain. "How far to the small peak? You're from this area, so you told me, right?"

"Yeah, I'm from a small village a little further east. To the Peak of the Wolf, the smallest, would be a day, more or less, from here."

"Can you get there and back in less than a day?" Egil asked him.

"Climbing as far as the peak?" Fulker asked. He was staring at them blankly, wondering where these questions were leading.

"Not to the peak, just as far as the snow-line."

"Hmmm... that would be a bit less... the steepest part is the last one... if we push the horses to their limit and climb the mountain the same way... maybe it might be possible. Why?"

"If we want to bring the fever down, we need to cool her body. For that we need ice, which we don't have at hand as it's the beginning of autumn, or else snow, and that's something we can get."

Egil pointed up at the mountain.

"Ah... now I see," said Gurkog.

"How much snow are we talking about?" Fulker asked.

"We need to cover her whole body with it," Egil explained. "That should be enough to bring her body temperature down enough and stop her from dying."

He looked up at the sky. It was growing cooler, as was usual at the beginning of autumn, but the temperature was not low enough to freeze Eyra. All the same, it ought to be cool enough to prevent the snow melting on the way.

"The plan's a little farfetched," Gurkog said to Egil. His tone of voice suggested that it would be a miracle if it worked.

Egil shrugged. "I can't think of anything else, under the circumstances..."

Gurkog exhaled loudly. "Okay then. We can at least try. We'll go for the snow. Since we need to bring enough, and part of it'll melt on the way back, I'll take most of them with me." He indicated the group, who had come closer to see what was going on after hearing Gurkog's shouts.

"Fine," Egil said. "Musker can stay to help. Valeria can go and fetch a surgeon from Icelbag."

"That seems fine to me. You others, come with me. We're going to bring snow. Empty all your backpacks and travel bags. We're taking them with us."

The Rangers looked at Gurkog as if he were out of his mind. The idea was totally insane, and they did not understand why they were doing it.

"We're off! We've got to go there and back as if we had wings!"

"We need the snow to lower her body temperature," Egil explained to them, "so that she doesn't die from the fever."

The Rangers gave him the same look they had given Gurkog, but said nothing. They did as they had been told and began to empty all the bags they were carrying.

"The ones for supplies too!" Gurkog ordered.

"Do you think it'll work?" Gerd asked Egil anxiously.

Egil put his hand on his shoulder. "I hope so. Get the snow. All you can, and then we may be able to save her."

"I'll bring you half the mountain!"

Egil smiled. "I wasn't expecting any less of you, my friend."

"Valeria, off you go! This minute!" Gurkog ordered her, shooing her off with his hands.

"I'll be back in the blink of an eye!" she told Egil, who nodded.

"Find the most experienced surgeon. We'll need him."

"Got it. He'll be here before you realize." She gave him an encouraging smile.

"Off you go!" Egil said. He smiled back gratefully.

A moment later, she was vanishing at a gallop toward the city of Icelbag. Gurkog and the others mounted, laden with all their backpacks and bags.

"Don't let her die! I'll bring you your snow!" Gurkog promised, and then they galloped away. Egil knew that he would keep his promise. They would race to the mountain, then climb up to the snow, as though this were a competition. They were Specialist Rangers, with the exception of Gerd, and Egil knew that they were tough and strong. Probably the one who would suffer most in the climb would be Gerd. His body was too big and he was not particularly good at climbing, but he would give it everything he had, and Egil knew it.

He settled down to prepare more potions for Eyra. When he had finished, he sat down in front of the fire and made himself a strong tisane, blew on the brown liquid to cool it off a little and took a sip. The smell was strong, as was the taste.

Musker came over from tending to the horses and sat down opposite him on the other side of the fire.

"How's the patient?"

"Sleeping. She seems a bit less delirious."

"Is it still burning?"

"Yes, her temperature's very high."

"Well, maybe her body will get over it. She's a tough woman."

Egil shook his head. "She's tough, but that's not usually what happens. When there's fever, particularly when it's the result of poison, the body can't cope with it."

"Then let's hope our comrades get back quickly."

"They will. I have faith in them," Egil said. He took another sip.

Musker had noticed the strong aroma of the tisane. "What's that you're drinking?"

"An invigorating tisane. An old Ranger's remedy. I haven't slept a wink, and I find it helps. Would you like some? It gives you plenty of energy and stops you falling asleep."

Musker nodded. "I could do with something hot, to give me some energy."

Egil smiled and began to pour a small bowl for him.

"Will you do me a favor and check she hasn't woken up?" he asked Musker, with a wave in the direction of the cage at the back of the cart.

"No problem." Musker got to his feet and looked inside the cage. Eyra was asleep, soaked in sweat.

"Is she asleep?"

"It's more that she's having nightmares, she's moving quite a bit. But yes, she's asleep."

"Thanks. Here's your tisane."

Musker took it in his hands and sipped it. "Very good, this invigorating tisane," he said, and took two more sips.

"It'll do you good," Egil replied. He took another sip of his own.

"So you're sure there's poison in whatever Eyra's suffering from?" Musker asked, his eyes half-closed.

"Yeah, it's almost certain. I've been analyzing samples from the wound, and it looks as though there's something very toxic in it."

"The arrow, then?"

"Everything points to that."

Musker scratched his head. "Maybe you're wrong, and the poison doesn't come from the arrow."

"That's an interesting theory. Where could it have come from, d'you think?"

"Couldn't she have poisoned herself?" Musker hinted. "Considering what's in store for her in the capital, which we can all imagine, and knowing what she knows about poisons and potions... it's the most logical thing."

"It might be the most logical thing, I'm not saying it isn't. All the same, it seems extremely unlikely to me, because she's been searched several times, precisely to avoid that happening. And also, I've been watching her closely. I haven't found any poison on her, and I can't see how she could have got hold of any."

"In that case it could have been somebody else who poisoned her. Somebody in the group..." Musker went on hinting. There was suspicion in his eyes.

Egil gave him a sudden hard glare. "You, for instance?"

PEDRO URVI

Musker was startled by this. "Me? Why should it be me?"

"Because you work for someone, and that someone could have asked you to kill her."

"I work for the Rangers, like all of us, like you."

"That's not entirely true, or rather not exactly. You're a Ranger like me, like all of us, but you work directly for someone else"

Musker was looking unsettled. "I don't know why you should say that," he said defensively.

"Because I've been watching you, and I know you've been spying on me."

"Spying? Me spying on you? Of course not!"

"There's no need for you to pretend." Egil gave their surroundings a wave. "Here we are, all by ourselves, just the two of us."

"I'm telling you again, I haven't been spying on you! I find that an offensive accusation!"

"I guessed you'd say something like that. Guilty people tend to make very simplistic defenses, such as denying everything."

"Guilty? Simplistic?" Musker wagged his finger threateningly. "If you don't want to regret it, I'd advise you to shut that know-it-all mouth of yours!"

"And now we move on to the threats... so predictable..." Egil commented, looking and sounding bored.

"You don't talk to me in that superior way! You're no better than me!"

"Right. I think the time has come to move on to the questioning. We won't have another opportunity like this for a very long time to have a talk all by ourselves, and we need to make use of the opportunity."

"What questioning? Are you out of your mind?"

"Far from it. My mind works perfectly well. I've never felt better, in fact. This is the moment when you tell me who you're working for. It's time to clear up a few unknown quantities."

"I've no idea what you're talking about," Musker yelled at him, "but I'm getting tired of putting up with all your nonsense!" He tried to get up, but his legs buckled underneath him.

"You'd better stay sitting down," Egil advised him.

"What's the matter with me?" Musker cried, his eyes staring wide. He tried to move his numbed legs with all his might, but without

182

success.

"You won't be able to move them for quite a while. You'll lose your arms as well before very long."

"You bastard! What have you done to me?"

"It's a highly effective paralyzing brew. One of Eyra's specialties, in fact. I remember when she taught it to us. I'm sure she taught it to you as well in your day."

Musker looked down at the tisane in his hands with hatred in his eyes, then hurled it at Egil. "You're out of your mind!"

Egil dodged the bowl easily and got up. "Spending time with Eyra reminded me about it: Limb-numbing Potion."

"You put it in my tisane!"

"Relax. It's quite harmless, except that you won't be able to move either your arms or your legs, so we'll be able to have a peaceful chat about our business."

"I'll gut you for this!"

"I doubt it. If I were you, I'd relax. None of your threats, insults, fighting talk and all that sort of thing will have the least effect on me. It's just one of those things. I'm like that. Let's say that the experiences I've been through have taught me a lot."

"You'll pay for this! I'll cut your eyes out!"

"Tch, tch... I see you're not following my advice. Don't worry. I'm going to fetch a couple of friends of mine who I think will help you see reason and decide to co-operate with me. They're really striking. You're going to love them."

"What friends? I'm not going to tell you anything!"

"Oh, but you are..." Egil went over to his horse and carefully took his black satchel.

"What are you doing? What's in there?" Musker had turned his head to see what Egil was doing. He was sitting with his legs stretched out and his arms hanging limp by his sides. He tried to move them, without effect. The only things he could move were his head and his waist.

"I have two friends I'd like to introduce you to. They're really charming, and I think they'll encourage you to speak sincerely, from the heart."

"I'm not going to tell you anything! Gurkog'll make you pay for this!"

"Gurkog will never know anything of this, because it's going to stay between the two of us. It'll be our little secret. It'll be just as if it had never happened."

"I'm going to kill you!" Musker yelled in fury, trying to move his limbs, without success.

Egil shook his head. "So much aggressiveness... that's very bad for your health."

With great care, he took out his two friends, each of which he was carrying in an individual pouch. He dropped Ginger on Musker's left leg, then Fred on his right.

Musker's eyes nearly burst out of their sockets. He opened his mouth wide to give a scream of pure terror, but like the experienced Ranger he was, knew that he was not supposed to do anything of the sort. He shut his mouth tightly and tried to control his terror. His teeth began to chatter from sheer horror, and he clenched his jaw and bit hard.

"I see my friends have made a good impression on you."

"Ven... venomous...?" he managed to stammer.

"Oh, yes. Very venomous. A sting or a bite from either of these two and it would be the end of you. Luckily for you, you can't move your legs, so they don't feel threatened and for the moment they won't either sting you or bite you. Well, that's what I'm hoping." Egil shrugged, as if he were not too sure of what was going to happen.

"Please... don't..."

"You see, the deal is a very simple one." He was helping Ginger to coil around Musker's right wrist. "You tell me what I want to know, and you come out of this alive. You lie to me, or you don't tell me what I want to know, and I'll let one of these two bite or sting you." As he spoke, he was guiding Fred with a stick so that he would not crawl off Musker's leg.

Musker nodded, his eyes staring. "I... I'll tell you everything..." he said. He was sweating profusely. He found the king scorpion even more frightening than the viper. The terror he felt, seeing them on his body and knowing he was utterly helpless, was more than his mind could take.

"Are you going to tell me the truth?"

"I swear I am... I don't want to die... not like this..." There was such terror in his voice that Egil knew he would tell him the last of his most intimate secrets, at least if he did not lose his mind before that out of sheer terror.

"Right then, let's begin. Who do you work for? Who told you to spy on me? The Dark Rangers?"

Musker shook his head slowly. His eyes went down to his arm, where the viper was slowly climbing up to his elbow. "It wasn't the Dark Rangers... I don't know anything about them... I don't belong to their organization..." He was watching the scorpion now.

"Oh, you don't? Are you sure?" Egil insisted. He moved Fred a little higher up the other's thigh by pushing him with the stick.

"I swear it! I've got nothing to do with the Dark Rangers!"

"So who ordered you to spy on me?"

"I'll tell you, but take them off me! By the Ice Gods! Take them off me!"

"The name...?"

Musker shouted the name to the sky.

Chapter 22

While he waited for Gurkog and the others to come back, Egil set about preparing new healing and revitalizing potions to try and help Eyra. Musker meanwhile was sitting on the other side of the camp. He had regained the movement of his legs, but not yet completely of his arms. He had stumbled away as best he could amid curses and oaths to the Ice Gods.

Egil watched him out of the corner of his eye to make sure he did not try to get his own back after the interrogation with Ginger and Fred. He was still in no condition to do anything, but later on in the day he would be able to, so that he knew he needed to be careful. He did not expect Musker to try to kill him, because he was not that kind of person. He was more the kind which can be corrupted up to a certain point, but not to that extreme.

Musker, who was trying to stir his right arm into action – though without much success – glared furiously at him. Deep down he was a Ranger: not one of the best in any single way, especially in the field of morals where he was no more than mediocre, but nor was he was one of the worst. The fact that he had been persuaded to spy on a comrade like Egil showed that his sense of honor was not highly developed. His values were not set hard as iron, but after all, most people were like that. As a result it was hard to find honorable people, people who kept their word, whose values were unshakable. This was true even among the Rangers, where such people existed. He could not expect everyone to be like the Snow Panthers. There was always one or another rotten apple, or at least one that was diseased.

He turned his attention back to Eyra and gave her a couple of potions he had just prepared. He had trouble making her drink them. She could barely stay conscious for a few moments at a time, and then would fall back into the world of nightmares brought on by her fever.

He left her sleeping and sat down by the fire in front of the cart to go on preparing more healing tisanes. It was best to be prepared in case the surgeon failed to arrive in time. Either way, if Gurkog did not come back with the snow in time, there would be nothing that could be done.

Musker had recovered the use of all his limbs by now. He gave Egil a furious glare.

"I'm going to keep watch," he muttered.

He picked up his bow, slung his quiver over his shoulder and began to patrol the camp perimeter.

The hours went by. Eyra was running out of time. The potions and mixtures he had given her did not seem to be doing anything to bring down her fever. For a moment she would appear to be improving, then a little later the fever would return. He still had no clue as to the cause, but he knew that one of those sudden flares of fever could kill her.

Musker came back to the camp, and Egil kept a careful eye on him in case he had hostile intentions. He had his composite bow in his hand and looked as though he was still furious, which was something Egil could hardly blame him for.

"Everything in order?" he asked.

Musker growled a 'yeah', took a water-skin and drank,

Egil went on preparing an ointment. He had used up everything he had brought with him and needed to prepare more. Luckily he had brought plenty of ingredients for the journey. *A wary man lives to grow old.* It was one of his favorite sayings.

Suddenly something moved behind Musker. Egil looked up from his ointment to see what it could be. The wind blowing a shrub, he thought. But shrubs did not move as much as that. He realized that it was not a shrub but a man, camouflaged with vegetation, approaching Musker from behind.

"Musker! Behind you!" Egil shouted in warning.

Musker turned, with the water-skin in his hand. "What?"

The camouflaged figure took a massive leap and fell on him like a born predator. Musker dropped the water-skin and reached for the Ranger's knife and axe at his waist. Before he could even draw them, he was dead. The figure had plunged two knives into his heart.

Egil saw that the assailant was a Ranger, one of the Dark Ones. From the camouflage and clothes he was wearing and the way he had carried out the attack, he must be a Natural Assassin.

The Assassin stared at him fixedly. Out of the corner of his eye, Egil looked for his bow. It was leaning on the wheel of the cart, too far away to reach.

Suddenly the assassin took another leap, rolled across the ground and vanished into the scrub forest to the west of the camp.

Egil drew the knife and axe all Rangers carried with them, even though he himself was not very good with them: certainly not good enough to fight a Natural Assassin. He would have given his left arm to have had Astrid there with him. What had he come for? To kill Eyra, or to rescue her? It must be to kill her, because she was in no condition to be rescued. In either case, the Dark Ranger would get rid of him first.

As he turned this over in his mind he was scanning his surroundings, turning round slowly because the Assassin had vanished into the undergrowth by now. He knew he had no chance of surviving that confrontation. He was going to end up like Musker. But he could not afford to give way to panic. He needed to stay cool, his mind clear and his nerves as much under control as possible.

He took a deep breath and looked left and right. Nothing. He took another breath and turned around, weapons at the ready, but still could not see him. Why did he hold back from attacking? Was he playing with him? Probably not. He must be waiting for the exact moment to catch him by surprise and kill him. One distraction, and he would be his next victim.

Egil went around the fire, where he was heating a pot of water, looking for an escape-route. Then he thought of Eyra. If he himself escaped, she would die. On the other hand, if he stayed, they would almost certainly die, both of them. He did not know whether to try and escape and save his own life, or stay and fight, even knowing that he would die. If he were to flee, he would sentence her to death. Logically, that Assassin must be here to kill her. If not, why send an Assassin and not a rescue team?

And during that moment of doubt the Assassin attacked, just as he had expected. He came from the east, rolling across the ground. Egil turned to face him. He saw the outstretched arm, and the image of Viggo came into his mind. The Assassin was throwing a knife at him, and instinctively he reacted, hurling himself to one side. He felt an impact in his shoulder and a sudden stab of pain, and fell to the ground. When he turned to try to defend himself, a new stab of sharp pain made him drop the axe. He stopped mid-way with his knife in his hand. The throwing knife was buried deep in his right shoulder.

The Assassin hurled himself on him, and he defended himself with his own knife. He was hit in the nose by two terrible punches, and the hilt of a knife dealt his temple a blow. His sight blurred, and a great dizziness came over him. His eyes were watering and he could barely think. He caught a glimpse of the Assassin above his body, pressing his knee down on the wrist of the hand that was holding the knife against the ground, immobilizing him. He saw him raise the knife, ready to kill him.

"Wait," came a voice. "I want to talk to him."

The Assassin did not deliver the final blow. He took his throwing knife out of Egil's shoulder, and his victim moaned in pain. The Assassin got up and left him writhing on the ground. When he rolled over, what he saw left him speechless.

Standing at the door of the cage, which was open, was a figure.

It was Eyra.

"Eyra... but... it's not..." Egil began to stammer.

"It's not possible? Is that what you wanted to say, my clever pupil?" she asked with her twisted smile.

"The fever... the poison..." He could not believe his eyes. Eyra was standing, which was practically impossible with the fever she was suffering. His eyes must surely be playing tricks on him.

"I know that at the moment you'll find it difficult to understand, but with time, seeing that you're who you are, I think you'll guess," she said with a smile as she came down from the cage with the Assassin's help.

"Shall I finish him off?" he asked.

She came up to Egil as he lay writhing on the ground and looked at him for a moment.

"Quite honestly, I ought to kill you, for the disgrace you've brought on me, for having found me out."

"Eyra... it was my duty..."

"Yes, I know, you were only doing your duty as a Ranger and you wanted to save Dolbarar at all costs. The loyalty and honor you've shown are truly impressive. You and your comrades of the Snow Panthers – a unique group, a special one, I have to admit. One of the few that pass through the Camp." She looked down at Musker's body. "Ah well, I see Musker wasn't so lucky. The truth is that I never particularly liked him. He wasn't one of the best Rangers..."

"Shall I finish him off?" the Assassin insisted.

Eyra sighed. "I hope I'm not making a mistake with you, Egil. I believe that someday, far in the future, you'll play an important role in this kingdom." She stared into his eyes, as if she were a witch and could read his fate in them. "Because of that, and because of the amazing care you've given me, which has helped me and without which I wouldn't now be able to escape, I'm going to let you live. You didn't realize the fact, but the more you helped me with all those potions you've been giving me, the faster I was recovering, and now I'll be able to get out of here."

"The fever... it wasn't..."

"The fever, yes... I'll let you think about it and how I managed to fool you. I'm not going to kill you. I've always had a soft spot for you. Of all those who've passed through the Camp in all these years I've served the Rangers, there's no doubt that you're the most intelligent and probably one of the most special, together with your friend Lasgol." She turned to the Assassin. "Let him live."

"Sure?"

Eyra sighed. "Yes, let him live."

Egil stretched out his hand as he lay there on the ground. "How...?" he asked. He needed to know how Eyra had managed to trick them in that way. Trick him in that way. He could not understand.

"You can't believe it, can you? You're left speechless in the face of what's happened. This old witch has deceived you. I've been cleverer than you. I've beaten you at your own game – one you're very good at, I should point out. The way you made Musker sing was masterly. A very good plan, to bring him here and interrogate him in that subtle way when you had the opportunity. Brilliant." She smiled maliciously. "You've always been very sharp and clever. I'd imagine it surprised you that he wasn't with us. As you can see, he wasn't. He was telling the truth." She pointed to him where he lay dead on the ground.

"I don't... understand..."

"Don't worry. All you need to know is that the teacher has defeated the student." She cackled with laughter.

With the terrible pain in his right shoulder barely letting him breathe, much less think, Egil muttered: "I'll find out how..."

"Maybe you will, and maybe not. We'll see."

"We'd better be off," the Assassin said to her. "The others'll be back soon."

"All right." She indicated Egil. "Get his horse ready." The Assassin hastened to saddle the horse. "One more thing, Egil. Don't make me regret having spared your life here today. If you interfere with my plans, if you go after me again, I will end your life. I give you my word that I will make him kill you. This isn't an empty threat. I have the means" – she indicated the Assassin, who was on his way back with the horse – "and I have the brains to do it. The same brains I've used to outsmart you. Remember. Always. I'll be watching your steps from the shadows."

Egil looked back into her eyes and knew she would keep her promise. He shivered.

She turned to the Assassin. "Help me mount. I'm still rather weak." He hastened to help her on to her horse, and a moment later they were galloping southwards.

Egil felt the wound to see how serious it was. It was agonizingly painful, and he nearly fainted. He lay there on his back, looking up at the grey sky with a question hammering in his mind.

How?

How had she tricked them all?

Chapter 23

"Egil! Wake up! *Egil!*"

The voice was very familiar, deeply familiar, but he could not open his eyes. He was very tired, and he needed to sleep so that he could recover.

"Come on, pal! Wake up!"

He felt someone shaking him. A sharp pain reached his mind. It came from his shoulder.

"Aagh..." he moaned, and managed to open one eye.

"Are you all right?" asked the huge figure above him. He recognized him at last.

"Gerd... when?"

"We've just arrived. What happened? Are you hurt?"

"My shoulder..."

"Hang on, I'll turn you over. We found you unconscious and Musker dead."

"Eyra's gone. What happened?" Gurkog asked harshly.

"A Natural Assassin... in camouflage..."

"Hellfire! One of the Dark Ones!"

Egil tried to see what was going on around him, but Gerd stopped him with a huge hand on his chest. "Wait, I'll tend to that wound first. Don't move. You've lost a lot of blood and you're very weak."

"I don't know how long..."

"Take it easy. Let me have a look at you. We need to clean the wound and put a few stitches on it before it gets infected."

Gurkog was looking around, trying to puzzle out what had happened there. "Eyra – has she escaped? Or has she been killed?"

"She got away with the Assassin."

"What do you mean, she got away?"

"Yeah, on horseback."

Gurkog's eyes opened wide. "Are you sure? Or are you delirious too?"

"I'm sure."

Gerd was already working on cleaning the wound, and Egil

grunted in pain a couple of times. He did not want to, but the pain was intense.

"How could she escape on horseback when she was eaten up with fever?" Gurkog said. "That's impossible."

"She tricked us... I've no idea how she did it, but she tricked us all."

"By all the Ice Gods! Search the area! Find their trail!"

Ibsen and Fulker set to it at once. Gurkog crouched down beside Musker and checked the wounds that had killed him.

"Don't worry, Egil, everything'll be all right, I'll see to it," Gerd told him as he disinfected the wound.

"Thanks... my friend."

Gurkog came over to Egil and looked down at him, his hands on his hips. "Why didn't he kill you too? He didn't give Musker a chance."

"Eyra... she let me... live."

"Why?"

"I... don't... know..."

"This is very strange. Suspicious."

Gerd stared at Gurkog in a very unfriendly way. "If you're hinting that there's been foul play on Egil's part, you're wrong."

"I'm not hinting at anything. I'm just saying all this is very strange. An old woman on the point of death gets up and tells a Natural Assassin to pardon his life? I saw the state Eyra was in, and it's simply not possible that she could have recovered so quickly, still less that she could have fled on horseback. That's unthinkable."

"Well, that's what she did," Fulker told him, indicating the trail on the ground. "Two horses, with two riders."

"This just can't be happening!" Gurkog cried in outrage.

Ibsen gestured at the bags full of snow, which was already melting. "It looks as if we're not going to be needing all this snow we've brought. And it was so hard to get it and bring it back before it melted."

"Don't complain," Gurkog said bad-temperedly. "At least you didn't end up like Musker." He turned to Egil. "Are you sure it was an Assassin, and not the Sniper who attacked us earlier?"

"Sure..."

Fulker pointed to a rider who was approaching from the west. "Look, here comes Enok. He'll be able to tell us."

When the Specialist arrived, he dismounted and looked around in amazement. At the sight of Musker lying dead on the ground, his expression changed to one of rage.

"Who killed him?"

"That's what we're trying to figure out. Could it have been the Sniper you were after?"

Enok shook his head. "He got away to the northwest. I was on his heels. It couldn't have been him."

"Then we've fallen into a trap," Gurkog said. "The Sniper was just a distraction, to keep us occupied and set up the next stage of the escape."

"She's escaped?" Enok asked in disbelief.

"That's right. A Natural Assassin killed Musker, wounded Egil and fled, taking Eyra with him."

"Hellfire!"

Gurkog turned to Ibsen. "Ibsen, cover Musker with a blanket. He deserved a better fate than to end up like this."

"What do we do now?" Fulker asked him.

"We're going after them! That's what we're going to do!"

"The horses are exhausted," Fulker pointed out.

"I know! We drove them to their limit!"

"We'll just have to wait till they recover a bit."

"How tired is your horse, Enok?" Gurkog asked.

"Tired, but not exhausted."

"Good. Get off. I'll take him."

"I beg your pardon?" Enok said blankly

"I'll go after them. I'll leave a clear trail for you, marked with my initials. As soon as the horses are rested, follow me."

"Oh, I see. Understood, sir."

"All of us?" asked Fulker.

"You three. Gerd, you stay with Egil and wait for Valeria to come back with the surgeon."

Enok nodded, dismounted and handed the reins to Gurkog.

"I can't believe this has happened," Fulker said sadly.

Gurkog stared at Musker's body, then at Egil as Gerd sutured his wound. "They'll pay for what they've done. Ibsen, you look after the horses. You won't start out before they're fully rested. The hunt may take some time."

"Yes, sir. Right away," Ibsen said, and took the horses away.

As he waited impatiently for his horse to be ready, Gurkog concentrated on going over his weapons and equipment in readiness for the chase. As he was one of the best Man Hunters, they all trusted him to find and follow the trail of the two fugitives. On the other hand, the more time that went by, the more difficult it would be.

"He gave you a good beating," Gerd said to Egil. Your nose is broken and you have a black eye. I'll have to reset your nose, and it's going to hurt."

"Go ahead."

Gerd pulled Egil's nose with two fingers and set it back in place. Egil cried out in pain, and his eyes moistened.

"Wow, it certainly does hurt..."

"I'll put some snow on your wounds to bring the swelling down."

"Thanks."

The moment came for Gurkog to leave. "Follow my trail, it'll be clear," he told his comrades, and he left at a gallop.

The others waited until the horses were rested. They were impatient to start, but they had to wait even though they knew that while they waited, their quarry was widening the gap between them.

In the distance they saw two riders approaching: Valeria and the surgeon.

"What's happened?" Valeria cried in astonishment at the sight of Musker's body covered with a blanket and Egil lying there wounded. The surgeon too was looking on with fear in his eyes

"Easy, Val. Get off your horse and we'll explain," Gerd said.

"Are you the surgeon?" Enok asked.

"That's right. My name's Albertsen, and I'm a surgeon in the city of Icelbag. This young Ranger requested my services, and that's why I'm here."

Enok indicated Musker. "That one doesn't need you anymore. This one" – he pointed to Egil – "has a nasty wound in his shoulder."

The surgeon dismounted with some care. He must have been in his sixties, and as a city man he was not altogether at ease when dealing with horses. "Right. I'll have a look at him this minute."

Valeria leapt off her horse. "What happened?" she asked. "I came as fast as I could, but the good surgeon isn't a great horseman."

"We're off," Fulker called back to them.

"Be careful, and don't be too confident," Egil said.

"Don't worry, we won't."

"Particularly now we've seen what that witch is capable of," Ibsen added.

The three left at a gallop, following Gurkog's trail.

"Now tell me everything, every last detail," Valeria said.

While the surgeon examined his wound, Egil told them the story, including his questioning of Musker.

"I can't believe you used Ginger and Fred again!" Gerd reproached him.

"That was the plan," Egil said apologetically.

"You and your, look how Musker ended up."

"True," Egil said, "but if it hadn't been Musker it would've been someone else. Perhaps you."

The giant thought about it and was forced to agree. "Fine, but even so, you shouldn't use those two to question people."

"It's a really effective method."

"One day you'll give someone a heart attack, you just wait and see."

"That could happen, true," Egil admitted.

"I don't know who treated him," the surgeon commented, "but he's made a very good job of it."

Egil nodded at Gerd. "It was him."

"Good work. I'll just go and get some tonics from my saddlebag."

Valeria was shaking her head. "How could Eyra have tricked us all like that? She had a fever, I checked her temperature myself several times. She wasn't pretending."

"Or maybe she knows how to create the symptoms of fever without actually having one," Egil suggested. "That's all I can think of at the moment."

"Could be," Gerd agreed. "She's an expert on poisons and healing potions."

"However she did it," Egil said, "she tricked us all, and we swallowed it hook, line and sinker."

The surgeon came back to them. "Here you are, two tonics. Take the first one now and the other one this evening, They'll help to hold off any fever."

"Let me ask you a question," Valeria said.

"Ask away, young lady," he replied amiably.

"You have a lot of experience in treating illnesses, and you must have seen plenty of fevers. Do you know if it would be possible to feign the symptoms of a very high fever?"

The surgeon looked at her in surprise. "Feign? Why would anybody feign a fever?"

"Don't worry about the reason. Would it be possible?"

"Well..." He scratched his partially-bald head. "In theory it could be done, I think, though it seems a very complicated business to me."

Gerd was listening with interest. "How would you do it?"

"You'd have to take something that would cause your body temperature to rise a lot, but without creating an infection. There are poisons that work like that."

"Snake venoms, for instance," Egil added. He was beginning to see what had happened.

"Exactly. Some venomous snakebites produce a reaction in the body that raises the temperature considerably, but don't produce a fever as such."

"So that's how she did it..." Valeria said.

"But the effect fades away, doesn't it?" Gerd asked.

"Yes, the system fights against the toxin and brings down the body temperature."

"And so?" Gerd looked at Egil.

"She's been taking some kind of venom," he said thoughtfully.

"How, though?" Valeria objected. "You've been keeping an eye on her day and night."

"I've no idea, but I'll find out."

"Any other questions for me?" the surgeon asked. His face showed the confusion all these questions had caused him.

"No thanks. You've been a great help," Egil said. He gave him a reassuring smile. "Thank you for treating me."

"You're welcome. A pleasure to be of help, it's my duty. Do you need me for anything else?"

"No, thanks, you can leave now," Egil said. "We won't keep you any longer."

"All right, then. A pleasure helping Rangers. Be careful, all of you."

Valeria helped him on to his horse, which caused him some difficulty, and he set off on his way back to the city.

"What now?" Valeria asked Egil.

"Now we wait till I'm feeling a little better, then we go on."

"Are we going after Eyra?" she wanted to know.

Egil shook his head. "Gurkog and the others will deal with that. We're going back to the capital."

"Yeah, in your state you're not exactly fit to chase anybody," Gerd pointed out.

Egil smiled. "Precisely, my dear friend." But the smile turned into a grimace of pain.

"We can wait a couple of days till you're better," Valeria suggested.

"We ought to leave as soon as possible. I'll get better on the way."

"Why so much hurry?" Gerd asked in puzzlement.

"Many and interesting vicissitudes are in store for us in the capital," Egil said with a smile.

"Vici... what?"

Egil winked at him. "Events. Major ones."

The giant snorted angrily. "I can't wait," he said with a look of horror.

Chapter 24

Nilsa was chatting cheerfully with three members of the Royal Rangers at the dining-room in the Tower. She always appreciated the attention she got from the tall, strong (and in some cases very handsome) of the best from among all the Rangers. And not only that: they had been selected to serve under First Ranger Gatik alongside the Royal Guard, protecting the King.

She smiled and giggled at the thought that there were handsome men in the Royal Guard too, bigger than the Royal Rangers, some of them the size of a Wild One of the Ice. But she preferred the company and the attentions of her own people. She felt far more comfortable with a Royal Ranger than with a Royal Guard, even if the latter happened to be better-looking. Lately she had been thinking a lot about handsome Norghanian warriors, which made her feel a little giddy.

"You're saying it's our turn to guard the throne hall today?" Hans asked. He was the ugliest of the three, with his nose broken in two different places, but apart from that he was the image of a strong Norghanian warrior.

"That's what Gatik told us a moment ago," Frey said.

Nilsa found him very attractive. He was blond, with his hair in two braids which fell as far as his strong shoulders. You could have lost yourself in his blue eyes, and his strong chin gave him the air of a tough guy.

"Well, isn't that just wonderful!" Kol grumbled. "We'll die of boredom listening to the nobles prattling and the King's usual outbursts. My toes end up going to sleep with spending so long on foot guarding the throne."

"Protecting the King in his home is a great honor," Nilsa pointed out with a playful smile.

Kol was the handsomest of the three as far as features were concerned. He had light brown hair, almost blond, worn loose. His nose and features were sharp, his brown eyes very intense. In fact, she could not decide which of the two she liked better, Frey or Kol, and hence spent plenty of time with both of them to see if she could make up her mind. Also to see which of the two put more effort into wooing her, which was something she greatly appreciated.

Kol smiled back at her. "It is, of course," he admitted. "Our pretty redhead's right."

"That's because she's very intelligent and discerning," Frey said at once, as though he did not want to be left behind when it came to paying Nilsa compliments.

"Oh, not especially," Nilsa said, pretending to dismiss this with a wave of her hand. Actually, she enjoyed the compliments that came her way enormously. "It's the two of you who really play an important part in serving the realm."

"Being Gondabar's personal messenger and liaison with the Rangers is an important job too," Frey pointed out.

"And you do it very well, so people say around here," Kol added.

"Is that what people say?" Nilsa was obviously keen to be told the gossip.

"They certainly do," Kol said. "They say Gondabar's had a lot of messengers, but they never lasted long because they usually displeased him. He's a demanding boss."

"Oh, he's certainly that. I've been at the receiving end of several outbursts over minor details. Well, and one or two others I deserved, because of my clumsiness..."

"What clumsiness?" Frey smiled at her. "You're as graceful as a gazelle."

She laughed. "Oh yeah, sure!"

Hans got up from the table. "I'm going to have another helping of moose stew. Today I'm absolutely starving." He got up from the table and went to fetch more food.

Kol laughed. "If he goes on eating like that he's going to get a real pot-belly."

Nilsa and Frey joined in the laughter.

"And when do you say you're going to have some free time?" Frey asked Nilsa seductively.

"Ufff, no idea. The only free time I have is this, my lunch-break. And that's only because I'd drop dead in front of Gondabar if I didn't eat. I go from one place to another all day long, what with all the preparations for the Great Council."

"Well, I'd like you to give me a proper account of everything you've been doing," Kol said. "It must be very interesting."

Nilsa gave a snort. "I wouldn't call it interesting exactly."

"More interesting than being on foot all day keeping watch on the throne hall, surely," Hans said as he came back with another full plate.

"I have a thousand things to do, from finding proper accommodations for the leaders, getting the Chamber ready for the Great Council, by way of security and endless small details that Gondabar wants to be perfect."

"Security?" Frey repeated. "But the Council'll be in the King's palace. There's no safer place in the whole continent of Tremia."

"That's what I think too," Nilsa agreed. "But there's enormous concern about the leaders' lives, after what happened to Dolbarar."

"That was a nasty business," Hans said, his mouth full of stew.

Kol shook his head. "I find it hard to believe Eyra's a traitor. To me it's... I don't know... almost unthinkable."

"Perhaps that's exactly why nobody ever suspected her," Frey said.

"I wouldn't have thought it could have happened in a million years," said Nilsa.

"That's because all of you are too reluctant to think ill of people," Hans assured them as he finished his stew." You ought to be more prepared to."

"I didn't have so much to do with her," Kol said. "I'm in the School of Archery."

"Your Specialty is Mage Hunter, isn't it?" Nilsa asked him. She already knew, but she wanted to hear it from his own lips again.

"That's right. The best of the specialties for protecting our leaders and the King. There's nothing more dangerous than a Mage."

"That's for sure!" Nilsa cried. She still hated Magi, although less than before. She remembered her dead father, and rage stirred in her stomach. Although she had begun to accept the use of magic, particularly after seeing what the Healer Edwina and Camu could do, she still felt a strong repulsion toward magi and sorcerers. However hard she might try to quell her hatred, she could not manage to completely. And in any case, she had to admit that not all magic was evil, and nor did all those who had the Gift turn evil, as she had previously thought.

Kol gave her a wink. "If you stay with me, no Mage'll be able to do anything to you. I'll kill him at over three hundred paces. You'll always be protected."

"Bah! Nothing'll happen if you stay with me!" said Hans. "Mage or not, nobody can get past an Infallible Marksman like me."

"Infallible at short range, you ought to specify," Kol pointed out. "If a Mage takes up a position two hundred paces from you, you're dead, and at that distance you're not quite as infallible as that."

"I am!"

"We all know that you Infallible Marksmen are only that at a hundred and fifty paces or less," Frey said.

"I am at two hundred too!" Hans shot back in annoyance, wrinkling his broken nose and looking like a bulldog.

"Don't argue, please," Nilsa put in. "I'm sure Hans is infallible at two hundred paces," she said in an attempt to calm him.

"I am, thanks," he said, and relaxed a little,

Frey jabbed his thumb at his own chest. "Whichever way, it'll better for our freckled beauty to stay with a Healer Guard."

"Healer Guard is a very difficult specialty," Nilsa admitted with a touch of admiration in her voice. On the other hand, she was delighted with the compliment she had been given.

"So it is. You have to study a lot, and if the King falls sick or is wounded or poisoned, my responsibility is to save his life. For that you need a lot of knowledge of healing and nature."

"It might be easier to prevent the King being wounded or killed," Kol said rather condescendingly.

"That's not always going to be possible," Frey pointed out ironically.

"It's possible at the moment," Hans put in. "I agree, healing is the secondary plan. It's better if they don't wound him or get close to him."

"Healer Guard belongs to the School of Nature," Kol said. "You studied under Eyra and Annika, right?"

Frey nodded.

"Did you ever notice anything strange about Eyra?"

"Not at all, quite the opposite. She helped me to avoid failing. I had one foot already out, and she helped me a lot during that final year at the Camp. Then at the Shelter things went much better for me."

"Eyra must have been pretending, so that Dolbarar wouldn't find her out," Hans said.

Kol frowned. "Pretending?"

"Well, of course." Hans waved his hands. "Making it look as though she was helping the ones with problems, that she was all goodwill, that she was incapable of doing anything bad, and all that sort of thing..."

"I hadn't thought of that," Frey admitted.

"Yeah, maybe," Kol said thoughtfully. "Perhaps that was why Dolbarar trusted her so much and never suspected anything."

"Well, we found her out," said Nilsa.

"That's because apart from being beautiful and charming, you're brilliant," Frey said shamelessly.

Kol rolled his eyes.

Nilsa blushed. She was delighted by this. "I wouldn't say brilliant. Discerning." She smiled. "Well, boys, I'll leave you now, I've got to get on with my work."

"If you need any help, let me know," Kol said. "I'd love to share some time with you," he assured her with a smile.

Now it was Frey's turn to roll his eyes.

"See you!" Nilsa said, and ran off.

Hans looked at Frey and Kol, who were watching her as she left.

"Can't you stop all that with Nilsa? You're like a couple of teenagers in love. You make me ashamed."

Astrid and Lasgol rode into the capital through the southern gate, with Camu and Ona camouflaged behind them. Lasgol had asked Camu to keep his sister invisible while they crossed the city, to avoid creating an uproar among the citizens. A snow panther the size of Ona would scare the most quarrelsome Norghanian. Lasgol was pleased to be back in Norghania, because now he would see his other friends. At the same time, part of him was sad because he and Astrid would not be able to spend so much time by themselves. They had enormously enjoyed those last few days together.

As they made their way to the Royal Castle the city around them was vibrant, with hundreds of people wandering the streets on their daily business. Lasgol wondered what it would be like to be one of them. It would probably be a quiet life. He would have a trade and be earning his living through it. No adventures, no running unnecessary risks every second moment.

"Would you like an easy life, like these people's?" he asked Astrid as they went up one of the main streets.

"You mean living in the city like them?"

"Yeah, you know, having a 'normal' job and living quietly inside the protection of these walls."

Astrid looked around for a moment and thought about it, then looked up at the cloudy sky, which was already threatening snow. She shook her head. "Perhaps someday, but not now," she said with a mischievous smile.

"Some day? With me?"

"If you behave..."

"I always behave well with you!" he exclaimed, looking offended.

Astrid burst out laughing. "I know that, I just like to tease you. You always fall for it. You're too good."

Lasgol shook his head. "In other words you'd rather have a life full of risks and mortal danger?"

Astrid looked amused. "Exactly."

"Well, that's all I needed..."

"I could point out that most of the risks and dangers I run come from either your direction or Egil's."

"Oh, come on! Blame us!"

"I'm only telling you the truth. I run more risks with you two than with the Assassin of Nature missions I'm given, and that's saying something."

"But that's not our fault."

"I know. And besides, I love it."

"You love it?"

"Of course. I can cover your back and be with you. What more could I ask for?"

"A quiet life?"

"Nah, that's not for me."

"And suppose I were to become an iron-worker?"

"Even then, danger would come knocking on your door. I can almost see it."

"Well then, I'll become a miner, like them." He pointed to a group of miners on their way back from work."

"Honestly, even if you were underground, trouble wouldn't stop coming after you."

"Well that's just wonderful..."

"Don't worry. You have me and the rest of the Snow Panthers. We'll always protect you."

"That's good, because I really don't see myself as a miner."

Astrid laughed. "Neither do I."

Once they arrived at the castle, Lasgol told Camu he could allow Ona to be visible. The panther showed her gratitude with a moan. Lasgol hoped that she would end up by getting used to it, but he knew it would take some time yet. There were certain things cats were especially sensitive to.

When they were stopped at the gate they identified themselves as Rangers, but unlike on previous occasions, that was not enough. Lasgol realized that there were twice the usual number of guards on the towers and battlements. Security had been reinforced, presumably because of the Great Council, since as far as they knew there was nothing threatening the realm at that moment. Then he reconsidered this. There was always some risk for the Crown and the nobles of Norghana, whether internal or external.

"They're being incredibly wary," Astrid said as they dismounted and waited patiently.

Camu, be quiet and well-behaved.

I always well-behaved, came the reply from behind him, as he had expected. He smiled and said nothing.

The officer at the gate came back with a Ranger. "The Liaison is in charge of identifying and accrediting all the Rangers who arrive," he announced.

Lasgol began to smile. He had recognized the Liaison, who was none other than Nilsa.

"Name and rank," she asked them very seriously in an official voice, although her eyes were sparkling with the joy of seeing them.

Lasgol gestured to Astrid to go first.

"Astrid, Specialist, Assassin of Nature."

Nilsa looked at her up and down, then made a note in the notebook she was carrying.

"Lasgol, Specialist, Beast Whisperer. This is Ona, my snow panther."

The redhead wrote this down as well. "Reason for your visit?"

"To attend the Great Council."

The officer turned to Nilsa. "Are they on the list of approved persons?" he asked sternly.

"Yes, sir. Here they are, both of them. They're approved."

"Right," the officer said. He turned to his men. "Let them in!"

"Permission granted," Nilsa said. "You may pass."

Nilsa went ahead of them into the castle, and the soldiers could not take their eyes off Ona. The panther already knew that she had to walk beside Lasgol, close to his leg as if she were his dog, to avoid spreading alarm. They made their way to the stables, still pretending. When they were safely there, Nilsa hurled herself on them, hugging and kissing them.

"How wonderful to see you!" she cried, and smothered them as if she had not seen them in years.

"The happiness is ours," said Astrid, laughing as she took the redhead in her arms.

Lasgol had to step back from the force of Nilsa's momentum. "The stable-lads are giving us strange looks," he told her as he hugged her.

"Yeah, I'd better keep myself under control." She moved away and pretended to pat her clothes down after those intense embraces.

"You're looking radiant," Astrid told her.

She put on a lunatic expression. "What I'm doing is losing my wits, what with all the things I'm having to do."

Lasgol laughed. "You'll have to tell us everything."

"And you have to do the same for me!"

"Have the others arrived?" Astrid asked.

"Ingrid and Viggo have arrived. Egil and Gerd haven't yet."

"How did things go for Ingrid and Viggo?" Lasgol asked, expecting the answer to be positive.

"Very badly."

Astrid and Lasgol stared back at her, surprised and worried.

"It'd be better if they explained. They're fine, but they were attacked, and... they'll tell you everything."

Astrid shook her head. "Uh-oh."

Lasgol nodded. "I can smell trouble."

"Hi there, Ona, my lovely," Nilsa said. She scratched her head and ears, and the panther chirped gratefully. "Let's leave the horses here and find out what happened to them."

Trotter, rest and eat as much as you like, Lasgol transmitted, and his strong Norghanian pony nickered happily and moved his head up and down.

"Is Camu here?" Nilsa asked.

I here, he transmitted. He brushed against her leg, and she gave a startled jump.

"Yes, I see he is."

Lasgol smiled at her. "As always."

Nilsa set off with them toward the Rangers' tower. "One of the few good things about being in charge of practically everything to do with the Great Council is that I've got you both excellent accommodation. We're all sharing one of the big rooms, so nobody'll bother us and we'll be really comfortable and quiet."

Astrid was stroking her friend's back. "That's wonderful."

Lasgol laughed. "Comfortable and quiet... two terms that don't often go with us."

"Very true!" Nilsa said. "Now you've got me in charge of a lot of things here, and we should get a few benefits out of that."

"Wonderful! Let's see how long that lasts."

Chapter 25

The tower was being guarded by six Rangers. When they saw that Nilsa was with them, they were allowed through without any trouble, although they looked at her for confirmation. Seeing a snow panther with them, one of the guards turned to Lasgol.

"Is that your familiar?"

"That's right. I'm a Beast Whisperer."

"Okay, but see that there aren't any incidents."

"Don't worry, there won't be."

Inside the tower were a couple more guards at the entrance. Nilsa pointed to the right. "Follow me this way. It's the room at the end, the largest one."

In it they found Viggo lying on one of the eight beds. In front of each was a trunk, and at the entrance was a sizeable armory for hanging up bows and quivers. Behind a wooden folding screen at the end of the room, Ingrid was washing herself from the waist up in a basin of water and wild-flower soap. Viggo was taking furtive glances at her.

"I told you not to look, you dumbass!"

"I'm not looking, I'm just checking that nothing's visible."

"That's looking!"

"If there's nothing to see, how can it be looking?" The familiar argument made Astrid and Lasgol smile.

Viggo fun, Camu transmitted.

Yes, he is, Lasgol agreed.

Nilsa cleared her throat loudly, to make sure they heard her, and Viggo half-sat up in his cot.

"Well, it took you long enough to get here!"

Ingrid poked her wet, soapy head out from behind the folding screen. "Welcome! We've got perfumed soap!" she added happily.

"Oooh, that's a real luxury," Astrid said.

Viggo was rubbing his hands in delight. "And these cots aren't the hard kind. Also they have fine, clean sheets."

"I told you I got you one of the good rooms," Nilsa said. She was very happy that they appreciated the fact.

"We certainly appreciate it, very much so," Lasgol added. "Sleeping between clean sheets and being able to have a wash is always welcome."

"Give me a moment to finish," Ingrid said.

Viggo came to greet them, and they all hugged cheerfully. "I'm glad to see you, weirdo," he said to Lasgol.

"And I'm glad to see you, little pain."

Viggo laughed. "Hah! That's a good one!"

"I've got more, saved for later," Lasgol said.

"Viggo, how's the most lethal assassin of all?" Astrid asked him. She spread her arms wide for a hug,

"Have I ever told you that out of all this lot, you're the one I like best?"

"I think you have," she said with a smile.

"Well, I'll say it again, just to be sure," Viggo said, and put his arms round her. At the same time Nilsa shut the door and bolted it.

You can become visible, Lasgol said to Camu. *We're safe in this room.*

The creature became visible all of a sudden, and Viggo gave a sudden start.

"By the cloudy skies, the bug's grown enormous!"

I no bug, Camu protested. *I dragon.*

"He says not to call him a bug, 'cause he's a dragon."

"Dragon? He thinks he's a dragon now?" Viggo asked in disbelief. "No way —"

He had no chance to finish, because Camu hurled himself at him, pushing him over backwards, and began to lick his face with his blue tongue. Ona, seeing him, joined in.

"Get... them... off me!" he told Lasgol, who was laughing.

"A little love will do you good," he pointed out.

"Or else he might get stomach cramp," Nilsa added.

"You just wait.... till I get up!"

Astrid, Nilsa and Lasgol laughed until tears rolled down their cheeks as he was given a course of licks by Camu and Ona. By the time they had finished with him his face and hair were soaked in saliva – but even though his protests suggested that they were eating him alive, he made no serious effort to clean it off.

Meanwhile Ingrid came out from behind the screen, now wearing her tunic, and greeted them all with hugs and smiles. "We need to catch up. Choose a cot, leave your bags and weapons and let's talk."

Ingrid and Viggo told them what had happened during the ambush.

Astrid shook her head. "Wow, they dared to attack the Elder Specialists, of all people..."

"What I find most worrying is how many of them there are," Lasgol said. "I hadn't imagined there'd be so many."

"It seems they've been recruiting among the ones who didn't manage to graduate," Viggo explained.

"That's pretty worrying," said Nilsa. "Do you think they've done the same with the ones who didn't manage to graduate as Specialists?"

"Could be," said Ingrid.

"Well then, we've got a major problem on our hands," said Viggo.

"That's what Gondabar said when we reported," said Ingrid.

Nilsa shook her head. "He was very angry, and he's sent urgent messages via birds and messengers to the Camp, to forestall another attack. All this makes me very nervous."

"Daring to attack the Elder Specialists is a full-fledged declaration of war," Ingrid pointed out.

"Gondabar had to explain what happened to King Thoran," Nilsa added. "You could hear the shouting from outside the throne hall."

Viggo raised an eyebrow. "Who told you?"

"Some Royal Rangers."

"Ah, I see you're still making special friends among the cream of the Rangers..."

"And among the Royal Guard. It looks as though my charm and personality are very attractive."

"Or maybe it's just that both Rangers and Guards are so tired of seeing the King, his brother and all those ugly, pompous nobles that the moment they see a friendly face, they start to drool..."

"I'm a lot more than a friendly face!"

"Of course you are. It goes without saying..."

"Your connections are a godsend for us," Ingrid said encouragingly. "Don't listen to anything this pumpkin-head tells you, and keep your eyes and ears open."

"Thanks, I will. Gatik has all the Royal Rangers on watch duty day and night. Not only to protect the King, but to protect Gondabar too. He's afraid of an attempt on his life."

Lasgol looked very worried at this. "On Gondabar?"

"He's our leader," Astrid said. "If the Dark Ones want to hurt us, it makes sense for them to try and kill him, the way they did with Dolbarar."

"That's if the King doesn't do the job first with his yelling," Viggo put in.

"Thoran's really furious about the situation," Nilsa explained. "According to the Royal Guards I know, it's because it makes him look weak in front of the court nobles. The Rangers are his elite corps."

"We all are," Ingrid said. "Good Rangers are losing their lives..."

"That's right," Lasgol said. "How sad about Molak and Luca. I'm sorry they were wounded."

"Will they recover?" Astrid asked. "Will there be any after-effects?"

"Luca will make a full recovery. Molak might have some trouble with his hip," said Ingrid.

"The surgeons who've seen him say that kind of wound usually leaves a mark," Nilsa said, sounding worried.

"Molak's tough and strong," Ingrid said confidently. "I'm sure he'll get over it and be back to what he was before. I'm going to see him in the infirmary later. Come with me if you want."

"Yeah, I'd like to say hi," said Lasgol.

"Me too," Astrid joined in.

"Oh yeah," Viggo muttered, "let's all go together hand in hand to say hi to Captain Fantastic."

"Viggo!" Ingrid said reproachfully. "He's a wounded comrade!"

"He's your little sweetheart, and just so you know, if he's been wounded it's because he isn't as fantastic as all that."

"He's not my little sweetheart, and I'm going to give you a black eye for being nasty about a wounded comrade!"

Viggo shook imaginary dust off his shoulders. "I was there, and look, not a scratch."

"Possibly that's just down to idiots' luck," Nilsa suggested.

Lasgol burst out laughing, and Astrid joined in. "Exactly," Ingrid said. The joke had relaxed her a little.

"Do we know anything about Egil and Gerd?" Lasgol asked. He was petting Ona, who had lain down at his feet. Camu had chosen a cot for himself and was snoozing on it.

"They haven't arrived yet," Nilsa said.

"I hope they haven't run into any trouble," said Lasgol.

Ingrid turned to Astrid and Lasgol. "And what about you two, everything all right?"

"No problems whatsoever," Astrid replied.

"Yup," Lasgol agreed. "We followed Egil's instructions."

"Does anybody know what the know-it-all's planning?" Viggo asked.

They all shook their heads, and Lasgol shrugged. "He didn't explain anything to me."

"It must be one of his secret plans," said Ingrid.

Viggo raised an eyebrow. "Hmm, those always come with a few surprises in tow."

"That's true," Astrid agreed. "You can see them coming."

"Have a rest now," Ingrid said, "then we'll go to the infirmary."

The next three days they spent resting, with the exception of Nilsa, who went back and forth without a break as she finished the last details of the preparations. The day of the Great Council was approaching, and though she had everything ready, there always seemed to be some other detail to sort out. Some of the group would have liked to go out and enjoy the city, but once you had entered the castle you could not go out again, while inside it, there was a curfew. Security was rigorous, with soldiers on guard everywhere. Moreover, as they were Rangers, and hence might belong to the Dark Ones, all the soldiers tended to look at them suspiciously. Nor could they even go wherever they wanted inside the fortress. They only had permission to be in the Rangers' Tower, the infirmary and the main courtyard, visible to all. The only one who was happy about this was Viggo, because it allowed him to rest and allow his exhausted 'lethal muscles', as he called them, to recover.

Two days later Egil, Gerd and Valeria arrived at the castle. Nilsa went to greet them, and as soon as Egil had explained what had happened, they went directly to inform Gondabar. Egil had already sent a pigeon from the city of Usters to warn him.

Gatik was with him, and both of them looked serious and worried.

"Tell us what happened in detail, however trivial the details may seem," Gondabar told Egil.

Egil told them everything he could remember, with the exception of his private conversation with Musker.

"It's really amazing that she managed to deceive you with that fever," Gatik commented.

"I'm certain she really did have it," Egil said.

"Eyra is a wise woman when it comes to potions, poisons and antidotes," Gondabar said. "If she wanted to give herself a fever and then get it to disappear, she's the most knowledgeable person in the whole north of Tremia."

"That's true – perhaps with the exception of Annika."

Gondabar nodded. "Correct. The Elder Specialist of Nature is the only one whose knowledge is comparable. I'm sure she could shed some light on this matter."

"We'll put the case to her," Gatik said.

"Before that, I'd like Gerd and Valeria to tell us their versions of what happened too. It's always good to get all points of view on the matter."

"Very true," Gatik agreed. "Go ahead."

Valeria's account was not as complete as Egil's, because she had gone in search of the surgeon. The same was true of Gerd, because he had been transporting snow when the events took place.

"A very well-planned and well-executed plan," Gatik said. "They knew we were bringing her to the capital, when the mission had been kept secret. We have a traitor among us."

"And he's here in the capital," Gondabar added, "because I sent the order to Dolbarar."

"One of your assistants?" Gatik asked

"Unfortunately it's possible."

"The Dark Ones have infiltrated every rank among the Rangers. Perhaps even your own trusted team."

The leader of the Rangers nodded heavily. "I don't want that to be true... but it's possible."

"What about Dolbarar, Angus and the Master Rangers? Did their travel plan come from here too?"

Gondabar shook his head. "As soon as I got Egil's message I sent another one to Dolbarar, explaining what had happened. I asked him to decide the route and day and not share it with anybody. It was the only way to keep it secret."

Gatik nodded. "It sounds like a very good idea. If nobody except the person who's carrying it out knows the plan, there's very little risk of betrayal."

"Dolbarar's on his way, and he ought to be here in a few days' time. I hope they don't fall into an ambush too."

"I don't think they will," Gatik insisted. "Nobody knows what day they set out, or what route they took."

"What do you think, Egil? I know you have a very good head for these things."

"If Dolbarar kept his journey a secret, he ought to be safe. But it's difficult to keep this sort of mission a secret." He was thoughtful for a moment. "The leader of the Camp is very intelligent and has a lot of experience. And in addition to that, after the enormous shock of Eyra's betrayal I'm sure he'll be more than cautious. He won't take any risks, particularly when he's travelling with the other Master Rangers, because their lives are very dear to him. Yes, I think he'll have done everything possible to keep the secret, in the circumstances."

Gondabar nodded. "I agree."

"Well, we'll soon know," Gatik said. "His Majesty will want details of what happened..."

"I'll give them to him. It's my responsibility," Gondabar interrupted him, looking worried.

"He's not going to like it at all," Gatik said. His expression suggested that Gondabar was in trouble.

"I know. I'll deal with His Majesty's anger."

"I could tell him myself..." Gatik offered.

"And burden yourself with my blame? No, it's my responsibility, and I'll deal with the consequences."

"It's the responsibility of all of us, my lord," Gatik said, and his gesture included himself.

"Ultimately the responsibility is mine, because I'm the Leader of the Rangers and I was appointed by the King to be in charge of them."

"As you wish, my lord. I'll be at your side in the Throne Hall. You'll have my support and my assistance."

"Thank you, Gatik. As for you three, go with Nilsa now. She'll have your rooms ready for you."

Outside, Nilsa was waiting for them, biting her nails.

"How did it go?"

"Fine. We told them everything," said Egil.

"Any clue? Any suspect?"

"Nothing for the moment..."

"It all points to someone close to Dolbarar," Valeria said.

"Wow, that's bad."

Gerd scratched his head. "Yeah, maybe one of his assistants..."

"But they've been with him for years!" Nilsa protested.

Valeria grimaced. "I don't think anybody's free from suspicion. Not even you, Nilsa."

"You can't mean that!"

"Yup," Egil said, "things are very tangled. Anybody might be a Dark One."

"I need to rest and clear my mind," Valeria said.

"Yeah, me too," Gerd agreed. "A nice nap'll work wonders for me."

"Follow me. I'll take you to where the others are," Nilsa said, and set off before she had finished the sentence.

Chapter 26

Nilsa came into the room where the group was resting, followed by Egil, Gerd and Valeria, who were trying to keep up with her. The cries of joy when they saw them filled the room.

"Egil! So good to see you!" Lasgol said as he hastened to throw his arms around his friend.

Egil was smiling from ear to ear. "I'm even happier to see you!"

"Gerd, you giant! You get bigger and uglier by the day!" Viggo said, and Gerd replied by trapping him in a bear-hug and lifting him off the floor.

"I'm glad to see you too!" the giant said with a huge smile.

"Put me down, you brainless giant!" Viggo protested as he was spun around in Gerd's arms.

Ingrid came over and threw her arms around Egil. "I see you all had as much trouble as we did."

"Yes, it was a troublesome mission," Egil admitted. He looked dissatisfied with the whole situation.

Ona and Camu looked for Egil and threw themselves on him. "Little fiends! It's so good to see you!" he said joyfully and began to make a fuss of them, while they licked his face and hair.

Ingrid went over to Valeria, who was hanging back a little. "I see you're keeping in good company."

She smiled. "Looks as though it's been my turn a lot lately, it's true."

Gerd put Viggo down. By now he looked dizzy.

"One of these days you'll make me throw up."

"You're exaggerating!" Gerd said with a laugh. He went on to greet the others with massive, affectionate bear-hugs.

Astrid greeted everyone except Valeria, whom she glared at darkly. The blonde Ranger shrugged it off as though it had nothing to do with her

"Why is she here?" she asked Egil.

"She came with us from the Camp," he explained. "She was part of the escort."

Astrid said nothing more, but it was clear from her expression that she was not at all happy about Valeria's presence.

"It's wonderful to be all together again, and still in one piece," Lasgol said. He greeted Valeria briefly, then hugged Gerd and Ingrid, because he could see that Astrid was staring at him.

"You can say that again!" said Nilsa.

The greetings, hugs, varied shows of affection and welcome went on for some time, but then they sat down and Ingrid told them everything that had happened to them. When she had finished there was a silence, and it was Egil's turn to tell the story.

"Wow...!" Lasgol said.

"D'you know whether they've caught her?" Gerd asked.

Nilsa shook her head. "I haven't heard anything about that, and if she'd been captured, I'm sure I'd have heard, even if Gondabar had wanted to keep it secret."

"We'll have to wait and see whether there's any news from Gurkog," said Egil. "And now, if you'll all excuse me, I need to lie down for a while," he added apologetically. "I'm rather tired, and there are a couple of matters on my mind I need to think about."

"Choose the bed you want out of those that aren't being used," Ingrid told him.

"Okay then," Nilsa said. "You've all got somewhere to stay, and I hope you'll be comfortable here. Anything you need, just ask me." She got up to leave.

"Oh no! She's not staying here with us," Astrid said, pointing at Valeria. Her voice was cutting.

"Hey! We have a cat fight!" Viggo cried, rubbing his hands together gleefully.

"Astrid..." Lasgol began, but the brunette turned a chilling glare on him.

"Don't worry, Lasgol," Valeria said. "I'm not a Snow Panther. I understand. I haven't earned my stripes yet. It's all right."

"You've done an excellent job on the missions with us," Gerd said gratefully, and glanced quickly at Astrid in case of an outburst. Though she said nothing, she gave him a stern look.

"I appreciate that," Valeria said.

"She may have done whatever you like," Astrid said, "but she's not staying here."

"I think this ought to be decided with a fight between the blonde and the brunette."

"Viggo! That's even unworthy of you!" Ingrid reproached him.

"What?" Viggo shrugged as if he had said nothing wrong. "It could be unarmed combat," he suggested, and gave her a mischievous smile.

It was Nilsa's turn to reproach him now. "You're a dumbass, besides being a complete idiot."

"A loving one," he replied cheerfully.

"Don't worry," Valeria put in, "I know when I'm one too many. I'm sure Nilsa can find me somewhere else to stay."

"Yes, of course..." Nilsa looked at Astrid in case she changed her mind and allowed Valeria to stay, but the icy glare she received left it very clear that she was going to do nothing of the kind.

"We'll see you tomorrow, Val," Egil told her, trying to ease things a little. "Thanks for the great job you've done."

She smiled. "You're welcome, Egil."

Before she shut the door behind her, she gave Astrid a look of hatred, then Lasgol a charming smile.

"She's a...." Astrid exclaimed, but Valeria shut the door behind her.

"She's a...? Finish the sentence, please," Viggo said.

Astrid was not in a good temper. She gave Viggo a look, then Lasgol another.

Lasgol waved his hands innocently. "Eh? I didn't do anything."

"Stop smiling at her like a halfwit!" Astrid snapped.

"But I didn't smile.... Did I really smile at her?" he asked Gerd, seeking his support, but suddenly they were all very busy with their own affairs and nobody was listening.

Over the next few days they rested and caught up with one another's news while they waited for the arrival of the remaining Leaders. Everything seemed quiet for the moment. Finally, through the great gate in the castle, they saw the retinue they had all been waiting for so anxiously. Escorted by thirty Rangers came Dolbarar, Angus and the three Master Rangers of the Camp. Before they had dismounted, word of their arrival had spread throughout the castle.

Nilsa ran to tell her friends. "Run to the courtyard! They're here!" she shouted as she opened the door to their room like a tornado.

Gerd jumped with shock at her hurricane entrance. "What? Who? What's up?"

"Who do you think? Dolbarar and the Master Rangers!"

Viggo leapt to his feet. "All in one piece?"

"Yes! Come on! Run, or else you'll miss it!"

Ingrid put away the weapons she had been sharpening. Egil and Lasgol, who were chatting beside Camu and Ona, got to their feet and followed the others, who were already running out of the door.

Camu, Ona, you stay here, Lasgol transmitted.

Want to see.

I know, but it's better if you stay here.

They not see.

The Rangers can't, but don't forget we're in the Royal Castle, and in the Tower of the Magi there are at least four Ice Magi who serve King Thoran.

Magi stupid, not see.

That we don't know for sure.

I know.

Okay, you know everything. Whichever way, you stay here, and that's that.

Lasgol ended the conversation and went out. In the great courtyard Dolbarar, Angus, Ivana, Haakon and Esben were dismounting. The remaining Rangers stayed on horseback.

"How wonderful to see you all safe and sound! Gondabar called as he came out of the tower with Gatik. From inside the main building of the castle came Sven and Duke Orten, the King's brother. They all wanted to see the arrival of the retinue, and particularly to find out whether anything had happened to them on the way.

"The joy is ours as well," Dolbarar replied with a cheerful smile. He shook the hand Gondabar offered him, and they embraced one another.

"I feared the worst, I won't deny it," Gondabar said.

Angus bowed respectfully, and the others did so as well.

"It's a pleasure to have you all here," Gondabar went on. "Did anything happen during the journey? No news reached me."

"Nothing of note happened on our journey," Dolbarar replied. "That's why there was no need to send any news."

"That eases my heart. I'm glad the mission ran into no trouble."

"As you requested," Dolbarar said, "I maintained absolute secrecy, and it seems that this time it worked."

Gondabar nodded, and his face showed how happy he was. Nor

was he the only one. Lasgol, Egil and the other Snow Panthers were also delighted to see the leaders of the Camp safe and sound inside the castle. None of them had been entirely confident. Lasgol snorted in relief, and Egil patted him on the back. Viggo, on the other hand, looked disappointed. He had commented that he would rather something had happened to give them more leads that would help them find out who was behind it all.

"The King welcomes you to his castle," Duke Orten said. "My brother wishes you to know that he wants to take part personally in the Great Council, and hence that he will be present whenever he considers convenient."

Gondabar gave a small bow. "Of course. That is the King's prerogative." He could not forbid the King's attendance, and this was what Orten was trying to make very clear.

"Let me know when the event commences and I will inform His Majesty," Sven said, and Gondabar nodded.

Orten and Sven went back inside the castle, while Dolbarar and the three Master Rangers set off to the Rangers' Tower. Nilsa ran to join them so that she could assist them.

"Looks as though we're all here," said Viggo.

"That's right," Ingrid said. "I'm glad they got here safely."

"The Council's going to begin soon," Egil pointed out.

"D'you think we'll be able to attend?" Gerd asked. "I'd like to be there."

Egil shook his head. "I don't think so. Only the leaders and a few guests will be there."

"You need a special invitation, which only Gondabar can give," said Ingrid. "At least so Nilsa told me."

"They'll want to keep it secret," said Astrid. "That's natural enough. Whatever they discuss in there will be important, and classified as secret."

"That's true," Lasgol agreed. "The fewer people who know what's discussed and decided there, the better."

"We're living in interesting times," said Egil with a half-smile.

"Yes, and complicated ones too," Ingrid added.

"We're always living in interesting and complicated times," Viggo objected. "Of course, all by courtesy of the weirdo and the know-it-all." He folded his arms.

Lasgol and Egil caught one another's eye. "He's quite right, you know," Egil said with a malicious smile.

"Don't pay any attention to this numbskull," Ingrid snapped.

"Don't you have to go and see your convalescent Captain Fantastic?"

"Well, actually, yes. Quite honestly, his company is a hundred times better than yours," she said, and set off to the infirmary.

Lasgol laughed out loud, and Astrid smiled, trying not to do the same.

"I think your approach to solving this problem is mistaken, or at least counterproductive," Egil pointed out to Viggo.

"And who asked for your advice?" Viggo replied grumpily.

"I'm just trying to help a friend... I think it's time to change your approach."

"What d'you mean, approach? That's what I'm like. There's no other approach."

"You can also be nice when you want to," Gerd pointed out.

"Even a good person, sometimes," Lasgol added.

"That's no use!"

Astrid winked at him. "You're making a mistake there. They're qualities a woman notices."

"Oh... well..."

"Listen to what Egil says and try a different strategy with Ingrid," Astrid said. She took Lasgol's hand and led him away.

As he watched them leave, Viggo was left looking thoughtful. He felt a healthy envy of what they had and he could not reach, even if it was at his fingertips. Perhaps it was time to change his behavior toward Ingrid. Yes, maybe it was time to be less biting. After all, he did not have much to lose... and things could hardly get any worse.

The next day Gondabar called all the leaders of the Rangers, one by one, for a private meeting in advance of the Great Council. It took him until well into the night. According to what Nilsa had been able to find out, it was the first stage of the Great Council, the preparatory one-to-one talks. Then the Great Council itself would begin with presentations by each member of the Council. These would be followed by discussions between all the members. Finally, the decisions would be made which had been agreed in the Great

Council. It was a long and complicated process, which would take days, and that was without taking account of the King's presence. If he attended, as was expected, it would be more complicated still. Or so said the rumors.

Two days later, Nilsa burst into the room the Snow Panthers were sharing with the renewed force of a hurricane. "The Great Council has been summoned!" she shouted.

Gerd, who was still asleep, fell off his cot with a start. Ona gave a roar and flattened back her ears. Camu camouflaged himself.

"Eh?" Ingrid said.

"The Great Council! It starts today!" Nilsa said, hopping up and down and clapping excitedly.

Viggo put his hands over his ears. "Relax, you're giving me a headache with all that yelling..."

Egil smiled. "Wow, they haven't wasted any time."

"Gondabar has just announced it! The leaders are all in the castle, and it looks as though they're all fit to attend!"

Astrid made a shushing gesture. "You're going to deafen us with all this excitement," she told her with a smile.

"It's just that I've been preparing it all for so long that I'm really excited!"

"We've got the message," Lasgol told her.

"Well," Ingrid said, "it seems the moment has come. I hope they get to the bottom of this ugly business."

Gerd got up from the floor. "You scared me out of my wits. Who on earth would think of bursting into a room like that? D'you want to kill me? My heart is galloping."

"Well, get a grip on yourself, because I've got another scare for you! We've been invited to attend!" Nilsa shouted. She gave an excited shriek.

"All of us?" Egil asked.

"Yes, all of us!" She took out the scrolls and handed them out one by one. "Open them! I've already opened mine, and that's why I know it's an invitation to the Council! Gondabar has just given them to me, and I ran here at once. That's why I'm out of breath!" She let her tongue hang out.

"You've been out of breath since you were five years old!" Viggo shot back.

The six opened their scrolls, sealed with the seal of the Rangers, and Lasgol read out the contents of his:

Specialist Ranger Lasgol Eklund:
By the present communication you are invited to attend the celebration of the Great Council as a guest. You will be able to listen to whatever is discussed, but you may only participate if so required by any of the members.

Signed:
Gondabar
Grand Meister and Leader of the Norghanian Rangers.

"Mine says the same," Gerd confirmed.

"Do they all say the same thing?" Ingrid asked, and Astrid and Viggo nodded.

"Yes, mine too," Egil said.

"Well, well, this is odd," Lasgol said.

"I'm sure it isn't good," Viggo said suspiciously.

"But it's a great honor!" Nilsa pointed out.

"I prefer gold," Viggo replied sarcastically." Honors are blown away by the wind."

"They probably only want us as witnesses," said Egil.

"To ask us about the incidents?" Lasgol suggested.

"Yeah, I guess so. They'll want to ask us questions first-hand."

"Then in that case I suppose we have no choice but to go."

"What do you mean, 'no choice'?" Nilsa exclaimed. "It's a real honor to be invited!"

"Okay, okay... don't shout, or you'll end up losing your voice."

"Is it now?" Egil asked Nilsa.

"At noon. In the Great Hall. Bring your invitations, and they'll let you in."

"Right, we'll be there," Egil said.

"Oh, this is really exciting! We're going to be there!" Nilsa cried, and ran out of the room.

Viggo put on a comic look. "That girl gets worse every day."

Egil smiled. "She's excited."

"Let's see what happens," said Lasgol.
"Yeah, let's see," Egil smiled, and his eyes glittered.

Chapter 27

The Great Hall of the Royal Castle was where all the grand Court events took place, from banquets to balls for the nobility. It was larger than the Throne Hall, considerably cozier, and better decorated. Norghanians were not exactly given to luxury – the opposite, if anything – but the Great Hall was considered sumptuous by the standards of northern taste. It was certainly the largest and best-prepared hall in all Norghana. It was one the Snow Panthers had never thought they would ever set foot in.

At the door, four soldiers of the Royal Guard stopped them. They had to show their invitations, then were allowed in one by one. Nilsa was already there, since to her surprise Gondabar had given her the responsibility of acting as an usher, which had excited her. She was delighted and was doing her job with great restraint, which was unusual in her. It must have been the effect of the hall and the event itself, which was a very solemn one.

The hall was huge, with space for over a hundred guests. The walls of rock, which rose to a great height to arched ceilings, were covered with enormous paintings of epic battles of the glorious Norghanian past against Zangrians and Rogdonians. There were also huge murals and tapestries depicting battles between the Norghanian kings themselves, as well as two very different ones which captivated everyone. One showed a group of warriors fighting a colossal silver dragon. The other one showed two dragons, one white and the other red, fighting in mid-air for supremacy.

An enormous and beautiful carpet covered the whole center, except for four massive square columns which supported the structure. The carpet represented an enormous oak-tree, complete with roots, trunk, branches and leaves. On different parts of the oak were circles, like crowns of laurel. On these were the chairs of the members of the Council. They were round, with high backs, carved with floral motifs. Lasgol became aware that each chair was made of a different wood and represented a different kind of tree: beech, ash, pine, cedar, yew, eucalyptus, chestnut and others.

Long benches with soft cushions had been prepared for the

guests at the southern end of the hall. A table had also been laid with food and drink typical of Norghana. The Council sessions would be long, and refreshments would be welcome. There were not too many guests, which made the presence of the Panthers even more significant.

Lasgol saw that at all four corners of the hall, Royal Rangers had been posted. They carried short bows, and their positions meant that they could shoot at any danger. There were only two doors: the southern one they had come through, and the northern one, which was locked from the inside. This meant that there was only one way in or out, and it was guarded.

"This is very well-arranged," Egil commented when they sat down on the long bench.

"Plenty of security," Lasgol agreed.

Viggo sat down beside Egil and smiled ironically. "It looks as though someone's nervous about what might happen."

"After everything that's happened, who wouldn't be," Astrid pointed out. She sat down on Lasgol's other side.

Gerd took his place at the end of the bench. "Comfortable, this cushion. Nilsa knows what she's doing," he said as he watched the redhead welcoming the attendants.

Then a figure sat down beside him. "Hi there, Gerd," said a playful voice he knew well.

"Val! Have you been invited too?"

"Yup. It seems they've invited us all." She waved her hand at the others.

Lasgol waved back at her and smiled. Astrid elbowed his ribs and glared at Valeria. The blonde Ranger ignored her.

Nilsa ushered in Gondabar and the other Ranger leaders. Gondabar took the second-highest chair amid the branches of the great oak, at the top. Then Gatik, the First Ranger, took his place on the higher reaches of the branches, below Gondabar.

Next came Sigrid, the Mother Specialist, and behind her the four Elder Specialists. Sigrid took the chair above Dolbarar's, which was where the trunk ended and the branches and leaves began. Annika, Engla, Ivar and Gisli – who seemed to have recovered from his wound – sat down amid the branches of the tree. The arrangement was two on the right and two on the left, under Gondabar, who was at the top of the tree.

Then it was Dolbarar's turn, and he sat down in the middle of the trunk of the great oak. Esben, Ivana, and Haakon took their places in the chairs on the roots of the great tree. One of the chairs on the roots – that of Eyra – remained empty.

Angus and Enduald came up to the tree and sat down on two chairs on a stream which ran beside the great oak and from which its roots drank. On the stream were several more chairs on the other side of the trunk, occupied by three people Lasgol did not know. These must be Rangers with important and specific functions which he had no idea of. Little by little they all came in, members of the Council and attendants, and sat down in their designated places. The entrance door was shut and locked from inside. Now nobody could go in or out.

Nilsa gave a nod to Gondabar. The leader of the Rangers stood up, and at once all the other members of the council did so too.

"Welcome, all of you, to the Great Council," he said. He struck the floor with a long staff ornamented with silver motifs, and suddenly the carpet seemed to come alive. Leaves and branches moved, swaying to the breath of an imaginary wind. The stream flowed, and even the grass swayed from side to side.

Lasgol shut his eyes tightly and opened them again, because he thought he was suffering some kind of hallucination. "Do you see the carpet moving?" he asked hesitantly.

"It's not so much the carpet itself," Egil explained. "It's the images represented on it that are moving."

"How's that possible?" Astrid wondered.

"This is Enduald's doing, I'm sure," said Ingrid, from the other end of the bench. "He charms fabrics. We saw him use one in the forest to camouflage himself. The carpet must have been charmed by him as well."

"That's absolutely fascinating," Egil said excitedly.

"I'm not sure," said Viggo." It's magic..."

"Nonsense," Egil said. "The effect is fantastic."

Gondabar went on with his introduction: "This Great Council has been summoned to discuss the extremely grave situation the Corps of Rangers finds itself in, and in consequence the whole realm of Norghana. It's known to you all, as I've met with each of you individually, as the leaders of the Rangers, to give you all the information I myself have about this ugly business which affects the honor of the entire corps. Hence all the members of the council know the danger we, as well as the whole realm, are confronting."

The other members, and particularly the leaders, nodded. Some murmured words of worry, even of rage.

"The Dark Rangers represent the biggest threat we have suffered in a hundred years. We need to unmask their leaders and put an end to them."

The statement received the support of everybody there.

"We've got to make them disappear," came a voice.

"Before we begin our deliberations, I would like to summon those people who witnessed the betrayal to give evidence before the council. The members of the council have the right to hear at first hand the information we have about this threat. The first one I want to call is Ranger Egil Olafstone."

Lasgol glanced at his friend as he stood up. "Courage," he whispered.

Egil smiled and stepped forward. He stopped at the feet of the great carpet, beneath the roots of the great oak.

"Egil, if you please, tell the Council everything you've found out about the Dark Rangers."

Egil cleared his throat and gave his account as clearly and simply as he could. When he had finished, the members of the Council asked him questions, which he answered. Then he withdrew to his place on the bench beside his comrades.

Next Gondabar called Gerd. As the giant walked up to testify, he was as white as a sheet. He did it as best he could, and answered all the questions. After him, Gondabar called Valeria, then Ingrid, Viggo, Lasgol and Astrid. Once they had testified, they returned to their places on the bench.

"As you see, the threat is greater than we had thought," Gondabar went on. "The Dark Rangers are not simply a few among us whom Eyra and the leaders of that group have managed to entice to their secret faction. They've been recruiting all those who didn't manage to pass the course at the Camp – and I very much fear, even those who failed to graduate as Specialists at the Shelter. That means their numbers are far higher than we'd thought."

"In addition to that, they've probably recruited members outside the Rangers among the King's soldiers," Sigrid, the Mother Specialist, suggested. "There are those who were expelled or dishonored or who are deserters there as well."

"Yes, that's a very real possibility we'll have to look into," Gondabar agreed.

"I won't say it's not possible," Sven said, "but I certainly find it very difficult to believe." The Commander of the King's Forces was coming into the Council. He went to stand outside the carpet formed by the members of the Council, as he was not a Ranger himself but belonged to the King's army.

"Many soldiers end their days expelled from the army," said Engla.

"That's true. It's a tough life, a soldier's. Deserters and those who are expelled with dishonor end up committing crimes, and pay for them."

"They might have been bought with gold," Sigrid said. "We've already heard that they have gold and they're well-financed."

"I find it hard to believe, but I won't say it's impossible," Sven admitted.

"Everyone on the Council will have their opportunity to express their own points of view, as well as suggest courses of action they feel are appropriate," Gondabar said. He could see that arguments among the members of the Council were already under way.

"That seems correct to me," said Sigrid, and Sven took a step back, off the carpet.

"We now begin our exchange of views with the roots of our noble oak," Gondabar said. "The Leaders of the Camp train the new generations of Rangers and mold our future leaders, and hence are the roots of our corps." He greeted Ivana, Haakon, and Esben, who in turn rose from their chairs and bowed respectfully to him. "In order of length of service in the corps, I call on Esben, Master Ranger of the School of Wildlife."

Esben gave his opinion. "The person who should really be speaking first in this Council is Eyra. I, in particular, feel a deep pain that she's unable to do so. I've puzzled over this for a long time, and I still can find no reason why she should have committed the atrocious acts she's accused of."

"They have been more than proven," Gondabar told him.

"I'm not saying otherwise, and her flight shows it. It's just that we've been united by a sincere friendship for many years, and I find it very difficult to understand what has happened. Her betrayal, her attempt to kill Dolbarar and occupy his place as Leader of the Camp... I would never have imagined it. Hence, and after thinking about it thoroughly, I believe we ought to be far more prudent and more vigilant than ever. There are snakes among us, and we need to find them out and cut off their heads before they poison us with their venomous bite. How this group of Dark Rangers was created I don't know, but they're among us, and hence we have to find them and finish them off before the evil becomes irreversible."

Esben's words stirred agreement among the other members of the Council.

"I call on Haakon, Master Ranger of the School of Expertise," said Gondabar.

"Those who know me well," Haakon began, "know I don't usually keep my opinions to myself, and hence there are some among our own people who already know mine. To fight against that secret organization and unmask their leader, we need to be able to count on very strong leadership. Otherwise we'll be unable to defeat them."

Several of the leaders protested at his words. "We have strong leadership," Gisli told him.

Haakon did not flinch, but let the murmurs of disapproval fade before he went on.

"We need to ask ourselves how it's possible for this to have happened in front of our own noses, without our realizing. There's only one explanation: we've allowed ourselves to relax. All of us. This relaxation, this lack of concentration, is due to the self-satisfaction of our present leaders. Without an iron hand guiding the destiny of the Rangers, we find ourselves facing this problem, and others that are worse."

Once again, words opposing his opinion filled the Council. "You're wrong," Annika told him. "You're young and arrogant. Our leaders are exceptional."

Gondabar, whose expression showed that those words had affected him, raised his hand to quell the murmuring. "Let Haakon express his opinion. He has the right to do so. We all need to express ourselves. That's the aim of this Council, and it must be respected."

Haakon nodded and went on. "That is why I propose that we must change the position of the King's Master Ranger and vote to elect a new leader who can guide us in these difficult times."

The proposal did not go down at all well with many in the hall.

They protested irately, waving their arms and showing their disagreement with Haakon's words.

"Thank you, Haakon," said Gondabar. "Now I invite Ivana, Master Ranger of the School of Archery."

Ivana addressed the council: "In my opinion, the situation we find ourselves in is in part our own fault. It's come about under our leadership, and hence is our responsibility. I understand Haakon's position, although I don't entirely share it. We must strengthen the leadership, that is irrefutable. But is choosing another leader the right way to do it? It may be, I don't deny it. Nevertheless, what I propose to the Council is that our leadership should be closely monitored by someone from outside the corps itself."

"What would this external entity be?" Gondabar asked.

"One that would monitor the leaders' performance and what is currently happening in the corps. It could be someone who has the confidence of His Majesty the King."

This suggestion did not go down well with many. It implied that the King would now take even more control over the Rangers, who although they served him, were independent from His Majesty's aims.

"The military powers must remain separate from those of the Rangers," Sigrid said, and there were voices of acceptance.

Gondabar now invited Dolbarar to speak, as Leader of the Camp. "Dolbarar has suffered the betrayal in his own flesh, and almost died as a result. Let us hear his words."

"Thank you, Gondabar, King's Master Ranger, and our leader," Dolbarar said.

He went on to describe all that he had been through, from the poisoning to the discovery of the betrayal, the pain, disappointment and suffering when he had found out what was happening, and the terrible threat posed by the Dark Rangers.

"I am alive by the grace of the Ice Gods and by the heroic performance of a group of young Rangers who went beyond the call of duty to save my life. I cannot thank them enough for saving my life and unmasking the traitor, Eyra. It breaks my heart to know that someone I trusted like a sister could have betrayed me in this way. It also shows us how dangerous they are, and I very much fear that they are among us. Even here, at this moment."

Dolbarar's words awoke an outburst of comment which Gondabar had to quell with firm gestures.

"He's a very good man," Lasgol said to Egil.

"He certainly is."

Dolbarar went on: "I feel that I am responsible to a considerable extent for what has happened, for not realizing that something was not right, that Eyra was conspiring, poisoning the minds of young Rangers, recruiting those we had rejected to join a secret organization which is acting against us and against the good of the kingdom. Because of that, I beg your forgiveness. I have failed you." His voice was choked by feelings of sorrow, rage and guilt.

"It's not your fault. You couldn't have known," Gondabar told him, and Sigrid and Oden added their support.

The remainder were divided between those in favor of Dolbarar and those against.

Gisli and Annika expressed their full support for the current leaders, both Gondabar and Dolbarar, and of course Sigrid. But Ivar and Engla were far more critical. Ivar suggested changing their system of organization for a more decentralized one, which would not depend on sending information to the capital and waiting for decisions to come back, but instead would allow them to make decisions quickly by themselves. This approach was not well received by Gondabar and Dolbarar, but was more popular with other leaders.

The one who surprised her own people was Engla. She, like Haakon, attacked the leadership, particularly that of Dolbarar and even more that of Gondabar. She asked for it to be renewed: both at the Camp, because that was where the greatest betrayal had occurred and where Eyra had been able to act undiscovered for years, and in the overall leadership, because Gondabar had completely failed to identify the threat posed by the Dark Rangers.

The arguments filled the hall again. This time the debate was more heated, with discordant voices which Gondabar had to appease with much gesturing.

Then came Sigrid's turn. Surprisingly, she brought up a subject which left everybody rather puzzled.

"These are extraordinary times, and times like these require extraordinary measures. As you know, I've always been in favor of improving our Specializations even further. What I propose for the fight against the Dark Rangers is to go on working on the improvement of our Specialists."

"You mean to go on experimenting on them?" Gondabar asked

her.

"Indeed. If we manage to develop Specialists who are ten times better than any Dark Ranger, they'll have no chance. We'll wipe them off the map."

Once again the murmurs of protest filled the hall.

"Your experiments and methods are extreme, to say the least," Ivar said.

"And very dangerous," Engla added.

"Great achievements also require great sacrifices," said Sigrid.

"Some sacrifices, such as the lives of the aspirants to Specialism, are not acceptable," Dolbarar told her.

"This is not the time to be cautious. Our enemies are not. They're trying to destroy us. With a force of Super Specialists, they'd have no chance. We'd destroy them. Think hard about it."

Again the murmurs filled the hall, but they were more divided this time.

"That proposal has always been considered too risky," Gondabar told her. "In fact you promised not to go on with those experiments after the problems which arose, and which involved the loss of human lives."

"More human lives have been lost, and more will be, in this entanglement with the Dark Rangers."

"That may be so, but the experiments cannot start again without the approval of the leadership," Gondabar reminded her, and there was a clear warning in his voice.

"That is why I'm raising the subject in the Council, so that it can be debated and I can be allowed to go on."

Gondabar had to agree, since all members of the Council had the freedom to express their ideas and propose initiatives to end the threat that hung over them.

"Now let us hear the opinion of our First Ranger Gatik."

"My opinion," Gatik began, "is that we have to confront this situation as though we were at war. We've been attacked, and they've declared war on us. We need to arm ourselves and finish them off one by one. Hunt them down, all of them, until not one of them is left alive. Somewhere there must be a list which shows the members of each group of them. Or maybe the list has been memorized by one person. I think the best thing we can do is to look for those lists and get rid of every single group of Dark Rangers. Only in this way will we manage to eradicate them."

"That's an interesting theory," Gondabar said.

"Yes, quite accurate," Dolbarar agreed.

Gondabar then called on the remaining members of the Council, including Oden, Enduald and the three people whom the Panthers did not know. The first of these turned out to be Bidean, who was in charge of the Rangers' logistics. The second was Diruer the Treasurer, whose job was to ensure their economic survival. This included taking on missions for other kingdoms in exchange for gold. This was something that the Panthers had not known, and which surprised them

"It doesn't surprise me," Viggo whispered nonchalantly. "Of course some neighboring noble or monarch would want to hire my services. They're hardly going to have anybody as good as me in their ranks."

Ingrid smiled. "Nor anybody as vain," she pointed out in a whisper.

"I'd heard something about that, said Nilsa. "There are Ranger Specialists who take on missions in distant lands, usually in groups of two or three. What I didn't know was that the missions were for gold."

"That means they send us on missions abroad for payment," Gerd said. He looked as though he was not very pleased with the idea. "That sounds like mercenaries."

"Look at it this way," said Astrid. "Thoran doesn't have enough gold to maintain the corps, and it's a good way of enabling us to be self-sufficient. I think it's a good idea."

"When you look at it like that it makes sense," Ingrid agreed. "We ought to send Viggo on all those missions. Then he'd be away for most of the year and we wouldn't have to put up with him."

He smiled from ear to ear. "My prowess would reach you in the songs of bards and troubadours."

Nilsa giggled.

"Either way, it's a good system of finance," Egil pointed out, "and it shows what a good reputation we Rangers have outside our borders."

"Yeah, I didn't know we were known outside Norghana," Gerd said.

"We certainly are," Nilsa said. "Gondabar receives messages from abroad, and even some from very far away."

Astrid's eyes were bright. "Interesting. Wouldn't you like to see a bit of the world?"

"I certainly would!" Nilsa said eagerly.

"So would I," Egil agreed with a smile. "Having the chance to study the different cultures and kingdoms of Tremia appeals to my vagabond soul."

Gerd folded his arms. "Well, my vagabond soul doesn't want to leave Norghana."

"Haven't we traveled enough?" Ingrid asked. She too did not sound enthusiastic at the prospect. "We've already got enough problems at home without embarking on others abroad."

The debate in the Council went on, and now it was the turn of the odd-looking woman who was by the stream, together with the director of Logistics and the Treasurer. She wore a white bearskin, and her hair, which was also white, hung in multiple braids on either side of her face. She looked like a witch of the snows.

Gondabar introduced her as Brenda Noita.

"Gondabar knows my opinion, and so do others in the Council. We need to resort to magical means to fight the forces of evil. We need to ally ourselves with the invisible forces which govern the destiny of the men of the North. To go on trying to solve complex situations like this one solely by mundane means won't lead us to our desired destiny. We need to call on the forces of magic so that they can reveal the destiny that awaits us, and whether in some way it's possible to alter it."

When Brenda had finished speaking, there was a silence as they tried to understand her strange words. A moment later they were arguing about whether using magic was something Rangers should or should not do.

"Who's that witch?" Viggo asked.

"No idea," Ingrid said. "I've never seen her before."

Gerd nodded. "Well, yes, she certainly looks like a witch, and she talks like one." He was looking at her out of the corner of his eye, as if he were afraid that she might catch him looking at her directly.

"Be careful she doesn't put the evil eye on you," Viggo said.

"Do you know her, Egil?" Lasgol asked.

"Only by name – well, by reputation too. I've never seen her before. She's a counselor to the Ranger leaders. She's summoned when some problem of a magical nature has to be dealt with."

"And they say she's a witch, a seer," Valeria added.

"A seer?" Nilsa repeated.

"Apart from being one who knows the magical world, they say her magic allows her to see parts of people's future."

"That's nonsense," Astrid said. "I'm sure she's simply a woman who's wise in arcane matters."

Valeria shrugged. "That's what I've heard. I've never seen her before either. She doesn't often leave her home."

"And where does she live?" Gerd asked.

"In a cave on Raven's Peak, so they say."

Nilsa frowned. "Remind me not to go anywhere near that particular mountain."

"Me too," said Gerd.

"Let's not jump to conclusions," Lasgol said. "If she's in the Council, it's because the leaders trust her. She must have great knowledge, like Dolbarar or Sigrid."

"Very probably," Egil agreed.

The deliberations went on well into the night and Gondabar finally called it a day. They all went back to their accommodation with their heads full of all the questions which had been discussed.

Chapter 28

The Great Council sat again the following morning. The hall filled with members of the council and guests, and Gondabar continued to act as Master of Ceremonies. The presentations and discussions went on throughout the day, until night fell once again. The discussion was open, with every member of the Council freely expressing his or her opinions, which gave rise to heated and very intense debates.

The Panthers listened with interest to all the discussions and commented among themselves in low voices on those issues which seemed most critical to them. The day was long and exhausting, but when the Panthers finally left, they went on debating among themselves in their room while they made a fuss of Ona and Camu, who had been locked up in there all day on their own. Little by little they all fell asleep, Lasgol with Ona's head on his chest and Egil stroking Camu who was stretched out beside his cot.

On the third day of the Council something happened which they were all simultaneously expecting and fearing: King Thoran appeared. The doors opened and two soldiers announced his arrival in loud voices. He was accompanied by Commander Sven and the Royal Guard, wearing his silver-scaled dress armor, with a red and white cape. He was also wearing the Norghanian crown on his head and a sword at his waist. Sven and the Royal Guard were also in full dress uniform, which was unusual for them.

Gondabar greeted him with an elaborate bow, and all the members of the Council rose to their feet and did the same.

"Your Majesty, welcome to the Great Council."

"Thank you, Gondabar. I have decided to take my place in the Council as King of Norghana and ultimate authority." He indicated his seat, which was above Gondabar's on the enormous carpet.

"Of course, your Majesty. It's your prerogative, as well as an honor for the members of the Council."

The King sat down in his chair and threw his cape over the back.

"What an entrance... worthy of a monarch," Ingrid commented in a whisper. She was obviously impressed.

"The only thing missing was for him to come in riding on a white courser," Viggo murmured. "Though the Council gave him a pretty cold welcome."

"That's natural," Egil explained very quietly, so that nobody else would hear, "because the King has the final word on the decisions that are taken, and generally he doesn't interfere. The fact that he's here isn't a good sign, and of course many of the Council aren't at all pleased. He might reject their decisions, or even annul them."

Nilsa was rubbing her hands together. "How interesting! I can foresee a political battle ahead."

"I don't like this business of the King coming at all," Gerd whispered. "I bet it'll mean trouble."

Lasgol and Astrid exchanged an intrigued glance. Why had the King come? Lasgol, like his friend the big guy, had an ominous feeling.

Valeria pretended to look horrified. "This is going to get very interesting," she murmured.

Gondabar made as if to speak, but the King raised his hand to stop him. "Before the discussions continue, I would like to know what matters are being dealt with, so that I can begin to consider my final opinion." It was very clear that he would be the one who made the decisions in the end.

"Of course, your Majesty," Gondabar replied. Calmly, he listed the main issues, at the same time giving the names of those who had presented them to the Council. As he did so, the expressions of most of the members of the Council turned grimmer. It was one thing to argue matters among themselves and arrive at some form of consensus, or at least partial agreement, but a very different one to persuade the King. And above all to persuade Thoran, who was one of those monarchs who did not allow themselves to be swayed and who enjoyed interfering and making the decisions he himself considered right. Not necessarily the best ones, or those which his counselors recommended to him.

"I think he's left things very clear to everybody here, with that direct style straight from the jaw so typical of our beloved king," Viggo muttered ironically.

"And many of them don't like it," Egil noted. He was listening intently.

"The King's the highest authority," Ingrid said. "They don't need to like it."

"It's a Council," Egil pointed out. "What they're seeking is consensus, not the imposition of ideas or decisions."

"That's all very well, but the one who has the final authority is the King."

"I don't think our monarch is much concerned with consensus," Viggo murmured sarcastically, "more with imposition."

"Very true," said Valeria.

When Gondabar had finished explaining, he fell silent. Thoran, sitting in his chair at the very top of the tree represented on the carpet, looked up at the ceiling and seemed to be lost in his own thoughts.

"He's thinking about it," Gerd commented. "Let's see what he says..."

"He has a lot to meditate on," Egil said. "The issues are profound and varied."

"He doesn't look to me like someone who meditates very much," said Viggo.

Finally the King spoke. "You've talked about a number of issues. I intend to focus on those which interest me, because some of them seem a waste of time and effort to me. As to the complaints about the leadership, I have to say that I share them completely. I'm very disappointed about everything that's happened." He looked at Gondabar as he spoke. "Those who criticize the leadership are absolutely right. The Dark Rangers should never have come into existence, still less have been recruited from among our own people. To rub salt into the wound, the last attacks and Eyra's escape are simply an irreparable humiliation and dishonor. I have half a mind to cut off the heads of the leaders of this organization on the spot, seeing how unacceptable the situation is."

He gave them all a furious glare. Nobody had the least doubt that he was capable of doing it. "Because of this, I have decided to make a harsh decision, but a necessary one. As of this moment, Gondabar, you are no longer the Leader of the Rangers. Your years of service are duly noted, and you are permitted to remain as a counselor at the level of the stream."

Immediately murmurs of protest rose, and Thoran stood up. "This is the King's decision!" he shouted at the top of his voice.

Everybody in the hall fell silent.

"He's dismissed Gondabar," Lasgol whispered in Egil's ear.

"I'm afraid there's going to be more..." Egil whispered back. He was watching Thoran with narrowed eyes.

Sven and the Guard reached for their swords.

"Of course, your Majesty," Gondabar said. There was sadness in his voice. "I will take up my new post at once." He got up from his chair and walked slowly to join Oden, who gave him an affectionate glance.

"Anybody who fails to obey my decisions will wish they'd never been born!" Thoran shouted furiously.

Nobody said a word, and everybody bowed their heads. A protest would mean death, or something worse. Everybody knew the King's temperament and how easily he lost his temper. Also, what could happen afterwards.

Nilsa could not bear what she was seeing, and put her hands to her face. Tears were running down her cheeks.

"Poor... Gondabar..." she mumbled, deeply moved.

"Good. I see I've made myself understood. Now let us continue with the Great Council. There are several more issues I want to deal with. Next comes the question of the leadership of the Camp. Dolbarar, it's unforgivable that you failed to see what Eyra was doing under your command, in front of your nose, laughing at you. For that reason I require your resignation, with immediate effect."

Lasgol looked at Egil in horror, and his friend nodded slowly, as if he had been expecting this to happen. The King was punishing the leaders instead of helping them to carry on with their work and deal with the problem. This, Lasgol realized, was precisely Thoran's style. He was not one to give second chances or forgive mistakes, very far from it. Along the entire bench where the Panthers were sitting, the expressions of disbelief and sadness were obvious.

"I can't believe it, it's not his fault," Ingrid whispered furiously.

"I bet now you don't think it's such a good thing that the king has the last word on everything," Viggo whispered to her.

"Dolbarar couldn't have known," Astrid said. She too was furious.

Valeria shook her head. "The King's like my father, he doesn't forgive people who make mistakes," she whispered, and Egil nodded in agreement.

Dolbarar rose from his chair and addressed the King. "I have always acted with the best interests of the Rangers at heart. I have done so following the Path and with honor. I hereby submit my resignation." He bowed respectfully to the King.

"Good. I don't doubt your loyalty and your honor. Otherwise you'd hang from a tree. And that goes for everyone." He looked defiantly at the other members of the Council. "Dolbarar, you go down to the stream."

"As you wish, sir," Dolbarar said, and went to stand beside Brenda. The White Witch put her hand on his and smiled at him. Dolbarar smiled back.

"And now we're going to move a few more pieces on this board," Thoran said in an overbearing voice. This did not please everyone there, but they said nothing to avoid provoking the King's rage afresh.

"Angus, for the good work you did during the time you were in charge of the Camp, I promote you to Leader of the Camp."

"My lord, I would like to offer my candidacy," Ivana said. "I have served the King for years..."

"Well, what d'you know!" Viggo whispered. "The icy blonde has aspirations."

"Strange that it isn't Haakon. I thought he'd be the one," Lasgol said. He was distressed at what had happened to Dolbarar, and also unable to understand why Haakon did not come forward.

"Esben's the one who ought to be the candidate," Gerd said. His eyes were moist.

But neither Haakon nor Esben said anything.

"Thank you for offering, Ivana," the King replied. "All the same, on this occasion and in the present situation, I would like someone with more experience in command. Your time will come, but not now."

"Thank you, your Majesty. In that case I withdraw my candidacy."

"Smart girl," the King said. He seemed to be pleased at having got his way. "Angus, take your place."

"It's an honor, your Majesty. I won't fail you."

"You'd better not, or else you too will end up in the river... drowned."

"What a temper..." Viggo murmured.

"If you can't get them to respect you, at least you can make them fear you," Egil whispered.

"Well, he's making a pretty good job of that," Lasgol said angrily.

"As to who is to succeed Gondabar in his post," Thoran said, addressing the members of the Council, "I have to make a decision, but first I'll listen to the candidates."

"Uh-oh," Nilsa muttered. She was biting her nails.

"This is getting interesting," Viggo said. He was watching very attentively and looking very amused at what was happening.

"It's not going to be anything good," Gerd said.

"It ought to be Sigrid, going by age and experience," Egil said. "But I'm afraid it won't be her who gets the title."

"Who else, then?" Ingrid asked.

"Someone younger and in line with the King," Egil predicted.

Sigrid stood up with a hard look in her eyes. "I present my candidacy," she said firmly.

"Thank you, Sigrid. Certainly an appropriate candidate. Does anybody else want the responsibility? It must be someone from the upper part of the tree." He waved at the carpet, then swept his gaze past Haakon, Ivana and Esben, as though challenging them to present themselves. Then he stared at Gisli, Ivar and Engla, until finally his gaze was fixed on Gatik. Everybody looked down, and only Sigrid remained standing.

"Apparently I'm the only candidate," she said with the light of victory in her eyes.

The King wrinkled his nose. He did not look very convinced. "I have nothing against you, Sigrid. All the same, you represent the old school, the old leaders who have failed me, even if you yourself have not as yet. Because of that, and because the choice is mine alone, my preference is for someone who has shown his worth and has not yet failed me. Someone with new blood, from a new generation which will revitalize the Rangers. My preference for this post is: Gatik."

Lasgol looked at Egil, who was nodding. He had already guessed it.

Everyone began to murmur. There was a division of opinion. Some, like Esben, Gisli and Annika, were in favor of Sigrid, as she was the best-qualified for the position because of her long career and wide experience. Others, like Haakon or Ivana, looked favorably on the King's choice of someone younger like Gatik. It seemed to be turning into a struggle between youth and experience.

"Discuss the matter," Thoran went on. "I want to hear your opinions."

It soon became obvious that nobody had anything bad to say against any of the two candidates: far from it. Everything said in support of one or another of them was made on the basis of their virtues. Nobody attacked the opposing candidate at any moment, and it became obvious that there were no weak points to attack, or at least no very obvious ones.

"This is really interesting," said Viggo, who was enjoying it all.

"Don't forget, whoever's chosen is going to lead all the Rangers," Ingrid said. She was looking at him very seriously." This is something very important."

"I'm taking it seriously. I know what's at stake and how it'll affect us."

Ingrid, who had been expecting some ironic retort, was surprised to hear him speaking seriously.

"I want to hear everybody's opinions," the King said, to encourage those who had not yet spoken.

And so they did, one by one. The Panthers listened expectantly to all of them, particularly Dolbarar.

"It seems to me that directing the Rangers requires first of all, experience and knowledge, both of the complex world of the Rangers and of life in general. These two virtues seem to me more developed in Sigrid than in Gatik. I'm not saying that our current First Ranger won't be a good leader, because he has all the characteristics to be that. All I'm saying is that his promotion at this moment seems a little too hasty. In my opinion Sigrid ought to be the one to lead us."

The King nodded and turned to Gondabar, who was the last to give his opinion.

"I have to say that I'm in full agreement with Dolbarar. Gatik is an exceptional First Ranger, and his worth is more than proven. He'll be a great leader someday, but I don't think that day has yet come. What we need now are experience and wisdom to lead the Rangers, and Sigrid is the most appropriate for the position."

When Gondabar had finished speaking, there followed a long silence. The King was looking up at the ceiling, and seemed to be deliberating.

"Good," he said suddenly. "I've listened to all the members of the council and assessed their opinions. They're correct. So is mine. And as my opinion weighs more, it will be the one which prevails in the end. My choice is unchanged. Gatik will be the new leader of the Rangers."

The murmuring filled the hall again.

"There's none so blind as the one who won't see," Viggo muttered.

"This time I'm going to have to agree with you," Ingrid said.

"He's come here with a single idea in his head, and he's not going to listen to the Council," Lasgol summed up.

"That's the prerogative of Kings," said Egil.

"Do you accept the position, Gatik?" the King asked him. "Or would you rather go on hunting bears in your free time, instead of leading the Rangers?" he added with a touch of sarcasm.

Gatik stood up and looked at his King. "Your Majesty knows that hunting bears is my favorite sport and that I enjoy it very much, as I do any task your Majesty entrusts me with which involves movement. I'm a man of action, not one who sits behind a desk and dispatches orders and messages. What my heart wishes is to use my bow to rid my realm of the enemy. But in the circumstances, and in the present difficult situation, I put my bow and my mind at the service of the Rangers and the King. If I'm required to act as leader of the Rangers and exchange my bow for a pen, I'd regard it as an honor to accept the position."

"That's the way to speak!" the King exclaimed. "The position is yours."

Egil was looking at Gatik intensely. The new leader of the Rangers was the one who had killed his father on the orders of Uthar the Shifter in the Frozen Continent, and he had not forgotten the fact. Nor would he ever forget it. He had been waiting for an occasion to have his revenge, but it had not arisen. Now, with Gatik rising to the leadership of the Rangers, his revenge would have to wait even longer, because it would be very difficult to act against him when he was the leader and enjoyed the King's support. Luckily Egil was a patient man. He would wait, just as he was waiting for the opportunity to act against Thoran and the Eastern nobles. Patience was one of his virtues, and he would have to practice it for some time.

"Do I understand that there's no opposition to my decision?"

Thoran asked.

The members of the Council were silent. They knew it was useless to oppose it.

"There is none, your Majesty," Gondabar said, trying to calm the monarch.

"It's an honor I wasn't expecting. I hope to rise to the occasion," Gatik said, and bowed deeply to the King.

"So you'd better. Don't fail me."

"I won't do that, your Majesty, you can rest assured of that."

"We shall see."

Viggo smiled wryly. "Wow, our King doesn't even trust the ones he chooses himself."

"It's a warning for Gatik and for all of us," Ingrid told him.

"The first thing I want you to do at this moment is to hunt down that traitor who managed to escape," Thoran said.

"Eyra, your Majesty?" Gatik asked.

"Yes. What do we know of her?"

"Our Man Hunters and Tireless Trackers have found her trail. She's in the Valley of Everlasting Winter."

"And why hasn't she been captured yet?"

"You see, your Majesty... there are thirty or so Dark Rangers with her, protecting her. Our Man Hunter Gurkog was wounded and had to withdraw. He's on the outskirts of the enemy camp. He sent one of his men, Ibsen, back to report. Eyra's still in that camp. We're going to organize an assault force to catch her."

"I don't want it to be just any old force. I want a very good group that won't fail. I'd like to have more Rangers like them" – he indicated his Royal Rangers – "the best among all the Rangers."

"Your Majesty... by your leave..." said Engla. "I've proposed the creation of a special group within the Rangers which would be in charge of 'sensitive operations'."

"Yes, that's an interesting idea," Thoran agreed. "I like it. What would be the functions of this group?"

"Those of being in charge of missions of a delicate nature, as for example catching the leaders of the Dark Rangers, or keeping a watch on the leaders of the Rangers themselves in case any of them started to behave strangely."

"Oh... I see... like a group which would make sure everyone behaves as they should among the Rangers..."

"That would be the idea, your Majesty."

"But that would imply spying on the members of this Council themselves," Gondabar protested. He did not like the idea in the least.

"That's correct," Engla said. "If there's nothing to hide, what's the problem? Also, it's a defense mechanism in case anyone abandons the Path or is tempted to do so. Weeds need to be pulled out by the roots."

"I like the idea," Thoran said with a nod. "Who would they report to?"

"Only to the leader of the Rangers," Engla said. "In that way, nobody could have any influence over them."

"Spying on your own people is not an honorable thing to do," Dolbarar protested. He too was unhappy with the idea.

"If anybody had been spying on Eyra, we wouldn't be here today," Haakon added. "I agree, it's a good idea. A group of Rangers whose missions come only from the leader, and with nobody else having any authority over them."

"It might be dangerous if as time went by they turned on us," Annika said in warning.

"They'd be assessed every year, and it would be decided whether they were still fit for their position," the King said.

"Your Majesty," Gondabar began, "we ought to discuss it further..."

"Nonsense. It's a very intelligent idea. The matter is decided."

"On that same subject," Sigrid began, "I'd like to be able to go on working on the creation of improved Rangers. That group would be an ideal candidate for that..."

"I have some knowledge of your experiments. I don't like them very much. On the other hand, having improved Rangers would give me an impressive advantage in the field, not to speak of the prestige we'd gain, the fear we'd create in our enemies and the gold we'd be able to collect for the Crown Treasury by leasing the services of those prodigies to other kingdoms." He gave a brisk nod. "I like the possibilities. Go ahead. You have the King's permission to go on with your experiments."

"Thank you, your Majesty," Sigrid said, and a gleam of triumph appeared in her eyes.

"Right. Unless there's anything else you'd like to discuss, I declare the Great Council at an end."

The members of the council looked at one another, but nobody had anything else to add.

"We seem to have a consensus. I'm sure the measures which have been created in this Council will be extremely beneficial for the realm."

"Not so much for the realm, for him," Viggo commented softly.

"Yeah," Ingrid agreed, "he's put the people in his trust in leadership posts."

"Hey, we're getting to agree more and more."

"Well, yes... I don't know what's going on," Ingrid said in surprise.

Thoran rose to his feet, and the remainder of the Council rose with him.

"Now all of you go and bring me that traitor Eyra back alive. I want to interrogate her, find out who the leader of the Dark Rangers is and hang him from the portcullis of my castle."

"As your majesty commands," Gatik said with a solemn bow.

Chapter 29

The assault force arrived at the entrance to the valley. Gatik was in the lead, flanked by his Royal Rangers. He had asked Thoran to let him carry out this last mission before he took on his new post as leader of the Rangers, when he would be sitting behind a desk and leading instead of acting. He did not seem to be very happy about leaving all the action behind.

Several groups of Specialists who had been chosen for this mission were with them. The Panthers and several other Rangers who had attended the Great Council had also been chosen to take part in the taking of the Dark Ones' camp and the capture of Eyra.

Lasgol had told Ona and Camu not to come with him this time, but there had been no way of persuading them to remain in the tower. Whatever happened, he was not going to let them take part in the battle.

You stay behind our lines.

No, we fight, came Camu's reply.

I want you to stay behind. I don't expect there to be any magic involved, and I'd rather not risk you being hurt.

Always risk.

I know, but today there'll be more of it. With so many Rangers on both sides of the fight, I can foresee an exchange of arrows, and I don' t want you in danger.

Exchange of arrows?

Arrows flying in all directions.

Many arrows, bad.

Exactly. That's why you're going to stay behind and wait till I call you. If I see any magic or think I'm going to need you, I'll let you know.

But —

No buts. This is going to be a very dangerous attack, and it's not your kind of mission. We've got enough Rangers with us to manage the assault.

Okay... Camu said resignedly.

Ona?

The good panther chirped once.

That's the way I like it, he told them, although he was not by no means certain they would obey. They sometimes made their own decisions. Not always the right ones, of course.

Gatik gave the order to halt. They had left their horses a league away and finished the last stage of the journey on foot. They were hiding in a maple-wood and were watching the entrance to the valley, which would surely be under observation. After some time, three figures came towards them from among the trees.

"Don't shoot!" Gatik ordered.

Lasgol was watching from a few steps behind, to the right of Gatik and the leading group. He did not recognize the three figures who were approaching at a crouch.

"D'you know who they are?" he asked his comrades beside him.

Egil craned his neck. "The first one's Gurkog, and he's wounded. To judge by the way he's moving, I'd say badly. With him are Fulker and Enok, two very good Specialists. They were with us the mission escorting Eyra. They went after her when she got away. They must have followed her trail here."

"They say Gurkog's very good at tracking," said Gerd. "Eyra couldn't shake him off."

"Well, he'd better look after himself," Ingrid said. "He's as white as a sheet."

"Ibsen was with them, and Gurkog sent him to the capital to report when they found the Dark Rangers' camp," Egil explained. "I spoke to him before we left."

Gurkog, Fulker and Enok talked with Gatik for a while. The Panthers could not hear what they were saying, but they guessed that they would be passing on information about the enemy camp to the leader of the Rangers. Finally Gatik made his decision.

"We've got to get rid of the watchmen to stop them sounding the alarm," the leader murmured to his Royal Rangers. "You snipers, find a position, in silence. They mustn't spot us."

One of the Rangers took out a Sniper's bow and ran to find an elevated position to shoot from. Two other Snipers from among the Specialists did the same.

"Assassins, spread out and help dispose of the watchmen who survive," Gatik ordered. "Don't give them a chance to sound the alarm."

Four of the Royal Rangers, the Assassins, disappeared into the wood. Astrid and Viggo followed them.

"You others, wait here in silence till the way in is clear."

The first of the enemy watchmen was in the crown of an oak. He fell to an arrow from a Sniper he never saw, three hundred and fifty paces away. The second was hit in the middle of his forehead at three hundred paces a little further west, also up in a tree. He fell dead without knowing what had hit him. The most amazing shot was from four hundred and fifty paces, which brought down the best-positioned watchman at the top of the highest tree.

Four watchmen who were at ground level saw the bodies of their comrades fall and ran to sound the alarm, but did not get very far. The Assassins had already slipped through the underbrush and hunted them down with the speed of a cheetah and the ferocity of a tiger. Viggo and Astrid fell on the last one as he was reaching the entrance of the enemy camp and opening his mouth, ready to sound a warning. He never managed to make a sound as the knives of both buried themselves in him, and he fell on his face, dead.

The Assassins took up positions which allowed them to watch the enemy camp. They found more than thirty armed Dark Ones in the tents and supply carts. They must have been preparing for action, because they were all armed and ready for battle, which did not encourage a frontal attack. One of the Assassins went back to Gatik and explained the situation.

"They're ready to fight?" he asked in surprise.

"That's right, sir. They're going on some mission or other."

"We can't allow that. We've got to end this now."

"A frontal attack isn't advisable in these circumstances, sir..."

"I know, but I'm not going to let them get away now. We'll attack with everything we've got. Pass the order along. We attack the camp at my signal."

Lasgol glanced at Egil, who was very quiet. In his eyes he could see that his friend was a little uneasy. He was out of his element here. He could not plan and direct the operation and he would have to fight, one of the things he liked least. Lasgol knew that his friend was going to have a hard time during the attack, but after all, he was a Ranger, so he would do well. Just in case, Lasgol was going to keep a close eye on him and help him if things turned complicated.

"Attack!" came Gatik's order.

They all moved as one, at a crouch and rapidly, toward the entrance to the valley which hid the camp. At the entrance they spread out like a fan, to give themselves a greater area of attack. The

Dark Rangers saw them and gave the alarm. The arrows began to fall on the enemy camp, while horn-calls and shouts of alarm filled the valley.

Lasgol released against one of the defenders and hit him in the chest. Egil was behind him, crouching, bow in hand, Ingrid and Nilsa on either side, and Gerd bringing up the rear. Astrid and Viggo had already vanished, while the Assassins were concealed and would be responsible for fighting from the shadows.

Gatik and the Royal Rangers were attacking the center like an impressive assault force, releasing to right and left with great accuracy.

The Dark Ones tried to repel the attack, but they were falling to the accurate arrows of the Rangers who were advancing toward the center of the camp. They sought protection behind tents and crates and toppled several supply carts to take cover from the rain of arrows falling on their heads.

"Don't let them take up covered positions!" Gatik ordered, and an arrow hit the Royal Ranger on his right. "Move! Spread out across the terrain, don't give them an easy target!"

The Royal Rangers began to race through the camp as they released, at the same time seeking cover from the Dark Archers, who were now all in protected positions.

Seeing a tent larger than the others, Lasgol made his way towards it. From behind it came three Dark Ones who had been in hiding. They raised their bows and aimed.

"Look out!" he cried as he released.

His shot grazed the head of one of the Dark Ones, but did not hit him squarely. Luckily he disturbed him enough to stop him shooting. He aimed again, but it was already too late for the Dark One, because Nilsa's arrow struck him in the face. The second was given no time to release, as Ingrid killed him before he could finish aiming. The third one, on the other hand, managed to release, and the arrow shot toward Lasgol's chest as he was in the lead. In a reflex movement he put out his right forearm to block the arrow, and it buried itself in the protection he was wearing.

"Get down!" Gerd ordered.

Egil and Lasgol ducked, and Gerd's arrow hit the archer in the heart.

"Thanks!" Lasgol said. He was in pain from the arrow which was buried in his forearm. It had pierced the protection, and the tip had entered the flesh.

At the tent, Lasgol signaled them to stop. Cries and arrows flew over the camp from side to side and in every direction. Lasgol broke the arrow so that he could use his bow, but could not manage to extract the tip. For that he was going to need a little camp surgery.

He looked inside the tent. "We did it," he said to the others as they released to defend themselves.

Egil put his head inside the tent and saw Eyra there. He smiled.

"We've come for you. If you'd be so good..." He offered her his hand so that she would come out of the tent.

"Surround the tent, and we'll defend it," Lasgol called to his friends.

Ingrid took up her position a couple of paces to the east. Nilsa did the same to the west, and Gerd went behind the tent. The three began to launch arrows against the nearest Dark Rangers behind their protective cover.

"Egil, I told you not to come after me," Eyra said as she came out of the tent.

"I had no choice."

"Well, it was a mistake, and you'll pay with your life."

"Why do you say that?" Lasgol asked her.

She pointed to Egil. "I've arranged to have him executed if I'm either caught or killed."

"The Natural Assassin?" Egil guessed.

"Exactly," Eyra said, with a malicious smile.

Several arrows passed close to them. They crouched, even though there was nowhere to hide. Fighting was breaking out all over the hollow as the fighters ran and released from one side to the other, or else leapt to seek cover behind barrels, toppled carts and crates.

"Why did you let me live?" Egil asked her.

"Because you can still be useful to me. You have influence in the West. Dead, you were no use to me."

"Use for what?"

"To protect my back. You always need to protect yourself from the enemy, and even more from friends."

"Are you afraid the Leader of the Dark Rangers will betray you?"

"Afraid he'll silence me forever, to be more exact."

Egil and Lasgol shared an uneasy glance. "Who is the leader,

Eyra?" Lasgol asked.

"What do you offer me in exchange for betraying him?"

"You'll have our protection."

"That's not enough. Thoran too wants my head."

Egil thought about this.

"I'll help you escape alive from Norghana," he said at last, and Lasgol stared at him in surprise. That was a lot to promise, and if Thoran were to find out, Egil would end up being hanged. He did not much like the deal.

He tried to dissuade him. "Egil..."

"Trust me," Egil replied.

Lasgol, who trusted his friend completely, did not insist. Egil would think of some plan which would get Eyra out of Norghana without hanging from a tree on Thoran's orders himself.

Eyra was silent for a moment, considering the proposition.

The battle in the camp was chaotic. The Dark Ones were resisting the attack with all their might. Arrows were flying everywhere

"Come on, tell us who he is and we'll protect you," Lasgol insisted.

Eyra nodded at last. "All right. I'll tell you." She opened her mouth to say the name, and an arrow buried itself deep in her chest with a sharp, hollow sound "Aaagh..." she groaned, and collapsed.

Lasgol seized her before she hit the ground and laid her gently on the grass. "Eyra, hold on!" he muttered, and began to examine the wound.

Egil was looking around, crouching down, trying to find out where the arrow had come from. From above, but from which direction?

"Who did it?" Lasgol asked him.

Egil scanned a group of Royal Rangers who were still exchanging arrows with the Dark Ones from behind the rocks and the protections they had improvised.

"I don't know. It could have been any of them."

"Was it an accident?"

Egil shook his head. "I doubt it. When this kind of thing happens it's not usually an accident. They shot to kill."

"I'm... dying..." Eyra mumbled.

Lasgol was examining the wound and putting pressure on it with his hands to stop her losing any more blood.

"Egil?" he said.

His friend knelt beside the old woman and checked the wound in turn. He shook his head, then bowed it. "It's fatal."

Gerd came at a run and hurled himself like a huge lion at two Dark Rangers who were coming close to Lasgol and Egil. One of them managed to get back on his feet and took out his axe to attack Gerd, who was also getting back up. He had no time to attack, because Ona leapt on to his back and brought him down on his face. Before he could turn over, she buried her fangs in the back of his neck and closed her jaws tightly. Gerd dispatched the other Dark One with a tremendous punch which left him unconscious.

"Eyra, tell us who he is," Lasgol pleaded.

"You have nothing more to lose," Egil said in a desperate attempt to persuade her.

Eyra in her death throes, with blood at the corners of her mouth, looked toward the Royal Rangers. She pointed a finger.

"Him..."

"I think she means a person," said Egil. "But who?"

Eyra let her hand fall and died with one last exhalation

"Hellfire!" Lasgol said, and closed her eyes.

Every moment the fighting was becoming more desperate for the defenders, who were losing. Astrid appeared, leaping like a tigress from a high boulder, and fell on top of two archers who were hiding behind it. The first died without knowing what had hit him on the head. The second one was lying wounded on the ground. He turned over and drew his knife and axe.

"It'll be quicker and less painful if you don't resist," she suggested.

"No way. I'm going to cut you into little pieces."

"As you wish," she said, and with another great leap she came down on to him. He defended himself with knife and axe against her attack, but unfortunately for him, he was not even half as agile as she was. She slashed his axe arm, and the weapon fell to the ground. He tried to retrieve it, but with a swift movement she slashed him again. Desperately, the Dark Ranger hurled himself at her to bury his knife in her. She moved to one side, and as he failed with his stroke, she buried her knife in his heart.

"Aaagh..." he grunted, and died.

"I warned you," she said.

At the back of the enclave, Viggo was slipping past like a shadow out of a nightmare seeking its next victim. He had already finished off several Dark Ones, surprising them from behind, the last direction they were expecting to be attacked from. One of the things that most amused him was to catch his enemies completely unawares. It was like a game for him, a dangerous and lethal game, and he loved it. He spotted three Dark Ones releasing from three different positions behind barrels and crates. He was creeping up to them from behind, and they had not yet noticed his presence. The three of them were five paces or so apart, and were giving the Rangers trouble because they were shooting from covered positions.

"We'll have to give those Royal Rangers a hand," Viggo murmured under his breath. He crept up to the one in the middle from behind, moving like a large predator, without the least sound, without the quarry realizing that its end was approaching, then stopped one step behind his prey and stared at him. The Dark One was so busy aiming and releasing without a break that he had not realized death was at the nape of his neck.

"Surprise," Viggo whispered in his ear.

The Dark One started in surprise. He did not even get the chance to call out. Viggo hurled himself on him and slit his throat with two precise slashes. He looked to left and right to see whether the other two had noticed anything, but they had not. They were still trying to reach the Royal Rangers, who never stopped moving and simultaneously releasing.

"Now I think we'll make a couple more surprise visits," he told himself, amused.

He began to slip aside like a black lion seeking his next prey. A couple of moments later he fell on the archer on the left. The one on the right died from his throwing dagger. He had tried his luck with a very difficult throw.

In the end the Dark Rangers were defeated. The Rangers took the ones who surrendered and tied them up in the middle of what was left of the camp. Gatik shouted orders to right and left. Escorted by four of the Royal Rangers, he came to where Eyra was lying. Lasgol and Egil were still beside her.

"Why did you kill her? We needed her for interrogation!"

"It wasn't us, sir," Lasgol said.

"A random arrow," Egil said, and showed him the wound.

"This is a serious setback," Gatik protested. "King Thoran wanted to question her and get to the bottom of who's behind this secret organization."

"He's not going to be happy," Egil said.

"I should think he isn't! I'll be the one who'll have to put up with his wrath! Hell! We almost had it!"

"Maybe we'll find some clue here in the camp," Lasgol suggested.

"That's true, there could be something. I want it all searched from top to bottom."

"Sir..."

"Yes Egil, speak up."

"It might be better if only a few of us searched the camp. It'll be tidier, and easier to find something significant. If everybody starts searching the place, it'll get trashed." He gestured at the Royal Rangers.

"Thank goodness I have people with a good head around me. Very good thinking, Egil." He turned to his men. "Egil alone and whoever he chooses are to search the camp!"

"Thank you, sir."

"Don't leave a single stone unturned," he told the two of them. "I'll go and see how many casualties and wounded we have, and what can be done for them. You start searching."

"Yes, sir!"

While Gatik attended to the Rangers, Egil, Lasgol and the other Panthers checked the whole camp, starting with Eyra's. It was a long task, and unfortunately a fruitless one. They found nothing that would indicate either who the leader was or what other members of the organization had infiltrated the ranks of the Rangers, or the Court.

Tired and disappointed, they had to give up. They sat down beside Eyra's tent.

"At least we gave them a good hiding," said Viggo.

"Yup, the victory's ours," Ingrid agreed.

"But it's a shame not to have found anything else," Astrid pointed out.

"Didn't Eyra say anything?" Nilsa asked hopefully.

Lasgol shook his head. "She didn't have time,"

"They silenced her forever," Egil said.

Gerd raised one eyebrow. "Wasn't it a stray arrow?"

"No, that arrow was to kill her," Egil said.

"One of her own people?" Viggo suggested.

Egil nodded. "Perhaps," he said mysteriously, "but it might have been one of our own."

Valeria had come close to listen. "One of our own? Are you sure?"

"At this moment I'm not sure of anything," Egil admitted.

Nilsa put her hands to her head. "Oh my, what a mess..."

"A big fat one," Egil agreed.

Chapter 30

Back at the Royal Castle from the failed mission to capture Eyra, the group withdrew to rest in the Rangers' Tower. Nilsa stayed in the main building to listen to the shouts King Thoran intended to dedicate to Gatik for having failed in his mission. Thoran was not one who forgave mistakes, particularly when there was so much at stake. He might even sack Gatik from the post of Leader of the Rangers, making him their shortest-lived leader of all.

The other Panthers threw themselves on to their cots and rested. After all the action they had been through, a little peace and quiet would be good for the soul. Ona and Camu were lying on the floor dozing, like two huge puppies.

Lasgol had not had the heart to scold them. They had disobeyed him and taken part in the assault on their own initiative. Luckily they had remained hidden until the last moment, when Ona had leapt to Gerd's aid. The fact that they were getting more and more independent and acting on their own pleased him, because it showed that they were maturing. At the same time it terrified him, because if they were acting on their own, sooner or later they would make a bad decision and put their lives at risk. The mere thought of losing either of them made his heart shrink.

He decided it was not the moment to contemplate such dramatic possibilities. They had enough trouble as it was.

He turned toward his friend, who was reading one of his books on the cot next to his own. "What d'you think, Egil?"

"That now we have no chance of obtaining information from Eyra, and we need to find the Boar and the Bear. They're the key to this whole business. Once we know who they are, we'll be able to find out everything else."

Gerd pushed himself up on his cot. "What 'everything else'?"

Egil scratched his head. "There's one thing in this situation that doesn't fit: those Zangrian assassins were paid a thousand coins for my head."

"I found those," Gerd said. He was listening to them, lying back on his cot.

"That's right, and it doesn't make sense."

"Why's that important?" Ingrid asked. She was sharpening her weapons as she listened to them.

"It isn't really, but..." Egil began.

"But?" Lasgol insisted.

"When a detail doesn't fit, it's for a reason. However much I puzzle over it, I can't seem to make that detail fit, and that tells me we're overlooking something. Something important."

"Well, if you have a funny feeling about a small detail, then it must surely be important," Viggo said. He was practicing with his throwing dagger, as he nearly always did whenever he had some free time. He was throwing it repeatedly at a target, which on this occasion was the frame of a mirror on the wall.

"For once I agree with Viggo. Small details are usually important."

Viggo smiled. "Wow, today's my lucky day." He had stopped mid-way in his dagger-throwing.

"Are you going to say something silly?" Ingrid asked him. The tone of her voice warned him not even to dare think of it.

"No, not at all. It's just that I'm delighted we both agree on something."

"What's wrong with you? You've spent days without saying any of your usual rubbish to me." She looked genuinely surprised.

"To me?" He smiled. "Nothing's happened to me. Nothing at all."

"Something's wrong with you..." She pointed her Ranger's knife at him.

"No, really. I'm delighted to be here chatting with you," he replied amiably, with a charming smile.

Ingrid stared at him. "Something odd's happened to you," she said.

Viggo shrugged and said nothing, but merely went on smiling, which puzzled Ingrid, who was expecting the usual out-of-place comment. Seeing that it did not come, she tried to make him jealous.

"I'm going to see Molak later on. The wound's going well, and he'll be able to get back on missions in no time at all. He'll want to know everything about the attack on Eyra's camp."

She glanced at Viggo out of the corner of her eye, but he did not seem to be affected. He simply went on smiling at her and throwing his dagger, without missing once.

"He's tough, he'll be back to normal straight away," he commented as he went to retrieve his dagger from the mirror. He had made the comment without irony.

This time it was not just Ingrid but all of them who turned to stare at him. They had not expected a reply like that.

"He must be running a fever," Ingrid said incredulously.

"Eh? It's true. Molak's a tough guy, he'll be as good as new in no time."

"You referred to him by his name? No 'Captain Fantastic' and all that nonsense?"

"His name is Molak, isn't it?"

"You're definitely coming down with something."

"No way, I feel great," he smiled.

"How's Luca doing?" Astrid asked. "I might go and see him."

"Well, his wound's infected, it seems," Ingrid said.

"Oh dear. In that case I'll call in to cheer him up. I hope it's not serious."

"Nasty infections from a weapon wound can make you lose your arm," Gerd said, more as though he were thinking aloud than talking to the group.

"You're not helping," said Ingrid.

"Oh, sorry. It'll probably be nothing. They'll cure the infection and he'll get well."

"Let's hope so,"

The door burst open and Nilsa came in, looking flushed.

"Wow, someone's been running along the corridors," Gerd said.

"It shows, does it?"

"Yeah, a little."

"I ran over to tell you that the King nearly ordered poor Gatik to be beheaded. Luckily his brother Orten and Sven between them managed to persuade him not to. You should have heard his shouts. This time I didn't need to talk to the Royal Rangers, you could hear him from a league away. He called him incompetent and an idiot, brainless, and other choice compliments like that."

"This King of ours is a little bit temperamental," Viggo said.

"Two little bits," Ingrid added.

"It's not Gatik's fault that Eyra died," said Gerd.

"Yeah," Ingrid said, "but it happened under his command, so it's partly his fault. That's how the chain of command works. He's responsible for what his men do."

"And just let me remind you, one of them's a rotten apple," Viggo put in.

"Is that what you think?" Lasgol asked.

"It looks like it. If Eyra's death was no accident, then someone killed her."

"Let's go by stages," Astrid said. "Was it an accident or wasn't it?" She looked at Egil in search of a reply.

"As I see it, and basing my view on the situation, I'd say with almost total certainty that it wasn't an accident. Simply and clearly because it was too convenient for the interested party who's trying to keep their identity hidden."

"Deadly accidents tend not to be just bad luck when you end up with an arrow in your heart, or your throat slit," Viggo pointed out.

"If you put it that way... my goodness!" Nilsa said, looking horrified.

"Well, we're already beginning to clear a few things up," Ingrid said, looking at Egil for confirmation. "It looks as if it was no accident, and that someone murdered Eyra. I gather the arrow that killed her came from her own side. They were looking to stop her tongue."

"That's not completely clear," said Astrid.

"No?" Gerd asked in surprise.

"I'm afraid the arrow could have come from either side," Egil explained.

"And as it was a scrum, it's impossible to know which side," Viggo added.

"Yeah, there were people running and releasing everywhere," said Lasgol. "I didn't even realize she'd been hit until I heard her moan."

"But it couldn't have been someone from our side, surely?" Gerd asked, more in hope than in the expectation of an answer.

"We can't say for sure that the arrow wasn't one of ours," Viggo said.

"But if – apart from us – they were all either Specialists or the Royal Guard, how could it have been one of them?" Nilsa asked.

"Because there's a Dark One infiltrated among either the Specialists or the Royal Guard."

"Or both. Or the Royal Rangers," Viggo added. He was now

playing with his throwing dagger, flicking it up in the air and catching it as it fell.

Nilsa folded her arms and shook her head. "It can't be the Royal Rangers. I know them all, and they're all above reproach."

"We can't rule anyone out," Lasgol said. "We don't know how deeply they've been infiltrated."

Egil nodded. "Correct."

"Well then, let's start with the Specialists."

"That's something we could do," said Ingrid. "We know who was there, and we know quite a few of them personally."

"That's a good idea," Astrid agreed. "They're all in the castle. Some are in the infirmary, others in the Tower resting, like us."

"I think it's a good idea to keep an eye on them, but they mustn't notice the fact," said Egil. "If whoever it was realizes we're looking for him, almost certainly they won't contact their leader."

"And that's what we want, so that we can catch him," Viggo added.

"And suppose he's not one of our side?" Astrid asked. "And suppose the arrow came from theirs?"

"In that case things get a lot more complicated," said Egil, "because whoever did it might already be dead."

"The ones who survived are in the royal dungeons," said Ingrid.

"We might try and talk with them," Lasgol suggested. "See what information we could get."

"I fear the Royal Guard wouldn't let us near them," Ingrid pointed out.

"It's Orten, the King's brother, who's going to be in charge of the interrogation," Nilsa said, looking appalled. "They say he loves that sort of job."

"You mean he'll use blows and yells to get the information out of someone?" Viggo asked ironically.

"Yeah, but I'd rather not go into details."

Viggo shrugged.

"Could you get anywhere near the prisoners?" Astrid asked Nilsa.

"Hmm, yes, they might let me. They know me all over the castle. I could try,"

"Then Nilsa can try to get information out of the prisoners," said Ingrid, "and we'll keep an eye on the Specialists and the Royal Guard."

"That sounds a good idea," said Lasgol.

"Egil, what do you think?" Astrid asked.

"That we need to keep an eye on them, and try to find out who killed Eyra."

"I can't believe she's dead," Nilsa said. Tears came to her eyes.

"You're shedding tears for her?" Ingrid said in surprise. "But she was a traitor who wanted to kill Dolbarar and was the second-in-command of the Dark Rangers."

"No... well... it's not just because of that, it's because of everything." She wiped away a tear from her cheek. "It's because of Gondabar and Dolbarar..."

"Because they've lost their positions as leaders?"

"Yeah... it's got through to me. Especially Gondabar. He's someone I value a lot. He's someone who's given everything for the Rangers. He worked day and night, non-stop. I know because I was with him, helping him. He was completely devoted to our cause, body and soul. He deserved better than to be dismissed like that..." Tears came back into her eyes.

"Well, and what do you say about poor Dolbarar?" said Gerd. "If there was anyone who didn't deserve to lose his position, it was him. There was no-one more devoted to the Camp than him, to making sure that the Rangers were properly trained and followed the Path."

"He was a great man, and we all owe him a lot," Lasgol said.

Egil nodded. "Some of us even our own lives."

"Yeah, that got to me too," Viggo admitted.

Ingrid stared at him in disbelief. "You?"

"Yeah, I've got my little bit of a heart too, you know."

"You? Since when?"

He shrugged. "Lately?"

"Dolbarar's an exceptional man," Astrid said, "and what the King's done, even though it's understandable, is hateful."

"Understandable?" Nilsa repeated.

"Eyra tricked him, and she was working for the Dark Rangers for years without Dolbarar knowing or suspecting anything."

"That wasn't his fault," Nilsa said defensively.

"But it was his responsibility," Ingrid insisted. "He should have found out, so as far as that's concerned we can't say Thoran was wrong."

"By that logic," Viggo said, "it's Gondabar's fault too. He's the one who's ultimately responsible for the Rangers, and so we can't blame Thoran for having dismissed him."

"That's true," Astrid admitted.

"If we're looking for culprits, or the people responsible for what happened, it's true that Dolbarar, and ultimately Gondabar, are the ones who have to answer to the King," Lasgol said sadly. "But I don't think that's what we ought to do. We need to analyze why it's happened and understand it so that it never happens again."

Egil nodded. "From a logical, rational point of view, that's a good approach."

"Yeah, just as Thoran's perfectly logical and rational," Viggo grumbled.

"Besides," Gerd pointed out, "he hasn't even taken into account all the good both Dolbarar and Gondabar have done over the years. All the good they've done for the Rangers and Norghana itself adds up to a thousand times more than that one mistake of not having seen what was happening with the Dark Rangers. At least I see it that way."

"Me too," said Nilsa. "They've both done so much for the Rangers, they deserve a lot better than to be judged for this, without all the good they've done before being taken into account."

"Well, I think Thoran did take it into account, in his own way," said Viggo.

"Why do you say that?" Ingrid asked in puzzlement.

"Because being Thoran, he'd have beheaded them or hanged them if it hadn't been for their past careers. In fact he's allowed them to stay in the Rangers, he's only demoted them, not even expelled them."

"And you think that's okay?"

"No, I don't think it's okay, but I'm saying that Thoran, considering what he's like, has been quite restrained in his punishment."

"That's because the King, though he's temperamental and prone to bouts of wrath, is no fool," Egil pointed out. "Very much the opposite. He knows Dolbarar and Gondabar are valuable men for the corps, and that's why he's keeping them on. Dead, they're no use to him. Alive, they'll help the Rangers as much as they can, and they're loyal to the core, so they pose no threat to him. In fact it benefits him to have them working for him."

Astrid nodded. "Yes, that makes sense."

"Well, he could recognize their courage and merit instead of treating them like failures," Nilsa objected.

Egil smiled. "That's a lot to ask for."

"You'll never see that in this lifetime," Viggo said.

"I don't think the King recognizes their value," Lasgol said, "when what he wants is to punish them to set an example."

Nilsa got up. "Well, I must leave you. Gatik's waiting for me. I have to prepare the King's journey, and his brother's."

"What journey is this?" Lasgol asked, intrigued.

"Well, Duke Orten and King Thoran are going away and I have to prepare everything, and you can't imagine the pressure I'm under, because if I make the slightest mistake – well, you know what they're like, those two."

Astrid gave an ironic grimace. "Yeah, the two little angels, they ought to be called."

Lasgol chuckled. "You can say that again."

"Where are they going?" asked Egil.

"The Duke's going to his fortress in the south. He says he's fed up with having to put up with so many court weaklings in the capital. He wants to go south to hunt Masig."

"What a monster," Ingrid said angrily. "The Masig are people like us. They may live a nomadic existence and have a different skin-color to ours, but that doesn't make them any less than us. They're still people, and as such they ought to be respected by everyone."

"According to Orten," Nilsa said, "they're wild animals that need to be domesticated. He often says it."

"He's the one who's the savage animal," Astrid said. "We ought to castrate him to stop him reproducing."

Viggo smiled. "That's a great idea. Add his brother to the list. Norghana'll be deeply grateful to you."

"Well, speaking of Thoran, offspring and the future of Norghana, Thoran's leaving the same day as his brother, for Count Volgren's castle. He's the most powerful noble in the court – after Orten, of course. The Royal Guards have told me there's a rumor in the court that Thoran's going to marry Ulrika Volgren, the Count's younger sister, and so ensure his power in Norghana, with Volgren as his family."

"That's a solid strategy," Egil said. "Power in kingdoms is

strengthened by marriages that unite powerful families, as in this case. Count Volgren has the second-largest county in the realm after Orten's, and he's the most powerful noble in the East."

"Well, with this wedding, Thoran would secure his throne," Lasgol commented.

"That is, if she says yes to that brute Thoran," Gerd pointed out. "Which I presume she won't."

"You're very naïve," Viggo told him.

"Me? Why?"

"That kind of marriage is usually arranged between families," Egil explained. "Between Volgren and Thoran in this case. Ulrika won't have any say in the matter, or at least they won't let her have any. It's politics."

"That's horrible!" Astrid cried.

Gerd shook his head. "That's very bad."

Viggo shrugged. "That's how arranged marriages work. It's not for love, but for power. In fact I don't think there's any love in this whole business."

"As I said, it's politics," Egil said. "A convenient alliance, sealed with an imposed marriage."

"It's an abominable practice which ought to be abolished," Ingrid said angrily.

"You're absolutely right," Astrid agreed, and the others nodded.

"Well, look on the bright side," Viggo pointed out. "If Thoran and Orten leave the capital, the city'll be nice and quiet."

"That's very true," said Nilsa. "I'll be able to rest a little."

"When do they leave?" Lasgol asked.

"In two days."

"I have to go too," said Egil, and they all looked at him in surprise.

"Go? Where?" Lasgol asked.

"I have an appointment I mustn't miss. I have to leave today."

"We'll go with you," Ingrid said.

"No, for this mission all I need is a bodyguard."

"Only one?" Lasgol asked him in concern.

"Yup, it's all planned. Don't worry."

"And does it have to be right now?" Astrid asked him. "We're in the middle of a very complicated situation..."

"I'm afraid it has to be now. It's one of the plans I set in action, and I have to finish what I began. It can't wait, I assure you."

"We believe you," Lasgol told him. "It's just that you ought to have protection on the way. They're trying to kill you, in case you'd forgotten... and Eyra's arranged for an Assassin to kill you."

Egil smiled. "No, I hadn't forgotten. In fact, it has to do with that. I'll take Gerd with me, if he agrees."

"Me?" Gerd asked in surprise.

"Yeah, big guy, you."

"But you've got Ingrid or Viggo..."

"True, but I'd rather it was you who came on this mission."

Ingrid and Viggo exchanged looks of puzzlement. "Are you sure?" they both asked.

"Yeah, sure," Egil said confidently.

"Oh, okay then," Gerd said.

"Good. Well then, off we go."

He and Gerd left the room, before the incredulous eyes of their friends. They were baffled. Where was he going? What did he intend to do? Why was he taking Gerd? Unfortunately they were not going to get answers to those questions.

Chapter 31

Egil arrived at the meeting-point at midnight, just as he had said he would in his message to Count Malason. He went to the middle of the clearing and watched the moon, partially covered by clouds on an autumn evening which was threatening a storm. It looked as though the sky was a premonition of what was about to happen. The evening was cool, and would soon turn cold. The storm was already hanging low over the plain and the two nearby woods: one of oak to the north, another of beech to the east.

His horse nickered restlessly, and Egil had to give him a few affectionate pats to relax him. It seemed that the animal too had a premonition of trouble. Everything about that evening looked ominous, and he knew his fears were going to come true. In fact he was expecting them to. He was not someone who allowed himself to be influenced by superstitions and bad omens: far from it. He believed in thinking long, hard and carefully, still more in planning, and then in reasoning to the very last detail. That way all sorts of unpleasant surprises could be avoided. Not all of them, because predicting everything that could go wrong in a complicated situation was practically impossible. All the same, the better prepared you were, the better your chances of coming out victorious. Even when something went awry, being prepared for many possibilities – even if it turned out not to be one of those – was a great help.

He breathed out heavily and tried to calm himself. He was rather worried. He had planned this meeting over a long time. The situation was complex, but he had turned it over in his mind a thousand times, considering every little thing that might go wrong and how to counter it. In the end he had decided to take the risk and carry out the plan. It was a calculated risk, he knew, but still a risk, when all was said and done. And a massive one. He could lose his life that night.

When he breathed in the cold air his lungs were filled with the smell of autumn in the Norghanian countryside, and he felt a little better. That risk, he reminded himself, was always present when he carried out one of those plans which centered on himself. Several parties had an interest in seeing him dead, and he was very much aware of the fact. For a long time he had believed that this interest was limited to King Thoran and the Eastern nobles. That was to be expected. By blood, he was the heir to the crown and considered by the West to be their legitimate King. Hence the court in the capital – which consisted mainly of Eastern nobles, together with King Thoran and his brother Orten – were against him. From there to wanting his death was only a single step.

He had been careful not to give them any reason to go after him. His work in the Camp had given him a perfect cover. There he was safe, among Rangers, where an attempt on his life would be difficult. Not impossible, but definitely difficult. At the same time, having access to the Camp communications had enabled him to keep very much up to date with everything that was going on, and to communicate with his allies secretly. This was crucially important, because without the support of his friends, and his Western allies, his chances of staying alive were limited. In fact they were minimal. That was why he had not left the Camp until Dolbarar's situation had become terminal. At that moment he had felt obliged to do so in order to save his life. Otherwise he would never have left a place where he enjoyed a certain amount of protection. He was very much aware that setting foot outside the Camp had put a target in the middle of his back. He was also conscious of the fact that the archers had been warned.

He huddled in his Ranger cloak. His hood was down, so that his face could be clearly seen. It was time to take a few risks. He scanned the surroundings with narrowed eyes, but could see nobody. He listened intently, but could hear nothing. It was time. Where was Malason? Was treachery lurking? A shiver ran down his spine. Had he made a mistake in his calculations?

Suddenly he heard hooves on the moist ground. He concentrated, seeking to establish where they were coming from. An Assassin sent to kill him? Or Malason himself? Doubt made him begin to tense. A rider appeared, coming into the clearing from the west. Egil held his ground and did not let the fear which was rising from his stomach take possession of him.

The rider came toward him, slowly. He made no sudden or aggressive movement, but stopped in front of Egil and nodded to him.

"My lord Egil, legitimate King of the West," he said respectfully, and drew back his hood.

It was Count Malason.

Egil returned the greeting with another nod. "Count."

They stared at one another for a moment, as if waiting for the other to make the first movement. In the end it was Malason who took the first step.

"I've come to this meeting as you requested, my lord."

"I was hoping you would," Egil replied with a certain satisfaction in his voice.

"If you'll forgive me, isn't this a rather strange meeting?" the Count said. He was looking around, where darkness was all there was to be seen.

"So it is. Have you come alone, as I asked you to?" Egil had narrowed his eyes and was looking past Malason's back in case some other rider should appear in the west.

"Yes, my lord. I've come alone as you told me to."

"Did my request surprise you?"

"Greatly, my lord. A meeting alone, in the middle of the night, isn't a thing which happens often, and it generally brings bad news with it."

"Indeed. I'm afraid this meeting is one of those."

The Count's face hardened. "What's going on? Why are we meeting like this?"

"Well now, you see, someone's tried to kill me several times. Luckily they haven't succeeded – so far, that is."

"I'm sorry to hear that, sir. I'm glad you're still alive. Yours is the future of the West and of Norghana."

Egil nodded. "As a result I began to look into who was behind the attempts, and my inquiries led me to a guild of Zangrian assassins."

"Foreigners?"

"Paid by someone from here, from the West."

"Oh..."

"I got hold of the name of the person who arranged the contract for my head with the guild. And hence this meeting."

"I don't understand, my lord... do you need my help to catch this person?"

"The name I obtained in Zangria is yours, Malason," Egil accused him, coldly and with a lethal stare.

The Count shook his head. "Mine? No, that's impossible."

"I'm afraid so."

"I don't know how my name has reached Zangria, but I can assure you I had nothing to do with this unpleasant business." Malason was waving his hands in denial.

"It was your name. I saw it with my own eyes in the Guild accountant's books."

Malason rose in his stirrups. "I swear, my lord, that I would never betray you. I'm loyal to you and to the West. I never arranged any contract for your life."

"So I thought... that you were faithful to me... but the evidence..."

"My lord" – now there was a mixture of disbelief and fear in Malason's voice – "you know me. I would never betray you."

"Never is a long time... and loyalties change..."

"Not mine! I swear it, on my honor!"

"That's a great disappointment," Egil said, shaking his head.

"Just think about it, if I were the traitor which it seems the evidence says I am, I'd have sent an assassin to this night meeting."

Egil bowed his head. "Very probably you would."

"And yet I didn't. I came here in person, as you requested."

"To find out how much I know about your treason?"

"No, of course not. Even at this moment – consider this – I have you alone with me. I could kill you. I'm better with the sword than you are. Even though you were trained by the Rangers, you wouldn't beat me..."

"I know."

"And so? I don't understand, sir..."

"I never believed you were the traitor."

"You didn't?" Malason's expression turned to one of astonishment.

Egil shook his head. "Too convenient."

"Convenient? I don't understand, my lord. You had to get the information from a guild of Zangrian assassins. That doesn't exactly sound very convenient to me."

"That's right. Getting the information was very difficult. Nevertheless, the fact that I found it was very convenient."

"Convenient for whom?"

"And that is the question."

"You're losing me, my lord," Malason said. He looked as though he had no idea what Egil was hinting at and where he was going with this.

"You and I are related."

"Yes... we're cousins."

"And if I die, who inherits the Western crown?"

Malason narrowed his eyes and seemed finally to understand. He nodded heavily.

"If you were to die, the next in blood with a right to the crown would be me."

"Now are you beginning to understand the strategy?"

"Yes and no. It's obvious that if you were to fall dead, everybody would turn their eyes on me. I wouldn't get away with being the traitor which – I repeat – I am not."

"Not necessarily. Not if it were done so that it appeared the East was responsible."

"Thoran?"

"Or the Eastern nobles."

"Yes... in that case nothing is gained for the West. I don't want the crown. I've never wanted it. I only want what's best for the West and for Norghana."

"Are you sure?"

"Yes, absolutely sure," Malason said with complete conviction.

"But if there's no longer a leader in the West, someone has to take on that role."

"Oh... I see... they'd force me to go on with the fight... they'd force me to take on your position of leadership..."

"That's right."

"I understand."

"Not entirely."

"No?"

Egil shook his head. "You would never be King of the West."

"Betrayal?"

Egil nodded. "The same as the one I'm involved in myself. The plot isn't only to get rid of me, but also of you. They're looking to kill both of us."

"Me? But why? I don't want the throne, I've told you that. My loyalty is to the West, but I don't want to rule."

"If I were to die, who's your only blood relative?"

"Direct blood relative?"

Egil nodded.

"My cousin, Count Olmossen."

"If I die tonight and you die, who inherits the throne of the West – and could even claim that of all Norghana later on?"

Malason was shaking his head. "Olmossen..."

"The plot is his. You and I must die so that it can work. In all probability making it pass as a treacherous action on Thoran's part, so that the West retaliates."

Malason was trying to take in what Egil had just told him, with his gaze lost in the distance. He swallowed.

"He was at my castle."

"I know. Astrid and Lasgol told me about it."

"I have nothing to do with all this," Malason assured him.

"That's what I wanted to find out. Whether this was only Olmossen's work, or whether you were involved too."

Malason nodded. "And hence this nocturnal meeting. To see whether I too had betrayed you and joined forces with Olmossen."

"Exactly. If you sent assassins, I would know you'd betrayed me. If you came alone and without an escort, it would mean that you were loyal to me."

Malason nodded repeatedly. Now he understood.

"I will never betray you," he said.

"It gladdens my soul to hear that," Egil said with a smile, and offered him his hand.

Malason looked into his eyes and shook his hand forcefully.

A new rider appeared, coming out of the wood to the north. Egil and Malason watched him approach. When he was near enough for them to identify him, they realized who it was.

"Olmossen," Egil said. He had recognized him.

Chapter 32

"Well, how strange to meet you two here in the middle of the night," Count Olmossen said with marked irony.

Malason frowned. "We could say the same to you."

"I feel a little rejected. I'd have liked to have been invited to this meeting between friends."

Egil raised one eyebrow. "Can we count you as one of our friends?"

"You'll have to decide that."

"I'd like it to be true," Egil said. "I've never wanted anything other than to see the Western nobles stay united, but I don't think you're our friend."

"You've found out the game, have you?" Olmossen said. His smile was sarcastic.

"I'd say I have," Egil replied with a shrug, almost as if he were sorry to have found out the Count's plans for betrayal.

"Very smart, Egil," Olmossen said. "You've always been that, I have to admit."

"Thank you."

Malason frowned. "You don't deny it?"

"No. I don't deny it. Don't get angry, cousin. It doesn't suit you, you turn very serious and look outraged."

"You're a traitor!" Malason accused him.

"Yes, it's time to change some things here in the West. In case you haven't noticed, things aren't going too well for us."

"That's not the way to change things!" Malason spat out. "It's just a filthy betrayal!"

Count Olmossen raised a hand. "Don't get upset, cousin."

From the wood to the north appeared fifteen or so riders. They were big and strong, armed with double axes. They were a frightening sight.

"I've invited some friends to the meeting," Olmossen said with a triumphant smile.

"You filthy traitor!" Malason shouted at him. He drew his sword.

"Don't try anything stupid."

"Don't," Egil said to Malason, who was looking at him as though waiting for the order to attack. "There are too many of them. We have no choice."

"That's what happens when you meet alone at night," Olmossen said. "It's dangerous, particularly in these turbulent times for the West."

The riders reached them, and Malason recognized one of them. "Osvald! What are you doing with them? You've sold me out!"

Osvald 'the whip' smiled from ear to ear. "Surprise. You weren't expecting this, eh?"

"Why did you do it? You've lived in my castle, eaten my food. I've treated you as one of the household, one of my family!"

"You've always treated me as if I were less than you and your own people! You only gave me cast-offs, the way you would have to a hungry flea-ridden dog!"

"I took you in when you had nothing. I gave you work to do, a position."

"Position? You put me in charge of the mines! You put me to work! Me, your own blood!"

"You're not my blood. I took you in when your parents died because our families were distantly related. I took pity on you. I didn't have to do it. And this is how you repay me?"

"Yes, this is how I repay you. You should have treated me with the respect I deserve. You should have given me title and position, as if I were your own blood."

"I repeat, you're not my blood. We're distant relatives. I owe you nothing."

There was hatred in Osvald's eyes. "That may be the way you see it, but I don't. And for that you'll pay."

"Well, now we know who told you about our little meeting," Egil said to Olmossen.

"That's right. Nothing like having a spy in the right place, at the right time."

Malason turned to Osvald in disbelief. "You spied on me?"

"Of course. I've been spying on you for him for a long time." Osvald laughed. "I copied the message about this meeting and sent it to him."

"You treacherous swine. After everything I've done for you!"

"You've never done anything for me!"

Malason indicated Olmossen. "And he will?"

"Of course I will," Olmossen said. "He'll have your title and positions." He gave a malicious smile.

At that moment Malason realized the scale of the betrayal. They were going to kill him, and everything he had would pass to Osvald. And Osvald would take his place, serving Olmossen.

"You swine!"

Osvald burst out laughing. "The very noble – and blind – Count Malason."

"It's time the West had a new King," Olmossen said. "One who will sit on the Western throne. To be more precise, it's time I regained the crown of the East."

"You'll pay for this," Malason said.

"I doubt that very much," Olmossen replied. "Now, Egil, tell your escort to come forward."

"My escort?" Egil said, as if he had no idea what they were talking about.

Olmossen smiled at him. "You don't think I'm going to believe you came to meet Malason alone, do you?"

Egil sighed, and Malason looked at him in surprise.

"Come on!" Osvald urged him. He threatened him with his whip.

Egil looked at the fifteen enormous Norghanians, and knew that if they tried anything it would be the end for them. He raised his hand and waved.

Twenty paces behind him, a dim mass that looked like a boulder moved. A man stood up, armed with a bow.

It was Gerd.

"That's much better," said Olmossen.

"Drop that bow!" Osvald shouted.

Gerd hesitated for a moment. The riders drew their huge axes and prepared to attack.

"All right," Gerd said, and dropped his bow.

"Perfect," Olmossen said. "It seems my plan has worked perfectly."

"Don't forget it was thanks to me," Osvald told him.

"Don't worry, I won't forget." He pointed to Malason. "You'll have his lands and titles, just as I promised you."

"You heartless, gutless scum," Malason said.

"Your insults hurt me, cousin. But I'll get over it when I'm on the

Western throne."

"So it was you who put the contract on my head with the Zangrian guild of assassins?" Egil said.

"It certainly was me. There's no reason to hide it any longer. It was me, but passing myself off as my dear cousin Malason. It took some effort, but I managed to trick them. They accepted me as Malason."

Egil nodded. "So they did."

"I see you found out," Olmossen said. He sounded a little surprised.

"Yes. I went to Zangria, found the Guild of the Blue Snake, the guild of assassins. I found out that they were the ones who were after me."

"Well, that surprises and displeases me. I took a great deal of trouble to get the job done by professionals from outside the country, and it cost me a great deal of gold."

"And it cost me a lot to find out about it, gold and a great deal of time," Egil said.

"You must admit that it was a very good idea," Olmossen said, and smiled proudly.

"It certainly was," Egil admitted. "It threw me off the trail and made me waste a lot of time."

"And that's why you organized this nocturnal meeting, isn't it? You came to see whether Malason had betrayed you or not."

"Exactly, that was the plan. Now I know he wasn't the one who betrayed me."

"Good plan, Egil... except that I already knew about it and decided not to let slip this unique opportunity to kill two birds with one stone." He smiled ironically. "There are some situations one can't let pass, and this is certainly one of them."

"What I don't understand," said Egil, "is that in the clothes of one of the guild assassins we found an order on my head for a thousand Zangrian coins. Why pay the guild twice if they hadn't done the job yet? There was no need, they'd have gone on trying till they succeeded."

Olmossen laughed. "For someone so intelligent, there are things that escape you. It's natural enough, you don't have all the information. The conspiracy is far bigger than you imagine. Far bigger than this." He indicated Malason, Egil and himself. "It goes far beyond that. This conspiracy is going to change Norghana forever. The country will never be the same again."

Egil looked at him in surprise. "Wasn't it you who paid those thousand coins?"

Olmossen shook his head. "No, it wasn't me. Somebody else wanted your death. He didn't want to wait, and gave the Zangrian assassins an extra incentive."

"Who else would benefit from my death, if not you?"

"Oh, you don't see it, eh?"

"I see that you want to get rid of me and Malason so that you can be King of the West, then you'll go for the Norghanian crown."

"Well, you see... I'm not particularly greedy. I'm more intelligent than that. I only want half the kingdom. I only want the West. That's enough for me."

Egil did not believe this story. Olmossen wanted the whole of Norghana. If he was limiting himself to only half, to the West, it was for some other reason. But what? Then he saw it clearly. Half was enough for him, because he had made a deal for the other half with someone else.

"You have a partner in this. One who'll keep the East in the share-out."

"Bravo! You really are brilliant! It's wonderful to deal with enemies like you."

"I'm not your enemy," Egil reminded him.

"True, in actual fact you're my rival for the throne, and that makes you my enemy."

"I see you've decided to clear the path by eliminating the two who are ahead of you in order of succession."

"That's right. I'll get there far sooner, and as I'll blame the East for your deaths, I'll have the support of the League and the whole West. I'll mourn your loss deeply."

Egil nodded. He had guessed that part of the plan already.

"Who gets the East?"

Olmossen smiled maliciously. "Wouldn't you like to know? Eh?" He was enjoying his victory thoroughly.

"Yes, I would."

"The Boar will have the East."

"The Boar?" Egil was thoughtful for a moment. "So that means you'll both go against Thoran and Orten, because they'll never accept such a division of the realm, and I understand they're not the Boar, because they already have the crown of all Norghana."

"That's right. The regicide is already under way. Soon those two brainless brutes won't rule in Norghana any longer. It will be ours." His voice had a victorious ring to it.

"Are you going to make an attempt on the lives of the King and his brother?" Malason asked. "Are you out of your mind?"

"Far from it. We've been planning this for years and waiting for our chance, and finally it's come. Years of preparation, years of spying and waiting in secret without being found out while we pulled the strings until the plot could be set in motion. And that day has come. Thoran and Orten will die very shortly, and the kingdom will be ours."

Egil was surprised by all this. He had known that there was a conspiracy to kill him and take over the leadership of the West. What he had just heard had implications that were far wider and more serious. It was not only the throne of the West they plotting to gain but also Thoran's, that of all Norghana. That meant enormous audacity and daring.

"Not that I don't believe it's possible," he said, "but we've already had a civil war, and even then we didn't manage to defeat Thoran."

"No, we didn't succeed, but it brought us closer to our goal," Olmossen said confidently. "Now we'll deliver the final stroke and skewer the rotten hearts of those two ignorant bullies."

"If the Boar gets the West, what about the Bear?" Egil asked, trying to get more information out of him.

Olmossen opened his eyes wide. "I see you know something, though not the whole of it. The Bear already has what he wanted, and he'll help us get what we're after."

"A plot with three important players, a trio of thinking minds: that's not easy to carry through."

"You're right there. But to launch a coup like that in Norghana you need influential allies, well placed at court, allies with power. That's what your brother and the Western League never understood, and they paid for it. For a regicide, there's no need for an army. What's needed is a master-plan and some exceptional players. Which is what we have."

The mention of his brother, who had died defending the West, hurt Egil deeply, but he said nothing. In fact there was something in what Olmossen had said. To overthrow a King, strength was often not the best approach. Subtle treachery was a great deal more efficient. Thousands of soldiers could not achieve what poison or a dagger in the night could, if everything was properly planned.

"If the Bear already has what he wants, he won't need to help you any further."

"There's still one little thing he wants. A whim, a death, which I've promised him he'll have. A friend of yours, in fact." Olmossen winked at him.

"A friend of mine?" But before he had finished speaking, Egil knew who he meant.

"Lasgol Eklund."

"I'll kill that stupid, spoilt brat myself!" Osvald shouted.

"You know he's already taken. You can't kill him."

"I hope he suffers!" Osvald said. He was so enraged that saliva flew from his mouth as he spoke.

Olmossen realized that in his delight at having beaten Egil, he was giving away too much. "But we've already chatted enough in this little night-time meeting."

Egil made a final attempt before Olmossen refused to say any more. "Who are the Bear and the Boar?"

"You'd like to know, wouldn't you?"

"Yes."

"How do you even know they exist?"

"The coins with the seal of the Bear and the Boar."

"Ah, yes. The ones he hands over to the Dark Rangers and other collaborators. I told them it was clumsy of them, that they could be traced to their collaborators or even to themselves. But they paid no attention. They like their secret games with their little coins and dark organizations. Although I must admit it's worked very well. One of those coins, and you don't need to know who you're talking to or who the message is from. You simply trust it. It's efficient, and it allows identities to be kept secret."

"Yes, it's a system I haven't cracked yet," Egil said.

"Nor will you ever."

"You're not going to tell me who they are?"

Olmossen shook his head. "No. I've said enough. You'll die knowing you've been beaten at your own games of strategies and secrets. You'll go to the kingdom of the Ice Gods with this last one unsolved." He smiled. "I suppose that's what happens to a lot of players who lose the game, they don't know how they were beaten or why. Don't let it embitter your frozen eternity."

"I've no doubt that one day I'll go to the kingdom of the Ice Gods. Luckily it won't be tonight."

Olmossen threw his head back in astonishment.

"I'm not going to be merciful to either of you. You must understand that I can't let you live. You know too much, and I don't need any inconveniences on my route to crowning myself King of the West." The Count looked aside confidently at his dozen warriors, who were waiting ready to kill them.

"I'd already guessed that. You can't leave us alive, now we know you're the traitor and part of a huge conspiracy. Unfortunately for you, your plans aren't going to succeed. You'll never be King of the West." Egil raised both arms and waved them.

"What the devil are you doing?" Olmossen asked him angrily.

Egil lowered his arms. "I'm signaling to some friends."

"There's nobody here."

"Not here perhaps, but in the beech wood over there."

Suddenly a hundred riders came out of the wood at a gallop. Everybody turned to stare at them. Olmossen opened his eyes wide in astonishment.

"Who are they?"

"They're the nobles of the Western League, with some of their men," Egil said. "I invited them to take part in this little night-time meeting."

"Yes!" Malason cried. By now he had lost all hope of getting out of there alive.

"No!" Olmossen said angrily. "How can this be possible? You didn't know I'd be here! You couldn't have known I was going to set this trap for you!"

Egil pretended to be surprised. "Oh, is that what this is? All this time I was under the impression it was my trap, not yours." He shrugged and smiled.

"Your trap? What do you mean, your trap?" Olmossen could not believe it. The riders were charging toward them, and they bore the banners of Dukes Erikson and Svensen.

"I've always known Malason was innocent. The message, this night-time meeting, using myself as bait, was just a trap to see who'd fall into it. I must say that it's worked wonderfully well, and I've trapped the person I thought I would."

"Nooo! You snake!"

"Have them killed!" Osvald shouted to him.

"That would prejudice your health considerably. I don't think my allies would spare your lives." Egil turned to the warriors. "But if you take these two traitors prisoner I'm sure nothing bad will happen to you, because you'll be doing the West a great service."

"No!" Osvald cried. He was staring at the warriors.

"Kill them!" Olmossen ordered his own men. As he did so, Gerd took his bow from the ground and nocked an arrow.

But there was no need for him to act. The warriors threatened Osvald and Olmossen with their axes and forced them to dismount. Osvald resisted, and one of the warriors launched a blow to his head with the flat of his axe which felled him and left him unconscious.

"I'm very grateful for your support," Egil said with a nod.

The Western soldiers arrived and surrounded them. "Dukes Svensen and Erikson," Egil said, and nodded in greeting.

"Is this rat the traitor?" Duke Erikson asked.

"That's right."

"Let me run him through with my sword," Duke Svensen begged.

Egil raised one hand. "No, I want him alive."

"We'll take care of him," Duke Erikson said.

"Take him somewhere safe and lock him up. Make it somewhere close to the capital. I need him nearby. There's still one last conversation I want him to have when the time comes. A very unpleasant one."

"And what do we do with the other one?"

"Hard labor in the mine for the rest of his life," Egil said.

"A very appropriate sentence," Malason said with a look of satisfaction.

"And now, sir?" Duke Svensen asked.

"Now, much to my regret, we have to stop this plot."

"Why stop it?" Count Malason said. "Let them take care of Thoran and Orten."

"There's nothing I'd like better, I can assure you, except that they'd get their wish. And we'd have another civil war, which at the moment we can't win. The West is still weak. We couldn't stand up to the forces of the East. They're better-manned and better-funded than us."

"Would they blame us for the regicide?" Malason asked.

"Certainly. It was planned to happen that way. They'll kill the King and his brother and then blame us. The Eastern nobles will try to make us pay with everything we have, and their new leaders, whoever they are, will come for us. It'll be a massacre. They'll destroy us, and the West would suffer anew, even more so than during the civil war. I can't allow it. I have to stop it."

"What can we do?" Duke Erikson asked.

"For the moment, nothing. Wait for my news. I'll get in touch with you. Remember, I'll send white owls."

"We'll remember," both Dukes said.

"Right," said Egil. "It's time to stop this conspiracy and unmask the other two leaders, the Boar and the Bear."

Gerd came to his side. "Before we go back, I'd like to ask you something."

"Ask away, big guy."

"Why did you choose me out of the whole team for this mission?" he asked. He was still in awe at having been chosen.

Egil smiled at him. "Because out of all of them, you're the only one who wouldn't have questioned this. I needed you to act as bait, which they'd have been against."

"Oh... I hadn't thought of that... it's not that I wouldn't question you, it's just that I believe in your intelligence."

"I know that, and you have my most heartfelt thanks."

"In other words I'm the one who gives you the least trouble, and that's why you want me at your side."

Egil winked at him. "Irrefutable, my dear friend."

Gerd beamed. "Maybe it's time I started questioning your plans."

Egil shook his head.

"Better not," he said, and gave him another wink.

Chapter 33

It was already mid-afternoon when Egil came into the room in the Rangers' Tower which the Panthers were sharing. With him was Gerd, still in his role as bodyguard. He found Ingrid and Lasgol looking after their bows. Astrid was playing with Ona, rolling on the floor in a panther-fight amid growls, human as well as animal. Camu was chasing Viggo, who was leaping from bed to bed trying to escape the little fiend, who was anxious to lick his face.

"Egil! Gerd! You're back!" Lasgol said delightedly.

"Hey, it's good to see you!" Astrid called, and ran to hug them.

Gerd beamed. "Even better for me!"

"Did you get into any trouble?" Viggo asked.

"None as big as the ones you get mixed up with."

"Hey! That's a good answer!" Ingrid said.

"Come in, sit down and tell us what you've been up to," Lasgol demanded impatiently.

Before they could sit down, the door burst open and Nilsa came in breathlessly.

"It's you! I thought it was you!"

"Yeah, did you see us arriving?" Gerd asked.

"From one of the upper windows of the tower. I went down at top speed, then tripped on the stairs from the excitement and nearly cracked my head open. Luckily I fell on top of two Specialists, and they cushioned the fall."

Viggo smiled. "That was a bit of luck for them."

"It's an honor for them to be able to help a comrade," Ingrid pointed out.

"Yeah, I'm not denying it..."

"Well, one of them invited me for a beer... to take the scare away, of course..."

Astrid laughed. "Hah! Yeah, of course, that would be exactly why."

Nilsa, who already knew what it had been to try and make a conquest of her, blushed. Her friendliness, her lovely red hair and the freckles that adorned her face seemed to have bewitched quite a few men at the Royal Castle, whether soldiers, Guards or Rangers. It was something which delighted her, and it entertained her greatly. Being made a fuss of was always a delight for the soul. She came in and shut the door.

"Tell us everything, Egil," she said, almost pleading. "I'm dying to know what you've been doing. I'm sure it was really exciting!"

Gerd was nodding emphatically. "Oh, it was certainly that."

Viggo raised one eyebrow and stared at him mysteriously. "And were there any surprises?"

"You bet there were."

"Tell us, Egil," Lasgol encouraged him.

"Before I do, I'd be glad to know what you've been able to find out about Eyra's death."

Ingrid encouraged Nilsa with a gesture, and she nodded. "I tried to get some information from the prisoners. It was a complicated business getting to them. Orten didn't want anybody to talk to them, and I had to persuade a couple of Royal Guards to let me get anywhere near."

"And they let you?" Gerd said in surprise.

"My first attempts didn't go well. They refused to let me into the Royal Dungeons, even though I asked two guards I know fairly well. The trouble is that they're afraid of what Orten might do to them afterwards."

"They're more afraid of him than they are fond of you," Viggo said with a smile.

"Oh, certainly."

"How did you manage to persuade them?" Gerd asked.

"I waited until Sveinn and Lars were on duty, because they're not exactly the brightest... I went up to them and told them I had orders from Gatik to make a recount of the prisoners and see how many had died."

"And they swallowed it?"

"That's right. I knew a couple of prisoners had died from the wounds they got during the fight, and also from Orten's horrible interrogation, so that gave me the idea."

"Very good thinking," Egil said appreciatively.

"So I went down to the dungeons and tried to speak with the prisoners. That was even harder. Of course none of them wanted to speak with me, I'm the enemy. And also some of them were terrified of the fate that was in store for them."

"Thoran will hang them all, as soon as his brother's finished his interrogation," Viggo said grimly.

"Orten had already finished. They look terrible. I think they've all talked, but I don't think they knew too much, The King'll pass judgment as soon as he comes back from his visit to Count Volgren."

"In that case they'll live a few days longer," Viggo said.

"So I concentrated on the ones who were terrified," Nilsa went on. "I could see the fear in their eyes. I thought they were the ones who'd give me a chance, and I wasn't wrong. I managed to make two of them talk to me. I promised to help them get out of there alive if they told me everything they knew. In the end, and because their situation was so utterly desperate, they talked."

Egil was listening with great interest. "What did they tell you?"

"From what they told me, and what I was able to guess, the arrow that killed Eyra didn't come from their side. They had orders from the Leader of the Dark Rangers to protect her at all times. She was the second-in-command. They confirmed that. Her escape had been planned so that she could go on working in the shadows. But Gurkog's too good, and he managed to follow her trail and find their camp."

"That's right, Gurkog has shown his quality," Egil agreed.

"Is he better yet?" Gerd asked.

"No, not yet" Ingrid said. "The wound was a serious one, but he'll recover. The surgeons say in eight weeks' time he'll be as good as new."

"I'll go and see him in the infirmary," Gerd said.

"That must mean the Dark Ones had orders to protect Eyra, not to kill her," Egil said thoughtfully.

"That's right. I asked them whether if they were surrounded, they had orders to make sure she didn't survive, and they said no. They didn't have orders to kill her under any circumstances."

"Did their explanations seem truthful to you?" Egil asked.

Nilsa nodded repeatedly. "Yeah, they were terrified. They'd been through Orten's hands, and their bodies were covered in cuts and bruises."

"Did he torture them to make them talk?"

"Yeah..." Nilsa said, shaking her head.

"That's cowardly," Ingrid muttered.

"You can't torture prisoners," Lasgol said. "There ought to be a code against it."

Nilsa nodded. "I'm afraid there isn't, and it's common practice."

"I think it's appalling, a totally unscrupulous thing to do," said Gerd.

"It certainly is," Astrid agreed. "Those Dark Rangers lost the battle and were captured. They don't deserve that. Let them be judged for their crimes, but don't lay a hand on them."

"Torture shows how black and rotten the hearts of violent, unscrupulous men are," Egil said bitterly. "It's disgusting."

"I believe they told me the truth," Nilsa insisted.

"Good work," Egil told her, and she smiled at him gratefully.

"As for the Specialists and the Royal Rangers," Ingrid said, "we haven't had much luck. But we've found something out, something significant. Astrid and I have been talking to the Specialists, and also some of the Royal Rangers. In fact if you invite them for a couple of beers at the castle canteen they tell you their whole story, then their parents' and even their grandparents, especially the Royal Rangers."

"They were probably trying to get off with you..." Viggo said with a mischievous look on his face.

"Get off with us?"

"Flirt with the two of you. Really, do I really have to explain everything?" He looked unable to believe they did not understand.

"Oh, were they? Well, I didn't notice," said Ingrid, who in fact had not noticed anything.

"They were definitely trying to flirt with us, no doubt about that," Astrid said to Viggo.

"See? I knew it. That's why they talk to you so much. They don't even say good morning to me!"

Astrid winked at him. "Well, you're not exactly the nicest person in the castle."

"I am when you know me well," he said with a smile.

"Oh, sure," Ingrid said with a look of total disbelief on her face. "As I was saying, after speaking to the Specialists who took part in our mission, two of them, Thorir and Vidar, had seen something very significant. According to their version of the account, the arrow that killed Eyra didn't come from the Dark side. It came from ours."

"Wow!" Gerd exclaimed.

"Go on," said Egil.

"They swear blind that although they didn't see who released, because they were looking at you, trying to protect you from the Dark Ones, they saw the arrow fly past them."

"Where was it coming from?"

"That's the interesting point. They say it was coming from the group of Royal Rangers in the center."

"And what do the Royal Rangers say about that?" Gerd asked.

"They deny it," Astrid said with a grimace of disgust. "They insist that the arrow couldn't have come from them."

"And if you argue with them, they get pretty stupid," Ingrid added. "According to them, they never release just for the sake of it and that every arrow counts, so that none of them released anywhere even remotely near Eyra, especially when she was with several Rangers, which is to say all of you."

"D'you believe them?" Gerd asked.

Ingrid shrugged. "On the one hand, yes, I do. Because it's true that it would surprise me if one of them had released against Eyra when she was with other Rangers, and I also think they're very good, and they'd never make as big a miscalculation as that."

"They're the best among all of us," Astrid said. "I agree. I don't think an arrow went astray and accidentally killed Eyra. Particularly knowing Thoran wanted her alive."

"Not accidentally," Egil said.

"On purpose," Lasgol guessed.

"That's what I'm afraid of."

"Well then," Viggo said, "that means we have a traitor among the Royal Rangers."

"And a very skilled one," Lasgol added, "because he released against Eyra and his people didn't realize it."

"More than skilled, someone extremely good with a bow," said Ingrid. "Taking a shot like that means an exceptional Archer."

"As I said, they're the best," Astrid agreed.

"That seems hard to believe," Nilsa objected. "I know nearly all of them."

"Relax, it doesn't have to be one of your beaux," Viggo pointed out.

"I don't have beaux," she snapped back, and poked her tongue out at him.

"Well, one of your 'special friends'."

"Nor those either!"

Viggo smiled and let the subject drop.

"Nilsa, we've got to find out which of them it was," Egil said.

"In that case," Lasgol asked, "are we accepting the theory that the arrow came from our side, and that it was one of the Royal Rangers?" He was keen to make sure they all thought the same.

Nilsa was shaking her head. "I still think it can't be a Royal Ranger."

"You have no say in this, because your friendships put you in a compromising position," Viggo said.

Nilsa wrinkled her nose at him. "Yes, I do."

"I think that's where the clues are pointing," said Astrid. "It was one of the Royal Rangers."

Ingrid wrinkled her nose in disgust at the implications. "I think so too, even if it means we've got an infiltrator among them."

Egil was listening and nodding.

"Wow..." Gerd was shaking his head slowly.

"If it's one of them, and that's what it looks like," said Lasgol, "we have to find him and unmask him."

"That's going to be difficult," Ingrid pointed out. "We're not going to be able to get very close to them."

"And don't forget, we still don't know who's behind all this," Astrid said.

"It's as if he were right there, and we couldn't reach him," Ingrid complained.

"It's like putting your hand in the pond and trying to catch some trout with it," said Viggo.

"They get away, they're very slippery," said Nilsa.

"That reminds me..." Egil began, but then fell silent, as though he had suddenly had an idea.

"What is it?" Lasgol asked.

"Something you told me... about your vision..." His expression was that of someone who was just becoming aware of something very important.

Lasgol had no idea what his friend was talking about. "Yes...?"

Egil turned to the group. "Wait here, all of you. Lasgol, you and I are going to have a talk with someone."

"Who with?" Lasgol asked blankly.

"With the Leader of the Hunt."

They stared at him in puzzlement as he left the room, with Lasgol following him.

Chapter 34

Lasgol followed his friend through the castle courtyard. They were on their way to the royal kennels, which puzzled him. What was Egil after? Or rather, what did he mean to find out there?

The kennels were located at the back of the castle, at a distance and out of sight both because of the noise the dogs made, and because they were not considered a suitable sight for the court nobles. But it was also better for the dogs, who were quieter. They found several kennel-lads cleaning and feeding the animals.

"I'm looking for the Leader of the Hunt," Egil told one of the boys, who was feeding some magnificent Spitzes.

The boy waved toward the end of a long wooden shed. "Master Aren is at the back."

"Thank you," said Egil, and walked in determinedly.

Lasgol was waiting for his friend to explain what he was up to, but since Egil sometimes dived in head-first and only explained things afterwards, he went in after him expectantly. Inside the wooden structure were endless cages, where dogs of different breeds were resting. They all looked well-fed and cared-for. Lasgol was surprised that they did not bark at them, though they whimpered as he and Egil passed their cages.

Two men were looking after a female dog and a litter of puppies who were no more than a week old.

"Hunt Leader Aren?" Egil asked.

The two men turned to look at them. The elder of the two said: "That's me."

He must have been bordering eighty, his hair very short and white as snow. He was tall and strong-looking, with a snub nose in a face full of creases from the passage of time, and the strong hands of a working man. He now wiped these with a rag. A pair of sea-blue eyes looked them up and down. The other man with him was dark, thin, with bulging eyes. Lasgol put him at around seventy, perhaps a little less, though he was distinctly weather-beaten from an outdoor life.

"Good morning. We're Egil and Lasgol, Rangers."

"Aren and Igor. I'm the Leader of the Hunt, and he's my assistant and deputy in the hunt for half a century."

"Pleased to meet you," said Egil and offered them his hand as a friendly gesture. They all shook hands.

"Are you in need of a hound?" Aren asked. "As a rule the Rangers have their own dogs, but if you need one of mine I'll be very pleased to help you. I have dogs trained in big-game hunting of any species, from tigers and boars to bears and reindeer."

"Thanks, but we don't need animals," Egil said.

"I thought as much."

"We wanted to ask you a couple of questions."

"Questions? About hunting? Big-game hunting?"

"Exactly."

"Go ahead. I'll answer as best I can, but it's a complex art and it needs a lot of experience."

"It's not so much the techniques and knowledge of hunting. We'd like to ask you about the past."

"About the past? Well now, that's pretty unusual. Nobody's interested in speaking to a couple of old geezers like us about anything." He jabbed Igor with his elbow.

"Two old geezers like us are of no interest whatever to young people," Igor said with a chuckle.

"Except when there's a hunting party to be arranged for the King," said Aren, "then everybody listens to us and our word is law."

"Does Thoran still organize hunts?" Egil asked.

"Not as many as the late King Uthar, but yes, every now and then he organizes one."

"It's usually to impress the Eastern nobles," Igor explained. "King Thoran has a good spear arm, though his brother Orten is much better than he is with it."

"And with the axe," Aren added. "With the bow, on the other hand, neither of them is outstanding, particularly if you compare him with the Royal Rangers who usually go with him on the hunts."

"Have the Royal Rangers always gone with the Kings on the hunts?"

"Not so much in Uthar's time, but now they always do. They don't take part as such in the actual hunt, but they make sure there are no accidents, especially if the quarry they want to kill is a tiger or a bear. That can turn out very dangerous."

"Who did King Uthar go hunting with?"

"Well, he always went with the First Ranger and a few others."

"Dakon Eklund?"

"Yes, he was an amazing hunter. His skill at tracking, marksmanship and everything to do with the hunt and the forest was impressive. In fact... now that I look at you, lad... you have something of him."

"He was my father."

"Ah. Well now, that really is a surprise. I'm glad you're following in your father's footsteps. I'm sure you've inherited many of his amazing qualities."

Lasgol blushed. "I'm not so sure myself."

"Your father was a legendary hunter," Igor told him.

"I don't think I'll ever get to be like him."

"The apple doesn't fall far from the tree, just you wait," Aren said.

Lasgol smiled. "If only!"

"I can tell you, your father was a good person too. He always treated us very well. Not like certain self-important noblemen who take advantage of their position to mistreat those of us who are beneath them."

"I suppose there's a lot of that," said Egil, "especially when a number of noblemen get together for a hunt."

"And when they compete among themselves, even more so. The losers always blame us. The dogs were bad, or else we led them badly, or any other excuse that puts the blame on us rather than admitting they're bad hunters themselves."

"The Frozen Continent will melt before a noble admits he's a bad hunter," Igor said, and Egil and Lasgol both smiled.

"Your father was always good to us and looked after us. He always gave us something after every hunt and treated us with respect, which was really kind and much appreciated."

"Yeah, sometimes they treat us just like dogs," Igor added.

"My father was a good man," Lasgol said. He was touched by what they had said.

"He was that," Aren assured him.

"Who else did King Uthar go hunting with, besides Dakon?"

"Well, it depended on the occasion and the quarry to be killed," Aren explained. "If there were no noblemen involved and it was just an escapade to let the King amuse himself, and the prey was a tiger, for example, a couple of Royal Rangers would go with them just in case."

"And if the quarry was a boar?"

"In that case Commander Sven always went as well, though at the time he was only a captain. Dakon taught him to hunt, and he turned out to be very good with the spear, one of the best I've seen. A lot better than Orten, in fact."

"Well now, that's interesting. And suppose the quarry was a bear?"

"In that case Dakon always took Gatik. There's nobody better than Gatik at hunting bears, with traps as well as the bow, a real phenomenon at killing bears. Dakon taught him too, and soon he was as good as he was, or better."

"Very interesting," Egil said.

Lasgol was beginning to understand what was going on there and what Egil was trying to find out.

"Any other person that comes to mind if I say that the quarry is a bear or a boar?"

Both veteran hunters looked at one another and were thoughtful. Aren shook his head.

"No. If it's a question of hunting boar, Sven is the best. If it's bear, Gatik's your man. One with the spear and the other with the bow. There's nobody else at the Court who even comes close."

"Many thanks for the information. I think I know as much as I need to now. We'd better be on our way," Egil said a little curtly, as if he suddenly found himself in a hurry.

"Oh, all right. If there's anything else you want to know about hunting, you know where to find us."

"Thanks, we'll bear it in mind."

"It was a pleasure meeting you," Lasgol added.

"It was a pleasure to meet Dakon Eklund's son," Aren told him. "You follow in your father's footsteps, young man, and you'll go far."

"Be like him, and there are plenty who'll respect you and follow you," Igor advised him.

"I'll try," Lasgol promised.

Egil left the kennels at a rapid pace. Lasgol went beside him, trying not to lag behind. From his friend's expression he knew he was engaging the gears of his prodigious mind, and something was not going altogether well.

"Problems?" he asked.

"Yes, a number of them. We need to act urgently. We have to get everyone together and prepare a plan."

Lasgol wanted him to explain, but he was heading straight to the tower with a determined look in his eyes. He was not going to stop to talk.

"Fine," he said. He was trying to puzzle out what Egil had found out in the conversation and which had stirred that sense of urgency in him, but he would have to wait for his friend to explain.

They went into the Tower of the Rangers like a gust of wind. Luckily the veterans on watch duty at the door knew them well and did not halt them. Once they were in the room the Panthers shared, Egil went straight to the far end, as far as the stone wall, without saying a word to anyone. The Panthers, who were resting on their cots, stared at him in surprise. He turned and walked back to the door, where Lasgol, feeling uneasy, watched him shut it.

"Are you all right?" he asked.

Egil turned around again and walked back to the far end, looking straight ahead, his gaze lost, as if he were not really there.

"He's out of his mind," Viggo commented. "It was bound to happen sooner or later, just a matter of time."

"Don't be stupid, you dumbass. There's nothing wrong with him," Ingrid said, although her words did not sound very convincing. She was looking with concern at Egil as he paced back and forth.

"Something's up with him," said Astrid, who was also watching him in puzzlement.

Nilsa leapt to her feet and began to follow him in his comings and goings. "Egil? Are you okay?"

Egil said nothing. He went on walking with his gaze distant.

Ona and Camu too began to follow him, as if this were a game. For them it was, but seeing Egil in that state was not something to be taken lightly. Lasgol was beginning to feel worried.

Gerd was watching his friend with narrowed eyes. "He's thinking, working out the problem..."

"Irrefutable, my dear friend," Egil said suddenly, and stopped dead in the middle of the room.

Lasgol gave a snort of frustration. He was beginning to think that they would have to do something to get Egil out of that state. Nilsa, Camu and Ona stopped behind his friend. Nilsa looked firmly into his eyes and put her hands on his shoulders.

"Are you all right?"

"Yes, perfectly. At last it all makes sense."

"Well, it would be nice if you told the rest of us," Viggo said with his head to one side, as if he were still wondering whether Egil had lost his mind.

"I'm really intrigued," Astrid said. She looked at Lasgol, who shrugged because he had no idea of what Egil had found out, beyond what he had deduced from the conversation with Aren.

"Sit down, all of you. I have something very important to tell you."

As if they were back at the Camp listening to an instructor giving a lesson, they all sat down around Egil, who stayed standing in the center of the room. Ona and Camu meanwhile lay down at his feet.

"I'm going to start by telling you what happened on the mission Gerd and I went on. It's important that you listen without interrupting me, because I'm afraid we don't have much time."

"Okay," Ingrid said, "go ahead."

When he had finished the story of his nocturnal meeting with Count Malason and the outcome of the ambush, his friends could not hold back their comments.

"Wow!" Nilsa said. "Count Malason turns out to be innocent! I was sure he was the traitor!"

"He might have looked like the traitor, but that didn't make him one," Egil pointed out. "We mustn't jump to hasty conclusions."

"But it was his name we found in Zangria, at the guild of assassins. I took it for granted it was him."

"Yeah, so did I," said Gerd.

"I knew Egil was planning something," Astrid said, "and that's why I wasn't entirely convinced Malason was guilty. Otherwise, why send Lasgol and me to deliver the message?"

"So that Malason would know it was from me, and that it was something very important," said Egil.

"And so that whoever was spying would know as well," Lasgol guessed.

"That's right. The fact that I sent you personally was proof that whatever I wanted to discuss with Malason was something very important. Both for Malason and for whoever was spying on him."

"And Olmossen swallowed the bait," said Viggo.

"Right. Osvald realized that it must be something important and spied on Malason. He read the message with the details of place and time."

Ingrid wagged her finger at him. "You set yourself up as bait, and that's very dangerous. You shouldn't have done it."

"To get a very smart fish to bite, the bait has to be a very juicy one," Egil said with a smile.

Viggo smiled. "And you're the juiciest."

"Olmossen saw his chance to finish me off once and for all, and in addition, as a bonus, to finish off Malason too. He'd eliminate two enemies in the line of succession to the throne in one blow. A very easy one, because we'd be alone."

"Yeah, you made it really, really tempting," Viggo said,

"And he swallowed it hook, line and sinker," Astrid added admiringly.

"That was the plan, to get him out of the shadows and see his face."

"Did you already suspect him? Olmossen?" Lasgol asked.

"Not at first. He's a noble who plays on both sides, and he's known to be untrustworthy. But I didn't suspect him specifically, though on the other hand I knew it might be him, because he's the third in the line of succession to the throne after me and Malason."

"If he killed you both, his path to the throne would be clear," Astrid said.

"Not quite clear," Nilsa said. "There are Thoran and Orten too."

"That's true. To the throne of the West, then."

"I suppose he'd blame your deaths on either the King or the Eastern nobles," Viggo guessed.

"That's right. That was his plan."

Ingrid was beginning to understand the gamble. "The West would turn against the East, and Olmossen would become their new leader."

"That's it. Olmossen had been waiting for the chance to get rid of me, and also of Malason. I haven't the slightest doubt that our deaths would have been at the hand of a false assassin of the East."

Nilsa, completely carried away, got up and patted him on the back. "Except that you set a trap for him, and he fell headlong into it." She sat down again and applauded.

Egil shrugged. "It was a risky stratagem, but it bore fruit."

"And suppose it had been Malason?" Lasgol asked him.

"The result would have been much the same. I hadn't told the Count about the trap. He had no idea the other leaders of the Western League would be there."

"In that case, why did you take me with you?" Gerd asked.

"In case the leaders of the League betrayed me."

"Oh..."

"Irrefutable, my dear friend. You can't trust anybody, I repeat, anybody. Barring present company, of course."

Viggo was smiling at him. "I can see that with every day that goes by, you're getting to be more like me."

"Thanks, my friend," Egil replied, and gave him a respectful nod.

Ingrid wrinkled her nose. "That's not exactly an improvement."

"For some things it is," Viggo replied, and Egil nodded in agreement.

Astrid was still curious. "And who are Olmossen's two associates in this conspiracy?" she asked.

"Yeah, who's he allied himself with to overthrow King Thoran?" Ingrid asked.

There was a silence, and Egil looked at them as if expecting one of them to come up with the answer.

Nobody spoke.

Chapter 35

Lasgol stayed silent, though by now he had guessed the answer. He had done this as Egil was describing what he had found out during his meeting with Olmossen. He left Egil to reveal the secret.

"It's a complex conspiracy, and a very well-planned one," his friend began. "That's why it's taken me so long to find it out. The key was in the coins. That was something I already knew, but I couldn't find the connection."

"The coins of the Dark Rangers?" Nilsa asked.

"Yes. The ones with the shields of the Boar and the Bear. That was the key."

"Who are they?" Gerd said.

"I've only just found that out. The Leader of the Hunt had the key to it. The Boar is none other than Sven, the Commander of the Royal Guard."

"Sven? But he's Thoran's faithful hound!" Ingrid said.

"Not so faithful as all that," said Egil.

"He wants the crown?" Astrid asked incredulously.

"That's right."

"But he can't have it," said Ingrid. "He hasn't got an army to overthrow Thoran with, and he isn't of royal blood, he can't come to the throne."

"Correct in both points. He knows that, which is why he's allied himself with Olmossen and the Bear."

Nilsa had put her hands to her face in surprise. "Wow... the Commander..."

"Now that's something I wasn't expecting at all," Gerd said, looking impressed.

"Sven doesn't want the throne of Norghana," Egil began. "He knows he can't accede to it because he doesn't have royal blood –"

"– but on the other hand he wants the throne of the East if the country splits into two in another civil war," Viggo reasoned.

"Exactly. He can lead the nobles of the East and stay on as Regent, while Olmossen does the same with the West."

"He still doesn't have either an army or any support," Ingrid pointed out.

"That's where the Bear comes in," said Egil.

Nilsa was biting her nails. "I'm dying to know who he is."

"That makes two of us," Gerd put in.

"The Bear is Gatik, our revered First Ranger."

"No!" both Ingrid and Nilsa cried in disbelief. "That's impossible!"

Viggo was nodding. He had already guessed what was coming next. "And he's the Leader of the Dark Rangers," he said, more to himself than to the others.

They all turned to stare at him, and Astrid grimaced.

"Is he?"

Egil nodded heavily. "He is. Gatik's the one who leads the Dark Rangers. His goal is to get hold of the leadership of the Rangers, and with them Sven would have his own little army that he could use to lead the West with."

Gerd was shaking his head. "Gatik? It's just not possible. He's the First Ranger..."

"It makes absolute sense," said Viggo. "In fact he's already achieved his aim. He's the leader of the Rangers now."

"Are you sure of this, Egil?" Ingrid asked him. She was finding all this hard to accept.

"Yes, I am. I've been thinking about it and analyzing it, and it all fits together. Olmossen wouldn't be able to achieve his goal of ruling over the West without help. Sven and Gatik couldn't reach their goals by themselves, so they joined forces."

"Sven and Gatik have known each other since they were young," Lasgol said. "I've seen it in the visions my mother's pendant showed. They could have been planning this for years."

"And Count Olmossen has always been playing at being sympathetic to both East and West," Egil said, "which means he's had contacts not only with King Thoran, but very probably with Sven too."

Nilsa put her hands to her head. "What an incredibly complicated plot!"

"The whole thing's very complicated," Gerd said, shaking his head.

"There's one item more that corroborates it. While we were transporting Eyra, I had the opportunity to enjoy a friendly chat with

Musker Isterton."

Gerd gave him a questioning look. "Friendly? Or did you bring out Ginger and Fred?"

Egil shrugged and looked apologetic. "The latter..."

"Egil!" You told me you'd behave!"

"The opportunity presented itself, and it was necessary... They didn't bite or sting him, if that puts your mind at rest," he added as an excuse.

"Sure, as if that would be enough. Poor Musker, he must have had a heart attack."

"Almost, but not quite. He just got a little cross."

"Yeah... a little, he says..." Gerd grumbled, not sounding at all happy.

"In fact I got the name of the person who'd ordered him to spy on me."

"Sven or Gatik?" Ingrid asked.

"No, if it had been either of them I'd have been on their heels by now, but unfortunately the one keeping his eyes on me is Orten."

"The King's brother? Why?"

"He wants to know whether I'm planning some action against his brother."

Viggo smiled sourly. "It looks as though you attract a lot of attention."

"It's the burden I carry for bearing the name of my family."

"And how does that confirm the conspiracy?" asked Ingrid, who did not understand.

"Because the other possibility, the most obvious one, is that it was the King who wanted me dead. For the moment, at least, that's not so. He just keeps an eye on me, or to be more precise his brother does. Musker had the order to report any movements of mine that involve the West. He didn't have any order to kill me."

"My mind's going to burst," said Nilsa.

"It's easy enough to understand," Astrid said. "Deduction by elimination. If one of them doesn't want to kill you, then by default it has to be the other one. In other words, if it's not Thoran, then it has to be either Sven or Olmossen, and hence it confirms Egil's suspicions about the conspiracy."

Lasgol looked at her, impressed, and Egil smiled.

"Very well deduced and expressed."

"And now what are we going to do?" Ingrid asked. "We have to tell Thoran about the betrayal."

"I'm afraid it's something a little more serious and urgent than that," said Egil.

Lasgol had not been expecting this. "What d'you mean?"

"From what I was able to get out of Olmossen," Egil said, "they're going to try a coup, and I think it's already started."

"Against King Thoran?" Nilsa was so nervous that she gave a sudden jump.

"Against the King and his brother. They want to kill them both so that there's no leadership left in the East, and in that way Sven can take the reins of the kingdom."

"The King and his brother have already left," Nilsa said. "The King's on his way to Count Volgren's castle, accompanied by his Royal Guard and a group of Royal Rangers. Orten's on his way to his own castle. Sven offered to escort him with a detachment."

"Well, I'm afraid they're both going to be attacked," Egil said. "It's the perfect occasion. They're outside the city, they only have a small guard with them because the areas they're going to are secure, and both brothers are separated from each other. It's a unique opportunity. The fact that Gatik's with the King and Sven with Orten at the same time is more than suspicious."

Astrid realized the strategy immediately. "They're going to be murdered..."

"We've got to go and stop this attempt at a coup!" Ingrid cried, with urgency in her voice.

"Do we have to?" said Viggo suddenly. His voice was very calm.

"What d'you mean, do we have to? Of course we do! They're going to try to kill the King!"

"Just give it a bit of thought. Really, do we have to?"

Lasgol understood what Viggo was hinting at. The argument had begun. He preferred to keep quiet and listen to his friends' arguments.

"It's our duty to protect the kingdom and the King," Nilsa said very seriously.   "Okay," Viggo objected, "but this king and his brother, he's probably one of the worst monarchs in the history, not just of Norghana, but I'd venture to say of all Tremia. Do you want him to stay on the throne?"

"Viggo has a point," Gerd said. "Thoran and Orten are a couple of heartless brutes. They shouldn't be on the throne."

"That's not something we either can or should decide," Ingrid countered. "He's on the throne because that's politics. Our duty is to protect whoever's King of Norghana. We can't choose who's going to rule, whether or not we like the fact."

"Besides," Nilsa said hotly, "who's to say Sven's going to be a better King than Thoran? I very much doubt it. Don't forget, Thoran came to the throne by chance, not by overthrowing the legitimate King. If we let Sven take the throne, we'll be helping a traitor and conspirator to rule."

"Very well said, Nilsa," Ingrid told her. "It's not us who decide who rules. We defend him. That's our job, and we have to act honorably."

"And suppose it was Egil who could take the throne instead of Sven?" Viggo asked her.

"But that's not the case!" Ingrid protested.

"But suppose it were?"

It was Nilsa's turn to come into the discussion. "If one day that happens, we'll decide then. This isn't the moment to think about that. What we have to do now is stop them killing the King!"

"You're too loyal," Viggo said, "and you're making decisions with your heart instead of your head. One day you'll find that things aren't black or white but different shades of grey."

"I don't think we ought to help Sven to gain power," said Gerd. "We're Rangers, and we have to defend the realm. Sven is a traitor and a conspirator. We have to stop him."

"Bear in mind that if they kill the King and his brother, they'll make it look like an attack by the West, and we'll have another civil war," Egil pointed out. "It's what both Olmossen and Sven are after, because that would give them power on both sides."

"It's a good plan," Astrid admitted. "Kill the King and his brother and take power in West and East. A very good one."

Finally Lasgol spoke. "Except that we're going to stop it."

"We are?" Viggo asked, trying to dissuade him.

"Yes, Viggo. We're going to stop this conspiracy, because it's our duty as Rangers and Norghanians, and because if there's another civil war, thousands of good people will suffer, and that has to be avoided at all costs. We'll do it out of honor."

Viggo fell silent and looked down.

"Everyone agreed? Lasgol asked. He stared at his comrades.

"I don't like Thoran and Orten any more than you do," Astrid said, "but we've got to do what's right. We should stop the conspiracy."

"Stop the traitors," said Ingrid.

Gerd nodded. "Yes, this has got to be stopped before things get even worse. We've got to stop people from suffering because of the greed of a few ruthless individuals."

"Very well said, Gerd. I totally agree," Nilsa said eagerly.

"Well, I'm against," Viggo objected. "I'd let Sven and Gatik kill Thoran and Orten, then we could deal with the two of them. It would be cleaner, and in the long run a lot better for everyone."

"That's a tempting approach," Egil said, smiling. "All the same, there's this thing in our hearts that obliges us to do good instead of evil."

"Yeah, it's called sentimentality," Viggo protested.

"Then that's decided," Lasgol said. "We act."

"Right," said Ingrid. "What's the plan?"

They all turned to Egil, even Ona and Camu.

"There's one important piece missing," he pointed out. "Where's Gatik now?"

"He's gone hunting," Nilsa said. "He's on his way to the Black Mountains, to go bear-hunting."

"Well, well... an odd moment to go hunting... or perhaps not so odd..." Egil was thoughtful, and the others waited while he worked out his plan.

"We'll split up," he said at last. "It's the only way to stop them being killed."

Astrid nodded. "Okay. What groups?"

"Ingrid, Nilsa, you go and warn King Thoran. You've got to stop them killing him."

"How are they going to try to do it?" Ingrid asked.

"That I have no idea of. Be very alert."

"This complicates things. If we don't know how they're going to try to kill the King, we won't know how to stop them."

"And besides, the King might not believe us, Nilsa added.

"I know. I'll go with Gerd after Olmossen and bring him here so that he can confess before the King. You make him get back to the capital at once. I'm sure they'll try to kill him before he reaches

Count Volgren's castle."

Ingrid nodded. "Okay. We'll stop it, one way or another. It's our duty, and we'll do it."

"If you don't bring him back alive, it wouldn't matter," Viggo muttered.

Egil looked at him with his eyebrows raised. "Viggo and Astrid, you deal with Sven. I've no idea what he'll have prepared to kill Orten, so be very careful. Lasgol..."

"What do you want me to do?"

"We need to find Gatik and see what he's up to. This hunting trip at this particular moment seems deeply suspicious to me."

"You think he's planning something, right?"

Egil nodded. "It's what makes the most sense. Either he's planning something, or else it's an alibi. Probably both. Either way, we need to find out what it is."

"Right. I'll take care of that."

"Be careful. He might suspect something."

"I'll be with Ona and Camu. It'll be fine."

"All right. A word of warning, pal: don't confront him, whatever happens."

"Are you afraid he'll kill me?"

"He's the First Ranger, the best among all the Rangers. He'll be sure to kill you, even with the help of Ona and Camu."

"Yeah, you're right there. He's too good."

"Don't confront him. Just find out what's he's planning, and don't give him any reason to attack you."

Lasgol nodded. "All right. Just keep an eye on him from a distance, no confrontation."

"That's the idea. We'll have plenty of time to go for him, but this isn't the moment. The crucial thing at this point is to save the King's life and convince him there's a conspiracy against him. It won't be easy, and that's why we have to deal with all these fronts at the same time."

"What are we going to do about Valeria?" Lasgol asked.

"I volunteer to explain her father's treason to her," Astrid said, with a glint of animosity in her eyes.

"I don't think the news would affect her too much," Gerd said. "She doesn't get along with him too well."

"That's true," said Lasgol, remembering the conversation he

himself had had about her with Olmossen.

"Even so, he's her father, and it'll be better not to tell her anything," Egil said. "They may hate each other, but blood makes a deep bond and Valeria's the kind of person who acts first and thinks afterwards. She could get into trouble. No, it's better if she doesn't know anything about this."

"Are you sure?" Astrid insisted. She was dying to go and tell Valeria.

Lasgol looked at her pleadingly.

"When it's all over, then you'll be able to do it," said Egil. "This isn't the moment."

"Fine. But nobody's going to rob me of my satisfaction." She glared at Lasgol.

"Everybody ready?" Egil asked.

"Ready!" they called, almost in unison.

"Remember, time's running out, and we've got to get to them and stop them being killed."

"Go, Panthers!" Ingrid shouted.

"Let's go!" they all shouted back, and went out of the room.

Chapter 36

Ona was waiting a few paces away as Lasgol loaded Trotter's saddlebags, and Camu was with her, though he was not visible. Lasgol was the last of the Panthers to leave. They had planned it this way to avoid arousing any suspicions. Each group would leave the castle at a programmed interval, and the others had already left. Lasgol was packing a campaign tent when someone talked to him.

"Ahem..." came a feminine voice behind him. "And where do you think you're going?" Lasgol turned and found Valeria looking into his eyes.

"Val! What a surprise! What are you doing here?"

"That's exactly what I was about to ask you. I've seen you all leaving the castle, very unobtrusively. I think there's something worrying and urgent going on, because you're all rushing off like mad."

"No... nothing's wrong," Lasgol tried to pretend.

"Yeah, that's what Ingrid and Nilsa told me when I ran into them."

"Well, that's right, there's nothing the matter," Lasgol said, trying to stay nonchalant.

"Oh yeah, and suddenly all the Panthers are leaving the Royal Castle at intervals and in a tearing hurry... not suspicious at all."

"Honestly, it's nothing."

"So where are you going?"

"Well... each of us is going to join our particular mission."

"Yeah, and you're a pretty poor liar, eh?"

Lasgol felt trapped. He did not want to lie to Valeria, but neither did he want to tell her the truth, particularly knowing what they had found out about her father.

"I'd like to tell you, but I can't."

"Secrets?"

"Well, yeah, Panther stuff, you know..."

"See how easy it is? Now I know you're telling me the truth. You're a terribly bad liar. I hope the enemy never captures you, because they'll just take one glance at you and know everything."

Lasgol smiled. "In that case, let's hope I'm never captured."

"So you're not going to tell me what's up?"

"I'm afraid not. It's nothing personal..."

"That much I already know. Well, it must be a little bit personal, or else you'd be telling me your secrets, and you don't always do that."

"It depends on the situation."

"Or on the mess you're in, yeah, I know."

Lasgol was glad she was taking it so well and not getting annoyed. Nobody likes not being trusted, particularly when it depends on the situation. Valeria had proven herself many times and had helped them greatly. It was a pity that because she was the daughter of who she was, he could not tell her everything that was going on.

"Well, I'd better go now. See you when I get back."

"All right. Try not to get caught," she joked, and walked away beaming and blowing him a long goodbye kiss.

Lasgol swallowed. If Astrid saw her blowing him kisses, it might lead to bloodshed. He mounted and left the Royal Castle.

Cover your sister so nobody can see her in the city, he told Camu.

I cover, Camu transmitted cheerfully. *Going adventure?*

We're going to find Gatik.

Gatik good?

I'm afraid not. Before, we thought he was good, but now we think he's bad.

Okay.

Ona chirped once, meaning she understood.

Right. We'll have to keep our eyes peeled.

No problem. I see and hear everything.

Either way, you see enough and Ona hears a lot.

I see and hear everything.

Oh, well... have it your own way.

Lasgol decided not to argue with Camu, who was so happy to be leaving the tower and the city at last, that now he felt he was a lethal adventurer. The funny thing was that Ona was certainly far more lethal than he was, but who was going to try to make Camu understand that?

Once outside the capital, they set off toward the Black Mountains. He would have to set a stiff pace for Trotter, but the strong pony was used to this.

Trotter, we're going to have to keep up a good speed.

The good pony nickered and shook his head up and down. He understood what he had to do. Lasgol thanked the Ice Gods for having three such wonderful companions. Well, two and a half, since Camu was half-torment.

They left the road and took a short cut through a couple of not-very-dense areas of woodland, trying to gain some time. Lasgol only had one thing in mind, which was to find Gatik and see what he was up to. He remembered what everybody said about the First Ranger: he was the best of all, quite exceptional: not only with weapons, but in every way. It was not going to be at all easy to find him, still less to spy on him. On the other hand he himself had Trotter, Camu and Ona. They were an advantage which Gatik did not have. Even so, he knew he was going to face an extremely difficult and dangerous situation. What would his father Dakon have done in his place? Probably have been as cautious as possible.

With luck, Gatik would only be looking for an alibi and not scheming anything. He relaxed a little. Suddenly he had a sense of something ominous. There was someone close at hand. Almost instinctively, he sought his Gift and activated his *Feline Reflexes* and *Improved Agility* skills. Two green flashes ran through his body.

Why use magic? came Camu's message.

I think someone's watching us.

I investigate.

Very carefully. If it's Gatik, don't attack, come back at once.

Okay.

Ona, you stay with me.

Ona grunted once.

Unobtrusively Lasgol prepared his composite bow as he went on moving alongside a stream. He nocked an arrow. Ona was very alert, her eyes flattened back on top of her head and her fur on end. Someone was nearby.

I find, Camu's message reached him.

Gatik?

No.

So who?

Valeria.

Lasgol turned in his saddle and aimed behind him. Valeria appeared from behind a group of rocks. She raised one hand.

"Don't shoot, it's me!"

"What the heck are you doing following me?"

"What do you think I'm doing? I'm coming with you."

"No way!"

"Of course I'm coming with you. I'm not going to let you get into trouble all alone." She rode toward him on her white horse.

"I'm not going to get into any trouble."

"Yeah, this has all the signs of one of Egil's plans. And those always end up in trouble."

"Valeria, honestly, you can't come with me."

She smiled. "Lower your bow in case you take one of my eyes out."

Lasgol lowered his bow and shook his head as she reached his side. "You know I always appreciate it when someone lends me a hand, but this time it's not possible."

"You can protest and argue with me as much as you want, especially because you get so cute when you're angry" –she smiled– "but it won't make any difference, because I'm coming with you."

"Val... please..."

"I'm not going to let you go on a dangerous mission by yourself. There's nothing more to be said." She tossed her golden hair to one side and raised her chin.

Lasgol considered his options. The only way to get her to let him go on his own was to antagonize her with a full-scale argument. He was not at all sure he would manage to pull that off. Valeria always got what she wanted, and what she wanted now was to come with him. On the other hand, she was a friend and a valuable comrade, and especially an Elemental Archer. Her help would come in very handy. The complicated thing was going to be to persuade her that they had to find Gatik and spy on him. And however he might put it, she was not going to think it was a good idea, particularly now that Gatik was the new Leader of the Rangers.

"And suppose I told you that the goal of the mission involves doing something you're not going to agree with?"

"Is it part of some plan of Egil's?"

"Yeah..."

"Then I'll do it."

"I doubt it..."

"Well, when we get that far we'll see. Anyway, what do you have to lose if I come with you all the way? I'll help you with whatever it is."

"I want you to promise you won't interfere at the end."

"Interfere? Me? Never."

"Well then, give me your word."

"Okay. You have my word that I won't stop you doing whatever it is you have to do."

"All right."

"Well then, let's be off."

"To the North," Lasgol said, and they set off.

"Have I ever told you you're really attractive when you argue with me?" she said playfully.

"Val..."

"Okay, okay... it's just that at times you're irresistible."

Lasgol looked at her pleadingly. "Don't make me regret it..."

"Okay... I'll keep my feelings to myself," She smiled at him gaily.

Lasgol snorted. This was going to be a very entertaining mission.

"Ona's a real beauty," Valeria said as they were going up a hillside. "Do you think I'd be able to stroke her when we stop for a break?"

"Big cats don't like to be touched. You need to earn their trust first."

Ona growled once.

"Hah, she seems to have understood us."

Lasgol smiled. "More than you'd imagine."

Valeria pretty, came Camu's message.

How do you know she's pretty?

I know.

Yeah, but how?

You ugly, Valeria pretty. I know.

Yeah... very funny.

Ona gave a chirp.

And don't you encourage him, 'cause that's all I need.

The route turned out to be quite easy, even at the stiff pace they were keeping up. The cold was not excessive, and there was not much snow – at least, on the lower reaches of the mountains. Higher up, things were different. Lasgol wondered as they rode on how he could make Valeria help him instead of trying to dissuade her when she found out that they were after Gatik. After giving it a great deal of thought, he had an idea. He waited for the right moment to act on it.

"I can see we're in a hurry," she commented.

"Yes, what I have to do is very urgent."

"And what exactly is it we're going to do?"

"We're going to find out what one of the Dark Ones is doing. The Leader of the Dark Rangers, to be precise."

"You're kidding me! You know who he is?"

"No," he lied. "But we have a lead on him. It's what I'm following, and with a bit of luck it'll take us to him."

"But that's incredible! They'll give us a medal if we catch him!"

"Yes, but he's very dangerous, so we need to be very careful. The plan isn't to capture him, it's to see what he's up to."

"I see. We're going to locate him and spy out what he's doing."

"That's right," Lasgol said. His strategy was to avoid telling her that the Leader of the Dark Rangers was Gatik. First they had to reach him, then he would explain. It was not the most brilliant of plans, but it was all he could come up with in the present situation.

"Okay, then."

"You follow my instructions and everything'll be fine."

"I'm going to check my elemental arrows. This mission has turned very interesting all of a sudden."

"Yeah, and it's going to turn even more so. If I can give you some advice, prepare some Air and Water arrows. We're going to need them."

She smiled. "You can always advise me about anything you want."

Lasgol shook his head and rode on.

When they reached the foot of the Black Mountains, without any setback, they stopped and stared up for a moment.

"Is it up there?" she asked.

"It looks like it."

"Well then, you tell me what to do."

"I'm going to find the trail. You wait for me here."

He dismounted and set off toward the nearest slopes, with Ona by his side and Camu behind them.

Ona, search for tracks, Lasgol transmitted to the big cat, and they both began to search for the trail of any recent hunter. It took them some time to find out where Gatik had set off up the mountain, but finally they were able to identify a trail. Lasgol had no doubt that it was Gatik's because it was barely discernible, as though he had tried to erase it, which there had been no need for him to do. Someone who walked so 'lightly' could only be a very experienced Ranger: someone like Gatik. It was pretty unlikely that two very experienced Rangers were in that same area at the same time. He went back to Valeria.

"I've got the trail now."

"You're fantastic, as Egil would say."

He smiled. "No, not really. It's my specialty. After all, I'm a Tireless Tracker."

"Yeah, and Beast Whisperer."

"Yeah, that too."

"Just what I was saying, phenomenal."

Lasgol shook his head. "We'll leave the horses here."

They tethered the horses to the trees and got ready to climb.

"Follow me. Now it's time for the hunt to begin."

"Awesome!" Valeria exclaimed, and nocked an Air Arrow.

Chapter 37

Lasgol began to follow the trail up the mountain, with Ona beside him and Valeria a little behind. Camu brought up the rear, camouflaged. Lasgol realized that Valeria knew nothing about Camu, because he had never told her about either his friend's existence or his Power. He might have to do so before the hunt was over. Or perhaps not. The less involved she was in his business, the better. She would be running less risk and would get into less trouble.

Camu, don't stray very far, and don't frighten Valeria.

She not see.

Yeah, and that's exactly why you mustn't appear suddenly, in case the shock makes her launch an arrow at you.

Launch arrow against me bad.

Yeah, exactly.

I camouflaged, she not see.

Good.

Ona smelt something and gave a loud growl. Her tail fluffed up, and Valeria noticed this.

"What's the matter with Ona?"

"She's found a trail."

"The Dark Ranger?"

"No, it's an animal's. A black bear."

"Wow... they're dangerous."

"We'll have to keep our wits about us and avoid it."

"Luckily Ona will warn us if it appears, right?"

"Yeah, she'll detect it a lot sooner than either of us," Lasgol said as he petted the Snow Panther.

He was wondering about the reason Gatik was on this particular mountain hunting bears. Seeing the landscape and thinking about a black bear nearby, the idea of the alibi began to take shape more clearly in his mind. It made sense. What Gatik was doing was making sure he had a good alibi. The murders of Thoran and Orten would be carried out at the same time as he himself was on this mountain. When he went back to the capital with a huge black bear as a trophy he would find out what had happened, and nobody would be able to link the murders to him, because he had been hunting a long way from where the events had taken place. It was a good bit of planning..

With this idea in mind he went on climbing. The ascent quickly became steeper and more difficult.

Ona, keep an eye out for bears. Warn us if there's one anywhere near. We don't want any surprises.

Ona growled once.

I also alert, Camu transmitted.

That's good to hear.

Gatik's trail vanished in a steep rocky area. Lasgol had to make a long detour until he found it again.

Valeria watched him as he bent over a patch of black earth. "Did you find it?"

"Yes, here it is." He showed her.

"It's an odd color, the earth on this mountain," she commented. "It looks as if they'd set fire to the mountain more than once."

He smiled. "I don't think that's the reason."

As long as they found no rocks, the trail was easy enough to follow. Unfortunately they came across several sharp slopes full of them, and Lasgol had to find the trail again while Ona and Camu stayed on the alert in case of bears.

Above the snowline the trails were much easier to follow, but they also had to go as carefully as they could to avoid slipping on the snow and falling down one of the steep slopes.

"Careful now," Lasgol said.

"Don't worry, I can manage."

"The snow's our ally now. It'll let us see the tracks from a distance. But it could also make us fall."

"We won't fall if we tread carefully. Well, I'll have to pay more attention because I like going behind you, following that cute tight little butt of yours."

"Val..." he said reproachfully.

"Sorry, it slipped out," she said mischievously.

Funny, Camu's message reached him.

It's not funny. Watch out.

Yes funny, and I watch out.

The trail was clearer now, and Lasgol found the tracks of other animals. Two were of bears, and Ona began to be very tense. Lasgol

315

told Valeria about the bears.

She aimed her bow in all directions, one after the other. "I can't see any."

They were on a wide snow-covered slope with a few trees and a little high-mountain vegetation. The wind was stronger at that height and it was beginning to turn cold, unlike at the base of the mountain.

Lasgol pointed to some trees higher up. "We'll go that way."

Their concern was a double one now: on the one hand Gatik, on the other the bears that lived among these mountains. Either of these two dangers was deadly. Among the trees Lasgol found something impressive. Behind them was a pass between the rocks which seemed to lead into a valley within the mountain.

"Wow!" Valeria said. "I wasn't expecting this!"

"Me neither."

"Do we go in?"

Lasgol checked the trail, which turned out to lead into the valley. On the right of Gatik's trail he found another, that of a sizeable bear. Probably Gatik was following that trail to hunt the bear. If he succeeded, he would come back with a very good trophy.

"We'll go on."

Crouching, they went along the pass. Grey rock flanked them, and the snow they stepped on sank with every step they took. It reached as far as their knees. Once they were in the valley, they sought protection behind a group of snow-covered trees.

"The trail goes on to the north. We'll follow it. Be ready to release against man or animal."

"Okay. I'm ready."

Get ready, the time has come.

I ready.

Ona growled once.

Lasgol set off, following Gatik's trail with his composite bow in his hand, ready to release if he had to, although he hoped he would not. All they had to do was locate him and see what he was doing. As he went forward, he called on his skills of *Improved Agility* and *Cat-Like Reflexes*. Camu saw the green flashes his body gave out, but said nothing. They were in danger, and Lasgol usually called upon his skills at this point.

Ona moved with a care and agility only possible in a great cat of the snows. Every time she placed her paws on the ground she seemed to be ready to leap on to some quarry. Lasgol wished he was as silent as she was. He had the impression that both he and Valeria could be heard a league away, even if it was not true. They were moving as carefully and silently as they could, but even so, at that height and amid that icy silence, it seemed that they would be spotted at any moment.

Suddenly it began to snow.

"Oh no..." Lasgol said sadly. This was going to complicate things.

"And it looks as if it's going to be heavy," Valeria said as she watched the snow falling around her.

"This is bad news for us. The snow will cover the trail and make it hard for us to follow."

"Well then, we'd better follow it quickly, before the snow covers the whole valley."

They began to follow Gatik's trail as quickly as they could. Or at least as fast as they could through the snow. Lasgol saw that the valley was a large one which ended in another climb toward a summit of snow-covered rocks. The trail went on until it went into a group of trees to the east. When they went into the trees, they saw smears of blood.

Lasgol crouched to inspect them and put his blood-smeared fingertips to his lips.

"Man or animal?" Valeria asked

"Fresh, from not long ago. It's an animal, and a big one to judge by its prints."

"The bear?"

"Yeah, I think he's wounded it."

"Well, wounding a big bear isn't a particularly intelligent idea," she pointed out.

Lasgol pointed to the trail on the ground which led between the trees. "It's gone after him."

"Well, he may be the Leader of the Dark Rangers, but he's not very bright. Why would he shoot an arrow against a black bear?"

"Maybe he wants to hunt one."

Valeria shook her head. "To prove something?"

"Who knows..." He did not want to tell her why Gatik was hunting a bear. There were too many explanations which would have been awkward at this point. "He must have his reasons."

"Well, it could cost him his life."

Lasgol wished this could be true, but something told him that Gatik was too good to let himself get killed by a bear in the mountains. Besides, hunting bears was his favorite activity, and although it was a very dangerous one, as Aren had said, he was exceptionally good at it.

"I don't think so. He'll probably have finished off the bear by now."

"If he has, we'll soon find out," Valeria said. She nodded ahead.

Beyond the trees, they found a small area of open land. The trail went on, and there were more spatters of blood on the snow.

Ona gave a warning growl, and Lasgol stopped.

"What is it, Ona?"

The panther gave another growl, long and sustained.

Lasgol called upon his *Owl Hearing* skill to hear better, but no revealing sound came to his ears. Then he saw it. Beside several large boulders which had fallen from the top of the mountain were the hind legs of a bear. The rest of the body was hidden by the boulders.

Valeria brushed the snow off her face and followed Lasgol's pointing finger. "I can see it. The bear."

To make sure there was no other dangerous animal anywhere near, Lasgol called upon his *Animal Presence* skill. The only thing it revealed was the dead bear, together with some birds in the nearby trees.

"I'll go over there. You stay in this position and cover me."

"You sure?"

"It'll be better if the two of us don't go, just in case. And Ona will come with me."

Lasgol, Ona and Camu moved very slowly and carefully toward the dead bear. Lasgol guessed that Gatik had released repeatedly against the animal while at the same time retreating at a run. He had done it with great precision, because it is not at all easy to kill a bear of that size, and several accurate shots would have been needed to bring it down. He guessed that Gatik had gone uphill to release his last arrows from there, so he needed to be very careful. He might be nearby.

Bent double, he went up to the bear's feet with Ona beside him and Camu right behind. Sudden there was a metallic click, and his heart went up to his throat.

"Trap!" he shouted.

The ground under his feet began to sink. Using his skills of *Improved Agility* and *Cat-Like Reflexes*, which were still active, he managed to propel himself forward as the ground sank beneath him. He lost his bow, which fell into the trench which was now opening up. Ona's reaction was the opposite. She leapt backwards out of pure instinct, while Camu, who had had no time to react, sank into the trap.

"Lasgol!" Valeria cried in alarm.

Lasgol fell on to his feet beside the dead bear. At once he heard another click, and a second trap clamped his right foot. He felt an explosion of pain in his leg and knew he would not be able to get free.

Ona and Camu fell into a deep trench, and when they landed at the bottom there were two more clicks.

"Oh no!" Lasgol cried out in fear.

There came two explosions from the Water Traps at the bottom, and Ona and Camu were enveloped in frost and ice.

Are you all right? Has anything happened to you? Lasgol messaged in alarm.

Frozen trap. Can't move legs.

Ona growled once.

Try to move, both of you, Lasgol told them as he bent over the metal clamp which had caught his leg.

"Lasgol, are you all right?" Valeria asked anxiously.

"I'm okay..."

"I'm coming to help you."

He held out his hand to stop her from coming any nearer. "Wait! This is full of traps!"

Ona and Camu were trying to move their limbs, but they were frozen because of the Water Traps. Even part of Camu's abdomen was frozen. However hard they tried to break free, they were unable to.

Can't move. Frozen, Camu warned Lasgol.

Relax and hold on. It'll pass in a while.

He realized that it was a double trap, a trench with Water Traps at the bottom. Not only did the prey fall in, it activated the icy traps, then froze and could not get out.

"What do I do?" Valeria asked. She was aiming her bow in all directions.

Lasgol saw a figure coming down from the mountain-top and knew that it was Gatik. He was coming to see what had fallen into his trap.

"The Dark One's coming down. Hide and put an arrow in him."

"Okay." Valeria said. She went to stand behind a boulder and aimed straight ahead.

A moment later a figure in a hood, with the lower part of his face covered by a Ranger's scarf, came up to Lasgol. In his hand was a composite bow, ready to use.

"Well, well, well, what have we caught here?"

Lasgol looked at his eyes, but with the snow falling, the hood over the figure's head and the scarf which covered his nose and mouth, he could not be sure that it was Gatik.

"A Ranger," he said.

"Exactly what I was hoping to catch today," the figure said, and Lasgol recognized the voice. It was Gatik.

"Release!" he called out to Valeria.

Gatik looked down at Lasgol, then to the far end of the valley, apparently without seeing her. Valeria had a clean shot, and she would not miss. Gatik went forward to the trench, ignoring Lasgol. He saw Ona trying unsuccessfully to move.

Gatik here, Camu warned.

"Release, Val!" Lasgol called again.

But the shot that ought to have brought Gatik down did not come.

"It's useless. You've lost," Gatik said.

Lasgol looked toward where Valeria was hiding. He did not understand why she did not take the shot. Then something happened that turned him to stone. Valeria got up slowly and began to walk toward Gatik, bow in hand.

He could not believe his eyes. Why was she walking toward Gatik?

"Val?" he said in puzzlement.

Valeria reached Gatik's side and greeted him with a nod. "My lord," she said.

"I see you were right," Gatik replied.

"I told you I'd manage it."

"And so you have. I'm delighted."

"I serve my Lord," she said respectfully.

And at that moment Lasgol knew that Valeria was not who she pretended to be.

She had betrayed them.

She was with the Dark Rangers.

Chapter 38

Orten led his retinue on an impressive black courser. He liked to ride in the lead so that everybody could see how formidable he was. With him were thirty of his best soldiers. They were Norghanians he himself had selected as part of his personal escort. They were massive and strong, and they were excellent fighters. He had no Royal Guard or Royal Rangers to protect him, but his own soldiers lost nothing in comparison with those of his brother. In fact his men were tougher, as well as somewhat more twisted, which gratified him.

He indicated the half-dozen Royal Guards who were accompanying the Commander. "Couldn't all those softies from the Royal Guard manage to beat my men?" he asked Sven.

Sven swallowed the insult and considered his answer.

"That could only be determined in a tournament," he replied. He did not want to offend Orten, nor did he want to lose face in front of his men, who had clearly heard the suggestion and were watching, grim-faced.

Orten looked back at Sven's men again with unmistakable scorn. "Bah! They don't look very tough to me."

The Commander, who was used to Duke Orten's contempt and even insults, did not flinch. "Only combat could decide that," he insisted.

"I've been told you've never lost a sword-fight in a tournament. Is that true?" Orten asked. His tone of voice suggested that he did not believe it.

"That's right. More than twenty duels, and I'm still undefeated."

"Well, you're not exactly the sort I'd bet on in a fight. You look too skinny to me. Any muscle under the armor?"

Sven smiled in a superior way. "A warrior's size has nothing to do with his skill in the battlefield."

"And what does that mean?"

"That a master swordsman, whatever his size, can deal with any warrior, even if he's double his size."

"I'm not sure if that's right."

"I can assure you. It's been shown."

"Bah, until I see it I won't believe it."

"I'll be delighted to fight the biggest warrior you've got at the next tournament, and I'll bet fifty gold coins on my own head."

"Excellent!" Orten exclaimed. He was sure he would win. "I'll take you at your word!"

Sven half-smiled to one side and looked at his Royal Guards, who were smiling in turn. They were well aware that brute force would not defeat their commander, who was a master swordsman.

The weather was good for the journey, and though it was beginning to turn a little colder, it was not raining which was very welcome. There was nothing worse for the journey than a heavy rain soaking everything.

"I'm looking forward to getting to my fortress."

"It's a magnificent one," Sven assured him.

"I prefer it a thousand times to the capital. The nobles of the court make me sick with their constant whining about everything and their soft ways."

"I've always said that the Court is no place for a land-owning nobleman."

"That's exactly what I say! And don't get me started on their dances and feasts!"

"I understand you perfectly, my lord," Sven said.

Their journey onward was trouble-free, because the peasants and traders they came across got out of their way as soon as they saw them coming. They came to a long gully and went in two abreast because of the narrowness of the pass. The road followed the middle, and it gave the impression of once having been a river which had dried up and then been turned into a road.

Sven and Orten rode at the head of the procession. After them came Orten's six soldiers. These were followed by Sven's six Royal Guards, then the rest of the Duke's soldiers.

"You didn't need to have come with me," Orten told Sven. "Nobody would dare to attack me with my men for protection."

"I'm coming with you because I have business to deal with in the south. I'm sure nobody would dare attempt anything against your retinue. When I found out you were leaving, I thought it would be sensible to travel under your protection."

"Ah, that sounds better. I thought it was strange that you should come to protect me. I don't need that."

"Of course not," Sven said with feigned concern. "All the same, these are troubled times, and this business of the Dark Rangers has left us all very restless. It's better to be cautious."

"My brother has already started to sort out that ugly business. He'll soon find the leaders and hang them from the main square in the capital as an example."

"That's what we're all hoping for, my lord."

"Well, don't you worry. With us, you'll reach the south without a scratch."

"That's my intention," Sven said.

They were half-way along the gully when there was a sudden landslide of earth and rock ahead of them. The horses reared at the noise.

Orten was having trouble controlling his mount, but in the end he managed it. "What's the matter?" he asked.

"A landslide," Sven said. He was having trouble controlling his own horse.

The column of soldiers stopped, while the noise of the crash died away, to be replaced by a cloud of dust.

"Go and see what's happened!" Orten ordered his men.

Two of them went ahead, but the enormous cloud of dust would not let them see what had happened, though they managed to get as far as the fallen rocks.

We can't get through!" one of the soldiers called back.

The other was about to say something, but only got as far as opening his mouth. Two arrows hit him full in the chest, and he fell dead from his horse. His comrade looked up and saw archers placed along the rim of the gully.

"Ambush!" he yelled, and two arrows from both sides killed him instantly.

"To arms!" Orten shouted as he drew his sword and grasped his round shield.

His soldiers drew their axes and shields as a dozen archers appeared at the rim of the gully and began to release on the column.

"Cover yourselves with your shields!" Orten shouted.

The arrows fell on the soldiers. Several of them had no time to protect themselves in time and fell, riddled with arrows.

"It seems that the Dark Rangers have dared to attack the great Duke Orten after all," Sven said. His smile was deeply ironic.

"Shut your mouth and defend me!" he ordered Sven, who was watching him nonchalantly from his saddle, sword in one hand and shield in the other.

"I'd almost rather watch them killing you, my lord."

"What? How?" Orten could not believe what he was hearing.

Sven turned to his men. Pointing his finger at Orten, he ordered: "Kill this arrogant pig!"

Orten turned his horse toward Sven's men. "Treason! Soldiers, to me!"

Orten's soldiers saw Sven's six men falling on Orten, and ran to help him. Meanwhile the arrows went on seeking lives among Orten's men, and succeeding. At the rear of the retinue several soldiers were falling. Orten was defending himself like a furious bear, delivering sword-strokes to left and right, while his powerful courser repelled the attack of Sven's men.

"Traitors! You cursed swine!" he shouted, red with rage. As a big strong man who knew how to use a sword, he was putting up a good fight. His soldiers attacked Sven's men from behind, forcing them to turn round and face them. The three-way fight between Sven's soldiers, Orten's and the archers turned furious.

Sven was watching the killing from his horse without taking part in it, waiting for his men and the archers to put an end to Orten and his people.

Orten got a cut in his arm, but he skewered one of the Royal Guards.

"Die, you traitor!"

Another of the Royal Guards killed one of Orten's soldiers and went for their leader. Orten defended himself, and was so big and strong that every stroke he delivered almost unsaddled his opponent. He had his back against the left-hand slope of the gully, but nobody was shooting at him. Puzzled, Sven looked up and saw that there were no archers in sight. Where were they? Orten's soldiers could not climb the slope to reach them. It was a magnificent ambush. All they had to do was release against Orten and his men until they were all dead. His Royal Guards had orders to distract them to stop them escaping through the entrance to the gully, and they were doing it well. So what was going on?

He looked to the right and saw two archers, but instead of releasing down into the gully they seemed to be doing so behind them. Had any of Orten's soldiers managed to climb the slope? It was unlikely, but not impossible.

"Kill them all!" Orten yelled. He had another cut in his shoulder and his face was spattered with blood, but he was still in the saddle, fighting like a cornered bear.

Sven saw that only a couple of Orten's soldiers were left alive, together with three of his own Royal Guards. He spurred his mount, went to the nearest soldier and attacked him. Two feints and a stroke to the heart, and the soldier fell dead.

Orten meanwhile killed another of the Royal Guards. "I'll kill you all!" he yelled furiously.

"There are three of us and only one of you," Sven said, looking at the two of his Guards who were still in their saddles. All Orten's soldiers were dead, most of them at the hands of the archers and the last ones at the hands of Sven's Royal Guards.

"You treacherous swine! Come and kill me if you can!"

"Of course I can," Sven shot back, very sure of himself.

"Come and fight, man to man!" Orten challenged him.

Sven glanced at his men and nodded. "I'll take it upon me to teach him the last lesson of his dishonorable life," he told them.

"I'm going to split you open from side to side!" Orten cried.

"I'm going to give you a short lesson in swordsmanship," Sven said with absolute iciness and certainty, "and then I'll cut your throat."

"Right! Let's see if you can!"

Sven urged his mount forward, and their swords met. Orten launched a massive blow, and Sven parried it with his shield. Orten struck again and again, but Sven parried all the blows with shield and sword, with amazing ease. Their horses crashed together and moved apart, and with each movement backwards and forwards the swords clashed again.

The two soldiers who were watching the fight were sure that Sven would finish Orten off whenever he felt like it. He was toying with him. They were so absorbed in the fight that they did not even notice the two shadows which leapt on them from the rim of the gully, one from either side. Both soldiers fell from their horses at the same moment. As they hit the ground they felt a second blow, this time a lethal one, and neither of them got up again. Their hearts had been pierced with Assassin knives.

The two shadows got to their feet. They were armed with knives.

Sven noticed that something was happening, and turned on his horse to see the two Assassins watching him

"It's time to hand yourself over, or else die," Viggo told him.

"Who are you?"

"Rangers, loyal to the King," Astrid said.

Orten pointed at Sven with his sword. "Yes! Kill him!"

"It's his decision," Viggo told Orten, and then to Sven: "You can either turn yourself in or die."

Sven glared at Orten, then at Viggo and Astrid. He knew that if he tried to kill Orten, the two Assassins would kill him. But if he charged them, he would still have a chance. He turned his horse, ready to attack.

"That's a bad choice," Viggo warned him.

"Surrender," Astrid said.

Sven gave Orten a look of profound disdain. "If I do, this heartless brute will torture me to death."

"You'd live another day," Viggo pointed out.

Sven pointed up to the edge of the gully. "You killed my archers?"

"Yes, me on one side, her on the other."

"Who sent you?"

"Egil," Astrid said.

"Olafstone?"

"That's right," said Viggo.

"I knew I ought to have had him killed. I paid a thousand coins for his death." He was shaking his head.

"Yes, but Egil's pretty sharp-witted and slippery," Viggo said.

"It's a mistake you're going to pay for dearly," said Astrid.

"Olmossen?"

"We have him," said Viggo.

Sven nodded heavily. "I guessed as much. Otherwise you wouldn't be here."

"Some conspiracies go awry, however well planned," Astrid pointed out.

Sven nodded. For the first time his eyes showed the shadow of defeat. He took a deep breath and composed himself.

"You won't be able to stop it happening in the end."

"We're dealing with it," Viggo said. "It's over for you."

"Surrender and save your life." Astrid told him.

Sven gave one last look at Orten, who spat blood at him.

"No, I'm not going to surrender!" he said, and charged at Viggo and Astrid,

"Bad choice," said Viggo.

He side-stepped like lightning to get out of the horse's way. Sven's sword sought his chest, but he bent backwards as the steel brushed it. Astrid, who had moved to the other side, gave a great leap and hurled herself on Sven. The Commander raised his shield and used it to repel her, but she managed to cut him in the thigh before she leapt backwards. Sven spurred his horse and fled.

Viggo lashed out at his arm.

"He's escaping!" Orten yelled. "Don't let him get away!"

Viggo bowed his head. "He won't get far."

Astrid got to her feet. "No, he won't make it to the end of the gully."

"What do you mean, he won't?" Orten thundered. "He's getting away at a gallop!"

Suddenly Sven swayed to one side of the saddle, and a moment later he fell off his horse.

"Eh? Is he dead?" Orten asked in amazement.

"Yes, very much so," Viggo said.

"How on earth did you do it?"

Astrid raised her knives. "Deadly poison."

"But I'm the one who killed him," Viggo pointed out.

"Throwing dagger?"

"Yeah, I got him in the back of the neck."

Astrid nodded. "In that case we both killed him."

Viggo gave her a wink. "All right, I'll allow you that one."

Orten was staring at them, utterly flabbergasted. "But who the hell are you two?"

"Snow Panthers. We deal with trivial problems in the kingdom, such as conspiracies to kill the King and his brother."

"They're going to try to kill my brother Thoran?"

"Yes, but don't worry, we've got that in hand too," Viggo said, and Orten's jaw dropped.

Astrid could not help smiling.

Chapter 39

"Valeria... no..." Lasgol said in utter despair.

She gave him a strange look, as if she did not recognize him, and shrugged. "That's the way things are."

Gatik beckoned to her, and they both came over to where Lasgol was lying, one on either side.

"I see my traps have worked," Gatik said. "Both of them. This delights me. It took me a long time to prepare them and hide them." He was staring into the trench, where Ona and Camu were trying to wriggle free. Gatik of course could see only Ona, trying unsuccessfully to move her limbs. "Your familiar won't be able to get free. I put a good load into those water-traps. Even if the effect wears off, she won't be able to get out of the trench. It's a deep one."

Lasgol tried to pretend, making his voice sound as convincing as possible. "Sir, we were coming to warn you."

"Oh, you were coming to warn me, were you? About what exactly?"

"About a conspiracy, sir. To kill the King." He was trying to find a way out, but could see none.

"Well, well, that certainly is serious."

"That's why we came to warn you," Lasgol said untruthfully.

Gatik turned to Valeria. "Did he come for that?"

Valeria looked at Lasgol, then back at Gatik. "No, my lord. He came to spy on us."

Gatik smiled. "I imagined someone like you might come after me. That's why I prepared these traps. The fact that it was you, Lasgol, is a bonus, though I had a hunch it would be you. Call it intuition, if you like."

Lasgol looked at them in bafflement. "Sir –" he began.

"You can stop lying," Gatik interrupted him. "I know you're here because of me. I also know about the conspiracy. I'm one of the leaders, which is something you must know too, because otherwise you wouldn't be in this rather uncomfortable situation."

"He knows you're the leader of the Dark Rangers," Valeria said.

Lasgol froze at hearing her betray him like this.

Gatik laughed. "And still he pretends he knows nothing. Worthy son of his father."

"Don't even mention my father, you traitor," Lasgol said angrily.

"Well, I think it's only fair to mention him. He died trying to save the kingdom from a conspirator. Now you'll die for the same reason."

"Valeria..." he pleaded. "You can't be with them. You can't be part of this."

"Sorry, Lasgol. I am. I'm one of them"

"It's not possible," Lasgol muttered. He was unable to believe what was happening.

She nodded. "It is, Lasgol."

"Since when?"

"For a long time. In fact since my first year at the Camp."

"No! I refuse to believe that!"

"You'll have to believe it. It's the truth."

Lasgol shook his head, so stunned he could not even think. "Why? I don't understand."

"It's complicated. I don't think you'd understand."

"Try. Explain it to me. Please. I need to understand. Why?"

"My father Count Olmossen sent me to the Camp. My situation was like Egil's when he came there. My father sent me, just as his own father sent him, as a possible hostage for Uthar if they joined the Western League. The difference between Egil and me was that in my case I came with a larger plan: to join the Dark Rangers. My father was already in touch with the leader and was already working towards seizing the throne."

"Your father sent you? But... you can't stand him, so why did you obey him?"

"I have to confess, that was a role I was playing. Actually, I get along really well with my father. I love him, and he adores me."

"And all that business about not giving you the title, that it would pass to your brother? That he was a male chauvinist?"

"All false. My brother isn't half as skilled as I am. And I mean in everything. And my father knows it. I've always been the apple of his eye. That's why he sent me to the Camp, so that I'd get in touch with the Dark Rangers and help them from within."

"Spying for him..."

"Spying, manipulating, acting, just as the situation required. Like today."

"That's why you wanted to be near me..."

"Don't feel bad, you're cute, but my interest was a different one. And it wasn't only you I was interested in..."

"Egil," Lasgol guessed.

"Exactly. He's very smart, our dear Egil. I had to stick to him like a limpet, to follow him and find out what he was planning."

"And you've done a magnificent job," Gatik told her.

"You've been spying on us this whole time, pretending to be our friend..."

"That's what my father and Gatik needed, and that's what I've done, that's right. Apart from a lot of other things you don't know."

"For the Dark Rangers?"

"Exactly."

"So... you were recruited by Eyra too at the Camp?"

"That's right. Eyra had already been informed of who I was and what I was there for. She enlisted me, trained me and took me under her wing. That was when our friendship was born. She did a good job. As you can see, I became a Specialist, and I'm an exceptional spy and Ranger."

Lasgol shook his head. "But you've been with me, on my side..." He was refusing to believe what she was telling him, even though his subconscious was assuring him that it was the truth.

"I'm sorry to disappoint you, but it was all a ruse. My mission since the Camp has been to get close to the Snow Panthers, and particularly to you and Egil. Eyra wanted Egil to be closely watched, and for some reason you too. I think she guessed you'd be a problem, or else – as has finally happened – that you two would turn out to be extremely troublesome."

"So your interest in me was totally feigned?"

"Absolutely. My orders were to get close to you and the Panthers and keep an eye on you. I had to get as much information as I could for Eyra."

"Especially after all that business about the Shifter," Gatik explained, "and your friend Egil becoming the King of the West after his brother's death in the civil war. You became an object of great interest for our organization."

"When Egil found out about the poisoning, I warned Eyra," Valeria explained. "She told me you'd never be able to prove it had been her."

"But then you appeared with those wretched flowers," said Gatik. "This posed a great problem for us. Eyra was left in the open."

"We had to improvise and think up an escape plan for her," Valeria added.

"So it was you who helped her escape?"

Valeria looked him in the eye. "Yes, it was me."

Lasgol was shaking his head. "I can't believe it." The more he heard, the more he was coming to realize the tremendous mistake they had made in trusting her.

"You'd better believe it. It was me, and it turned out not to be easy in the least."

"How did you do it?"

"The most difficult part was getting myself into the escort group. Eyra was very skilled there. She begged Dolbarar to allow a woman to be in the escort, as a courtesy to her and for reasons of modesty, to help with a woman's specific needs. I wasn't expecting them to accept, but they did. They looked for a woman who was a Specialist, who was totally trustworthy and who was in the Camp at the time. There were only two of us, because there aren't that many women, and even fewer who match those requirements. Angus chose me, because I'd been part of Egil's mission in Erenal."

"But how did you trick Egil, and everyone else in the escort?"

"It wasn't easy. Tricking Egil looked like being very complicated, and so it turned out to be. All the same, we managed it. The Sniper's role wasn't to kill Eyra. He was a distraction, so that she could be taken out of the cage and I could give her the toxic substance she needed to take, to make it seem she had a fever."

"How did you give it to her?"

"Egil helped me himself, without knowing. He asked me to get her out of the cage so that the Sniper wouldn't kill her. Of course that wasn't our agent's intention. I got her out and hid her under the cart to 'protect' her. What I really did was make the cut on her forehead and then give her the poison, so that she could use it while we were under cover and nobody could see us. She hid the two phials among her clothes so that she could start taking the poison."

"Oh..."

"Egil attended to the wound, but then as soon as she was alone, she took the poison and put a little in the wound so that it got infected. Dear Egil thought the arrow had been poisoned, which is what we wanted him to believe. In fact it wasn't, it didn't even touch her. I was the one who gave her the wound."

"The aim was to make it appear that she was sick."

"That's right. It would make Egil and the escort act. As they did. The Natural Assassin who had to free Eyra had been following us from the Camp. He was waiting for the opportunity to act."

"The fever was feigned? It can't have been. Egil would have realized."

"It wasn't. The poison brought it on. It's a special one Eyra discovered while she was experimenting at the Camp. It can kill a person with fever without leaving any trace. It's used for assassinations. The victim contracts a fever from some unknown cause, and then dies. However, if it's taken in small doses, it causes peaks of fever which then fade away. Eyra took a little, her fever would go up, and Egil would prepare potions and tisanes for her to bring it down again. She was able to control when to take it and the exact amount she needed. Which wasn't much, because it's a powerful toxin."

"You fooled everybody."

"Exactly. Egil is very intelligent, in fact brilliant. But so is Eyra, and with my help she succeeded."

"Why did she leave Egil alive? Why didn't she kill him?"

"That's a good question." Valeria turned to look at Gatik.

The leader of the Dark Rangers went on with the story. "Eyra knew her plans might fail, and that if they did, it suited her to have one player who was still alive."

"Egil?"

"Yes, because he's the King of the West."

"I don't follow..."

"It was a safeguard. If Thoran and Orten survived the conspiracy, Eyra knew it would suit her if the King of the West were still alive, because he'd pose a problem for King Thoran."

"She decided it would suit her if her enemy's enemy was left alive."

Gatik nodded. "That's right. But she did it without consulting me. I'm not in favor of leaving an enemy alive. And that was Eyra's great mistake. One she paid for with her life."

"You gave the order to have her killed," Lasgol reasoned.

"I killed her myself when we attacked the camp. I saw her with you and Egil, and I knew I had to silence her forever. There's no better Archer in all Norghana than me, and in the confusion of the battle nobody saw where the arrow that killed her had come from."

"We thought it had come from the Royal Rangers."

Gatik smiled. "And there I was among them." There was a gleam of triumph in his eyes.

"So... Egil... you're going to kill him?"

"Of course. We can't leave a pretender to the crown alive. The crown will be ours."

"Is that what you're after? The crown?"

Gatik laughed. "No, I'm not interested in the crown. I want to lead the Rangers and change them, improve them."

"Turn them Dark," Lasgol said.

"Yes, that's a good way of putting it."

"You want to transform the whole organization of the Rangers and remake it in your own image."

"That's right. Kings come and go. Look at what happened to Uthar, to Egil's brothers. Thoran and Orten too will disappear before long. The Rangers remain. One day they'll be so powerful that they'll appoint and overthrow kings at will."

"At your will," Lasgol said more exactly.

"You're clever. That's right. What kings and nobles don't understand is that in order to rule, you need strong support behind you. That's going to be my role. I'll support whoever I want and put him on the throne. Or else I'll withdraw my support and he'll fall in the mud. I'll have the power, not them. Kings will be my puppets."

Lasgol nodded. Now he understood. Gatik was the greediest of all, because not only did he want to lead the Rangers, but he also wanted to manipulate the future kings of Norghana. With a strong body of Rangers carrying out his orders, there was no doubt that he could.

"An ambitious plan..."

"That's why I allied myself with Sven. It's why we've been conspiring all this time behind the backs of Thoran and the Rangers."

"The Bear and the Boar," Lasgol said.

"That's right. I'm the Bear and he's the Boar. I see you'd already found that out."

"We found out, that's right."

"That's why you're here now."

Lasgol had to admit this.

Gatik gave him a self-satisfied smile. "You know the reason for those nicknames?"

Lasgol shook his head. He needed to gain a little time. To think of a way of getting out of that situation. His right foot was trapped in the clamp, and he could not get it out. He knew that type of trap well: it was a man-trap. Once it was in place there was no way the prey could open it and escape. It was one of those most often used by Man Hunters.

Gatik indicated the dead animal beside Lasgol. "The animal I enjoy hunting most is the bear. That was my specialty, ridding Norghana of aggressive bears. That's what I concentrated on during my first years as a Ranger. There was no-one better than me in the corps. I used traps of all kinds to limit their mobility, or even immobilize them completely, as in your case, and then I took care of them. I gave them either a quick death or a sweet one."

"A sweet one?"

"Poisoned honey. One of the specialties Eyra taught me. Did you know we were very good friends during my stay at the Camp?"

"I didn't know, but I'd guess you must have been, for all the rest to be able to happen afterwards."

"She recruited me for the Dark Rangers."

"Did you create them together?"

"No. Eyra created them even before I ever came to the Camp. She didn't like the way the leaders of the Rangers were doing things, particularly their total obedience to the crown, whoever the King happened to be. At the time it was Uthar, who wasn't an entirely bad king, although neither was he one who could bring back the splendor and greatness the kingdom of Norghana deserves. He wasn't a warrior king, and he'd never have given us back either the glory our people deserve or its dominant position as one of the powers of Tremia. Obviously I'm talking about the time before he was taken over by the Shifter. That was a big surprise, and one none of us had either foreseen or seen coming. One of those unexpected things that happen in life, and we must confront them. I believe we owe you one for ridding us of him. At that time Eyra already had Dark Rangers infiltrated and ready to act. When she recruited me, a long time ago, she already had her secret organization up and running."

"So how did you become their leader?"

"She handed her position over to me a few years ago, to strengthen the organization. You need new blood to lead those youngsters who come in and want to see changes. Also so that I wouldn't betray her. She was a very clever woman. She pulled the strings from the shadows, and until you found her out she oversaw recruiting new, promising adepts for the group. She was very good at it."

"And you killed her."

Gatik shrugged. "She was going to betray me. She was going to talk. It was nothing personal."

"Still..."

"You and your friend Egil are going to share the same fate too. Don't worry." He smiled maliciously. "I'm not the kind to leave any loose ends."

"Are you the one who's been trying to kill us?"

Gatik laughed. "It's Olmossen who's been trying to kill Egil, and recently Sven too has paid to put an end to him once and for all. He's slippery as an eel."

"And me?"

"You? Oh, that was me."

Lasgol looked at him uncomprehendingly. "Why?"

"The reason is a very simple one. Because you're who you are. Because you're the son of Dakon, the best First Ranger Norghana has ever had, and my mentor. He taught me a lot, and he helped me to become First Ranger like him. When I left the Camp he helped me to get into the Shelter, and when I became a Specialist he went on helping me. I owe him a lot. Thanks to everything he taught me, I've reached the position of Leader of the Rangers."

"If you owe my father so much, why kill his son?"

"Precisely because you're his son. You're like him. I've followed your development, and it's as clear as a summer's day. You'll be as good as he was himself, if not better. That makes you into a direct enemy. Not only because you'll search for the truth like a hound, as he did, but because you'll want my position of leadership."

"I don't want your position."

"Maybe not now, but one day you will. Either way, I wasn't wrong. Here you are, following my trail and unearthing the conspiracy. I knew this would happen. Your father couldn't stop sniffing out Uthar, and look what happened. The same thing's happened to you. You didn't stop sniffing around, and here you are. If it's any consolation, you'll die like your father, heroically, trying to save the kingdom. Unfortunately he didn't succeed, and nor will you."

"I don't regret the fact that I'm the person I am, or that that it's led me here."

"I believe you, but I don't care. It's time to put an end to your uncomfortable existence."

"Isn't there any other way out?" Lasgol asked, desperately trying to find some escape-route.

"I'm afraid not. You and your friends have become a major problem, you've interfered in our plans and caused us a great deal of damage. It's time for you to die."

Chapter 40

Lasgol, who had fallen to one knee, raised his hand. The pain from the trap was unbearable. He clenched his jaw.

"Your betrayal isn't going to work. The plan's going to fail."

Gatik smiled in disbelief. "You don't really think I'm going to believe you?"

"We have Count Olmossen."

"What do you mean, you have my father?" Valeria asked with a look of hatred.

"Egil found out about his treason. The nobles of the Western League have detained him."

"You're lying."

"I'm not lying. Egil set a trap for your father, and he fell into it. He gave himself away when he tried to kill Egil and Count Malason."

"The next two in line for the throne of the West..." Valeria muttered.

"He couldn't resist the opportunity of killing both of them with one shot and clearing the way for his ambitions."

"Don't believe it," Gatik told her. "He's trying to confuse you."

"You know I don't know how to lie," Lasgol said to her. "It's the truth. You can see it in my eyes."

She came a little closer and looked into his eyes. "He's not lying."

"How long has it been since you last had news of him?" Lasgol asked them.

"That proves nothing," Gatik said. "We communicate very little. It's safer."

"We know about the conspiracy to kill the King and his brother Orten. Egil managed to get Olmossen to tell him all about it when the Count thought he had him and was going to kill him."

Valeria and Gatik exchanged a serious glance.

Can't move, came Camu's message, along with a feeling of great concern for him.

Relax, I'm still alive. I'll try to make things last longer.

I try to move. Ona too.

Keep trying.

"What do you know?" Gatik asked him menacingly.

"I know that at the moment they're going to try and kill King Thoran and his brother Orten. I know that's why you're here, so that you can go back with that bear as an alibi. I know that if you succeed, you'll blame the West for the attacks and we'll have another civil war. I know that you won't succeed, because we've found out about the plot."

"That's a lot to know, and a lot to assume," Gatik said. His expression was no longer that of a confident man but of a very worried one.

"What do you mean, we're not going to succeed because you've found out about us?" Valeria asked.

"The Panthers have sprung into action to stop the murders. At the moment they're intercepting Thoran and Orten's retinues. You won't be able to kill them."

"And what about my father?"

"Egil's gone to look for him. He'll take him to the King so that he can confess."

Valeria turned to Gatik with a look of concern.

"They won't get there in time to stop it," he told her. "What he's not telling us is that he doesn't know how the murders are going to be carried out. He's just guessing."

"We've got to stop my father from getting to Norghania. Thoran'll torture him and then hang him."

"Thoran? Thoran will be dead. And so will Orten."

Valeria was seriously worried about her father by now. "Can you give me an assurance that Sven will have the East?" she insisted.

Gatik nodded. "Sven will take over the reins of the East and free your father. The plan will go on just the same. We'll kill Olafstone and Malason, then Olmossen will take the West. Everything'll be ours. Don't let him confuse you."

Lasgol realized that he could not argue against this without proof that the murders had been stopped. They were not going to believe him. He tried to see whether his two friends had managed to free themselves from the ice trap.

How are you doing?

Bad, only one leg free, Camu messaged.

And Ona?

Two free, two frozen.

Lasgol swallowed. His friends would be unable to help him, and he was running out of both arguments and time.

"I can't believe you tricked me right up to the end," he told Valeria.

"I'm sorry things have turned out like this. We come from two very different lineages, you and me. You loved your father very much, and I love mine. I have to help him."

"Don't let him trap you with his words," Gatik told her. "If you want to see your father alive, you know what has to be done."

Valeria nodded. "Yes, my father's got to live."

"Then we have to put an end to this and go back to Norghania." He looked Valeria in the eyes, an icy look. "Kill him."

Valeria snorted. "You want me to be the one who kills him?"

Gatik nodded. "That way you'll prove your loyalty and courage. Remember, your father's life depends on it."

Valeria turned to Lasgol. She changed the elemental arrow she had nocked for one with a specially penetrating point. A shot with it would pierce Lasgol's heart as if it were paper.

"I'm really sorry," she said.

"Valeria, no!"

He reached out with his right hand, but there was nothing he could do. He was unarmed and trapped. His skills were no use to him without a weapon. In his desperate state he tried to send a message to her mind using his *Animal Communication* skill, to try to dissuade her in some way, or at least to confuse her and gain time. When he concentrated he was able to see her auras, which glowed intensely. He tried to communicate with that of her mind by focusing on it. For a moment he thought he had succeeded, but there was no green flash and the skill failed in affecting her mind in the way he wanted it to.

She was now aiming her bow at his heart.

"What are you waiting for?" Gatik ordered her angrily. "Kill him!"

"I..." She seemed to hesitate. She was staring at Lasgol, but did not release the arrow which was aimed at his heart.

There was a tense silence.

In desperation, Lasgol tried to use his skill again. He probed for the aura of Valeria's mind and focused on it with all his might. This was his last chance. He tried with the despair of someone who knows he is going to die the next moment. The skill failed. Nothing was transmitted, and he knew that he was going to die.

"I told you to kill him! That's an order!" Gatik shouted at her.

"I... can't..." Valeria stammered. She began to lower her bow.

"Don't you dare lower that bow!"

"I can't..."

"There's no place for weakness among the Dark Rangers! If you don't kill him, I'll finish you off myself this moment! Raise your bow and release!"

Valeria turned and saw that Gatik was now aiming at her.

"Gatik..."

"Kill him, or it's your own life!"

Valeria knew that if she did not kill Lasgol, Gatik would kill her at that very moment. She sighed and looked into Lasgol's eyes.

"I'm sorry," she said, and raised her bow.

She exhaled, spun like lightning and released. Her arrow was aimed at Gatik's chest, but he had already released against her. His arrow caught her in the collarbone, and the force of the impact made her stumble and fall backwards. Her own arrow grazed Gatik's shoulder, but did not hit him squarely. The First Ranger had seen her movement and stepped a little aside to his left.

"You fool! How dare you?" Gatik shouted at her furiously. He already had another arrow nocked, and was aiming at her.

"I'm sorry... Lasgol..." she said from the ground. She had lost her bow, and her hands were on the arrow. She was losing a lot of blood, and the wound looked serious.

In a desperate act, Lasgol drew his Ranger's knife from his belt and prepared to throw it. The First Ranger saw him, shifted his bow and released. His arrow caught Lasgol in the hand, and the knife was deflected.

"You fool, do you really think you can reach me like that?"

Without yielding to the sense of impotence he was feeling, Lasgol drew his short axe and made the same movement, ready to throw it.

"You have your father's guts, but not his skill with weapons," Gatik told him. He released again as he stepped forward toward his victim, catching his hand so that the axe flew off to one side.

Gatik nocked another arrow rapidly and came to stand above Lasgol, ready for the final, point-blank shot.

Lasgol let his head and hands hang as if he were defeated. He put his hands on the ground. They were bleeding from the cuts he had received when Gatik had disarmed him.

"Give my regards to your father when you see him in the realm of the Ice Gods."

Gatik was about to kill him, but he had made a small mistake. He had come too close, close enough for Lasgol to use his *Dirt Throwing* skill. He called upon it, and a green flash ran through his hands. He raised them towards Gatik and threw a handful of soil, dirt and dust which flew straight to the First Ranger's eyes and face.

Caught by surprise, instead of releasing, he took a step backward and shut his eyes in a reflex act. But it was too late to protect them. The skill had already affected him, and he was half blinded.

"You swine! I'll run you through all the same, even if I can't see you!"

Lasgol threw himself on to the ground, and Gatik's arrow buried itself in his left thigh. He groaned in pain.

Gatik took another step back to wipe his eyes and clear his sight.

Lasgol could not free himself from the man-trap, but it had a hole for a key. Gatik must have it. He swore under his breath. If Gatik got his sight back, he was dead.

"I'm going to riddle you with arrows!" Gatik yelled..

At that moment Ona burst out of the trench. She had climbed up Camu's body. He had managed to straighten up, although his limbs were still frozen. Her front legs were still half-frozen, but she had regained the full use of her hindquarters and tail, which she had used to give herself impetus for the leap.

Ona. Attack. His neck, Lasgol ordered.

The panther dragged herself along the snow, passing in front of Valeria, who was stopping her wound with both hands to stem the bleeding.

Gatik meanwhile was beginning to get his sight back.

Ona took another leap with her hind legs, using her huge tail for balance, and fell on him. Before he could turn round, she buried her fangs in his throat and bit with all her strength until she had killed him, as if he were her own prey.

Chapter 41

Ingrid and Nilsa knew they had to reach King Thoran and his retinue before it was too late, and they were riding as fast as their horses would go. The route the King intended to take was no secret. They were going by the Royal Way, which linked the capital and Count Volgren's castle. King Thoran did not often leave the Royal Way, which was well-kept and made the journey a great deal easier. The secondary roads and shortcuts through forests were for the common people, not for the high-born.

On the other hand, since the two riders knew the route, they took cuts through forests and waded across rivers to try to reach the king as quickly as possible. If they did not arrive in time and he died, not only would it be a terrible failure for the Panthers, but the kingdom would be plunged into chaos once again, causing thousands of innocent deaths. This they needed to prevent at all costs.

Night was falling, and they had not yet reached the royal retinue This was worrying them, because soon they would have to stop to rest their exhausted horses.

Nilsa pointed. "Look, Ingrid! To the east!"

Ingrid craned her neck and followed Nilsa's pointing finger "It looks like a military camp. Yeah, that could be them."

Riding at top speed, they were soon able to confirm that it was the royal camp after all. They could see three tents, one very large and elegant, displaying the Norghanian royal banners and the one which bore Thoran's arms.

At the camp, Four Royal Guards came out to intercept them with spears, and several others aimed at them from their posts nearby. They tugged hard at their reins and halted.

"We're Rangers!" Ingrid called, raising her hand so that they would not be shot at.

Nilsa raised both hands too, to show that they had no hostile intentions. The situation was very confused, and they might end up with a friendly arrow buried in their hearts at the slightest badly-judged move.

"Rangers, eh?" one of the Royal Guards said.

"That's right."

"The Dark Ones?" said another. The four were keeping their spears pointing threateningly at them.

At that moment an officer of the Royal Guard strode over to them, looking very serious. "What's the matter here?" he asked.

"They say they're loyal Rangers, Captain Uldritch," said one of the guards.

The Captain looked them up and down. "Dismount," he barked.

"Is the King still alive?" Ingrid asked immediately.

Uldritch looked at her in surprise. "Of course the King's alive. Now you're going to have to explain to me why you should ask a question like that."

"I need to see King Thoran at once."

"Dismount. I'm not going to say it again."

Ingrid nodded at Nilsa, and they both dismounted. "Who are you?" Uldritch demanded.

"Specialist Ingrid Stenberg, and this is Ranger Nilsa Blom."

One of the Royal Rangers came forward with three others. "We know Nilsa well," he said.

Nilsa recognized him. It was Kol, the handsome Mage Hunter who was trying to woo her.

Ingrid wasted no time. "It's a matter of life and death. The King's life's in danger."

"King Thoran is resting in his tent and is perfectly all right," the officer replied. "He can't be disturbed."

"He needs to be disturbed right now," she insisted. "His life's in danger."

"If we disturb the King while he's resting," Uldritch said, "it's our lives that'll be in danger."

"Listen, there's a conspiracy to kill the King. He's got to be warned."

The Guards and the Royal Rangers looked at one another. "Are you serious?" Uldritch asked.

"Of course I'm serious. D'you think I'd dare come here to the King's camp in the middle of the night with a story like this if I wasn't serious?"

"Nilsa, what do you say?" another of the Royal Rangers asked her.

"I say that what she's saying is the truth. There's going to be an attempt on the King's life, and we've got to stop it!"

The Royal Rangers tensed. They believed Nilsa and did not know how to react to the news. Despite this, Uldritch himself did not seem to be impressed.

"Take us to the King," Ingrid insisted. "We'll explain it all to him."

"And how do we know you aren't the ones who're trying to kill him, and this is just part of your plan?" the Captain of the Guard demanded.

Nilsa waved at the Royal Rangers. "Because they know me. Do you really believe I'd take part in an attempt on the King's life?"

"Well... quite honestly, no...I don't think you..." said Hans, the ugly Royal Ranger and Infallible Marksman Nilsa also knew.

"No, I don't think you're a Dark One," Kol agreed.

"It doesn't matter whether they believe you or not," Uldritch said adamantly. "I'm in command here, and nobody's going to disturb the King."

"Take us to the King!" Ingrid shouted furiously.

Several Royal Guards who were guarding the King's tent stared at them in amazement.

"You know I wouldn't make up a story like that," Nilsa pointed out.

Hans pointed to Ingrid. "Make up, no, but she might have told it to you, and you believed her when in fact there's no truth in it."

"If you try to suggest I'm lying one more time, I'll knock your teeth in!" Ingrid said, with a murderous look in her eyes.

"If you try that, it'll be the last thing you do," Hans said. He was wrinkling his nose and jutting out his jaw, so that though he was naturally ugly, now he looked even more so.

Uldritch was eyeing them both. "Nobody's going to do anything. Unless it's me." He turned to Ingrid. "I'm not in the mood for hanging anybody tonight, but I'll do that if you insist on seeing the King."

"Wait!" Nilsa said, getting in between the two of them. "You needn't go as far as that. The King's safe and sound, right?"

"Of course he is," Uldritch assured her.

"And we can't disturb him."

"No, you can't," he said flatly.

"In that case we'll wait till dawn to speak to him."

"That seems a better solution to me. What does your friend think?" Uldritch said, as if testing Ingrid.

Nilsa gave her a pleading look. "Ingrid... we can wait till morning..."

Ingrid took a deep breath, put her hands on her hips and exhaled. "Fine, we'll wait till morning to speak to the King."

"That's much more rational and acceptable. You can camp with the Royal Rangers. But let me warn you" – he pointed to a huge oak – "if I see you ten paces from the King's tent, I swear I'll hang you from this tree myself."

Ingrid said nothing, but the look she gave the Captain showed that she was not in the least afraid of him. Nilsa dragged her away from there before things reached the point of no return. They took their horses and followed Kol, who led them to where he and four other Royal Rangers were resting under another oak.

Nilsa smiled at him. "Thanks."

"What an entrance that was! It was worth seeing," Hans said as he joined them.

"We didn't mean to," Ingrid explained. "We just wanted to see the King."

"The Captain's tough and inflexible," Kol said, "but he's a good officer. He has his orders, and they come directly from Thoran. He's not going to disobey them."

"Not even if the King's life's at risk?"

"Well, at the moment I don't think it's at too much risk, is it?" Hans reasoned. "He can wait till morning to be told."

Ingrid shook her head. "I don't agree. Something as urgent as this ought to be passed on at once."

"Well, I'm not going to argue with you," Hans said. "I can see you're the unfriendly sort."

"I'm sweet as honey," Ingrid said. Her expression was ironic.

Kol gave a guffaw. "I can tell. Thank goodness our beautiful Nilsa managed to pacify you. If not, you'd both have ended up hanging."

"That remains to be seen!" Ingrid said. She was still annoyed.

"Relax, Ingrid," Nilsa said. "We're still in time to save the King."

"Sit down beside the fire and tell us what's going on," another of the Royal Rangers said.

They sat down, and were grateful for the warmth and the rest after their intense journey.

"Don't take this the wrong way," Ingrid said, "but I don't trust you. It's not a situation for sharing secrets blind."

"Nilsa trusts us, don't you, Nilsa?" Kol said.

"Yeah, sure, you and Hans and Frey," she said with a wave at the Royal Ranger who was sitting beside the fire with three other comrades. The Healer Guard returned the greeting with a broad smile. Once again Nilsa wondered which of the two she liked better, Kol or Frey. Both of them were so handsome, each in his own way.

"And what about us?" asked Ulsenk. He was another of the Royal Rangers she knew, but had had less to do with.

"Yeah, sure, you too," she said. In fact she trusted them less, but she did not want to admit it openly.

"I don't care who Nilsa trusts," Ingrid snapped. "The situation's critical. There's a conspiracy to kill the King, and we have to tread very carefully."

"Are you sure of that?" Kol asked. "It's not that we don't believe you, it's just that it's highly unlikely."

"Absolutely sure. We have proof, and we know who's behind the whole thing."

"I hope you're not wrong," said Hans. "The King's not one to forgive mistakes, particularly one like this."

"If you go to the King with this conspiracy and it turns out not to be true," Ulsenk said, "I'd say he's quite capable of hanging you on the spot."

Nilsa rushed to support Ingrid. "It doesn't matter. We're positive there's going to be an attempt on the King's life."

"And if we don't step in, they'll succeed. That's something else I'm sure of," Ingrid said very seriously.

"Well, let's say we believe you," Kol said. "What do you suggest we do?"

"We need to be very alert. We could be attacked at any moment, and right now I don't see you on watch duty."

"Uldritch has already posted sentries all around the camp," Hans explained.

"How many?"

"One at each point of the compass, as usual," said Ulsenk.

"I don't think that's enough. If they send a Natural Assassin, he'll kill the sentry on his side of the camp with no trouble."

"One of our Natural Assassins?" Kol said in amazement.

"Yeah," Nilsa explained. "We know that at least one of them belongs to the Dark Rangers and works for Eyra."

Hans shook his head. "Wow... that's nasty..."

"And a Sniper too," Ingrid added.

"Well, that certainly poses a problem," Ulsenk said. "He could shoot at the King from a distance, and we wouldn't realize until it was too late."

"That's why it's necessary to widen the area under watch," Ingrid pointed out.

"We can't do that without persuading Uldritch," said Kol. "He's the one who's in command here."

Ingrid stood up. "Well then, we've got to persuade him."

"Wait," Hans said. "I don't think you'd be able to."

"Why not?"

"Because of that peace-loving nature of yours." He gave her an ironic smile.

Ingrid frowned. "So who?"

Kol pointed to Nilsa. "Her."

"And why her?" Ingrid protested. She did not understand how Nilsa could achieve something she herself could not.

"Because she's sweet and kind?" Kol suggested.

"And knows how to make friends," Hans added.

"Yeah," Ulsenk said, "I agree, it would be better if it was Nilsa who went to talk to the Captain. He won't listen to any of us. He's narrow-minded. The chain of command and all that..."

Ingrid frowned angrily. "Well, for goodness' sake..." She was not at all happy about not being able to be the leader and do things the way she wanted to.

"I could try," said Nilsa.

"It'll be hard to convince him," Kol said. "He's stubborn, but if you approach him the nice way... he might lower his guard. Use your charm and smile at him," the Mage Hunter added with a wink.

"Wait a bit till he's gotten over the first impression," Hans recommended.

Nilsa agreed reluctantly.

As they waited, they scanned the camp in search of anything odd. It was well-organized and well-guarded. There must have been twenty or so Royal Guards and a dozen Royal Rangers there. Uldritch had put ten sentries around the King's tent and the surrounding area. Ingrid could not accuse him of incompetence, except that she herself would have doubled the number of sentries at the perimeter.

She saw that the Captain was retreating to his tent, and turned to Nilsa. "I think it's time to talk to Uldritch."

"Okay, I'll deal with it."

"Good luck."

"Thanks."

Chapter 42

Nilsa ran to Uldritch's tent to catch him before he went in to rest. If she were to make him come out again once he had gone inside, he would not be in a very good mood and she would be unable to convince him about anything. That was certain.

She raised her hand. "Captain! Just a moment!"

Uldritch turned and saw her running toward him. He looked at her with narrowed eyes.

"Yes?" he said in surprise.

Nilsa slowed down when she had almost reached him, but unluckily she tripped on a root and fell forwards, toward him. Wide-eyed, he caught her in his arms.

"Eh? What on earth are you doing?"

"Sorry! How clumsy of me!" Nilsa apologized as she tried to regain her balance.

Uldritch helped her back on to her feet. "For a moment I thought you were going to stab me."

"Oh no, not at all! It's just that I'm very clumsy."

"Well, that's better than being a murderer," the officer joked.

"Talking about murderers..." Nilsa took her chance and told him their fears about the Natural Assassin and the Sniper. She did it as eloquently as she could, trying to convey the urgency of the situation. She did not press him to take any action, she simply explained their fears, based on what they had found out and been through. When she had finished, she looked at him expectantly.

The Captain looked thoughtful. "And you say they were working for Eyra?"

"That's right, sir. Hence our concern."

"And you're genuinely convinced they're going to try to kill the King?"

"Yes, we are. We have evidence and information to prove it."

"But you're not certain."

"No, not absolutely certain, but now would be the best moment to try to murder him."

"I'm not saying it wouldn't be a good moment, seeing as we're on a journey in the open air and not protected inside the Royal Castle, but even so, without convincing proof I find it hard to believe."

"Either way, what harm can it do to strengthen the watch around the camp?"

Uldritch took a deep breath and looked up at the sky. He seemed to be going over the matter in his mind.

"Well, that's true. Strengthening security's never unwise. We have nothing to lose..."

"Better safe than to be sorry," Nilsa said with a shy smile.

"Yes, we need to be cautious these days. The Dark Ones pose a problem that's difficult to handle."

"That's why we're begging you to strengthen the sentry positions away from the camp."

"All right... I'll follow your advice and reinforce the perimeter positions with more sentries."

"Many thanks!"

"If the King's life really is in danger, I'd be a fool not to listen to you, so I'm going to do that."

"Thank you, sir."

"Tell your partner you've persuaded me. And also, make sure she stays calm. I don't want any kind of disturbance in my camp."

"Of course she'll do that, sir," Nilsa said very seriously.

"I don't like high-handedness."

"I understand that, sir. There won't be any trouble."

"Perfect. I'll go and take care of it."

Uldritch went away to reinforce the perimeter watch, and Nilsa went back to the fireside.

"How did it go?" Ingrid asked as soon as she saw her coming.

She smiled. "Better than expected. He's agreed to do what we asked."

Ingrid was duly impressed. "Wow! That's great!"

"That's because Nilsa has a special charm which is very hard to resist," Kol said with a provocative smile.

"And because even though Uldritch is tough, he's competent," Hans added.

Nilsa blushed a little.

"He listened to me, which is what counts," she said happily.

A Royal Ranger came over to the fire and indicated two other Rangers. "Ulsenk, Kol and you two, come with me. We're going to strengthen the perimeter watch."

Kol got to his feet. "Yes, sir." He looked at Nilsa. "See you at dawn," he added with a wink.

"Be careful," she said.

The Royal Rangers left, leaving Nilsa, Ingrid and Hans by the fire. At two other fires the same thing happened. Practically all the Royal Rangers were sent on sentry duty, leaving only the Royal Guards to keep watch on the interior of the camp.

Ingrid turned to Nilsa. "You seem to be very popular with the Royal Rangers."

"Oh, don't think that..." Nilsa said, and blushed slightly.

"She's more than popular. She has a retinue of followers, me included," Hans said with a smile which instead of flattering his face, made it uglier.

"Yeah, I'm beginning to see that," said Ingrid.

"It's just that she's adorable and beautiful besides," Hans said,

"I'm not beautiful. Ingrid's more beautiful than I am."

"Not at all," Ingrid objected.

"You have a warm beauty," Hans said, "like that of the embers of a fire on a cold winter's night. She has a cold beauty, like the Norghanian winter itself."

Nilsa giggled. "Wow, you're a real poet."

"Those of us who aren't very attractive physically have other virtues."

They chatted for some time about beauty and other trivial topics while the camp slept and the night rolled on. Ingrid and Nilsa could not sleep because of the tension of the situation. Every few moments they would look in all directions, as if expecting to see a horde of Dark Ones suddenly appear to capture the camp. Hans was drowsing by the fire, but he could not sleep either. He was restless. They all were.

Little by little, night engulfed everything, and darkness and exhaustion combined to make them fall asleep. Suddenly they heard shouts.

"Watch out!"

"Archer!"

The shouts were coming from the east. They were from the sentries posted there. Nilsa and Ingrid leapt to their feet and picked up their bows. It took Hans a moment to arm himself.

"What's going on?" he asked.

"They've sounded the alarm," Ingrid informed him as she scanned the direction the shouts had come from.

"To the east," Nilsa said.

The three looked toward that direction, arrows nocked, but they could see no enemy.

Uldritch came out of his tent with two other Royal Guards. "Royal Guard, with me!" he called, and they ran to his side, armed with swords and shields.

"Sniper!" came the alarm from the east.

"Three casualties!" came another voice.

The Captain turned toward the King's tent, where five Royal Guards were on sentry duty.

"Stay where you are," he told them. "You others, come with me." They set off toward where the calls of alarm were coming from.

"He's going after the Archer," Hans concluded.

"I'm not sure that's a good idea," said Ingrid.

"Shield formation!" Uldritch ordered, and they advanced into the night toward the east behind their shields.

"What do we do?" Nilsa asked.

"Do we go and help?" Hans suggested.

Ingrid looked around the camp. All except the Royal Guards who were protecting the King's tent, as well as themselves, were moving toward the archer's location.

"No, we stay here," she said firmly.

Hans pointed to the east. "But... the Sniper's over there."

"On the other hand the King's here," Ingrid said. She pointed to the royal tent.

"Look," said Nilsa.

Thoran's head peered out of the entrance to the tent. The Royal Guards outside it explained what was happening.

"How dare they!" he cried. "Those bloody traitors! Uldritch can brief me as soon as he's finished off the archer!" He went back into his tent again.

"We stay here and keep an eye on the King's tent," Ingrid said. "But let's find better positions for ourselves. Nilsa, you go to the west of the tent. Hans, you go behind it, and I'll take the east. Stand beside the Guards who are already on duty there. There are two Royal Guards at the front as well, and they ought to be able to stand up to an attack. That way we'll be able to check whether anyone tries to get as far as the King."

"Are you afraid the Assassin will attack?" Nilsa asked.

"Yeah. He might try to slip through, taking advantage of the confusion, and get as far as the royal tent."

"Understood," said Hans, and Nilsa nodded.

They took up the positions which had been arranged. The Royal Guard round the King's tent did not object. Having Rangers' bows available was always a welcome addition.

There were more cries from the east. "Guard wounded!" came a warning call.

"Don't move forward!" came another.

"Surround him!" Uldritch shouted.

Nilsa was very nervous. The situation was getting tenser and tenser all the time, and she was having trouble staying still. She was scanning in all directions continuously and trying to keep still, but it was impossible. The Royal Guard beside her gave her a number of questioning glances. In the end she began to make him nervous.

"Keep still, you're confusing me," he reproached her.

Nilsa nodded and took a deep breath. The soldier was right. She had to control herself. The situation was critical, and she could not allow herself to be carried away by her nerves. She looked toward the back of the tent and saw Hans talking to Frey. Nilsa relaxed at the sight of the handsome Healer Guard. Everything would be all right. They had the King's tent well-covered. The Assassin would not reach Thoran with them there.

She breathed out heavily. She did not like tense situations like that at all. She stretched her legs to stop them cramping with the tension. Anyway, Frey was there and could heal any wound, which made her feel even safer. She sighed, feeling more at ease. It was sheer luck to be able to count on a Specialist like him. She recalled the conversation with him in the capital, and his mentioning that Eyra had helped him to avoid failing and succeed in graduating as a Ranger.

That thought stayed in her mind, as though she were not fully able to process it. She wrinkled her nose. Something strange was happening to her. Why had that idea come into her mind and was now refusing to go away? And suddenly she realized. She turned to Hans and Frey, but could see neither of them.

"No!" she cried, and ran to the back of the tent as fast as she could. She had made a mistake, a very serious one, an unforgivable one. How could she not have realized? She reached the back of the tent and almost tripped over Hans' body.

His throat had been slit.

"Treason!" she shouted, and found that the canvas of the back of the tent had been torn. She opened it and went in.

"You...bloody..." the King was muttering.

Frey was on top of the King, who was lying on his back on the ground. The Ranger had one hand over the King's face, partially covering his mouth, to stop him from shouting. In his other hand was a knife, which he was trying to bury in Thoran's heart, and the King was not wearing his armor. He had been surprised while he was dressing, because part of it lay beside him on the floor. Thoran was clutching the wrist which held the knife with both his hands, struggling to avoid being killed.

Without stopping to think twice, Nilsa released almost without aiming, instinctively.

The arrow caught Frey in the back of his head, above the nape of his neck. For a moment he went on trying to stab the King. Nilsa nocked a second arrow and raised her bow, but it was not necessary. Frey collapsed to one side, dead.

Thoran stared at her.

"Great shot!"

Nilsa might have been paralyzed.

Ingrid came in and aimed her weapon. "Nilsa?" she said.

"It's Frey... he's the infiltrator."

Thoran pointed at the floor. "That bloody Royal Ranger is a Dark one!"

The Royal Guard came into the tent and helped the King to his feet.

"Are you wounded, your Majesty?" Ingrid asked.

Thoran looked at his clothes, which were bloodstained. "No. The blood's his."

At that moment Uldritch came into the tent.

"Uldritch! Where the hell were you?"

"Catching the Sniper, sir."

"You idiot! That was a distracting maneuver! I was attacked in my own tent!"

"Your Majesty... I..." the Captain stammered in an attempt to apologize.

"I was almost killed! You're an idiot!"

"Your Majesty, the threat..." he stammered, but he knew there was no possible defense.

"That's enough! I don't want to hear your excuses! If it hadn't been for this redhead here I'd be dead!"

They all turned to look at Nilsa, who still could not fully take in what had just happened. Frey was a Dark Ranger, and had been on the point of killing the King.

"There are two dead bodies behind the tent, sire," another Royal Guard reported. "A Guard and a Ranger."

"What good are my Guards if they let a murderer into my own tent to murder me?" Thoran yelled, waving his arms furiously. He began to insult the Captain and his men uncontrollably, and his shouts could be heard a league away.

"Well done," Ingrid whispered to Nilsa, while the King went on shouting at his men.

"Thanks..."

"How did you realize?"

"I'm not sure. Suddenly I remembered something he'd told me, and I worked it out from there."

"Well, that was a near thing."

"You can say that again."

At last Thoran calmed down a little. He stopped insulting and cursing his guards and turned to Nilsa and Ingrid, who were watching the scene in silence.

"The redhead. I want a word with you," he said to Nilsa. "Tell me everything you know about what's happened."

Nilsa turned to Ingrid, who nodded. "As you wish, your Majesty. It's a little complicated..."

"Complicated? What d'you mean, complicated? Wasn't it those accursed Dark Rangers?"

"There's more, your Majesty," said Ingrid.

Thoran stared at them and realized that something really serious was afoot.

"Uldritch, secure the camp. And do it properly this time!"

"Yes, your Majesty," the Captain replied, and left at once with his head down. If he had stayed inside, he might have lost it.

Thoran indicated the two girls. "Everybody out of the tent except you two."

Once they had all gone out, he said to Nilsa and Ingrid:

"Now tell me everything, from the beginning."

Chapter 43

When Egil and Gerd reached the top of the mountain it was snowing lightly, and even though it was not particularly cold by Norghanian standards, the air at this height was cutting. Gerd led the way, and Egil sheltered from the wind and the cold behind his friend's huge body. Long trudges through the snow were not exactly Egil's specialty and he was having a tough time during the climb. Nor did it help that he was carrying a backpack full of supplies and medicines. Gerd was carrying one too, but he was much stronger and over time had become a lot tougher. For him this was a pleasant stroll.

They reached a group of trees and saw a pass behind them. It led between the rocks to a valley within the mountains.

Gerd stopped and turned. "What d'you think?"

"Interesting. A lost valley up here."

"Do we go in?"

Egil looked around, but saw nothing that gave any sign of what they were looking for.

"Yeah, we keep going."

"Sure? Wouldn't it be better to try another direction?"

"No, I'm almost certain we're going in the right direction."

"Practically sure?"

"Certainty's rarely my traveling companion, my dear friend."

"Don't go all philosophical on me. I've got enough worries already without having to worry about you as well."

"Why should you worry about me?"

"Because you've been a bit strange lately..."

"I don't know what you mean. I've always been quite strange, or rather *different*, as I prefer to regard it."

"Well, you have some very strange new friends... Ginger and Fred... and now you go all philosophical when we're in the middle of a really critical situation."

"My dear friend, I can assure you that I'm in top form, and you have nothing to worry about. As for the situation being critical: well, that's true, it's something that happens to us too frequently. It's not good for the nerves."

"So you're all right?"

"Fantastically well."

"And I needn't worry?"

"Irrefutable, my dear friend."

"That's not an answer."

"You needn't worry about me," Egil assured him.

"Okay then, on we go."

The two friends entered the pass, with the snow falling more heavily on their cloaks and hoods. They found a snow-covered valley and went into it determinedly. Both of them held their bows at the ready as they went. Their leather boots sank into the snow a hand-span deep.

Gerd wiped away the crystalline flakes which were clinging to his face. "I can see something," he said.

"What is it?"

He pointed ahead through the trees. "It looks like a Ranger's tent."

Egil took a good look at the snow-covered tent. It was normal-sized, so that it could accommodate four people. Rangers carried them when they were making long or complicated journeys.

"Yup, it looks like one of ours. Let's get a closer look."

They approached the tent stealthily, not knowing what they might find. It could be a trap. The door was shut. Egil gestured to Gerd to be ready to release, and his big friend went to stand in front of the door. Egil counted to three on his fingers, very slowly and without a sound, then opened the door to reveal what was inside. Gerd meanwhile stood ready with his bow.

What they found left them stunned. Inside the tent were Lasgol and Valeria, their bodies bloodstained and their faces ashen. Huddled against them to provide them with some warmth were Camu and Ona.

The panther growled when the door opened. When she recognized Gerd, she moaned. Camu too looked out, and when he saw Egil and Gerd, his bulging eyes opened even wider. There was great delight in them.

Lasgol opened his eyes and looked out. "Gerd..." he muttered, as if coming out of a deep sleep.

Gerd lowered his bow. "Lasgol! What happened?"

Egil put his head in through the door and analyzed the strange scene as he stared at the extensive bloodstains on their clothes and the blanket which covered them. "Lasgol, how are you? I can see blood. Are you wounded?"

"Egil..." Lasgol tried to sit up. "I'm fine. Don't worry about me. It's Valeria, she's lost a lot of blood. I tried to save her... don't know whether I have... I think she's seriously hurt."

Egil came into the tent as best he could, because the four of them filled it almost completely. Valeria's face was ashen, and she looked as though she were more in the other world than in this one.

"She has a pulse. She's alive, but unconscious."

Gerd gasped with relief from the door. "Thank goodness!"

Egil checked her wound very carefully. Lasgol's bandages were rudimentary but efficient, and they had stopped the bleeding.

"I see you treated the infection and the loss of blood."

"I did what I could..."

"But you didn't take the arrowhead out."

"I was afraid she'd bleed to death if I did..."

"Well, I think we have no choice but to take it out," Egil said.

"Can't we carry her?" Gerd asked. "I could do it. She's not that heavy."

Egil shook his head. "I'm afraid not. We're too high up in the mountains to take her down. She wouldn't survive the journey in the state she's in. She's lost too much blood. She's barely alive."

"Oh no..." Gerd said sadly.

Egil turned to Lasgol. "Where are you wounded, pal?"

"How do you know I'm hurt?" Lasgol asked. He sounded surprised, and a little awed.

"Because you look bad, and because you've been forced to stay here and wait for someone to come looking for you. If you weren't hurt, you'd have gone down for help."

Lasgol sighed. "You're always right." He gave Egil a shy smile and indicated his leg.

Egil raised the blanket and saw that it was bloody and very swollen.

"The thigh wound is well healed," commented, examining it.

Gerd bent to look at the leg wound closely. "Ufff!" That's a trap wound, and a nasty one."

"A man-trap..." said Lasgol.

"Bad business, in that case. Those are the worst. There's no way to get free unless you have the key."

"I got the key. Gatik had it on him."

"Was it Gatik's trap?" Egil asked, raising one eyebrow, and Lasgol nodded.

"Where is he?" Gerd asked. Alarmed at the mention of the conspirator, he was aiming his bow everywhere.

"Relax. He's dead."

They stared at him.

"Dead? You faced up to him?"

"More or less."

"I told you not to, that it was too dangerous. All you needed to do was watch him."

"He set a trap for me. He guessed we'd come after him."

"What a dirty business," Gerd said. "How did you get the key to open the trap?"

"Ona dragged his body to me, and I searched for the key in his clothes."

"Was it you who killed him?" Egil asked. He was puzzling over how it could have happened.

"It wasn't me, it was Ona, when he was about to finish me off."

Egil bent to stroke her. "Well done, Ona," he said, and she moaned in gratitude.

"And you too, Camu," Egil said, patting his head.

I give heat. Lasgol and Valeria not die cold.

"He says he gave us heat, and that's why we haven't died of cold."

"Well done, Ona and Camu," Egil told them.

"Where's Gatik's body?" Gerd asked. "I want to make sure."

"A few paces to the north there's a trench. You'll find him inside. Be careful not to fall in, it's quite deep."

"A trap?"

"Yeah, a double one. Trench, plus elemental traps of water at the bottom."

"Wow, he knew what he was doing. I'm going to make sure. I'll leave you my backpack. There's some supplies in it, and a blanket."

Egil went out to fetch his own backpack, which he left on the floor beside them. "I've brought medicines and some food. Relax."

"I'm fine..."

"I'd better treat that wound, or it'll get infected. You don't want to end up like Ulf, do you?"

"You mean his character?" Lasgol joked. "Much better not."

"Well, if you can joke about it, it can't be as serious as that," Egil said. "I meant lame."

"And not that either."

"Right, we need to treat it, and do it properly. The wound's a nasty one, even though you may not think so."

Very happy Egil here.

I'm even happier, Lasgol transmitted back.

Egil very smart.

Yes, he certainly is.

Ona chirped once.

"What are they saying?" Egil asked as he took out his medicines and set to work.

"They're very happy to see you."

"And so am I to see you. We've been very worried."

"I guessed that when I didn't get back, you'd come looking for me."

"The Panthers don't leave anyone behind," Egil said, and gave him a wink.

Lasgol smiled. "Thanks for coming."

"Don't mention it. When Gerd and I got back to the capital with Count Olmossen and handed him over so that they could put him in prison, I saw you hadn't come back yet. I was a little worried, but we waited a day and then I had a bad feeling. Perhaps because Gatik was too dangerous. So I told Gerd we'd come looking for you, just in case."

"But you're not the sort of person who goes by hunches," Lasgol said in surprise.

"No, nine times out of ten I follow reason."

"Exactly."

"But this time it was that one in every ten, and I came looking for you."

"Well, you did the right thing."

He did very right thing, Camu transmitted, and licked Egil's face with his blue tongue.

Egil smiled and petted him. "For once I followed my instincts and was right, and we don't need to attach too much importance to it."

"What about the others? Are they okay?" Lasgol wanted to know.

"I don't know anything about them. We left before they got back."

"I hope they're all right."

"They will be, don't worry."

"Seeing how I ended up myself, I do worry."

Egil gave him a wink. "The others don't attract as much bad luck as the two of us do."

Lasgol smiled back. "That's very true. The two of us are far and away the most problematic."

Egil went on chatting with Lasgol as he prepared everything he needed, and after a while Gerd came back.

"I found him. He was covered by snow, but very dead."

"Did you go down into the trench to make sure?" Lasgol asked him, as if he were afraid Gatik might get out again.

"That didn't seem a very good idea to me. I'm not very good at getting out of traps," Gerd joked.

"Then how do you know he's completely dead?" Egil asked.

"I shot two arrows into him, to make sure."

Egil and Lasgol looked at him in amazement. "You shot a dead man at the bottom of a trench?" Egil asked him in disbelief.

Gerd shrugged. "Eh? I had to make sure, and that Gatik was very dangerous. It was better not to risk it."

Egil shook his head. "Every day you get more like Viggo."

"I'm fine with having one or two of Viggo's 'qualities', or yours too," Gerd said pointedly.

Egil chuckled. "Touché. Let me work on the wounds for a while, and we'll see how we get on after that."

Lasgol's wound was a nasty one, but after treating it, and with the initial attention Lasgol himself had given it, he managed to sort it out. It was different in Valeria's case. He had to take the arrowhead out, and it was in a very tricky place. If it was not done with surgical precision, he would cut through a major artery and she would bleed to death. In fact she was so weak that as soon as the infection spread – it had already started around the wound – she would die.

Egil passed this news on to them, looking worried.

"Do it," Gerd said. "I'll help you."

"She might not make it," Egil said.

Lasgol gave an impatient snort. "Do it. If we don't try, she's dead anyway."

"Gerd, we need a fire," Egil told him.

"I've already started on it."

Egil cleaned the wound with boiled water and left the blade of his Ranger's knife in the fire. "It'll disinfect it," he told Gerd and Lasgol, who were watching him.

"D'you think she'll wake up?" Gerd asked.

"Let's hope she doesn't. This is going to hurt a lot. Ona, Camu, Lasgol, I need you to leave the tent. We need to make some room."

Lasgol managed to limp out of the tent with Gerd's help. Outside, he got to his feet as best he could, limping heavily. Ona and Camu came out as well. Suddenly the tent seemed enormous with only Valeria left in it.

Stretch legs good, Camu transmitted.

Ona leapt once and then again, checking that her legs were well. They seemed to be.

Egil disinfected the area around the wound by pouring on a mixture he had prepared specifically for this. He took the knife and then, as if he were an experienced surgeon, made an incision in the wound so that he could take out the arrowhead. Valeria was still unconscious, but shifted as she felt the pain.

"Gerd, hold her down. This is going to hurt her. You've got to stop her moving."

"No problem. I'll take care of it." The giant grasped one arm and the opposite shoulder.

Egil began to extract the head very carefully. Valeria moved again, but Gerd held her down. Egil wiped away the blood which was oozing out of the wound.

"Get ready, Gerd."

"Ready."

Egil took the arrowhead out, trying not to harm any internal organ as he did so. Valeria opened her eyes suddenly and screamed in agony, and Gerd pressed down harder to hold her in place.

"Got it!" Egil said, and took out the bloodied arrowhead.

Lasgol poked his head in through the tent door. "Well done!" he called.

"We have to seal the wound," Egil said. He pressed it with the cloth to staunch the bleeding, then put his knife back in the fire.

"Are you going to seal it with hot iron?" Lasgol asked.

"It's the best way. She'll have a nasty scar, but it won't get infected."

Egil waited until the blade was red-hot, then applied it to the wound. A dreadful smell of burned flesh filled the tent. They all covered their noses, and even Ona and Camu turned away. Valeria gave another heart-rending scream, but Gerd held her firmly until she passed out from the pain.

"I think that went well," Egil said.

Lasgol was watching Valeria. "We'll soon know," he said. If she woke up in a few hours, she would live. If on the other hand she failed to, at least they had tried.

"Now what?" Gerd asked.

"We go back to the capital." Egil said. "We need to find out what's happened to our friends."

"We can't take Valeria to the capital," Lasgol said.

"What d'you mean? Why not?" Gerd asked.

Egil raised one eyebrow. He had already suspected that something unusual was going on. "What happened up here?" he asked Lasgol.

"I'll tell you both... but you're not going to like it."

He told them everything that had happened, right to the end. When he had finished, Gerd stared at him in horror and disbelief.

"It can't be! Not her!"

"Sorry, big guy," Lasgol said.

Gerd was shaking his head. "I can't believe it!"

Egil, on the other hand, had thought it through and understood it. "It makes sense, after all. It makes complete sense. She fooled us completely with that story of her enmity towards her father. Very clever."

"I just couldn't believe it when it happened," said Lasgol. "I still can't..."

"I can't believe it even now!" cried Gerd. He began to gesticulate around the tent, punching the air out of the enormous frustration he was feeling.

"If we take her to the capital," Egil said, "she'll hang with her father."

"It's what she deserves," Gerd said, carried away by rage at her betrayal.

PEDRO URVI

Egil glanced at Valeria lying unconscious in the tent. "I'm not saying she doesn't, but perhaps we ought to discuss it before we hand her over."

Lasgol nodded. "Let's not hand her over yet. We need to talk about it."

Egil nodded. He looked at Gerd, who was so furious and outraged that he was still pacing the tent.

"We trusted her! She was our friend! Why? How could she do a thing like that?"

"Loyalties of blood are difficult to understand," Egil said.

Gerd cursed to the heavens, but finally managed to calm down.

"And on top of all that, we just saved her life. She doesn't deserve it. Why didn't you tell us before?"

Egil looked hard at his friend. "So that we wouldn't be tempted not to help her and simply let her die."

Lasgol nodded. "Yeah, that's right. I couldn't let her die, in spite of what she's done. She saved my life in the end."

"Do whatever you want. As far as I'm concerned she's dead," Gerd said.

Egil watched her a moment longer.

"I'll deal with her. Leave it all in my hands."

Chapter 44

A week later, a very important meeting was held in the Throne Hall, which had been taken over by the Royal Guard. King Thoran was on the throne, with his brother Orten on his right. On one side the Royal Rangers were lined up, and in front was a group of selected guests whom the King had asked to attend: none other than the members of the Great Council and the Snow Panthers. The nobles of the realm had not been invited, because the matters to be dealt with were of a delicate nature, especially for Thoran. There had been an elaborate conspiracy to end both his life and that of his brother, which had come close to succeeding. Revealing this information to the nobles would make him appear a weak King, which was the last thing he wanted.

"I'm furious about everything that's happened," Thoran began, opening the session without beating about the bush.

"It's an unthinkable outrage," agreed his brother, who clearly shared his anger.

Everybody else said nothing, to avoid incurring the rage of either the King or his brother. They all knew the outbursts both were prone to: particularly those of Thoran, which were to be feared.

"There has been a conspiracy at the highest level, and they've tried to murder my brother and myself in order to get hold of the throne of Norghana."

The members of the Council, who had heard rumors but were not sure about anything, were perplexed and deeply worried. The news was not just serious, it was inconceivable.

"And not only that," Thoran added. "They've also attempted to take over the leadership of the Rangers."

There were murmurs and cries of surprise among all the members of the Council, who were unable to believe their ears.

"Count Olmossen, my Commander Sven and the newly-promoted Leader of the Rangers Gatik have betrayed me by conspiring against me behind my back and have attempted to put an end to my rule."

Sigrid, Gondabar, Dolbarar and the other members of the

Council were left petrified by the news. They were speechless, attempting to understand the magnitude of it all.

"I'll spare you the details, because they're insignificant, but you need to know that they united with the aim of dividing my kingdom. Olmossen intended to take over the West, Sven the East, and Gatik the Rangers."

"They're a bunch of stinking, treacherous swine," Orten said. "If I could, I'd rip their guts out!"

"Gatik and Sven died in the course of their attempts on my brother and myself. As for Count Olmossen, we have him in the dungeons. He's being questioned. He'll hang in the main square when we've finish extracting all the information he has about the conspiracy."

Orten punched his right fist into his left hand. "He hasn't got much left to confess," he said with an evil smile.

"What we have found out is that Gatik was the leader of the Dark Rangers, and that Eyra was his right hand. They've been conspiring for years."

"And they've paid for it with their lives," Orten added.

"And once the dog's dead, the rabies has gone, as the saying goes. With the deaths of Gatik and Eyra, the Dark Rangers are over and done with. However, I don't want to take any risks, and we're going to hunt them down until the last one is eliminated."

"This is terrible news," Gondabar said mournfully, almost unable to believe the King's words.

"Gatik's betrayal is a dishonor to us all," Sigrid said firmly.

"What could have driven them to act like this?" Dolbarar wondered, more to himself than to anybody else.

"Greed and hunger for power, that's what's driven them to act like this," Thoran replied. "And let this be a warning to all, that anyone who allows themselves to be seduced by them will end up in a nameless pit, like Gatik and Eyra."

"And Sven and Olmossen," Orten added.

"The throne is mine. and nobody is going to take it away from me!" Thoran thundered. "Anyone who tries is going to end up as food for worms!"

"You'd better all understand that!" Orten yelled. "Or else I'll tear your guts out with my own hands!"

The members of the Council and the Panthers fell silent. It was clearly not a good moment for comments or interruptions of any kind.

"To dare to go against me! Behind my back! To try to kill me! Accursed traitors!" Thoran shouted at the top of his voice. "I'll kill you all at the first suspicious sign! Every one of you!"

It took Thoran a moment to bring his rage and frustration under control. At last he managed to calm himself down to the point where he could sit down on the throne again and stop yelling at his audience. His brother Orten, his arms crossed over his powerful chest, looked as if he would like to kill half of Norghana.

"Nilsa and Ingrid, present yourselves before your King," Thoran called in a more neutral tone of voice.

Both of them came forward to stand before the throne. They were wearing formal dress: Ingrid as a Specialist and Nilsa as a Ranger. They knelt before the King.

"Rise. You have earned the honor of not having to kneel before your King."

They stood up, and Thoran acknowledged their salute with a nod.

"These two brave people saved my life by stopping a traitor among the Royal Rangers from assassinating me from behind. I want everyone here to know this. What the kingdom needs is more loyal soldiers like them. For their efforts to save my life, they have my gratitude and that of the kingdom. Their intervention saved me just in time. In addition to this, they are part of the group which found out about the conspiracy against me and informed me of what was going on so that I could take appropriate steps. For all this, I intend to grant them the Norghanian Star of Courage. They will also receive a notable amount of gold for their meritorious action."

Everybody applauded the King's words, and comments of appreciation and murmurs in praise of their work could be heard.

"Thank you, your Majesty," Ingrid said.

"It's an honor," said Nilsa. She was very moved.

Thoran beckoned to one of the Royal Guards, who came forward holding a crimson cushion embroidered in gold on which lay the medals. They were in the form of two silver stars, and they gleamed under the light which came in through the high windows of the hall.

The King took the decorations, rose from the throne and came down to where Nilsa and Ingrid were waiting, erect as stakes, with their chins held high. Thoran pinned the stars to their chests, above their hearts.

"The King and Norghana are grateful for your devotion and sacrifice," he said.

Everybody applauded once again as Ingrid and Nilsa went back to their comrades. Nilsa's eyes were moist with emotion, and Ingrid could not have been prouder. When they showed their stars to their friends Gerd's eyes opened wide, and Egil and Lasgol admired them with great satisfaction. Viggo bit Ingrid's star to make sure it was real silver, not an imitation, and this earned him a jab in the ribs.

Thoran waited a moment and then went on: "On the other hand, my brother Orten has told me that two Specialist Assassins, working alone, prevented the filthy traitor Sven and his minions from murdering him in a very well-planned ambush. I am very glad to know that we have among us such worthy and capable Specialists."

"I thought I was as good as dead," said Orten. "If it hadn't been for them I wouldn't be here to tell the tale, though I'd have taken that treacherous swine Sven with me to the world of the Ice Gods."

"Let the two Specialists who saved my brother's life step forward," Thoran proclaimed.

Astrid and Viggo went to stand before the throne. They too were wearing formal dress, as the King had requested. They knelt, but Thoran gestured them to rise, and they exchanged the salute for a bow.

"There's nothing I love more than my brother," Thoran said. "You saved his life, and for that you have my eternal gratitude."

"And mine, of course," Orten added.

"I grant you both the Norghanian Star of Courage as well, and the reward in gold for those heroic acts which stopped the ambush on my brother from ending in tragedy. More Specialists like you are what we need. That is beyond doubt."

Astrid and Viggo accepted their Stars gracefully, deeply honored. After they had withdrawn, Viggo whispered that the Star was not going to be much use to him, that what he wanted was the gold, and where on earth was it? Which earned him another jab in the ribs from Ingrid.

"I also wish to congratulate the rest of the group who helped to uncover the conspiracy to murder my brother and myself. Be pleased to step forward."

Gerd, Egil and Lasgol exchanged hesitant glances.

"Go on," Ingrid encouraged them.

"We explained everything to the King," Nilsa assured them.

Viggo raised one eyebrow. "Everything?"

"Almost everything," Ingrid corrected herself.

"In that case we'd better do as the King requests." Egil said.

The three friends advanced to the throne. Lasgol was limping from his wounds that were still unhealed. They bent one knee and bowed their heads. This time Thoran did not tell them to rise.

"Names?" Orten demanded. He was staring at them intensely.

"Gerd Vang, your Highness," said the giant, without raising his gaze.

"Lasgol Eklund."

"Egil Olafstone."

"He's the youngest Olafstone," Orten informed Thoran, who had probably investigated them already.

"I know. One finds oneself among strange allies now and then," Thoran said. "As I understand it, he's the mastermind of the group. Isn't that so, Egil?"

"I like to puzzle out enigmas, your Majesty," Egil said very calmly.

"That's what I've been told. I find it curious that someone with your surname should have helped me in this particular situation..."

"My surname is a thing of the past. It has nothing to do with who I am now. I'm a Ranger, and I defend my kingdom and the throne."

"I'm glad you think like that, not like that traitor Olmossen, who will hang very soon for his attempt to gain power in the West. I hope you'll never have that temptation."

The King's threat was unequivocal, both for Egil and for everybody else.

"My only temptation is the acquisition of greater knowledge. My weakness is books. Politics is not something that arouses my interest. There's already been enough tragedy in my family."

"Wise attitude. Stay on that path and you'll live," the King advised him. But his tone was one of command.

"I'll be keeping an eye on you so that you don't take your eyes off your books," Orten promised him.

"I won't disappoint you," Egil said. He knew that he had been under observation by Orten ever since his conversation with Musker, and was sure that the King's brother would send another agent to spy on him. It did not worry him particularly. He would find out who it was and see how he could deal with the inconvenience. He might even use him in his own favor to trick Orten, now that he knew he was the one who was spying on him.

"The three of you have done an exceptional job in uncovering the conspiracy and saving the kingdom from traitors," the King said, "and you will be duly rewarded for it."

"It was our duty, your Majesty," said Gerd, and the others nodded.

"Now rise," Thoran said.

They did so, and waited as the King and his brother looked them up and down.

"Let the decorated Rangers come forward too."

"We seem to have a nice group of young Rangers here," Orten commented when Nilsa, Ingrid, Astrid and Viggo had come forward to join their friends. From his tone of voice, it was hard to tell whether he meant it seriously or whether he was being sarcastic.

"To be honest, I'm impressed by their performance," Thoran said as he stared at them. "I've had an idea," he added suddenly. "At the Great Council I mentioned that I wanted to create a group of good Rangers, loyal to me. You've shown yourselves to be both, and for that reason I've decided that you seven are to form that group from now on. You are to be a group of Special Rangers who will carry out secret missions both within and without the kingdom, whenever required. You are also to ensure that no more conspiracies arise, either among the Rangers, the nobles or the army."

They were all taken completely by surprise.

"Us, your Majesty?" Ingrid said.

"Yes, you."

"I'm not sure we —" Ingrid began, but the King interrupted her at once.

"This is not a request, but an order,"

She bowed her head. "Of course, your Majesty."

"You will only report to the Leader of the Rangers, and of course to me. Nobody else in the realm will be able to give you orders."

"Not even the nobles or the army, your Majesty?" Viggo asked.

"Not even him," Thoran said, indicating his brother Orten. "In that way he'll never get any strange ideas, because he'll know you're keeping an eye on him."

Orten expression suggested that he was not at all happy about this. "As you wish, brother," he said grudgingly.

"I must think of a name you can be known by, so that everybody knows who you are... let me think..."

"We're known as the Snow Panthers, your Majesty," Ingrid said.

"Hmm. Not a bad name, but not sufficiently intimidating. I want a name that when they hear it will make my enemies, conspirators, traitors and suchlike quake till their teeth rattle."

"How about the Black Snakes?" Orten suggested. "Since the Rangers use names of animals for their teams."

"Better. That name is much better..." Thoran went on thinking. "I have it now. There's an animal that eats black snakes. The Eagle. You will be my Royal Eagles. You will eat the snakes which are my treacherous enemies. You will take out the eyes of spies and conspirators. Yes, the Royal Eagles."

Orten nodded. "I like it. A magnificent animal, and also a regal one."

"Which brings us to another important matter," Thoran went on. "With the death of Gatik, we're now without a leader among the Rangers. Hence we need to choose another." The King turned toward the seven. "Who do you trust? It must be someone you trust completely, because he's the only one you'll be reporting to, and your lives will be in his hands. Think carefully about it."

The Panthers formed a circle and talked among themselves in whispers. The situation was an uncomfortable one, because they were not only in the presence of the King and his brother but of all the members of the Council, who were watching them with great curiosity. After a brief deliberation, they turned back to the King. Ingrid was the one they had chosen to communicate their decision.

"Your Majesty, we have complete trust and faith in Gondabar and Dolbarar. Our wish would be that they might regain their positions, since they're loyal to the Rangers, to the realm and to the throne."

Thoran looked at them, frowning. "That doesn't please me at all. I demoted them for their incompetence."

He was silent for a moment, considering, then he turned back to the members of the Council. "Incompetent they may have shown themselves to be, but on the other hand, you're right in that they're loyal and trustworthy. For this reason, and because I owe you a favor,

I shall give them a second chance. With this, my favor toward you is paid for. However, if I see the least sign of incompetence among them, not only will I dismiss them, but they'll also end their days rotting in the royal dungeons. Is that clear enough?"

The members of the Council fell silent, and Gondabar and Dolbarar, who were surprised by the turn the situation had taken, stammered an affirmation,

"Come forward to the center, so that you may be seen and heard," Orten said.

"Let us make it official," Thoran said. "Gondabar, kneel to show your respect."

Gondabar bent his knee and bowed his head. Luckily he had his staff with him and was able to lean on it to keep his balance and rest his bones. At his age, it was not easy to kneel.

"Your Majesty, I am always at your service."

"Your King hereby grants you a second chance, in order that you may redeem the mistakes you have made. From this moment on, you are once again the King's Master Ranger, Leader of all the Rangers of Norghana."

"Your majesty, it's an honor. I'll serve the Rangers, the throne and Norghana with honor, to my final breath."

"Remember what I've told you. I'll be watching everything that goes on among the Rangers, and if you fail me again, you know the end that awaits you."

"Thank you, your Majesty. I won't fail you."

"I hope so, for your own good. You may withdraw."

Gondabar stood up slowly and went back to Dolbarar's side.

"Dolbarar, come closer."

"Your Majesty, always at your service," he said respectfully.

"From this moment, you once again take up the responsibility of being Leader of the Rangers' Camp. I do this at the request of these young people. Do not forget it, and do not make any more mistakes, or else I'll be forced to make you pay."

"I am grateful to these young Rangers for their support, and to your Majesty for giving me a second chance. I shall work without rest, honorably, for the Rangers and the Realm, and will do my best to train the new generations so that they may serve you as excellent Rangers."

"I hope so. Give me good Rangers to protect me and defend me from my enemies."

"So I will, your Majesty."

"You may withdraw."

"Thank you, my liege," Dolbarar said, and went back to Gondabar's side.

Thoran stared at the members of the Council, then at Angus.

"Angus, this means you lose your position. You'll help Dolbarar in his functions."

"It will be an honor, your Majesty," Angus said with a bow.

"Very well. Other concerns await me, so I hereby declare this audience at an end."

"Go, and serve your King and Lord," Orten told them.

Everybody began to leave the hall: first the members of the Council, then Gondabar and Dolbarar, and finally the Royal Eagles.

Chapter 45

In the ante-chamber the members of the Council were waiting for the group, while they discussed everything that had happened inside and the repercussions – of which there were many – which the King's decisions would mean for all of them.

Gondabar and Dolbarar came up to Lasgol and the group as soon as they came out of the throne hall.

"Thank you very much for what you've done," Dolbarar told them, with deep gratitude in his eyes.

"We are deeply indebted to you," Gondabar added.

Ingrid waved this aside. "It was nothing."

"It's the best thing for Norghana," Egil said.

"And for all of us," Nilsa added with a smile.

"What we are today we owe to our leaders," Lasgol said. He bowed to both of them, and there was gratitude in both his voice and the expression on his face.

"I wish we had more Rangers like you," Dolbarar said. "You're an example to be followed. A blessing for both the corps and the realm."

"I don't want to get emotional, which is not a good thing at my age," Gondabar said with moist eyes. "You have my eternal gratitude."

"How is this business of the Royal Eagles going to work?" Nilsa asked him. She was already beginning to imagine it.

"That's a good question," Gondabar replied. "As long as there's no special mission, just go back to your usual tasks. When I have need of you, I'll call you. I think that'll be the best way to manage things, because there won't be special missions very often. I hope so... because if there are, it'll mean there's serious trouble in the realm. We'll figure outhow to do it as we go along, and then adapt. This is something new for all of us."

"Wonderful!" Nilsa cried. "It's just that I love my work here with my leader

He smiled kindly at her. "The feeling is mutual."

"Now that the Great Council is over and this conspiracy has been dismantled," Dolbarar said, "we must all go back to our posts and work hard to re-establish everything we've lost. I miss the Camp."

"You'll see me there soon, starting work again," Egil said.

Dolbarar smiled at him. "That's simply wonderful. Your help is invaluable to me."

"Thank you, sir. I'll be happy to be back at my post, by your side."

Several other members of the Council, among them the Master Rangers and Oden, came over to congratulate them. Dolbarar and Gondabar moved away a little to give the others the chance to talk to the leading figures of the day.

"Great work!" Esben congratulated them, and clasped each of them in an embrace. It was a crushing one.

"Thank you, Master Ranger," Gerd said, delighted with the recognition he had been given.

"You've done a great job, I have to admit," Haakon said, almost despite himself, "although I'm not completely in agreement with the leaders staying in their positions. I still think we need new blood to guide us toward a new era of prosperity and peace."

"Thank you, sir. We think Gondabar and Dolbarar are the leaders we need," Lasgol replied. He was trying not to show how glad he was that Haakon had not gotten his way.

"They might be better for now," Ivana said, "but a time of change will come soon enough, and then things will go even better. In any case, you've shown that you're very competent Rangers, as should be expected of those who have passed through my School." Her eyes were on Nilsa and Ingrid as she said this.

"Thank you very much, Ma'am," they replied, almost in unison.

Haakon pointed to Astrid and Viggo. "And you two, you've shown your worth. I see what I taught you in the School of Expertise has served you well."

"More than well," Viggo said with a smile of satisfaction. "Although if there's good material to begin with, it helps."

"We're grateful for the training we were given," Astrid said, more humbly.

"Serve the corps and the realm, and don't get into trouble," Haakon said, looking at Egil and Lasgol, as if the warning were more for them than for Astrid and Viggo.

"Of course. So we will," said Astrid before Viggo could make one of his sarcastic comments.

The Master Rangers left them and gave way to Sigrid, the Mother Specialist, who came to their side together with the four Elder Specialists.

"Royal Eagles," she greeted them with one of her good-witch smiles. "Allow me to congratulate you on all you've done. The kingdom's in debt to all of you."

"Two Assassins alone who are capable of stopping a deadly ambush and saving the King's brother all by themselves," Engla said. "Impressive. Really noteworthy. I expected as much of Astrid, but you, Viggo, never cease to surprise me."

He smiled ironically. "Positively, I hope."

Engla laughed. "Yes, positively. This time, at least."

"Thank you, Ma'am," Astrid added respectfully. "Your teachings are a great help to us."

"Keep practicing every day, and don't forget what I taught you. If you need to improve in anything, pay me a visit and I'll see what else I can teach you."

"That would be an honor," Astrid replied.

Viggo nodded. "We will," he said, but it did not sound as if he really wanted to go back to the Shelter to go on learning.

"Well," Ivar said, "saving the King himself is quite a feat too, even if he was protected. Very good work, and my sincerest congratulations to my pupil."

"Thank you, Master," Ingrid replied, pleased with the recognition.

"Keep up the good work, and you'll go far among the Rangers."

"I'll try to do that," Ingrid said, feeling very honored.

"How are Ona and Camu?" Gisli asked Lasgol. "Happy to be with a Hero of the Realm who's unmasked the leader of the Dark Ones?"

"As mischievous as ever, but I think they're very happy too. They've grown a lot, and they seem very well physically and emotionally."

"Do you think I could visit them before we leave? I'd really like to see them and say hello to them."

"Of course, Master."

"Wonderful. I appreciate that very much."

Annika came over to Egil. "Even if you weren't able to enter the Shelter as a specialist, I think that now you're a Royal Eagle, and seeing the great potential you've shown and how intelligent you are, you should consider visiting me. There are many aspects of the Specialties of Nature you could learn, which I am sure would be very useful to you in the future."

"Thank you very much for the offering. It's an honor. I know there are very few who are offered this privilege after not having been chosen to become Specialists to start with. I'll bear it in mind and see if I can."

Annika smiled. "My doors will be waiting open for you."

"I extend the offering to the rest of the Royal Eagles," Sigrid said suddenly, and the group stared at her in surprise.

"Does the Mother Specialist want us all to go to the Shelter?" Lasgol asked. He had an inkling of the reason for that strange invitation.

"Indeed. It will be an honor to welcome you, some once again and others for the first time. You've shown what you're capable of. I never had any doubts about Lasgol, Astrid, Ingrid and Viggo, because they're exceptional Rangers and hence were able to become Specialists, and among the very best. You others have proved yourselves worthy of the opportunity to become Specialists, as Annika has quite rightly said to Egil. So I extend the invitation to Nilsa and Gerd."

"Oh, thank you!" Gerd said delightedly.

"I feel very honored," Nilsa said.

"You've earned it," Sigrid assured her.

"Is there anything else the Mother Specialist wants of us?" Lasgol asked her. He was still doubtful.

"Yes, my clever pup," she said. "I have the King's permission to continue my studies and go on experimenting with the creation of Improved Rangers. Who better than you to help attain that goal?"

"Mother Specialist... the experiments..." Lasgol began. He did not want to go through them again, still less to have his friends suffer in the same way.

"I'll be extremely careful. I've been working with my brother Enduald on a way to control them with the aid of enchantments that greatly reduce the risks."

"But don't completely eliminate them," Ingrid put in.

"Absolute certainty doesn't exist, and total safety is an illusion. All the same, I can assure you that the risks are now minimal."

"Those experiments aren't something I'd like to go through again," Lasgol pointed out.

"These would be completely different, and much safer," Sigrid insisted. "Think of the gain, of the improvements you'd gain. You could achieve the mastery of several specialties simultaneously, even ones of different schools. Think about it. You could all be phenomenal with those skills."

"That sounds interesting," said Viggo, who suddenly seemed very interested in the proposal.

"You could have all the specialties of Expertise and become the best Assassin Norghana has ever seen."

"Well... I already am that... but the proposal's very attractive."

"I think it's interesting too," Ingrid said. "I'd like to complement my Specialty with others like Nature, or even Expertise."

"I can offer you that if you agree to work with me and be a part of my studies and experiments."

"It's dangerous," Lasgol repeated.

"Think about it. You don't need to decide now. The invitation is there, and the doors of the Shelter will be open for you if you decide to try it."

"Thank you," Ingrid said. "We'll think about it."

Sigrid winked. "And Lasgol, if you bring Camu, I'd like to see him."

Lasgol nodded, but he had no intention of going back to the Shelter and taking part in experiments, much less of taking Camu with him so that she could experiment on the poor creature as well. He would have to persuade his partners to forget about the idea, however tempting it might sound.

Sigrid and the Elder Specialists left after congratulating them again for everything they had done. They were left alone at last in the ante-chamber.

"Well, it seems we're Royal Eagles now instead of Snow Panthers," Nilsa commented.

"I liked Black Snakes better," said Viggo. "With a name like that our enemies would wet themselves."

"Don't be gross," Nilsa said.

"How can you like Black Snakes?" Ingrid asked.

"Because it generates fear. We want to be feared."

"We want to be respected, not feared," Ingrid corrected him.

"Well, I want both."

"Well, I'm not too happy about the change of name," said Gerd. "I was quite fond of Snow Panthers."

"We'll always be the Snow Panthers," said Egil. "We'll only be the Royal Eagles when we're on a 'special mission' for Gondabar or Thoran."

"True..." said Lasgol. He was still thinking about it.

"Whether we're Panthers or Eagles, it doesn't change who we are," Ingrid pointed out. "We're still the same as ever."

"The only thing that'll change is what we're doing," Viggo said.

"I think it's okay," Nilsa said. "We can tell whether it's a Panther kind of mission or one of the special Eagle ones."

"Yeah, it's as if we could change roles," Astrid agreed.

Gerd spread his arms wide. "The Panther ones will be the usual ones, and the Eagles will be the complicated ones."

Astrid raised one eyebrow. "Is that what you think?"

Gerd considered this. "Yeah... well, in fact the Panthers' missions are usually quite complicated and tangled..."

"It's going to be hard for the special missions to be less hazardous and tangled-up than our usual ones," Nilsa said with a chuckle.

"Who knows," Ingrid said, "maybe we'll stop having Panther missions now we've disrupted the regicide and revealed the conspirators – who by the way are either dead, or else will be soon."

They all turned to Egil, waiting for his opinion.

"Well now... the situation's going to be a lot more peaceful now... or so I expect. The conspiracy has been stopped. Olmossen and Sven, who wanted to kill me, won't trouble us any longer. Gatik, who was trying to kill Lasgol, won't be a problem either, and with him and Eyra dead, the Dark Rangers aren't a threat any longer, they're finished. The few who remain will be hunted down and executed. There's a truce between West and East, and the Zangrians seem to be quiet lately. Unless something new happens in the Frozen Continent that requires us to step in – and I hope not – it seems to me that we can breathe easily for a while."

Viggo shook his head. "That won't be for long."

Astrid was moved to support him. "I'm not sure why, but I have that same feeling too."

"I'm hopeful that for once we might have a bit of peace and

381

quiet," said Gerd.

Nilsa was much less trusting. "Well, I want to be optimistic like Gerd, but we'll soon find out what kind of special missions they give us."

"Don't we have another front open?" Ingrid asked.

"There's Eyra's promise that she'd have Egil killed," Lasgol pointed out uneasily.

"Well, that was a threat," Gerd said, "but d'you really think she'll carry it out from the grave?"

"I hope not," said Nilsa.

"It's pretty unlikely," said Egil. "With Gatik and Eyra dead, I don't think the Assassin will carry out the threat."

"He'd better not try, or else he'll have me to deal with," said Viggo.

"You're always so sure of yourself," Ingrid snapped.

"Of course. That's what I am."

"You need to be a little less so," she advised him.

He smiled, looking grateful. "Thanks for your concern, but I'm fine."

"You're still being very strange," Ingrid said. She was staring at him with narrowed eyes, as though trying to read within him and know what he was up to.

"I'm very well, actually. I appreciate your concern about my wellbeing."

"Very, and I mean very, strange..." Ingrid was obviously mystified.

"Apart from this question of life or death, I don't think we have any more complications," Lasgol said. He turned to Egil in case he wanted to disagree.

Egil nodded. "The time has come to resolve one final matter we've left hanging."

Chapter 46

It was midnight when Egil arrived on horseback at the meeting point in the middle of the plain. He had a strange feeling that he was reliving a scene he had experienced before. In a way he was, because this was the same place where not long ago he had met Count Malason. And it was the same time. This evening he was meeting him once again, but he hoped that unlike the previous time, they would not be betrayed. He smiled. Fate was always so unpredictable that no-one could ever be sure of anything.

He gazed up at the moon, which was barely visible behind dark masses of cloud. The bad weather was beginning to dominate, and probably there would be a storm soon. He stroked the rump of his horse to soothe it. As he did so, he heard another horse behind him, and saw a rider coming. He did not need to look closely to know at once who it was.

"All calm behind us," Gerd said as he reached his side.

"I'm not expecting trouble tonight."

"Never a bad idea to make sure. Don't forget, there are people who want to kill you."

Egil smiled. "Fewer and fewer of them."

"True, they're all dying one by one."

"That's because I have a great bodyguard," Egil said, and gave him a wink.

"Don't be too trusting," Gerd said very seriously." And stay close to me."

Egil gave him a small bow from the saddle. "Yes, my dear partner."

Two riders appeared from the West. Egil and Gerd watched them arrive calmly. They had already recognized them, because behind them trotted a panther and reptilian-looking creature the size of an adult lion.

"Good evening," Astrid greeted them when they reached their side.

"Lasgol, Astrid, a pleasure to see you," said Egil.

And us? Camu messaged.

Egil saw that Camu was staring at him intensely with his bulging eyes and guessed that he was waiting to be greeted. "And of course hello to Ona and Camu too, our magnificent companions."

Yes, we magnificent.

"Don't flatter them," Lasgol said. "They'll get swollen heads."

Head not swell.

Yours will burst.

No swell. Ona and I magnificent.

Ufff... yes, you're both magnificent.

"If they're both fantastic, how can I help showing them my affection?" Egil asked.

See? We fantastic!

Ona chirped once in delight, and her long, powerful tail swished from side to side.

"Egil..." Lasgol protested. "I'm the one who has to deal with them afterwards."

Gerd was smiling. "They're great," he said.

"And delightful," Astrid added.

We great and delightful, Camu transmitted to Lasgol

Yeah... yeah...

Gerd pointed. "Two riders coming from the East."

They saw that the riders were women.

"Hi there, partners!" Nilsa called out.

"I'm glad to see you all well," Ingrid said.

"Any trouble getting to this night-time meeting?" Egil asked them.

"I thought Gondabar would think of something to stop me," Nilsa said, sounding surprised, "but no, it looks as though we're free to do more or less what we want now."

"Yeah, I didn't have any trouble either," said Ingrid. "I said I was on a 'special' mission, and hey, not one word more!"

Egil smiled. "That's what we get for being chosen by King Thoran to be the Royal Eagles. Nobody's going to get in our way or ask what we're doing."

"Which comes in extremely handy," came a voice.

They saw Viggo arriving from the north, dressed completely in black and riding a horse which was also completely black.

"Hey!" Gerd called out. "You startled me! I can't even see you!"

"That's the idea," Viggo said. He drew back his hood and

lowered the scarf he was wearing over his mouth and nose.

"You looked better with your hood and scarf on," Ingrid commented.

"Yes, you're right, when I'm mysterious–looking, I'm really breathtaking. That's what they always tell me."

"I wouldn't say breathtaking exactly..." Nilsa muttered under her breath.

He winked at her. "Deep down, you know I'm a lot more mysterious and attractive than those Royal Rangers and Guards of yours."

Nilsa burst out laughing. "You wish you were half as handsome as them!"

He smiled. "Being twice as smart is good enough for me."

"I see we're all here, and apparently in a very good mood," Egil said.

"Nothing like a meeting in the middle of nowhere, at midnight, with secret business in hand, to put me in a good mood," Viggo said. His smile was deeply ironic.

Astrid too burst out laughing.

"Very good," Gerd said. "Actually, all this secrecy makes me rather nervous."

"I don't know why," Viggo pointed out. "You ought to be more than used to it by now, big guy."

"There are some things I never get used to," Gerd complained. "This is one of them. If we're here it's because Egil's got something in mind, and I bet whatever you want it's nothing good."

They all turned toward Egil, who beamed at them. "Irrefutable, my dear friend," he said.

"Egil, tell us," Lasgol asked him. "What are we doing here?"

He pointed to the west. "You'll know very soon."

Seven riders were approaching at a trot. They were soldiers.

Before Egil could say anything Ingrid and Nilsa had armed their bows and Astrid and Viggo had drawn their knives, Lasgol took it more in his stride as he watched the riders approaching. They were armed, but they seemed not to have any hostile intentions, because they were not carrying weapons. He saw that Egil was calm. He was obviously expecting them.

Relax, they don't look like enemies.

Hide?

Yes, Camu, hide, just in case.

Okay.

"Don't worry, they're friends," Egil told them.

"Your friends tend to have treacherous ideas," Viggo pointed out.

"Very true. All the same, this evening I hope it won't be one of those rather alarming moments."

"Just in case, I'll stay on the alert.," said Viggo.

"Me too," Astrid added.

Ingrid said nothing, but she did not lower her bow either.

As the riders came closer, Lasgol recognized the one in the lead, and felt a little more at ease.

"Good evening, Count Malason," Egil greeted him.

"My lord calls me, and here I am," the Count replied. He stopped his horse in front of Egil and bowed from the saddle.

"I trust you had no trouble."

"None, my lord."

"I'm glad to hear that." Egil turned to the riders who were with the Count. "And the cargo?"

Malason beckoned, and one of his soldiers approached him. With him was another rider. This rider's hands were tied behind his back and a hood covered his head, so that they could not see who it was.

"Uncover the cargo, if you please," Egil said.

The soldier took off the rider's hood and a mass of blonde hair appeared, shining in the moonlight.

"Valeria!" several of the Panthers exclaimed as they recognized her. Jaws tensed, and several fists clenched.

The girl looked at them and sighed. She seems to have recovered from her wound, though not completely, because her complexion was not entirely healthy.

"As you requested, my lord," Count Malason said. "Safe and sound."

"I'm grateful for your help and your loyalty."

"I serve the King of the West, now and forever."

"Thank you. You've done me a great service."

"Always at your disposition, my lord. Do you need anything more of me?"

"No. You may leave. We'll take charge from this point."

"All right, my lord. But be careful. The East won't rest in its aim of dominating the West..."

"I know. You be careful too. We'll be in touch."

"I'll await your orders," the Count replied. He saluted Egil and left with his men, leaving Valeria on her horse.

"Hey, it looks as though Egil's organized an execution for us," Viggo said. He was watching her with a lethal gleam in his eyes.

"If you're going to kill me, do it quickly," Valeria said, looking down. She looked defeated, hopeless. Her natural beauty had gone from her face, which looked consumed by defeat and despair.

"I'll take care of that," Astrid said.

Egil raised his hand. "Stop! Wait a moment!"

Astrid looked at him and hesitated. But she stopped.

"This isn't an execution. This is a trial by the Panthers."

"What do you mean, a trial? She's a traitor, and she has to die!"

"I agree," said Viggo. "Anyone who betrays us dies. It's as simple as that, and that's the way it has to be if we're to live in peace."

"We all know what Valeria has done," said Egil. "We've talked about it, we know about her betrayal, and I told you I had her in custody. I allowed King Thoran to believe she'd died with Gatik so that he'd lose interest. It looks as though he believed me."

"We should have delivered her to him the way we did with her father," Ingrid said.

"Then she'd have been hanged in the square, just as he was in the end," Nilsa said. "That's a horrible death."

"Reserved for a horrible crime like the one they both committed," Astrid pointed out.

"She also saved Lasgol," Gerd said, trying to make a point in her favor.

"That doesn't exempt her from her crimes," said Ingrid.

"True," Egil said, "but on the other hand it's something to consider before we sentence her to death."

Gerd turned to Lasgol. "What do you think, Lasgol? You were there when Gatik had you at his mercy."

He looked at Valeria. "I think we ought to let her speak before we condemn her. I want to understand why she did it. And I want to know why she defended me at the last moment and almost lost her life because of it."

"I don't want to hear anything," Astrid said furiously. In her green eyes there shone a murderous gleam which left no doubt that she wanted to kill the treacherous blonde at that very moment.

"Let her explain herself," said Nilsa.

"Yeah, I want to know why too," Gerd agreed.

"It'll be a complete waste of time," said Viggo. Like Astrid, he wanted to finish Valeria off and put an end to the whole business.

"The prisoner always has a right to say a few last words," said Ingrid. "Let her speak and say what she wants."

Camu and Ona, who did not fully understand what was going on, were watching with great interest. Lasgol had explained the story of Valeria and her treason. They had found it hard to understand, and so had he. He knew it had happened, he had lived through it, but he could not understand the reason why. He was having nightmares in which Valeria betrayed him all over again, and this time he really did end up dead.

"Valeria," Egil said, "if you want to say something, now's the moment."

Valeria looked at the seven Panthers one by one. In exchange she received glares of rejection and even hatred, together with others of bafflement and sorrow. She took a deep breath and decided to speak.

"I can understand that you hate me. I can understand that you want to kill me because I betrayed you. You took me in as another partner – well, almost all of you," she added pointedly, looking at Astrid. "That's something that does you credit, and I'm grateful for it. What I intended when I approached you was never to betray you, it was simply to get information. Especially about Egil and Lasgol, who were two people of special interest: Egil for Sven and my father, and Lasgol for Gatik. They ordered me to stay close to them and spy on them. That's what I did. I had no choice. I've always been involved in the conspiracy, even before I joined the Rangers, because I was already working for my father and that's what he arranged. I'm Olmossen's daughter, just as you're Olafstone's son, Egil. We have to bear the weight of our family names on our shoulders. That's not an excuse, it's the truth. My father raised me as a son, because my younger brother doesn't have either the physical qualities or the character that are needed to become a Norghanian warrior. I had them, and my father had realized that ever since we were children. When I said I was better than my brother at everything, I wasn't lying. It's the truth. When I said my father would give him the title, I wasn't lying either. That was his idea during Uthar's rule, and that's why I ended up in the Rangers, because of that and also because my father wanted me to work for the Dark Ones and learn things from Eyra. Then everything changed with Uthar's death and Thoran's coming to the throne. My father, Sven and Gatik planned the conspiracy and began to get ready to topple him. I was involved in what happened then. I couldn't betray my father. He was a hard, ambitious man, but he was my father. A daughter doesn't betray her father. I loved him very much."

"But you knew you were doing wrong," Ingrid pointed out.

She nodded. "Yes, I knew that. I felt remorse for what I was doing, but I couldn't turn my back on my father. He was risking his life, and if he were found out, he'd hang."

"As he has, in the end. Was it worth it?" Viggo asked her.

Valeria sighed, and a look of enormous sadness came into her eyes.

"I always feared this end, and unfortunately, now it's come. I'm sorry about my father's death. He wasn't a bad man, and he loved me deeply. Ambition for the crown of the West destroyed him. It's happened to others. Don't let it happen to you, Egil."

"That's something I think about all the time, and I see the dangers," Egil said quietly.

"Do you really want us to believe you care about either Egil or Lasgol?" Astrid challenged her.

"I care about them, even if you don't believe me. It's what happens when you spend too much time with good, exceptional people like them. You grow fond of them."

"You were with them, not because you were fond of them, but so that you could spy on them and betray them when the time came," Astrid insisted.

"I couldn't kill Lasgol when Gatik ordered me to, and nor could I have killed Egil if he'd told me to. I don't have it in me. I don't have that kind of evil that would be needed for something like that."

"Why didn't you let Gatik kill him?" Ingrid asked. "You had no reason to defend him."

Valeria sighed. "I don't know, quite honestly. I saw that Lasgol was going to die. If I didn't kill him, Gatik was going to, and something lit up in me."

"Remorse?" Nilsa asked.

"Something stronger. I couldn't let him kill Lasgol. So I turned and shot Gatik. Unfortunately he dodged the arrow and hit me. He was very good."

"But you didn't save Lasgol," Viggo pointed out.

"Ona saved me," said Lasgol. "Thanks to her fur and the fact that she's so used to bearing the mountain cold, the ice-traps didn't stay frozen as long as they should have in her."

"Whatever the case," Astrid said, "Valeria belongs to the Dark Rangers, and we have to hand her over to them so that justice can be done."

Gerd was still trying to understand Valeria. "Didn't you realize you were doing wrong when you were with them?" he asked.

"Yes, I realized... but it's not so easy to do what's right when your father and your mentors tell you to do what's wrong. You convince yourself that you're doing it for them, and that if they tell you to do it, it's for a very good reason."

"It's hard to go against your own father if you love him," Nilsa said.

"Nobody's saying it isn't," Ingrid told her, "but you had thousands of opportunities to tell us, and if you'd done that, we wouldn't be here today."

"If you're going to kill me, do it. If you're going to turn me in, do that too. I'll accept my fate."

"I say we should kill her for being a traitor," said Astrid.

"Killing her now will save us problems later on," Viggo agreed.

"Killing her isn't the solution," Ingrid objected. "We can't take justice into our own hands. I say we turn her in. We'll say she didn't die, as we'd thought, and now we've caught her."

"That's a horrible fate," Nilsa pointed out. "She'll be tortured to get information out of her."

"So what do you want to do?" Ingrid asked. "Let her go? We can't, she's a traitor."

"We also need to take into account that she tried to save Lasgol's life at the last moment," Gerd insisted. "We can't forget that fact. If our friend's alive, it's partly because of her."

"True. Otherwise I'd have died," Lasgol agreed.

The discussion turned heated. At last Egil spoke. He had been silent all this time.

"There's one option that could resolve this situation."

Ingrid gestured at the others to stop arguing. "We're listening."

"I think Valeria has to pay for her crimes. I also think we should be magnanimous because she helped save Lasgol's life. I propose that we sentence her to exile. She'll leave Norghana at once, never to return, and if she does, then we'll hunt her down and kill her. That way there's an appropriate punishment. We pardon her life for having saved Lasgol's, and we won't have to deal with her later on. I should think this ought to satisfy all parties."

"Not me," Astrid snapped.

"It seems a little light, that particular sentence," Viggo objected.

Ingrid looked thoughtful. "I don't know..."

The others said nothing.

"I propose that we vote," said Egil. "Those in favor, raise their hand."

Nilsa, Gerd and Egil himself raised their hands. Astrid, Viggo and Ingrid were against. Ingrid was in favor of turning her in.

"It's three for and three against," Egil said. He glanced at Lasgol, who said nothing. "The decision is yours, pal."

There was a moment of silence. Lasgol looked at Ingrid, who was shaking her head, telling him not to let her go. Then he looked at Valeria, who was watching him in silence.

"I can't condemn her to death. She tried to kill Gatik to save my life and I have to repay the favor. I vote for exile."

Astrid, Ingrid and Viggo raised their voices in protest.

Egil raised his hand. "It's a clear vote, four against three. It's decided. Valeria, go and leave Norghana forever. If you ever set foot here again for whatever reason, the Panthers will hunt you down and execute you for treason wherever they find you. Is that clear?"

Valeria breathed out heavily. "Very clear."

"Gerd, cut her ties and let her go," Egil said.

The giant nodded. He went to Valeria and cut her loose. "Leave," he told her.

"Thank you. I'll never forget this."

She looked at them one last time and galloped away into the night.

Astrid made as if to raise her bow, but Nilsa moved her horse in front of her to prevent the shot.

"Hell, this is a mistake," she said bitterly.

"Maybe it is," Egil said. "But it's the Panthers' decision."

Chapter 47

A few weeks later, Ingrid was sitting on the bed in the room at the inn they had taken in the city of Bilboson, in eastern Norghana. She was sharpening her weapons. It was a large city, one of the largest and most handsome in the kingdom. The Panthers were to report there to begin their first mission as the Royal Eagles.

Ingrid and Egil had arrived in the city early and were going to spend the night at the inn. It was always a pleasure to be able to rest in a bed, a real luxury in the busy life of the Rangers, and especially so in theirs.

Egil came into the room, which was plain but functional. "I've asked them to bring dinner up here," he said.

"Wonderful. Something hot to put in our stomachs will be really welcome."

"The innkeeper told me we make a nice couple," Egil said with a smile.

Ingrid laughed. "Seriously? He thinks we're a couple?"

"I think he was surprised when we asked for a room for both of us, and he probably wanted me to confirm it."

"And did you?"

"Of course. I told him you surrendered to my intellectual charms."

Ingrid's laughter filled the room. "Yeah, surrendered completely."

Egil smiled. "I don't think I convinced him, and I really tried to sound as convincing as possible."

"That's because most of the brutes in this realm don't know how attractive an intelligent man is."

"That's true."

"And you're the most intelligent man in all Tremia," she said flatteringly.

"I wouldn't say the most intelligent..." Egil said, blushing.

"I can assure you, you are. But don't let it go to your head, because this is a country of brainless brutes."

"In the country of the blind, the one-eyed man is king."

Ingrid chuckled. "Exactly."

The innkeeper brought their dinner up a little later. Two good servings of lemon chicken with fresh bread, and mature cheese with nuts for dessert. A feast, for a place like that. They sat on two plain stools and enjoyed their dinner. As they ate, they talked about the possible mission they were going to be entrusted with. As it was their first special mission, they were a little nervous.

"Let's hope it's not too complicated," Ingrid said rather uneasily. "I'd imagine it could be anything, seeing that it's a special one."

Egil was savoring the dinner as if it were an exquisite delicacy.

"There's no need to worry too much. It'll be a normal mission. It'll probably be connected with something the King wants us to do."

"Yeah, and that something... what could it be?" Ingrid wondered, taking a sip of the cider the innkeeper had brought up with their dinner.

"The best thing we can do is enjoy our dinner and not worry about the mission, at least until we know what it is."

"Right, but I find it hard to relax with all this uncertainty."

"You'll find out that it's a lot less than we think," Egil assured her with a smile.

"I'll drink to that," Ingrid replied, and they both raised their cider.

"These wooden tumblers are a bit rustic for toasts, but there you are..."

"It's the life of a Ranger, non-stop luxury," Egil laughed, looking at the wooden tumbler in his hand.

Suddenly he dropped it on the floor and stared at it.

"Egil? Is something wrong?" Ingrid asked him in surprise.

Egil raised his head and stared at her. There was a strange expression on his face, as if he could not focus his eyes properly.

"Ingrid..." he said, and collapsed on to the floor with a thump.

"Egil!" she cried and stretched out her hand, but it never reached him. She stood up to help him and suddenly felt utterly dizzy. She gave one stumbling step toward him and fell to the floor.

They were left stretched out on the wooden boards, unconscious.

The door of the room opened slowly, without so much as a creak. A hooded figure slipped inside and closed it behind him. He took two stealthy steps, moving nimbly and with perfect balance and looked down at the two bodies on the floor. With a swift movement he drew two long knives and took a step toward Egil.

Suddenly the window burst open violently. Another hooded

figure entered, and came to stand in front of the intruder with a somersault.

"It seems you've come to finish your mission after all, Assassin," Viggo said as he drew his own knives.

The figure had turned toward him and seemed to be looking him up and down.

"I'm an Assassin, and I was given this mission."

"I see you're one of the old school. The drug you've given them isn't enough for you. You want to slit his throat with your own hands."

The other pointed to Viggo's knives with his own. "I see you're an Assassin as well."

"That's right. I'm the best Assassin in the Rangers."

"That's a lot to say. I wouldn't be so sure."

"Natural Assassin?" Viggo asked.

"That's right. You?"

"The same."

"Well then, this is going to be interesting."

"You know I can't let you live, don't you?" Viggo said.

"Because of your friend?" the other said, gesturing at Egil on the floor.

"Yes. You see, I like him very much, and my life would be very boring if you killed him. I like entertainment, so I can't let you carry out your mission. And I can't let you get away either, because I know you'd try again."

"That's right. I have to complete my mission."

"Yeah... it's just that I can't let you do that. Nothing personal," Viggo said with an apologetic gesture.

"Same here. I have to kill my target. If I have to kill you first, so be it."

"Right. In that case everything's clear," Viggo said, and gave him a nod.

The other Assassin returned the gesture, then with a lightning move slid toward Viggo to launch a slash at his neck. Viggo reacted with the same speed and bent backwards, so that the knife merely grazed his chin. The Assassin followed with a thrust to the heart which Viggo deflected with his own knife, countering with another directly to his opponent's heart. The other blocked the attack and slid to one side, aiming to strike his face. Viggo slid aside in turn and saw the blade pass his eyes a hair's breadth away from cutting him.

Both Assassins deployed all their ability and knowledge of the art of knife-fighting, and the fight became a lethal dance which appeared synchronized. Every slash was blocked, every strike was deflected, every attack countered by a defensive thrust. The two opponents were both outstanding Assassins: certainly two of the best in the whole of Norghana, if not the best.

Viggo defended himself well, but could not succeed in cutting the other Assassin, while his rival was getting closer and closer to him all the time.

"You're good, but you're not going to be able to reach me," Viggo said as he blocked a speedy attack.

"If you're telling me that, it's because you know I'm going to."

"No way."

"You're only voicing your fears," the other Assassin said. "Don't worry, you'll be dead before long, and your doubts will be over." He launched a frenetic attack with slashes to right and left, trying to get Viggo in either the head or his supporting leg.

Viggo had trouble dodging the attacks. With a pirouette he leapt up on to the bed, gaining some advantage from the height. He was beginning to feel worried. This rival was too good. He delivered several swift attacks with the advantage of his raised position, but the other deflected and blocked them all. Then, with a gesture so rapid Viggo almost missed it, he reached for his belt and threw a black powder at him. Viggo somersaulted on to the floor, and the black dust formed a cloud which hung suspended over the bed. It was some substance that blinded and stunned.

Seeing that Viggo had escaped and was now at a safe distance, the other held both knives in one hand, then with the other threw a small dagger at him. Viggo just managed to turn his head to one side and the dagger buried itself in the door, a hair's breadth from his ear. Seeing that he was losing the fight, he decided to resort to something which was not taught to the Assassins at the Shelter. He decided to try what he had learnt to survive as a child in the slums of the city: to play dirty.

The other Assassin prepared to attack, but Viggo refused to go on running around the room.

"I see you've understood you're about to die."

"No way," Viggo replied. He was now fleeing once again from his opponent's slashes, putting as much distance between the two of them as he could.

He began to move around Ingrid and Egil, still unconscious on the floor.

"You've put your comrades in the middle? That's for cowards."

"It's for smart ones."

The Assassin stopped. Viggo was opposite him, but between them were Ingrid and Egil on the floor.

"Bad strategy," he said, and bent over to stab Egil.

At that moment Viggo threw his right knife with all his might. The Assassin corrected his move to avoid it, and though it grazed him, it did not cut him. But he could not kill Egil either.

He saw Viggo holding a single knife. "I've got you," he muttered, and leapt at him over the two unconscious figures.

Viggo saw him coming and crouched down. At the same time, with his free hand he grabbed the stool beside him, and as the Assassin fell on him he smashed it on his head. Both of them rolled across the floor. Viggo leapt to his feet and grabbed the other stool as a shield. The other Assassin, still stunned, attacked him, but Viggo deflected the knife with his own. When his opponent was about to cut him with the other knife, he smashed the second stool on his head. The Assassin stayed on his feet, with his eyes shut. He took an irregular step to one side, then fell to his knees, trying unsuccessfully to remain conscious.

Viggo saw his opportunity, leapt across and buried his knife in the other's heart.

The Assassin fell backwards, dead.

He smiled in triumph. "That's called defense and attack with a stool. They don't teach that at the Shelter."

He turned to his friends on the floor and felt a sharp pain in his leg. He looked down at his thigh and saw that the Assassin had cut him there.

"That doesn't look good..." he muttered under his breath, took out a cord from his belt and made a tourniquet. He grunted in pain a couple of times before he had it properly tied, then bent down beside Ingrid.

"Wake up, Ingrid," he whispered in her ear.

Ingrid did not seem to hear him. Viggo decided to shake her to wake her up.

"Come on, Ingrid, wake up!"

One of Ingrid's eyes opened a little.

"Viggo...?"

"Yes, it's me. Open your eyes, I need you awake."

"What...?" She tried to open her eyes but could not manage to.

"Come on, make an effort. I need you."

Finally she was able to open her eyes, and was looking around blankly. "What happened...?"

"They drugged your food so you'd be defenseless."

"Who? How?" she asked restlessly.

He pointed to the dead Assassin on the floor. "That one."

Ingrid leapt to her feet when she saw him, but suddenly felt very dizzy and nearly fell back on to the floor.

"Gently, don't move," Viggo said. He held her in his arms. "Don't make any sudden moves, or you'll feel dizzy."

"Egil..." she said, gesturing at him on the floor.

"He's all right. The Assassin didn't get what he wanted."

"He came for Egil?"

"Yes. He's Eyra's Assassin."

"Hell! I've failed him!"

"Don't worry. I dealt with him myself."

She realized that there was a tourniquet on his thigh. "What happened to you? Did he hurt you?"

"Yeah, he turned out to be quite good. Not as good as me, of course – look how he ended up – but yes, he was good."

"Are you all right?"

"Well, that's what I wanted to talk to you about..."

"What? What's the matter?"

"You see... the cut itself is no big deal..."

"Then why the tourniquet?"

"Because he was a Natural Assassin..."

Ingrid realized, and her heart skipped a beat. "Poison! In the knives!"

"That's what I'm afraid of. I'm beginning to feel bad... which confirms it..."

"No! Viggo!"

"I knew the Assassin would go after Egil. The Assassins always finish their missions, particularly if they're murder ones."

"Don't talk! We've got to give you an antidote!" She was trying to think what to do.

"I followed Egil ever since he left the Camp. I did it without him seeing me. And I was expecting the Assassin. Tonight he showed up at last. I've given him what he deserved."

"Then you knew he'd come."

"Yeah, I was sure."

"Why didn't you tell us?"

"Because then you'd all have stayed close to Egil all the time and the Assassin wouldn't have made an appearance."

"That's not a bad thing!"

"It is, though, because eventually we'd have thought he wasn't coming, and at that very moment he'd have come on the scene and killed Egil. My system was better. He's dead now, and we don't have to spend our lives waiting for him to appear out of nowhere."

"You're an idiot! Why can't you act like any normal person?" She forced him to sit down on the bed.

"Because... I'm not normal?"

"I hate you!"

"My sight's beginning to get blurred..."

"Don't you Assassins carry antidotes?"

"Yeah... I've taken them all... they don't seem to have any effect..."

"Viggo! Come on, hold on!" She went over to Egil and began to shake him.

"I'm going to lie down for a while..." Viggo said, and collapsed on to he bed.

"Egil! Wake up! I need you!" Ingrid was still shaking Egil on the floor.

"My head's spinning..." Viggo said.

"Don't you die on me, you numbskull!" she shouted at him

"If I don't make it out of this..."

"Viggo!" Ingrid hastened to his side. "Don't leave me!"

"I want you... to know..."

"Viggo!"

"That I love you..." He closed his eyes.

"Nooooo!" Don't you dare die on me!" She began to press his heart with the palms of her hands.

Egil looked around him. He was coming to at last. "Wha'... wha's going on..."

"Viggo's been poisoned! He's dying!" Ingrid shouted desperately. Her blue eyes were beginning to fill with tears.

"Poisoned? What kind of poison?" Egil asked her. He had managed to get to his feet by now.

"I don't know! An Assassin one!"

"Assassins... the most common poisons are..." He thought for a moment and began to search in his belt.

"Quick! He's drifting away from us!" Ingrid cried. She was weeping now.

"Keep pressing his heart keep it beating," Egil told her.

"You're such an idiot! Why on earth did you do that?" she shouted at Viggo.

Egil hastily picked up a number of phials and came over to the bed. "You keep on massaging his heart. Get on top of him. I'll give him the antidotes."

Ingrid went on with the massage. She was now astride Viggo.

Egil made him swallow all the antidotes he was carrying. "Since I don't know what poison they used, I've given him all I have with me."

"He took all of his own."

"Let's hope one of them works," Egil said, but he did not look very convinced.

"Come on, Viggo! Fight!" Ingrid yelled at him with tears running down her cheeks as she tried to keep his heart beating.

Egil watched helplessly while she went on applying pressure. But the minutes passed, and he was still unresponsive.

"I think... I think he's gone..." Egil told her very sadly.

"No! I refuse to let him go!"

"Ingrid..."

"No!"

"Too much time has gone by..."

"I can't give up. He's got to live."

"If he were alive... he'd have come round by now."

"He will!"

Egil bent his head mournfully. "He was a great friend and partner..."

"He's going to live, I know he is!" Ingrid went on applying pressure.

Egil fell silent, letting her go on, but he was already certain that it was too late.

"He's gone," he said at last.

"Nooooo!" she howled in grief.

"Let it be. There's no point..."

Ingrid stopped pressing, and her head fell on to Viggo's chest.

"Why? Why didn't you say anything?" she reproached him amid sobs.

Egil stared at the dead Assassin on the floor. "He gave his life to save mine..." he said, and tears began to stream from his eyes.

Ingrid was unable to answer. She was weeping over Viggo's body.

Egil sat down on the floor and put his hands to his face. "He was... a phenomenon," he said amid tears.

There was a long silence, broken only by their sobs. Sorrow at their loss had overwhelmed them.

Suddenly they heard a great intake of air. Egil turned to look at Ingrid, thinking it had been her. But no.

Viggo had opened his eyes wide and was taking in all the air in the room to fill his lungs.

Ingrid realized this. "Viggo! You're alive!"

Viggo took another deep breath of air, this time through his mouth.

"Of course I'm alive... why are you sitting on me...? Is it a loving gesture?" he said with a smile.

Ingrid stared at him and could not hold herself back. She kissed him with all her being. Viggo put his arms around her, and she put her hands on his cheeks. They kissed tenderly and passionately.

"Ahem..." Egil said, seeing that they were not moving apart. "I'll have to check on the resuscitated one, to see if he's all right..."

"I'm... better than ever..." Viggo said between kisses.

"Still, I insist. I'll have to have a look at you."

Ingrid loosened her embrace. "Let him have a look at you."

"You party pooper," Viggo protested. "I was in the Realm of the Ice Gods, enjoying incredible happiness."

Ingrid got up and let Egil examine him. "How is he?" she asked.

"Well now, he ought to be dead, but I think one of those antidotes we gave him must have had an effect, because now his heart's beating strongly and his pulse is back to normal."

Viggo sat up on the bed.

"I feel fantastic, except that my chest hurts like mad." He touched the spot Ingrid had been pressing. "It's probably because of the kiss. My heart nearly jumped out of my chest." He gazed at Ingrid, who rolled her eyes.

"It was your life that nearly left you, not your heart," she said very seriously.

Viggo stood up, stretched his arms and legs and smiled. "I feel perfectly well," he said.

Ingrid and Egil stared at him, unable to believe their eyes.

"Well, you were dead for a while," Egil told him.

"Hey, that's another skill I didn't know I had. Sometimes I surprise myself." He was still beaming.

Egil nodded. "And others as well."

"Right then," Viggo said, as though he had just woken up after a refreshing nap. "When do we start this special mission? I'm looking forward to a bit of action."

"You really are hopeless, my dear dumbass," Ingrid said, and kissed him passionately once again.

The end Book 10

The adventure continues:
Click the image or the link above to preorder the next book in the series!

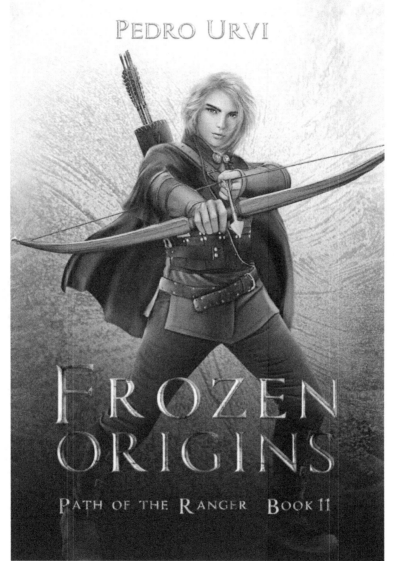

Click the image to preorder

While you wait for the next installment of the Path of the Ranger, I invite you to explore my other series that have different protagonists, but are related:

THE SECRET OF THE GOLDEN GODS

This series takes place three thousand years before the Path of the Ranger Series
Different protagonists, same world, one destiny.

The Ilenian Enigma

This series takes place several years after the Path of the Ranger Series. It has different protagonists. Lasgol joins the adventure in the second book of the series. He is a secondary character in this one, but he plays an important role, and he is alone...

Acknowledgements

I'm lucky enough to have very good friends and a wonderful family, and it's thanks to them that this book is now a reality. I can't express the incredible help they have given me during this epic journey.

I wish to thank my great friend Guiller C. for all his support, tireless encouragement and invaluable advice. This saga, not just this book, would never have come to exist without him.

Mon, master-strategist and exceptional plot-twister. Apart from acting as editor and always having a whip ready for deadlines to be met. A million thanks.

To Luis R. for helping me with the re-writes and for all the hours we spent talking about the books and how to make them more enjoyable for the readers.

Roser M., for all the readings, comments, criticisms, for what she has taught me and all her help in a thousand and one ways. And in addition, for being delightful.

The Bro, who as he always does, has supported me and helped me in his very own way.

Guiller B, for all your great advice, ideas, help and, above all, support.

My parents, who are the best in the world and have helped and supported me unbelievably in this, as in all my projects.

Olaya Martínez, for being an exceptional editor, a tireless worker, a great professional and above all for her encouragement and hope. And for everything she has taught me along the way.

Sarima, for being an artist with exquisite taste, and for drawing like an angel.

Special thanks to my wonderful collaborators: Christy Cox and Peter Gauld for caring so much about my books and for always going above and beyond. Thank you so very much.

And finally: thank you very much, reader, for supporting this author. I hope you've enjoyed it; if so I'd appreciate it if you could write a comment and recommend it to your family and friends.

Thank you very much, and with warmest regards.

Pedro

Author

Pedro Urvi

I would love to hear from you.
You can find me at:
Mail: pedrourvi@hotmail.com
Twitter: https://twitter.com/PedroUrvi
Facebook: https://www.facebook.com/PedroUrviAuthor/
My Website: http://pedrourvi.com

Join my mailing list to receive the latest news about my books:

Mailing List

Thank you for reading my books!

Note from the author:
I really hope you enjoyed my book. If you did, I would appreciate it if you could write a quick review. It helps me tremendously as it is one of the main factors readers consider when buying a book. As an Indie author I really need of your support.
Just go to Amazon and write a short opinion.
Thank you so very much.
Pedro.

See you in:

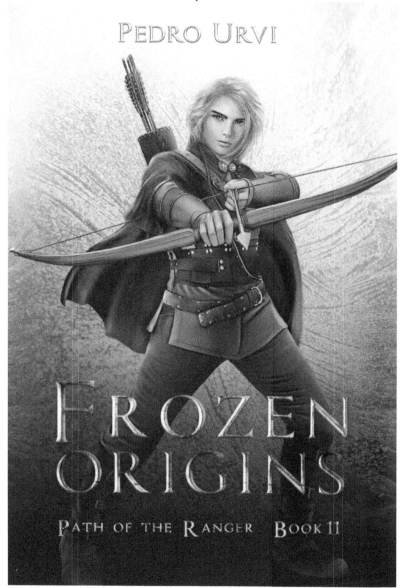

Made in the USA
Las Vegas, NV
04 February 2024

85310292R00226